Flight Path

By
Ian Andrew

D1080869

Dedication

For
Nancy & Nita
and
Jean & Jesse

Nothing is more precious, nor more worthy of protection, than an innocent.

June 2015

Stowmarket, Suffolk.

As dawn broke on his thirty-third birthday, paratrooper Darren Caistor stormed up Wireless Ridge on East Falkland. It was the last of the three battles he fought on those far-away islands and when the soft glow of the South Atlantic sun revealed the carnage, he had barely managed to stifle his tears. He always said it was his toughest birthday. He was wrong.

His wife's head leant on his shoulder, her chest heaving in quiet misery. The soft sobs of his daughter and son-in-law echoed off the sterile walls, muffling the gentle sounds of the nurses as they moved around the bed.

Through blurry eyes, Darren watched shadowed shapes gliding across his vision. He knew, in a detached way, that the room was almost silent, yet his head was filled with a screaming rage. A roar of blood, thoughts, frustrations and a desperate desire for revenge thundered inside him. As a nurse moved past the window, the curtains swayed and the briefest of glints from the rising sun shone through. It caught the swirling dust motes, twisting them in a soft-yellow lance of light that flashed across the length of the room, like a heavenly

1

sceptre. Its point came to rest on her soft face.

The sudden light cast a warming glow, gentle and reviving, but her eyes remained closed, her heart still. The curtain swayed back into place and the light was gone. Its sudden removal breached the last of the old soldier's defences. Tears streamed down the former Company Sergeant Major's stubbled cheeks, dripping unheeded as the room fell back into darkness.

On the dawn of his sixty-sixth birthday, Darren Caistor wept for the soul of his seven-year old granddaughter.

1

Camden, London. Wednesday, 18th November.

Kara Wright looked through half-closed venetian blinds at the busying street-scene below. The weak, wintery November sun hadn't yet managed to rise above the tops of the buildings, but a limp infusion of grey crept down the Kentish Town Road. It gave just enough light to pick out the heavily-cocooned early-risers, struggling against the wind that threatened to freeze them before they reached the warmth of their work.

She frowned at the weather awaiting her, but for now, wrapped in her dressing gown, towel atop her head, cup of tea in one hand and a slice of toast in the other, she was quite content. Her day didn't promise much.

A half hour from now she would venture out for a run with her business partner, Tien. The rest of the morning would be spent working on some background-checks for a City-based HR firm, followed by an afternoon meeting with a financial advisor called Shonel, who was trying to inform her about the best way to plan for the future. Kara was yet to be convinced about share portfolios, unit trusts or Government bonds.

She took a bite of toast just as her mobile phone vibrated

its dull drone on the coffee table. Chewing quickly and taking a swig of tea to wash it down, she made her way across the room and noticed the incoming call had its number withheld. Placing her cup on the table, she retrieved the phone.

"Hello."

"Hello Kara. It's me… Today?"

She had spoken to the old man only twice before. Once in the Huntingdon Police Station when he had first approached her and once in a pub in early August, when they had established their communication protocols. Since then there had been nothing. Her life had continued, seemingly unchanged, yet immeasurably different. She had waited, not patiently, but waited. Now, his calm voice sent a frisson of excitement through her and she felt her heart quicken.

She glanced at the phone screen to check the time before putting it back to her ear, "Yes, today. I make it 6:27?"

"I concur. Zero?" he asked.

"Zero is fine," Kara said and the call disconnected.

She sat in her favourite squishy armchair and reached for her tea. The towel on her head sagged against the soft upholstery and the tight tuck released, allowing gravity to drape the damp cloth down over her shoulders. Kara didn't notice. She was busy running through the procedures that had been agreed at their last meeting. They had determined that their relationship, not quite illegal, yet not quite above board, not exactly clandestine, but certainly not open, needed secure means of communication. Electronic telecommunications didn't provide that in the present day.

They decided to reinvoke the best of the old tradecraft skills, practised for decades during that often hot, Cold War. No one could bug everywhere in London, so all they needed was a way of establishing meeting points without having to mention them plainly in phone calls. That needed a code but one that had to be cipher-less. They weren't in the game of swapping code books, or driving past dead letter drops. The old man had had a good laugh when she had suggested chalk marks on benches or lampposts. She remembered him sitting

4

opposite her, in the rustic and charming surrounds of a real-ale house in Pinner, his thumbs tucked into his waistcoat pockets like a Dickensian patriarch, 'Oh no my dear Kara. My days of looking in rain swept vistas for a dab of chalk are long gone. We shall be simpler. You and I shall choose a suitable mix of locations and use them to our advantage.'

The resultant system was indeed simple, yet robust. A phone call made by either to the other's normal mobile number, from an untraceable burner phone. That eliminated the two being tied to each other by traceable phones, yet allowed them each to call a single, easy to remember number.

The caller would request a meeting. The date of the meeting determined the location. The rendezvous time would be plus four hours from the time of the call.

To work, it only required a list of thirty-one prearranged locations. Dependant on the day or the time they could modify the date-location by adding or subtracting numbers. If the meeting was to be on a Sunday at 09:00, there was little chance of using one of the pubs on the list.

Other than knowing the locations, the code needed nothing else and it gave enough variables to make counter-surveillance a practical impossibility. They built in a single contingency for meetings that needed to be called in dire emergencies, but strived to keep things as simple as possible.

Kara had used a memory-story placement technique to memorise the thirty-one locations. The meeting was today, the eighteenth, and the modifier had been zero so it was the eighteenth location, the identity of which came easily into her mind. Finishing her tea and toast, Kara picked up her phone and dialled the first number on her favourite's list. It rang three times.

"Hi, what's up?" Tien asked.

"Want to go for our run now and keep it short?"

"Yep, I'll be there in five."

The call disconnected and Kara hustled to get changed. As she was lacing up her running shoes she smiled at the thought of her friend. Never one to enjoy long runs, Kara's offer of a shortened effort would certainly have pleased Tien but that wasn't what made Kara smile. The two of them had an instinctive awareness of each other. Tien had known it was more than a shortened run, she had known something significant had occurred but shut down her requirement to ask anything about it. There was no, 'why, what's going on, is everything alright' on the phone. Just an acceptance and confirmation. It was true they had been partners for a long time, but they had always had an intuitive link. Kara could clearly recall their first brief meeting, when what looked like a walking Bergen had come through the flaps of a tent pitched on the edge of Basrah Airport.

It was February 2006, Southern Iraq was pleasantly warm but the dust was being whipped about in strong winds, assisted by the jets and propellers of a seemingly constant stream of aircraft arrivals and departures. Out of this swirling yellow maelstrom appeared a lightly-built, delicately featured girl with the rank of Lance Corporal and a look of nervous determination.

Kara had almost laughed at the size of the rucksack she had been lumbered with, "You must be our little helper, sent over from the Int Corps?"

"Yes Sergeant."

"Well, thanks for being volunteered. I'm Sergeant Kara Wright, but you get to call me Kara, this," Kara pointed to the woman sitting at a desk just behind her, "is Lieutenant Commander Victoria Oxford. You get to call her Ma'am or Lieutenant Commander Oxford. All good?"

"Yes Serg-, I mean, Kara."

"Great. Dump your gear and grab a brew. I'll take you through what you're going to be doing for us. What's your name?"

"I'm Lance Corporal Tien Tran and given the ranks in here, I guess you can call me whatever you want."

Kara was still smiling at the memory when she went out

her front door into the freezing cold of the November morning. The sun, still not visible above the rooftops, was lending the street a strange silvery hue, mirage-like, as Tien rounded the corner.

"I'm not stopping, it's too cold," she called out in puffs of condensation as she passed.

Once Kara had caught up they settled into a comfortable side-by-side rhythm, heading north to the open spaces of Hampstead Heath.

"Good morning to you. What's occurring?" Tien asked.

"Franklyn called, it appears we have a meeting," Kara answered, watching her friend as she said it. The reaction was as she expected.

Forgetting the cold, Tien pulled up quickly, eyes wide and eyebrows raised, "Seriously?"

Kara, jogging on the spot, nodded, "Yep, seriously."

"Do we know anything?"

"Not yet, but we will when we get to location eighteen at 10:27. I just need you to confirm that my memory is correct."

Tien set off jogging again. She too had memorised the list using her own technique, "I think today is a lovely day for a trip to Canons Park," she said.

2

Stanmore, London.

Tien pulled out of her parking bay and drove northwest. She liked systems and especially simple, elegant systems. She considered the meeting-code a simple, elegant system and especially liked that it didn't dictate transport options. That meant she could initiate all manner of security sweeps and dry-cleaning runs before Kara set foot near the meeting place. It was one reason why there was a four-hour gap between the call time and the rendezvous.

She also knew the precautions probably weren't strictly necessary, but Tien and Kara had routines. Well-practised and much used, their extensive pre-meeting security procedures had not let them down, be it in Iraq, Afghanistan, or much closer to home. Besides, it was how they were trained to operate and Tien still wasn't all that comfortable with the idea of Franklyn and the shadowy people he represented. People who formed a deniable organisation for purposes that may well have been admirable, but certainly fell outside of the law. They, whoever they were, had decided that the law and justice were often incompatible and on occasions it would be necessary to step in to redress the balance of the scales. Or rather, necessary for others to step in.

Tien had no problem believing that the UK Legal system was neither simple nor elegant. It was often overly-complicated, flawed and ugly but, it was still the law and that gave her cause to be cautious. Although she was the first of her family to be born in the UK, she was the product of her heritage. Her Mother's parents had both been lawyers in colonial Vietnam. They were born to a society that had been skewed toward their French masters, yet, they had gained education and worked from within, trying to make a bad system better. When they had met as lecturers in Saigon University, they had found kindred spirits. Passionate for the plight of the common people as much as for each other, they had begun to organise peaceful protests, but time had been against them.

Tien slowed for the double-roundabout, the powerful BMW automatic dropping effortlessly through the gears. She steered without having to use what she still referred to as the *suicide knob* and it caused her to smile. Her new prosthesis gripped the leather of the steering wheel as well, if not better, than the left hand she had lost in Afghanistan. Relaxing and firming her grip through sensors in her upper arm muscles, the Bebionic hand was a quantum leap in technology and had instantly relieved the mounting frustrations she had been encountering. Tien had come home from the London clinic after the final fitting and, in the privacy of her own apartment, cried with a mixture of joy and relief for nearly three hours. The intensity of the emotions had surprised even her.

As the car accelerated she passed a turn that led to the expanse of Highgate Cemetery, with its most famous internee. She mused on Franklyn and the organisation he represented. Perhaps he just wanted a better, more just society, like Marx, who was turned to dust over her right shoulder. Perhaps, but actions always had consequences and those worried her. She doubted Franklyn's actions would have the ramifications of Karl's. But she also doubted Karl had foreseen what would come of his impact on society. How his theories would be manipulated, leading to wars and non-wars, the mass slaughter of peoples and enforced migrations. She steered the car onto the dual-carriageway and wondered, if Marx had not lived, would she be here, driving past his resting place. Her Grandparents, on both sides, had been the victims of communist regimes sweeping through their homeland.

Tien shook her head and decided that philosophical musings on the reasons why she was in London, or on whether Franklyn was a safe bet, were not what she needed now. Besides, when Kara and she had discussed Franklyn's offer back in July, the day after the initial Police Station meeting, she had agreed to support her friend. There had been no coercion, no pressure. Kara, sitting in the wrecked old armchair that still held pride of place in her apartment, had been plain-spoken, eventually.

"Tien, this offers us a chance to do something that could make a difference. Something that matters."

"And what else?"

"And get paid for it?"

"We don't exactly need the money now, do we?" Tien had said, uneasiness in her voice as she spoke about the windfall they had received courtesy of their last case.

"No, I suppose not," Kara had conceded, "But we can help when things aren't fair. We can be a force for good."

"Great, shall I rush and get us some capes, a mask maybe? I look good in an all-in-one cat-suit."

Kara had laughed and reached for her drink, toasting Tien, "I'm sure you do."

"What's the real reason?"

There had been a pause. Kara had stared down at the gently swirling, golden-brown bourbon.

"It's okay Kara, just tell me."

Continuing to stare at the glass, Kara had said, "I miss the rush, Tien. Following the odd cheating partner or finding the employee who's dipping the till isn't enough. Last week, when we were working with the old team, it was a thrill, a buzz.

Franklyn's cases are likely to provide more of that. I want it."

"No you don't."

Kara looked up, frowning.

Tien continued, "You don't want it, you need it. Simple as that. You need it and to be honest, I enjoyed last week more than any other since I left the Army, so yeah, it's okay by me. On one condition."

"Name it."

"We both have to agree to every case. No agreement, no case."

"I wouldn't have wanted it any other way," Kara had said and downed her bourbon.

They'd set up a second meeting with Franklyn, sorted out all their protocols and then waited, but there had been no word from the old man. No contact, no excitement to get worked up about. Just silence. So they went back to doing routine. Not that they strictly needed to. The cash they had acquired while tracking down a less than respectable middle-aged couple meant they could have retired for good, but that would have driven both women insane. So now Franklyn had called and Tien had instigated the security measures that might not be necessary, but that she was going to oversee anyway.

Reaching to the steering wheel controls she pressed a small button marked with a telephone symbol. The BMW's head-up display in her windscreen showed a 'Dial by Name' command box.

"Call Jacob Harrop," Tien instructed. There was a small pause before a sultry voice responded with, 'Calling Jacob Harrop'. Tien needlessly said, "Thank you Marlene."

When she had taken delivery of the new car she had cycled through all the available voices, from the austere clipped English of an actor whose face she could see, but whose name she couldn't remember, through to an over-emphasised robotic voice. She had finally settled on the velvet tones of the female she had christened Marlene.

"Hi, how's it going?" Jacob answered, his Essex tones

neither sultry nor velvety.

"Good. You in place?"

"Roger that. Toby too. All is clear. You?"

"I'm about ten away. I'll confirm when I'm there. I make it ten-hundred hours," she paused and waited for the digital numbers on the head-up display to roll over, "now."

"Roger that."

She disconnected the call without any further formalities. The elegance and simplicity of using trusted colleagues on outer protection screens meant that she didn't have to waste time explaining the situation. They knew their job and Tien trusted Jacob and his brother Toby, both former Royal Air Force Regiment gunners, to protect Kara. Their role was to be the equivalent of the Seventh Cavalry and she knew they would come charging if required.

Tien's job was to be near with a vehicle. The Central London locations on the list would make that difficult, but out here in the North West suburbs, it was altogether easier. In the weeks that followed the second meeting with Franklyn, Tien had spent her time researching all thirty-one locations. Visiting each in turn she had assessed their surroundings, how many entrances each had, where the nearest parking spots were and based on what she found, she graded them into easy, medium and hard. The hard ones were those she dreaded due to the difficulty in protecting Kara, or being able to remove her from harm's way. She began to put rudimentary plans in place and then set about refining those plans as time allowed. Because Franklyn hadn't called in months, she had refined and improved her counter-surveillance plans for the complete list. The Canons Park location, a small coffee shop next to a Tube station, was graded as 'easy'. Open, above ground, a single front entrance and an exit door to the rear, albeit accessed through the kitchen, good road links surrounding it, parking in sight and no issues with mobile signals or line-of-sight radio communications. Tien would have chosen it herself for the first rendezvous.

She drove past the Tube station entrance and continued to

the next roundabout, mentally registering the cars and vans parked within the vicinity. Looping back, she pulled into a parking area adjacent to a long row of shops called 'Station Parade'. The small café was located midway down its length, sheltering between a newsagents and a picture framing business. Her position gave her a clear line of sight to the café entrance and allowed her to scan all the vehicles in the immediate vicinity. Being a Wednesday, the morning activity had slumped into a post-rush-hour-post-school-run hiatus, so activity around the Parade was minimal. She was parked directly in front of a car-parts shop that had been forlornly abandoned some time ago. The rest of the businesses in the row were still trading and there was light foot-traffic into the newsagents, the bookmakers, the florists and the rest of the sundry shops. The patrons toing and froing were wholly unremarkable.

Across the street a Number-79 bus slowed to a stop, then pulled away again having deposited a young mother with a baby-buggy and two older, sari-attired ladies. As the bus moved off Tien noted a white male still sitting in the shelter, his head down looking at his mobile phone. He looked about mid-twenties, had short dark hair and was wearing black trainers, jeans and a dark-blue padded ski-jacket.

She checked the London Transport sign at the near end of the shelter. It showed three route numbers so she relaxed a little, considering he may have been waiting for one of the other buses. She pulled her own mobile and searched for the routes. According to the online timetable the Number-186 was due in two minutes and the Number-340 two minutes after that. She relaxed some more and dialled Jacob's number.

"I'm here now. You still good?" she asked.

"Yep," he said.

"I have one possible. You?"

"None, I'm clear. Toby's happy their trail is clear too. Do you want me to come take a walk-by?"

"No," Tien answered. "Hang tight. If he is a sighter he won't be on his own. I suppose we should expect our guest to be running safety too."

"Okay, your call. I'll let Toby know."

"Good, talk soon." Tien disconnected and watched as an iconic red double-decker bus came into sight at the far end of the road. She could see '340 Harrow' in the vehicle's window display and thought it was typical that the second one due was the first to arrive. As it moved around a parked car she caught sight of the Number-186, a single-decker, following close behind.

An elderly couple, probably in their early seventies, had joined the young male at the shelter. The dapper old man stepped forward and raised his arm to signal the approaching bus. His wife waited a few steps behind. The young man didn't move.

Both buses trundled to a halt and although her view of the stop was obscured, Tien could see the elderly couple getting on to the first bus and making their way unsteadily to a seat. She was impressed that the driver waited for the couple to sit down before he hauled the double-decker back into traffic. The Number-186 trundled behind like a half-height sibling, patiently following in the tracks of its bigger sister.

The young male still hadn't moved. His eyes were sweeping from his mobile phone to the front entrance of the café. He hadn't yet looked up the opposite length of the street to where Tien was ensconced. She watched his hands. They held his mobile down on his lap but his fingers weren't moving the way they should if he was texting or surfing the net or accessing any other type of app. Then he raised his right hand to his mouth and spoke into his cuff. At the same time he turned in her direction. Tien, behind dark tinted side windows, scrunched down, making her movements very slowly, but he wasn't looking at her. He was watching a dark-maroon Jaguar XF saloon as it cruised down the road. When the car slowed and stopped outside the Tube station's entrance, the nearside front and rear passenger doors opened and two men, also in their mid-twenties, stepped from it. They glanced across to the man at the bus stop and nodded in acknowledgement. It was a quick gesture, but unmistakeable. The Jaguar pulled away as soon as the doors were slammed shut.

Tien called Jacob again, "Hi, I have two more males, short dark hair, wearing suits, making their way to the café."

"Do you want me to come to you?"

"Negative. You stay on the rear entrance. I think these two are doing a less than covert sweep. We should probably offer them some advice. This is not how to avoid attention."

Jacob laughed, "Have they even noticed you yet?"

"Nope, they've just walked straight for the café. One of them is standing outside, like a bad impression of a US secret service guy. The other one has just ducked inside," she paused, waiting. "And now he's back out. And they're going over to talk to their friend at the bus stop. Oh dear, this is amateur hour. All they need is mirror-sunglasses and they'd be perfect."

"What do you want to do?" Jacob asked.

"We'll wait until I'm sure they're our main guest's escorts. If not we'll abort. I have," Tien glanced at the car's clock, "10:17, so we have a few minutes. Give Toby a heads-up."

"Roger." The line disconnected and Tien knew that Jacob would call his brother who was currently at the next Tube station down the line, providing eyes-on protection for Kara.

Tien in turn called Kara, who answered on the second ring, "Yep?"

"We have company at the RV. Three tall, slim males, mid-twenties, behaving like they've read the easy-reader book of bad security details."

"Still, three young guys. I could maybe teach them a few moves?" Kara interjected with a laugh.

Tien couldn't help smiling, "Concentrate Kara," she mock scolded. "I'm going to get you to stay where you are until I know they're with our guest. Okay?"

"Yep."

Tien kept the line open but said no more. Instead she waited and watched. A few minutes later the Jaguar reappeared. The two men in suits left their colleague at the bus stop and crossed the road. As the car stopped level with the Tube station the rear, nearside passenger door opened and an older man, thin, with a receding hairline, stepped out. He nodded at the two younger men who got back into the car. It pulled away.

"Kara?" Tien asked.

"Yes."

"Our guest has arrived. He still has a plus-one in situ. I thought the old man trusted us?" Tien said with a laugh.

"Yeah, guess he trusts us like we trust him. Are we still going?" Kara asked.

"I think so. Seems okay. The other two were confirmed as his and they've left. When you talk to him you might suggest he ups his game. Those guys were dreadful. Wait," Tien watched the older man, dressed in a dark three-piece suit and carrying a slim document folder, walk purposefully towards the café. He carried himself with the poise of authority and despite Kara and Tien's assumption that he was way past retirement age, he walked with the bounce and vigour of a much younger man. He entered the café without a single glance around. "Okay, you're on," Tien said and disconnected the call.

From where Tien was parked she could see the elevated train line leading to the above ground station of Canons Park. At 10:24 Kara's train came into view.

Tien was satisfied the meeting place was secure. Jacob Harrop was positioned to the rear of Station Parade. He'd been in the vicinity of the shops since eight that morning. For the last hour he had been in a concealed vantage point that allowed him to get to the rear door of the café in less than thirty seconds if needed. His brother Toby would step from the train just behind Kara and be in loose contact with her until she was within sight of Tien. Then he would turn away and, having been briefed by his brother, knew to find a spot where he could keep an eye on the man at the bus stop. His job was to prevent anyone getting in the way of a rapid extraction. Tien was in overall control and as she saw Kara walking towards the café, she flicked a small switch on a compact radio transmitter. Each of the four wore a concealed earpiece and an omnidirectional mic that didn't require you to speak into your cuff, unless you wanted to look strange. It was much more convenient than using mobiles but had a limited range. Given their proximity now, the range was of no concern.

"Hi all, we're up on comms, how read?" Tien asked.

"Fives," answered Jacob.

"Same," answered Toby.

"Just dandy," Kara answered with a light tone as she looked into the florist's window.

"Thanks for that professional assessment," Tien said. "Anyway, you're cleared in. Time now is 10:27."

Tien watched Kara step through the café door and cross to a table set back from the window, about halfway into the small establishment. The older man rose and extended his hand. As he spoke, Kara's voice-activated microphone transmitted. Tien heard the distinctive 'Tic' as the mic switched on.

"My dear Kara, it is so good to see you again."

"You too Franklyn. To what do I owe the pleasure?"

"I'd like you to make sure the dead are really dead."

3

Canons Park, London.

Franklyn slid a document folder over to her. It contained a set of photographs, a coroner's provisional report, a number of newspaper cuttings and a handwritten letter. Kara closed the cover when the waitress appeared at her elbow. After Franklyn had ordered for both of them, Kara scanned the letter.

> 'To my family, friends and fans,
>
> I'm sorry for all the hurt that I have caused. There is no excuse. I succumbed to greed and my addictions. I should have reached out earlier but it is too late now. I am so sorry for disappointing you all. The money is gone and I cannot face any of you again. Especially not the parents and children who were relying on it. On me.
>
> I know you can never forgive me for I can never forgive myself. It is better that I end it like this. I am so sorry.
>
> Derek Swift'

"Okay, who's Derek Swift?" she asked.

"He was a radio broadcaster and sometimes television presenter in Suffolk. Strictly provincial but well known within his region. A local lad and a local celebrity," Franklyn said.

"And according to this, I assume he committed suicide because of some money he squandered?"

"Yes," Franklyn hesitated. "Well, that's what the official police enquiry and the initial coroner's report concluded."

Kara looked up from the file, "But you don't think so?"

"I don't know. I just think it's too convenient."

"Alright, let's begin at the beginning then?"

Franklyn smiled across the table at her and Kara, as she had done the first time they had met, found herself reciprocating the expression. There was something charmingly enigmatic about this old man which she found at once relaxing and intriguing. She knew practically nothing about him and despite Tien's and her best efforts they had failed to uncover anything. She didn't even know his full name. But then again, she didn't need to.

"Ever the practical one Kara," he said.

"I like to think so," she agreed.

"All the details we could recover are in the folder, but the general gist is this; Derek Swift was born in a village just outside of Ipswich, Suffolk in 1970. From age fourteen he volunteered at the local cottage-hospital radio station and after leaving school he moved permanently to Ipswich and started working for Radio Gippelwich."

"Never heard of it," Kara said.

"Well you wouldn't. It services the town and about twenty miles around. But it's second after BBC Radio Suffolk in popularity, so as Derek progressed from teaboy to DJ he began to be known in and around the town. He covered the local sports events, did outside broadcasts from the Suffolk Show, judged the occasional pageant, baking competition, you get the idea."

Kara nodded.

"Eventually he had his own breakfast show, 'The Swift

Start', which quickly became the most listened to radio show in Suffolk. After a few years he received offers to move to London and join the big national networks but he turned them all down. There's a newspaper cutting in there saying that he loved his home county and that he was happy. Ambition and money were second to family and friends."

"That's quite refreshing," Kara said. "What family did he have?"

"Parents and an older sister. That was it, no long-term partner although he was often seen in the company of women at functions and events," Franklyn paused as the waitress came back with his pot of tea and Kara's latte. He thanked her and poured himself a cup. Kara added a sugar to her coffee and watched Franklyn sipping his hot tea with no sugar or milk added. As he set the cup down he continued.

"He diversifies by going onto the local commercial television station. Chairs local-interest panel shows, a debate at election times, interviews the manager when the town football club was doing well, or badly. Eventually they offer him his own local-television talk show on a Friday night, 'A Swift Seven Days' taking a look at the events of the past week. Again, it does well and again he's offered to move to bigger things but again he turns it down."

"Sounds like he was doing okay. So what went wrong?" Kara asked.

"As you can probably imagine, Swift was always involved in local charities. Last year there was a cluster of kids in the Ipswich and greater Suffolk area all diagnosed with the same rare cancer. It made the national news, but the Scottish Independence vote was at its height so it was rapidly pushed from the newsfeeds. Locally it was still a significant story because four kids in a thirty-mile radius had a cancer that normally would affect only ten in the entire country per year. The progression of the disease was advanced and the normal treatments weren't successful."

"How old were the kids?" Kara asked.

"A four year old, two five year olds and a seven year old,"

Franklyn lifted his cup again.

"This isn't going to end well, is it?" Kara asked, dreading the answer.

Replacing his cup in its saucer the old man refilled it from the small pot, "No. Not well. Derek Swift headed up a fund-raising drive to get enough money to send all four kids to America. A hospital in Washington State had pioneered a new treatment and was having some success with it. The only problem was the cost of seventy-five thousand dollars per child in addition to the travel and accommodation costs. All in all they needed to raise a quarter of a million pounds. It took a while, but in May, the week before the UK's General Election, the parents were presented with one of those big promotional cheques for a total of two hundred and fifty six thousand pounds. That was on Saturday, the Second of May. The following day, Swift, and a friend called Amberley, went out deep-sea fishing, but Swift never made it back to harbour."

Kara frowned, "He fell off a boat?"

"So everyone thought. Your old colleagues in the RAF launched an immediate air and sea search but it was near dusk when he was reported missing so there wasn't much chance. Then on the Monday the police found the suicide note in his house in Ipswich. The reference to the money being gone and the children being disappointed raised obvious concerns. Swift had been one of the custodians of the charity account and sure enough it was empty. Nobody else involved had even checked and other than a few bank officials being reprimanded over shoddy audit practices, there was nothing anyone could do. The money was gone and so was Swift. The thinking was that he had been aiming to pay it back at some point, but the final total was reached quicker than expected. The loss would have been discovered as soon as the parents went to draw down the funds. With no time left, Swift took the decision to kill himself rather than be found out."

"Why didn't this make the news?"

"It was the General Election the following Thursday," Franklyn said with a shrug, "The media had bigger things to pursue than some provincial celebrity committing suicide."

"How did the police rule out that he hadn't done a runner, instead of drowning?"

"As he was boarding the boat, a passer-by had taken a, umm," Franklyn hesitated.

"Taken a?" Kara prompted.

"A photo of Swift and himself, as a memento of meeting him. I know there's a name for it."

Kara laughed, "A selfie, Franklyn, had he taken a selfie?"

"Yes. Quite. A selfie," he said the word self-consciously.

"So this convenient photo puts Swift on the boat, what else did the police turn up?" Kara asked.

"The witness testified that Swift and this chap Amberley were on the boat when it left. The boat had a full communications suite and a GPS trace available, a result of the navigation equipment on board, so they knew where it had been. According to the printout, it had gone into a well-known fishing area, then circled around looking for Swift, then eventually came back into harbour. They had the time of the first distress call from Swift's friend back to harbour and when the boat returned it was met by local police. All rather neatly packaged."

Kara drained the last of her coffee, "Do you want a fill up for your tea?"

"No, I'm fine thank you."

Kara caught the eye of the waitress and ordered another latte, but in a takeaway cup.

"Okay, so we have a dead minor celeb and a chunk of missing money. He spent it on a drug or booze or gambling debt if we believe his note and then dived off a boat. Why am I here Franklyn?"

"Because it's all too neat for me to be sure he's dead. If he paid off a debt for drugs or illegal gambling or whatever, then he was paying it off presumably to prevent being killed, or at least beaten to a pulp. Yet he pays the debt off then commits suicide? It doesn't sit quite right."

"Perhaps not, but guilt and remorse and who knows what

could have been rattling around in his head. But that's not quite what I meant."

Franklyn's brow creased, "I'm sorry, what did you mean?"

"I meant why am I here now? This money went missing in May, the man died, or didn't, in May. It's sad that he stole all the money, but it was six months ago and it's hardly the type of case that I thought would have concerned you."

"The children all succumbed to their disease," Franklyn said, his voice neutral of emotion.

"Well, yes, I assumed that," Kara said, her own voice reflecting Franklyn's. "But that still doesn't explain it."

"All four passed away before further funds could be raised. The eldest was the granddaughter of a former," Kara noticed he paused fractionally, "colleague of mine, but I only found out recently. I'm a grandfather too Kara. I don't know what losing a grandchild feels like and I don't want to know, but I can imagine. So, yes you're correct, this isn't necessarily the sort of case we had discussed. In fact the reason you're here is personal. I'd like to know if this Swift chap is really dead. I want to know if the money is really gone. It won't bring any of the children back, but it might allow for some closure. For the families." Franklyn folded his hands together on top of the table and held Kara in his gaze.

She found herself looking down at the old man's hands. He had long, slender fingers that matched similarly long, slender facial features. The liver spots on the backs of his hands betrayed his age much more than the rest of him. He was trim in his waistcoat, and although his hair had receded, his face was not severely lined or creviced. Each time Kara had met him, he had worn a three-piece suit with a fresh white shirt. This time his tie was a plain dark blue, on the previous meeting a maroon and on the first occasion she thought he had worn a regimental pattern, but hadn't been certain. Now she considered it was more likely than not.

"You said you heard about this recently. Would I be right in thinking you found out ten days ago?" she asked, trusting her instincts and playing a hunch that Franklyn had heard

23

about the events at a Remembrance Day reunion.

Franklyn nodded. As Kara silently considered her options he sat still, almost reverential and patiently awaited her decision.

"I'll have to-," she didn't finish her sentence as there was a small 'Tic' sound in her ear.

"Kara, if you're going to say you need to ask me, don't worry. I think we should take it," Tien's voice sounded softly in her ear.

"I'm sorry Kara, what were you saying?" Franklyn asked.

"Nothing. It's okay. We'll take the case. Can I assume this is all the information on file," she said patting the document folder.

"Yes," Franklyn nodded, "The police had little to go on and processed it by the book. They classified it as a high-risk missing persons, searched Swift's house, cars and work area but found nothing of consequence. The details of the friend who owned the boat are in the file, but it all came up clean. They kept it active for three months and then dropped it down to a low-level missing persons file."

Kara hesitated as the waitress came back to the table with her takeaway coffee. Once they were alone again she said, "Which in effect means no one is looking at it."

"Exactly," Franklyn confirmed. "Basically they might take it out and dust it off every so often but it will probably stay as it is for seven years. Then the coroner will review it, assess it for what it appears and declare Swift legally dead."

"Okay. Well, we'll take it from here. I'll be in touch," she said, pushing back her chair and standing.

Franklyn stood too, "Thank you Kara."

As she reached into her jeans pocket for money, he said, "It's okay, I'll look after the bill. I do appreciate you taking this on."

"It's fine Franklyn, no need to thank me yet." Kara put the folder under her arm and picked up her coffee. Halfway to the door she stopped and looked back, "The grandfather of the eldest child, who was he?"

Franklyn, still standing at the table, seemed to be considering how much he was willing to share. Eventually he said, "My Company Sergeant Major."

Kara nodded and left the café.

4

Woodbridge, Suffolk.

It had taken Tien less than half an hour to track down Francis Matthew Amberley. He was the owner of the *Heather-Anne,* a twenty-two foot fishing boat that was the last place anyone had seen Derek Swift.

According to the police file, Amberley and Swift had been friends since high school and had regularly fished together. Amberley was the deputy-manager of the Woodbridge marina, a job title, which as far as Tien could work out from the interview transcripts, meant he looked after all the maintenance issues. His social media presence was non-existent, but she had built up a profile of him from Franklyn's file, a biography on the marina's website, a few media reports about the company and the local Suffolk newspaper reports about the Swift case.

"So, what you're saying is, he's a local boy who has stayed local. Likes fishing, works with boats, plays with boats, is that it?" Kara asked.

"Pretty much," Tien nodded. "His interviews with the police paint a fairly bland picture. He lives in a modest terrace house that used to be his parents and is now his. He's single, keeps himself to himself. Likes pub quizzes at his local and that's about it."

"You've just described every serial killer on the planet," Kara quipped. "Quiet bloke, kept himself to himself, liked gardening, always digging up his patio he was," she said in an affected west-country accent.

Tien laughed, "It sounds like that, doesn't it? Seems our Mr Amberley is just a quiet chap."

"How does he afford a fishing boat?"

"I looked it up, you can get a boat like his for less than twenty grand, second-hand. So not much more than a car, which he doesn't own by the way. He lives within walking distance of the marina and just around the corner from the railway station, should he need to go further afield. The boat is parked in the marina too, so I imagine he gets that as a perk of the job."

"I think that's docked, or moored, or berthed, not parked," Kara said with a grin.

"Yeah, it's all wavy navy stuff, so no matter. How do you want to do this?"

"He's our only lead. We have nothing except he was out on the boat with Swift and therefore the last person to see Swift alive. From what I read here," Kara said, flicking through the police interviews, "he gave nothing to the cops other than he went below into the galley and when he came back up, his friend was gone. Simple story and he didn't waver from it."

"Maybe he didn't waver because it's true," Tien said.

"Maybe, but all we can do is go talk to him."

φ

It was always their preferred method to know the ground environment before setting up a meeting. In their previous lives they could have spent weeks getting familiar with the territory, planning contingencies, ensuring their options for extraction were well considered. But Suffolk was not southern Iraq, nor Helmand Province, nor any of the other less than permissive environments they had operated in.

To balance the reduced threat they had reduced assets. When they'd been with the Field Intelligence Tactical Team, they could rely on deployed teams of a dozen or more, and when they ran short, as Kara had in Iraq in 2006, they could borrow from the nearest Intelligence Corps billet. Now, in the constraints of a civilian operation, they were limited. People they might call on to help had lives to lead. They couldn't just drop everything, like they often had whilst in the Service.

Kara and Tien's first choice of protection was always Dan and Eugene O'Neill. The brothers were ex-paratroopers and had worked on security details with both women during their time in the military and extensively afterwards. But Dan and Eugene were currently attending their eldest sister's wedding in Perth, Australia, so they weren't an option.

Toby and Jacob had filled in for the O'Neills on a number of occasions, like with the Franklyn meet, and Kara and Tien had always been impressed, but Toby's wife Sally was due into hospital early the next morning to have an impacted wisdom tooth extracted, so Toby was looking after his three young kids. That meant for a short-notice, potentially overnight trip to Suffolk, only the younger Jacob was available.

There were others that Kara and Tien could call on but the job was low-risk and they decided it wasn't worth the extra logistics or the delay to get them in place. So it was that Jacob, Tien and Kara drove the couple of hours north and east and now sat in the converted barn accommodation of a Wood-bridge pub called the Beech Tree Inn. Given it was November, they had the place to themselves.

Kara finished briefing Jacob on the case.

"I remember him from when I was growing up," Jacob said, looking at a couple of photos of Derek Swift.

"How come?" Tien asked.

"He had a talk show. It was a local round-up of the week. My Dad used to watch it. Who knew he'd turn out to be a thieving toerag… Swift I mean, not my Dad."

Tien giggled, "Well, obviously." She flipped open the

laptop and brought up overhead satellite imagery of the town. The barn accommodation was less than three hundred yards from the house she zoomed in on.

"This is Francis Amberley's end of terrace. There's no practical way we can get an eyes-on recce of the place. His back garden is a postage stamp and the front door opens onto the street," Tien said, pointing out the features as she spoke.

"Are those football pitches on the other side of his garden wall?" Jacob asked.

"Hockey I think," Tien said. "They're the sports fields for this private school," she continued to manipulate the image so that it scanned out, "located in the same grounds as this church," she said, as the image revealed an expansive school building surrounded by manicured lawns and sitting next to a late-14th century church with a solid, square tower reaching over one-hundred feet into the air. The whole scene encapsulated biscuit-tin images of little England.

"Bit posher than my old Alma Mater," Jacob said with an appreciative low whistle.

"Yeah? Where was that?" Tien asked.

"Hylands Comprehensive, Chelmsford."

"Umm, yeah," Tien said with an over-exaggerated nod of her head. "I'd say this one's a bit more exclusive. Given the wide open playing fields and the lawn fairway right up to the main building it's definitely lovely, but of no use to us for mounting observations from."

"Can't we just go knock on his door?" Jacob asked.

"I'd prefer not to," Kara said. "I'd like it if the location was more neutral. Especially if we can't get a look inside the house first. It hands all the advantage to him, makes it difficult to get a tell on him and we don't know what he's got access to in there."

"What about the marina where he works?" Jacob offered.

"Same deal as the house really," Kara said.

"That leaves the pub it says he goes to," Tien said.

"Yes, that's an option," Kara nodded, "Do we know where it is?"

"No, but there can't be that many places within walking distance from his-" Tien cut herself off.

"What's the matter?" Jacob asked.

Tien turned the laptop around to show a Google map of the town. "I was going to say there can't be too many pubs within walking distance of his house, but it turns out there are ten."

"Good old Woodbridge," Jacob said. "It's a wonder anyone can walk anywhere."

"How many host quizzes?" Kara asked.

"Already ahead of you," said Tien, her fingers dancing over the laptop keyboard. "Three. One of which is this pub we're staying at, the others are the Angel, about a mile north of here on the main street and the Old Seafarer, which is practically right outside the marina's main entrance."

"Don't suppose any have their quizzes tonight?" Kara mused.

"Nope. Seems to be Fridays or Saturdays from their websites."

Kara reached back into the document file she had received from Franklyn and leafed through the cuttings, "Do we have a picture of Amberley?"

"Not in there, but I have a casual headshot of him from the marina website," Tien answered.

"Well," Kara stood and glanced at her watch, "I make it 16:00 now, what says we go for a bit of a pub crawl?"

φ

They didn't have to crawl very far. Kara didn't even have to show the picture, she merely had to mention Amberley's name to the landlady of the pub they were staying at. Mrs Spore, who insisted on being called Daphne, 'with no Y dear' and who reminded Kara of a somewhat worse-for-wear, brunette-from-a-bottle version of Barbara Windsor, told them all they needed. And much more besides.

"Oh yes dear, I know little Franny Amberley very well. Now why do you want to know about him?"

"Oh, it was one of our friends that said there was a real star of a quiz team up here," Kara lied effortlessly. "When she knew we were coming to Woodbridge she recommended we go have a try. We're keen on pub quizzes." Kara said, pointing over at Jacob and Tien. "We always enter at our local and this friend said she'd never come across a team as good as the one in this town. Said their star player was this chap Amberley. So do they come in here?"

"No dear, he doesn't come in here for his quizzing, or even for a quick drink, more's the pity. His Dad did, lovely man he was, big Franny. May the Lord keep him," Daphne halted her sing-song Suffolk lilt of an accent, which had the tiniest trace of a Cockney edge to it, just long enough to bless herself.

Kara noticed she used her left hand for the sign of the cross and was fairly sure, from having seen Tien do it many times, that Daphne had got it back to front. She also noticed the woman didn't seem to take a breath before she started talking again.

"He used to come in here every night dear. But then again he worked just a walk down the road at the plant nursery. Oh he had such a way with those plants, you never saw the like. He could charm a daisy out of the ground and as for tr-"

"Sorry Daphne," Kara interrupted as gently as she could. "Is this little Franny we're still talking about?"

"Oh no dear, that's his Dad, big Franny. No," and she let out a considerable laugh for a woman who couldn't have been more than five foot tall, "Oh no, not little Franny. That boy would curl a daisy by looking at it. Oh no. He never took to his Dad's work. Big Franny used to say, when he came in here and sat at that stool," she indicated the stool that Jacob was sitting on, tucked into the corner of the bar counter. Jacob involuntarily stood up and Daphne ploughed on, "That stool there, he would sit there and tell me that little Franny wouldn't know a daffodil from a dandelion."

"So you've been here a long time Daphne?" Kara interjected, trying to steer a conversation that she felt had the opportunity to last a week.

"What's that? Oh yes dear. Fifty-five years. I've seen them all in here."

"And little Franny doesn't come in here, Daphne? He's not part of your quiz team?" Kara said, leaning on the bar and laying her hand on the old woman's upper arm.

"No dear, that's right. He doesn't come in here."

"Why's that Daphne?" Kara said, again leaning in slightly as she asked the question.

"Well dear, he might not be able to grow plants like his old Dad, but he is like him in another way. He's no drinker. No, definitely not. That lovely young Mrs Amberley, God bless her," Daphne paused for another back-to-front-crossing, "yes, she had two good 'uns there. A husband and a son who are not drinkers is a good result for a woman. A good result in anyone's book. Big Franny would take one pint on the way home and that was all he would take and I think the son is the same. More's the pity though because he's a great quizzer from what I hear."

Kara leant her hand gently on the woman's upper arm again, "What happened to Mr and Mrs Amberley, Daphne?"

"A car accident dear. They both died, let's see, oh it must be twenty years ago now. Maybe more. Little Franny was so brave at the Church. Almost the whole town was there and rightly so for big Franny was well liked and Mrs Amberley was such a lovely lady. Up in front of that big crowd he stood and did a reading. Very good he was, well spoken. I remember it like it was yesterday and him only just eighteen and them both still so young and her such a beauty. Ah well, you can't have it all now can you?" Daphne finally paused for breath and took a sip from her cup of tea behind the bar.

"I'm sorry Daphne, how do you mean?"

"Oh now, that's just me saying what we all thought. Little Franny was such a quiet boy, like his Dad. He got quieter still after the accident but he started working at the marina and it settled him. He obviously got his Dad's brains but he got none of the looks of his Mother. Still not married now and I always think that's sad for a man. Such a shame for them not to have a woman to look after them."

Jacob looked to Tien and jokingly nodded in support of Daphne's suggestion of domestic bliss. Tien folded her arms and gave him her sternest stare. Then broke into a grin.

Kara decided to try to push things forward. "So do you know which pub Franny goes to for his pub quizzes, Daphne?" She asked as gently as she could.

"Oh yes dear," said Daphne reaching for her cup and taking another sip of tea.

Kara waited but there was nothing more forthcoming. She considered pressing the point but then thought better of it. There were only two other pubs to check out and the walk would probably be pleasant.

"Daphne, we've got to go out, but you've been marvellous. Really marvellous. Thank you. Would it be okay for us to catch up again and hear more about the town?" Kara enthused.

"Of course dear, of course. It's my pleasure."

Kara nodded to Tien and Jacob to head for the door.

"Excuse me, dear," Daphne called.

Kara turned, flanked by the others, "Yes Daphne?"

"You and your friends, you're not journalists are you?"

"No, Daphne, we're not. Why do you ask?"

"Oh, I just wondered dear," Daphne said distractedly. Kara began to turn away but the old lady continued, in a much firmer voice, "it would have been normal for a fuckin' journalist to lie to me. Treat me like some old fool. I can't stand fuckin' journalists. So if you were, you'd be finding somewhere else to sleep tonight."

Kara knew her face had registered a look of disbelief at the old lady's use of expletives.

"You look shocked dear, but I've run a pub less than a mile from a docks for the last half century. I can swear like a sailor if I need to. If you aren't journalists, why do you want to know about Francis Amberley?" The Suffolk burr had fallen from her accent and she was pure East End now.

Kara walked slowly back to the bar. Daphne was standing straighter, her arms stretched out and her palms down on the counter top. She hadn't grown in stature but her body language was so much less the frail old woman than it had been during the previous discussion. It was rare for Kara to be suckered-in by anyone, but this landlady had done it easily. She had let Kara see what she wanted to see and reeled her in. The one thing Kara knew for certain was that to lie to her again would be a singularly stupid thing to do.

"No Daphne, we're not journalists. We're private investigators, hired to look into the circumstances surrounding the death of Derek Swift. We just want to talk to Francis about what happened. That's it."

The old lady nodded slowly.

"Is anything that you told me true?" Kara asked.

"Yes, all of it. I just don't like the press looking about the town. The way they muckrake is bad for business."

"Is there anything to muckrake?"

"I don't know about that necessarily, but the only thing Francis Amberley ever did to be of interest to passing strangers is to be on a boat when a man fell off it. A man who swindled a lot of money from some very sick children, so I can't imagine any stories surrounding him would be positive."

"Fair enough," Kara said. "We're just here to make sure that man really did fall off that boat."

Daphne considered what Kara had said. She glanced over to Tien and Jacob. Then she looked up at the ship's clock on the wall, "Well, if you leave now you'll more than likely catch him at the Old Seafarer. I wasn't lying when I said he drops into a pub for a drink on the way home. Though I'm not sure who told you he was part of a quiz team. Francis Amberley has never been on a team in his life. He takes part in the quiz at the Seafarers on his own. Always on his own. Wins more than he loses, or so I hear. Our quiz is for teams of four or more. Same with the one at the Angel. That's why he doesn't play our quizzes. But the Seafarer let him be on his own."

"Thanks Daphne. I appreciate it."

"Just one more thing."

"Yes?"

"If you want to be discreet, I'd leave Tien outside."

"Pardon?" Kara said, feeling the instant spike in her temper. If there was one thing certain to rile her it was someone discriminating against her friend.

"This is Suffolk, dear. Not London. And rural, coastal Suffolk at that. Take a good look around you as you walk down the street and count how many non-whites we have here. I've run this pub for a lot of years and I can tell you that a non-white person is going to attract attention. We're not racist, but we will notice."

Kara's temper subsided as quickly as it had threatened to rise, "I owe you more thanks Daphne. You sure you've always been a landlady?"

"Since I was twenty-five dear. Before that I was a secretary, before that a schoolgirl and before that an evacuee from Hackney sent up here during the blitz. Came back here and ran this pub with my Terry, God rest him, after we got married. He'd been an evacuee here too. What made you ask that?"

"You have a particular skill for reading people and the situation surrounding them," Kara smiled.

"You don't run a pub and not acquire that dear, but off you go now or you'll miss him."

"Thanks Daphne. When we get back, you and Tien can catch up. She's born and bred in Hackney." Kara turned away but not before she caught the surprise on the old lady's face.

5

Jacob and Kara sat on either side of the Old Seafarer's main bar. The exposed timber beams testified to the building's Tudor heritage, and although it had been considerably expanded over the centuries, the main bar was still the original heart of the place. A long L-shaped counter looked like it was crafted from one of King Henry's ships of the line. A solidity emanated from it that anchored the rest of the room. The left hand edge of the long leg of the bar disappeared whole into a bulbous deformity in the white-washed wall. Halfway along that wall and midpoint down the length of the room, was a huge fireplace with a mantle six foot high. What looked like half a tree's worth of logs nestled in a heap of brown and grey, orange and scarlet. Occasionally the random lick of a flame cremated a small piece of unburnt bark to a wisp of ash. The smell of wood smoke and the gentle babble of voices gave the pub a homely, comforting feel.

Jacob was at a corner table between the fireplace and the front wall of the building. His view commanded all of the bar area with its six small tables which could sit three or four people each and currently had nine patrons in total. To his

36

right, the main entrance door, with its internal portico, was situated between two double bay windows. Opposite the fireplace and set back about five feet from the bar, was a long step that led down to a larger room filled, yet not crowded, with a further dozen or so small tables, a quarter of which were in use. Beyond this was a wall with a centrally mounted glass door that had 'The Seafarer's Fare' etched into it and led through to a separate ten-table restaurant. Kara sat to the left of that door, diagonally across the room from Jacob. Between her top-right and his bottom-left location, they had eyes-on the whole of the space. Crucially, Kara had a direct line of sight to the entrance door, whilst Jacob could see anyone coming in from the restaurant. Apart from the one behind the bar, the only other door was just to Kara's right and led to a corridor that in turn led to the toilets.

Tien was in the car, parked in the carpark, "Can you still hear me okay?"

Kara lifted her mobile phone to her ear, even though Tien's voice was coming through the communications earpiece. It was less noticeable to be talking into a phone than talking into thin air.

"Yes Tien, I can hear you."

"Is the fire nice?"

"It's lovely. You should see it. All warm and inviting."

"I really don't like you at times."

"How many coats have you got on?"

"Three."

Kara supressed a giggle, "Aww. We'll make it as quick as we can. I promise."

"I'm sure I can sue you. Leaving me in a car in November is tantamount to leaving a baby in a hot car in the summer."

Kara saw Jacob raise his hand to his mouth. Like he was scratching his chin. "I appreciate you taking this on Tien," he said in a soft whisper. "Really, I do. Oh sorry, excuse me, I just need to take my jacket off, it's soooo warm."

"I hope you boil," Tien said in her best imitation of a huffy child. "And as for you Kara, I-" she stopped and swapped from joking teammate to efficient operator. "Heads-up we have our target. He's just crossing the road from the marina. Dark boots, jeans, heavy donkey-jacket. Picture we have of him is a relatively good likeness. He's about five-five, medium build, slight paunch although that might just be his hands in his pockets. He's hunched over slightly, but that might be the temperature out here. Rectangular face, long chin, slightly protruding ears, small forehead, thinning dark hair. He's about ten feet from the front door. Copy?"

"Copy that," Kara confirmed.

As the door of the pub swung open the patrons that faced it looked up momentarily. Recognising the figure coming in from the already dark evening, they ignored him and looked back down. Except Kara. She continued to watch the man as he went straight to the bar.

Francis Amberley unbuttoned his jacket and Kara could see Tien's assessment had been correct. He had a paunch beginning to show under a cream, heavy-duty fisherman's jumper. The slight stoop to the man's stance apparently wasn't due to the cold for he maintained it in the heat of the room. He was bent at the waist to an angle of a few degrees. Kara thought it looked like a doll some child had bent forward and forgotten to straighten properly.

He didn't appear to speak before the barman lifted a round-bodied pewter tankard from amongst a dozen or so different shaped and sized tankards hanging from hooks on the low ceiling. After a couple of long pulls on the old-fashioned handle of something called Woodforde's Wherry, the tankard was set in front of Amberley. He looked at it but didn't touch it. Neither did he make small talk with the barman. He just reached into his jean's pocket, retrieved a small pile of coins and stacked them carefully on the solid counter. Then he stood still, slightly bent forward, watching his beer. The barman was moving about behind the bar doing those odd things barmen did when no customers were present. Dusting or wiping surfaces that appeared to Kara to be clean enough, moving glasses and bottles forward fractions of an inch to straighten them when they weren't crooked to begin with.

The entrance door opened and closed again and two young men, not more than early-twenties bustled in, hand in hand and making 'Brrrr' noises. The patrons once more looked up, but this time greeted the newcomers with warm smiles and the occasional nod, before returning to their own conversations.

The barman stopped doing his behind-the-bar-fidgeting and also greeted the men with a warm smile and a precise report of the weather conditions they'd just come from, "Hello Dylan, Rohan. It must be minus three out there and that wind's doing nothing to make it feel warmer. Get in here and get the chill out of you. What can I get for you both?"

Amberley looked out from under hooded eyes, his head moving a fraction so he could see the two men approaching to his left-hand side. Kara saw the faintest sneer contort his lips. Reaching out for the tankard, he took a long drink, then moved away from the bar and slouched to the bottom-right corner of the room. Between him and Kara were four empty tables.

Jacob raised his hand to obscure his mouth, "I can't see him. He's blocked by the small portico of the entrance door."

Kara nodded the most subtle of acknowledgments.

Over the next ten minutes the main door opened and closed a number of times as the pub began to fill with a steady stream of customers. Most looked like workers on their way home and most appeared to know each other, at least by sight, as shared smiles and nods were exchanged, a greeting and sometimes the mimed offer of a drink. An open hand tilting to the mouth and a nod of encouragement, normally met with a raised hand, a shake of the head, a mouthed, 'No, I'm fine' and another point to a half-full glass on a table. The little act ended with a mouthed, 'Thanks anyway' and the benevolent, would-be buyer continued their journey to the bar. It was a theatre and one that Kara warmed to, not just because of the fire. She loved to observe the interactions of people and could happily sit for hours watching unspoken language fill a room.

When Kara had come back from her final tour of Afghanistan she'd gone to stay with her parents in Somerset for almost a month. Most afternoons she had taken to dropping into the Royal Oak pub that was on the same street as her family home. She'd perch herself on the plush green velvet, deep-buttoned corner seat and quietly read a book, sipping tea. The sight of her, a single female reading in the pub, never turned a head nor garnered an unkind word. Occasionally she might be convinced to have a stronger option than tea, but the drink was of no consequence. It was the stability of sitting in a building that had been in the same spot for hundreds of years that she craved. The comfort of knowing most, if not all, the faces that came through the door was like a balm for her spirits, which were still rattled after she had come so close to dying.

Her family weren't of ancient Crewkerne lineage. Her parents often joked that having moved there in 1975, the locals might stop referring to them as drop-ins in another thirty years, but in reality they were part and parcel of the community. Kara had been born and bred in the town so she knew most of the patrons of the Royal Oak by name, or at least by family connection. She would smile and chat without reservation, yet she was often left to her own space and company. During those afternoons she would spend more time observing the people than reading words on a page. The comfortable friendliness, the shared banter, the unspoken antagonism, the furtive glance, the flirtatious laugh. It enthralled her. It was true that she had been trained in observation, reading body language, eye mapping, neuro-linguistic programming and many other techniques to establish rapport and elicit information, but the simple act of sitting and watching people casually was a soothing pastime in its own right. But, by watching closely you could tell so much about the society that was forming, for every space was its own society.

What she knew now, sitting in this Suffolk pub, was that the society of the Old Seafarer was a society plus one. The space, at 17:30 on a Wednesday evening, wasn't exactly full, yet there were enough people to generate a vibrant buzz of overlapping chatter and comfortable conversation. According to the 'events' board above the fireplace, there were no live football matches on tonight, no karaoke, no quiz, so it was unlikely to become packed. That meant people had a relatively free choice of seats. In addition to her and Jacob, Kara counted another five single drinkers. Two were seated on high stools at the bar and chatted amiably to one another, the barman and many of those who came up to buy drinks. One was seated at a table next to a group of two older couples and appeared content to look at his smartphone, catching up on whatever social media platform held his attention. Another was at the table next to Jacob. She had sparked up a casual chat with him.

Kara was pleased to see Jacob could maintain a perfectly natural conversation and still remain alert to the security job he was there to do. It was one of the best covers to adopt. Just a guy, and Kara had to admit, Jacob was quite a good-looking guy, having a laugh with an attractive girl.

Kara was on her own, a hi-ball glass of lemonade on the table to her front and an open paperback in her hand. Not knowing anyone in the pub meant she wasn't greeted like she would have been in the Royal Oak, but people still made eye contact with her when she looked up and would nod and smile in acknowledgement of her presence. Woodbridge was obviously welcoming to strangers.

That left Francis Amberley. The plus one to the bar's society. Kara was shocked at how stark the exclusion was. Granted, he sat at a small circular table in the corner, his back to the majority of the bar, looking out of a window. Or actually looking at his reflection in the window, for the only feature visible through the glass was the fuzzy halo of a dim streetlight across the carpark. Yet other people also had their backs to the bar and they were talked to, interacted with. No one sat within two tables of Amberley. No one looked towards him, no one smiled at him, no one nodded, no one said hello. Kara had the definite feeling he wasn't being snubbed by the rest of the pub's clientele, but that they were acting in response to his attitude to them. She couldn't be certain, but she was fairly sure it was Francis doing the excluding.

Holding her book so it looked like she was reading it, but in fact was reading Amberley, she watched him as he took slow drinks from the tankard. That too confused her. It was obvious this was his own tankard. Kara knew that many rural pubs would stock their regulars' favourite drinking vessels. A fraternity thing, almost homely, so at some stage, somehow, at some time, Francis must have been on speaking terms with the bar staff at least. She considered aborting the task for the evening and spending more time on research, but in the end she dismissed it as an option. They knew as much as they were likely to find out about him and, from the looks of the bar, not many in Woodbridge would be able to add anything more. Closing her book, she lifted her glass and walked over to his table. She sat down in the chair adjacent to him before he had a chance to react.

"Good evening Mr Amberley," she said and smiled.

He was halfway to reaching for his drink and his hand wavered in mid-air. He retracted it and set it on his lap whilst he looked out from under half-closed lids at her face. Tien's description had been accurate, as had Daphne's assessment. No good looks had been passed on from an attractive mother. Plain was the politically correct term, decidedly unattractive was Kara's thought. He smelled of diesel and sea-salt. The hand that had wavered was that of a manual worker. Long hours of being outside and longer hours of fixing engines had ingrained a blackness into every fingerprint crease.

He leant back slightly in his chair and looked down at her feet. Kara was dressed in boots, black trousers, a white blouse and a wool wrap. Her padded and insulated jacket was back at her original seat. She watched as he slowly gazed the length of her. His eyes stopped at her breasts. He didn't attempt to make it discreet. He stared at them, then raised his eyes to meet hers, then dropped his gaze back to her breasts.

Kara felt her skin crawl. She had to concentrate to restrain herself from shivering or from reaching across and smacking him with the glass she held in her hand. She couldn't restrain her tongue, "My face is up here Mr Amberley. Perhaps you'd be so kind as to look at it?"

He slowly brought his chin up, "Who are you and what do you want with me Missy?" he asked in his prominent Suffolk accent. Kara had been hearing those tones all afternoon and had thought they conveyed a quaint rustic charm, an old-England country idyllic, but in Amberley's care they were dull, lifeless, heralding a slowness of thought and action.

Tien and Kara had discussed their strategy for getting information from Amberley, but come up with little. Other than his boat, his quiz exploits and his modest house they had nothing concrete to work with. So they had decided a direct approach was their only opening. Direct didn't mean truthful.

"My name's Eve Allen and I'd like to talk to you if I may," Kara said, using a favoured alias.

"You a journalist are you?" he asked with an obvious disdain to his voice.

"No, not a journalist," Kara said, wondering why everyone in this part of Suffolk seemed to have a dislike for the fourth estate. Not that she completely disagreed. She had little time for the sleazier sides of that profession herself. "I'm working on behalf of the families of the children involved in the Derek Swift scandal." Kara noticed Amberley's whole body stiffen at the mention of the name. He looked away from her.

She continued in as neutral a tone as she could manage, "They want me to look into the circumstances of Mr Swift's death. They, and the company responsible for Mr Swift's life insurance, are keen to resolve the final status of Mr Swift as quickly as possible." Kara paused. There had been a small flicker to his right eye when she had mentioned life insurance, but other than that Amberley remained still. She pressed on, "As I am sure you know, a suicide without a body is not a recordable death for seven years. With no death certificate, there can be no payout of life cover. Even if there is a certificate, were it to be confirmed as suicide then that also precludes a payout of the cover." She stopped and watched the strange little man next to her. He was lost in his own thoughts

43

and made no reaction to the fact she had stopped talking. She prompted him, "Do you understand, Mr Amberley?"

"What's all that got to do with me then?" he finally asked, looking down at his tankard.

"I would have thought that was obvious Mr Amberley. The parents of the children wish to sue for the missing money out of the insurance settlement."

"What for? All their kids are dead ain't they?"

Kara managed to suppress the surge of anger she felt at the dismissiveness of the comment. In her ear, Tien's calming voice sounded softly, "Deep breath my friend. Concentrate on the task." Kara did as advised and nearly smiled in recognition of just how well Tien knew her.

She controlled her voice to reflect a neutral, business-like demeanour, "Yes Mr Amberley, sadly all the children are indeed dead, but the parents feel that if they can make good on the money raised, then it could be redistributed to other children who may be diagnosed in the future."

"Lovely I'm sure. Very Christian of them. Still don't know what it's got to do with me though," Amberley said, disdain still in his voice. He leant forward and picked up his tankard.

"As I said, I would have thought that would be obvious. As the sole beneficiary named in Derek Swift's insurance policy and with no other will and testament, it would be *you* that the parents will sue for recovery of the missing funds."

The effect of Kara's words were exactly as she had hoped. Amberley's eyes widened over the brim of his tankard and he coughed mid-drink. Some of the Woodforde's Wherry spilled down his jumper and more slopped over the sides of the tankard as he dropped it back onto the table. The crash of it against the wood caused a few of the other customers to look around, but only momentarily.

Shocked he may have been, but he managed to control his voice into a low growl, "What fucking insurance policy?"

"Mr Derek Swift was insured for one and a half million pounds, which would be doubled in the event of an accidental death, or reduced to zero in the event of a suicide. You are named as the beneficiary on that policy. I'm sorry Mr Amberley, I assumed you knew."

"No I didn't fucking know. You think if I knew I was due three million quid I'd have let hi-" Amberley stopped. His face, weather-beaten and oaken-coloured, infused purple.

"I'm sorry Mr Amberley. I didn't catch that. If you had known you'd have what?"

Kara watched his eyes dart from the tankard, to the window, to the ceiling then back to the table. She could almost hear the gears turning in his head. She waited for another few seconds. "Mr Amberley? You were saying?"

"Nothing. I wasn't saying nothing. They can't sue me, I don't have his money."

"No, I know Mr Amberley but as you can see, it would be a win-win for all if we could prove that it wasn't a suicide. Well, apart from the insurance company I suppose, but that's the game they are in. Certainly a win-win for you and the parents. I imagine if we can prove it was accidental and you get your three million, you'd happily settle out of court for the two hundred and fifty six thousand the parents want?"

Amberley didn't seem to have heard her. His lower jaw was clenching and grinding while his eyes continued to dart around. Kara tried again, a little louder, "Mr Amberley?"

"What? What are you saying?" he semi-growled.

"I said, I imagine if we can prove it was accidental and you get your three million, you would be happy to settle out of court for the money the parents want?"

"Yes," he said, still distracted. Then he refocussed, as he thought about what she had actually said, "Yes, of course. If it means it would all be over quickly then yes."

"So you will assist me?" she asked.

"What do you want?" he asked.

"Our main thrust is that the suicide note that was found by the police wasn't left prominently. We will argue that Mr Swift wasn't intending to fall overboard, that the note was never intended to be found and he never intended to commit suicide. You will be pivotal as you can tell us what mood he was in on

45

the evening."

"But I already told the police what happened. I said he was being quiet and withdrawn, not like himself at all. I already said all of that."

"Yes, yes you did… But you didn't say he was depressed or suicidal, did you?"

There was a pause and once more Kara could almost hear gears whirring. Eventually she saw a realisation in Amberley's eyes. He looked directly at her for the first time since she had mentioned Swift's name.

"No, I didn't say anything like that, you're right enough there Missy. I did not. Not one word."

"Well then," Kara stood, "I need you to have a good think about what happened and then I will need to take some notes. Would it be convenient for me to meet you tomorrow to discuss this further?"

Amberley remained seated, "Yes it would. I can get some time off, they owe me enough. Where do you want to meet?"

"I thought the restaurant here. We could meet for lunch?"

"For lunch, you say? Are you paying Missy?"

Kara kept her voice as toneless as before, "Yes Mr Amberley, I will pay. Shall we say one o'clock?"

Amberley nodded and reached for his tankard again.

Kara walked back over to her original table to get her coat. As she was putting it on, she angled her face to the wall and said quietly, "Tien, we're on our way out." Then, she walked to the door and saw Jacob making similar moves to leave. Exiting the pub she crossed to the car that Tien had already started.

"Bloody hell, it's cold in here," she said as she got into the passenger seat.

"That's enough out of you," Tien said. "You think we'll get him to talk?"

"Oh yes. He'll tell us every detail of that night without doubt. The horrid little slime of a man."

"That bad?"

"Worse. He looked at me like I was a piece of meat, had

no concern for the children and is a cheapskate to boot. I struggle to find any redeeming qualities so far."

"How did he react to the bait?"

"Exactly what we expected. It was a real shock to him. He had no idea there was a policy."

"I guess the shock of finding out we made it all up and that there isn't a policy will be equal in measure," Tien said and smiled at her partner in the dim light of the car's dashboard.

"Yep, but hopefully we'll have all we need by then."

The heater of the car made wheezing noises as it tried to bring the internal temperature up.

"Come on Jacob, where are you? Leave that nice young lady that was sitting beside you alone and get your butt out here. I'm freezing." Kara called out, wrapping her arms around herself and hunkering down in her seat.

"Kara, Tien, standby, standby," Jacob's voice was clear and controlled.

"Jacob, what's going on?" Kara asked, immediately sitting upright and swapping a concerned glance with Tien.

"I was delayed leaving. It seemed polite to break off my conversation with manners and not just run for it. Good job too, because as I was getting up, Amberley went to the toilet."

"And?" Kara asked.

"And he pulled an old model Nokia mobile from his pocket as he was making his way to the door. I followed him into the toilet but he's gone into a stall. He wasn't speaking, so I reckon he's texting. I've backed out and am standing by the restaurant door, looking as if I'm making a phone call. What do you want me to do?"

Kara had a decade of field intelligence experience, Tien just one year less. The benefit of it was mostly visible in the pre-planning that went into jobs, but it was truly visible when things went off-piste. So it was now as Kara began to control the situation, "Hold your position, keep your comms open. Where's his tankard?"

"What?" Jacob asked.

"The tankard that he was drinking from, is it still on the

47

table he was at?"

'Um, no. No the table's clear, he took the tankard back to the bar before he went to the loo."

"Is there a back exit out from the toilets?" Kara asked.

"Only the fire exit and it's fitted with an emergency bar-push handle. It's wired and alarmed. He's not going out that way without us knowing about it."

Once more Kara thanked the good sense Tien and she had in using professionals that they could rely on. "Good work Jacob. Now, what pocket did he pull his phone from?"

"Umm, his left I think."

"I need you to be sure Jacob. Very sure. If you don't know just say, it's better than guessing."

There was a small pause, "Definitely left pocket Kara. That's how I saw it so clearly."

"Okay, that's good. He has to come back out the front. You stay put, let us know when he's on his way and then follow semi-close behind, okay?"

"Yep."

"Tien?" Kara swivelled in her chair.

"Already there," Tien said, switching off the car and reaching for the door handle. Kara stepped out and leant against the side of the car. After a few minutes the small 'Tic' sounded again in her ear.

"He's moving," Jacob said.

As Amberley came out through the door and into the near darkness of the dimly lit carpark, Kara bumped into him almost head on.

"What the fu-" he said and put his hands out to fend off whoever it was to his front.

"Oh! Mr Amberley. I'm so sorry. I was just heading back inside to ask you if we could make it one-thirty tomorrow instead of one. My apologies, I didn't even see you." She remained in front of him and felt his hands on her torso.

"Bloody hell Missy, you nearly had me over there. You need to be careful walking around in the dark like that."

Kara felt his hands moving up the front of her jacket. "Yes, you're right. Sorry. I didn't mean to knock you," she sounded contrite. "Anyway, is one-thirty okay?" She stifled the urge to take the hand that had just slipped over her left breast and break it into its constituent parts.

"Yes Missy, one-thirty's fine," he said, completely unaware of Tien stepping away from him and re-entering the shadows of the pub's eaves.

"Thank you Mr Amberley, I believe you can let me go now. I don't think I'm going to fall," Kara said.

The Pub door opened again, creating a pool of light that illuminated their small tableau. Jacob walked past them and into the night.

Amberley pulled his hands away like Kara had become electric, stammered that he would see her tomorrow and walked off, stooping forward, in the direction of his home. Once he was out of sight the three met back at the car.

"All good?" Kara asked as Tien pressed the ignition button and the car once more began the effort of heating its interior.

"Yep, all good," Tien said and shifted the car into drive.

"Want to let me into what we just did?" Jacob asked from the backseat.

"Tien pickpocketed Amberley's phone," Kara answered.

"Really? That was pretty slick. What happens if he misses it?" Jacob asked.

"Well it's not so much of a problem," Tien said as she pulled out of the carpark and drove back to their accommodation. "If he does miss it, he'll return to the pub to look for it. He won't find it and so he'll go home. By that time I'll have figured out what he was up to, if anything, and if he's legit, Kara will give him his phone back at the meeting tomorrow, saying she found it after he left."

"And if he's not legit?" Jacob asked.

"Then I suspect we'll bring our meeting forward," Kara said.

6

It took six seconds for Tien to break the lock code on the mobile phone. "Ah, don't you miss the Nokia 3310? What a wonderful old friend it was," Tien said, giving the small phone a pat and disconnecting it from the cable that attached it to the PC.

Jacob looked sideways at Kara and smirked, "Is geek or nerd the right term?" he asked.

"I'll pretend I didn't hear that," Tien said, as she flicked through the Nokia's menus. "Oh, that's interesting. It's clean."

"How clean?" Kara asked.

"Totally. No call logs, no texts in or out. No contacts, not so much as a hint of any use."

"Interesting indeed," Kara said as she watched Tien plug the phone back into the PC's cable.

"What now?" Jacob asked.

Tien looked up and gave him a benevolent smile, "Clean doesn't mean empty Jacob. The idea that you delete call logs and texts and whatever else you think you've deleted from a phone is just an illusion. Just like you can recover files on a PC you can recover almost anything back from a mobile. You just

50

need the right software."

"And we have it?" he asked, already knowing the answer.

"Oh yeah, we have it, but first things first," Tien said as she began to type rapidly. The action was quite unusual to watch. Her prosthetic left hand, with extended index finger, prodded the keys in the style of a one-finger typist. Meanwhile, her right hand was the fully functional hand of an experienced touch typist. The resultant speed was much faster than most and much slower than Tien had once been.

The laptop screen displayed a new interface and a mobile number appeared in a box on the top left. Tien highlighted it and dragged it into another search box at the top right. A small egg-timer appeared and rotated for a few moments before another dialogue box popped up.

"This is an unregistered, pre-paid mobile, first activated for use in June," Tien read off the screen.

"Unregistered?" Jacob asked.

"Not on a contract. A burner phone that isn't in anyone's name so it's untraceable to an individual," Kara explained. Jacob nodded.

"And," Tien said as she continued to type and the display of the laptop changed again, "it's only ever made one call and only ever sent five text messages. The call," she paused as she transferred another phone number into another search box, "was the initial activation call to the network in June. The first text was also in June, loading on credit with an over-the-counter top-up. The rest of the texts were sent tonight," she checked her watch, "twenty minutes ago. Ties in with Amberley's trip to the toilet." Tien turned the laptop around so Kara and Jacob could see the screen. "The messages on the right are outgoing, the ones on the left incoming," she said as she zoomed the display in.

```
                                    This is Francis 44619
Hello Francis, Pin?
                                    826
Not quite.
```

Excellent.

Get a message to Del 44128
Contact me URGENT
A woman snifn about
Says there is money?
Insurance?
Need to talk

OK.

Tien closed the text display down and brought up a further interface. She opened a browser window and pasted yet another number into a search box. "Okay, these texts were sent to a mobile in Holland, or at least one with a Dutch country code," she said and leant back from the laptop.

"Thoughts?" Kara asked.

"The fact that everything was deleted off the phone is significant in itself. The texts look like a challenge and response protocol, which infers a set of security procedures and our Mr Amberley was quick off the mark to reach out for help," Tien said.

"But who's he calling for help from?" Jacob asked.

"Don't know yet, but I would say it's more than likely Del is short for Derek. Whether that means Derek Swift and that he's alive and well in Holland is something we're going to have to ask Amberley about," Kara said.

"When?" Jacob asked.

"No time like the present. I don't think we can afford to wait, just in case whoever is on the other end of these texts decides to contact him by some other method."

"So we're going to go knock on his door?" Jacob asked.

"Yep," said Kara. Conscious of her earlier reasoning to Jacob, she added, "He won't have any home advantage this time. We're going to be way less than polite visitors. I'll brief you on the way."

φ

The street had tightly packed, three-storey terraced houses

to the north side of the narrow road and much more substantial, detached houses to the south.

"It's like Coronation Street versus Quality Street," Tien said as they made their way along the ridiculously narrow footpath. The only light came from behind curtained windows, or the occasional faux-Edwardian porch light on the southern side.

"Why are there no street lights?" Jacob asked, in almost a whisper as he walked in the middle of the three of them, strung out in single file.

"Where would you put a pole? There's hardly enough room for one person to walk on the footpath let alone sticking a light pole in. It would have to go in the road," Tien whispered back.

"I'll take it as a lucky omen. It certainly works to our advantage," Kara said softly over her shoulder. "All set?" She asked, receiving whispered agreement from her two followers.

They crossed the road to the terrace side of the street. Jacob walked out and around her, going to the far side of the single ground-floor window. Tien stopped short, once more hidden in shadows. Kara stepped up and raised the dulled brass knocker that was mounted on the faded black door. She rapped twice and waited.

The venetian blinds on the window to Kara's right twitched and Amberley's face looked out into the night. His hand against the glass to see better, he looked at her and frowned. She faced him, illuminated by the window's light-spill, and raised the mobile phone. Giving her best fake-smile she waggled the phone as if to say, 'look what I found'. The blinds dropped back into place.

"Jacob," Kara said softly and he came to stand to her left-hand side. The sound of a deadbolt being withdrawn at the top of the door and a chain being released from the latch were the precursors to the final Yale lock being turned. As Amberley opened the door fully, Kara took a step to her right. The stockily built Jacob exploded into the tiny hallway, his left arm went around Amberley's waist while his right hand clamped over the shocked man's mouth. Jacob's momentum and the six inch height advantage he enjoyed, allowed him to lift the smaller man easily. Kara followed close behind. Tien stepped into the hall, casually shutting the door to the outside world.

ϕ

The house was a traditional Victorian terrace but with additions. The original living room to the front, facing the street, was connected to the kitchen by a narrow hallway which also accommodated the stairs. At some point in its history the house had had a two-storey extension added to the rear, hence the back garden being reduced to what Tien had called a postage stamp. The rear extension housed a small dining room on the ground floor, accessed through an arched opening from the kitchen. Upstairs, the extension accommodated a bedroom, which had allowed one of the original two bedrooms to be converted into a mid-landing bathroom with toilet.

A further flight of stairs led up to a third storey with a single long, narrow attic room running from front to back of the house. As Kara glanced into it she saw it was fitted with dormer windows to both the front and rear elevations and crammed with cardboard boxes. By the time she returned from her quick look around and entered the dining room, Amberley had been secured by Jacob and Tien.

"Hello Francis," Kara said as she pulled a dining room chair out from the small round table and sat down facing him. "So nice of you to have proper wooden dining chairs. Makes securing your hands behind you so much easier. It even lets my friends here tie each ankle to its own proper chair leg. How thoughtful of you!"

Amberley's mouth was covered in grey duct tape but his eyes were clearly visible and they were darting around much as they had in the Old Seafarer. He looked at Tien who stood in the archway leading to the kitchen, then he strained to see Jacob, who stood behind him. Not able to twist around, he focussed again on Tien, then Kara, the ceiling, the floor and back to Kara. His breath was ragged through his nose and his body, even though restrained, was still bent slightly forward from the waist.

Kara waited for his eyes to settle back on her. "Now Francis. You have some explaining to do, but I have some facts for you to contemplate first. We are not the police. We do not give a damn about the Police and Criminal Evidence Act. We do not consider that you have any rights and even if we did, we wouldn't uphold them. We *do*," she stressed the word as dramatically as she could, "care about a few things that you *should* know about." Amberley's eyes darted off her again to Tien. Kara leant forward and slapped the flat of her right hand against the wooden dining room table. The force of the blow sounded like a whip crack. At the same time she raised her left hand to within inches of Amberley's face. The effect of the movement and noise caused the man to flinch so dramatically he almost tipped his own chair over. Jacob reached out and steadied it. Despite no physical blow hitting him, Amberley's nostrils flared and his eyes glistened with tears.

"Pay attention Francis. You look at me when I am talking. You don't look anywhere else. Are we clear on that?" Kara paused and counted inside her head. She hadn't reached three before Francis Amberley nodded his agreement.

"That's good Francis. Well done. Now, as I was saying, there are some things my friends and I do care about. We care about the money that went missing and we care about what happened to Derek Swift. That's all. That is all we care about. We do not care about you or what part you played in it. We have no desire to see you go to prison or even for you to talk to the police. Not at all. We only care about Derek. That's it." She paused again, waiting. She heard Tien turn on her heel and saw Amberley's eyes momentarily flick towards the movement, but almost instantly return to her. Kara leant forward with her hand raised and watched him flinch his head away. She reached forward and patted his cheek, "There, there Francis, I wasn't going to hit you, sit up straight, look at me."

Amberley brought his head up to face her. His eyes locked on hers as Tien returned to the room and placed something down on the dining room table before she walked back to the arch. Amberley never dropped his gaze from Kara.

"It's okay Francis. You can look at what my friend has brought," Kara said indicating the table with a wave of her hand. Although muffled by the duct tape, there was no mistaking the terror of Amberley's choked scream.

7

Jacob had to hold the chair still as Amberley thrashed against his restraints. Tears spilled from the man's eyes while wailful moaning battered and broke against his sealed mouth in waves of despair.

"Sssh Francis, sssh," Kara soothed him and stroked his cheek. "These are only here if you don't listen to me and don't do as I ask." She waved her hand once more to indicate the table, and this time she let her fingers rest on the handle of the bread knife that Tien had set down next to an old-fashioned, wooden-handled corkscrew, a straight-blade screwdriver and a couple of forks. "Come along, be quiet now, or I'll have to make you be quiet Francis," she said, the soothing lull of her voice replaced with a sternness that had immediate effects. Amberley looked at her, wide-eyed but silent. The panic in his stare was enough for Kara to know she had arrived at the point where she needed to be. It hadn't surprised her how quickly the man had capitulated.

"Is Derek dead?" she asked, holding the man's stare.

Amberley shook his head.

"Did he abscond with the money?"

He nodded.

"Do you know where he is?"

He shook his head. Kara knew there had been no deception, no hesitation. Amberley didn't know where Swift was. It made sense when considered along with the text messages. If he had known where Swift was, he wouldn't have asked a third party to get a message to him.

"I'm going to take your gag off now Francis. If you scream I shall put it back on and never take it off again. I shall spend the rest of my night seeing how many ways I can hurt you with the tools my friend brought me from your kitchen. Are we clear?"

The nodding was instant and protracted. Jacob reached around and ripped the duct tape off.

"Who did you text, Francis?" As soon as she asked the question she saw his eyes dart away and back again. He hesitated just fractionally and breathed in to speak. She cut him off, "Careful Francis. Be very careful," she paused and placed her hand on the man's knee. Despite his restraints he recoiled from her touch. "If you say no one, I will not wait to reapply your gag. I will have my friends kill you." She said it calmly, like it was a perfectly normal thing for her to say. The impact on Amberley was anything but calm or normal. His eyes widened again and he bit back whatever words had been forming in his mouth. Kara continued, "There will be no second chance. You need to realise that some questions I already know the answer to. I am only asking to see if you are staying honest. If you answer those questions with a lie, I will no longer need to talk to you at all. I can't talk to you if you lie to me. My friends will kill you and then they will hang you from your stair bannisters. You will be found with a proper suicide note. No one will ever suspect." She paused again and counted silently to three. "Now, who did you text?"

"Rik. I texted Rik in Holland."

"And who's he?"

"He arranged for Derek to get out."

Kara's hand shot out, grasped the serrated bread knife and

hammered the butt of its handle into the wooden table. Amberley let out a pained whelp, reared away from the glistening blade and again Jacob had to prevent the chair falling over.

"I didn't ask you what he did, Francis. I asked you who he was. You need to pay attention."

Tears were streaming down Amberley's cheeks. He sniffed as hard as he could but the mucus from his nose was forming thick bubbles at his nostrils. His breath came in short snatches, "I'm sor- I'm sor- sor- sorry."

Kara nodded and repeated herself, "Who is he?"

"I don- I don't know. It does- it doesn't work- it doesn't work like that."

"It? What's it, Francis? How many more of your friends have you helped to disappear?"

Amberley's brows creased together and he looked genuinely confused, "Non-, none. None. I don't have-" he stopped himself and Kara felt the smallest twinge of sorrow for a man so obviously lonely and devoid of human contact. She stifled it and went to get on with the job, but was stopped by Tien's hand on her shoulder. She laid the knife down flat, stood and walked towards the kitchen.

Tien used a handful of paper towels to wipe Amberley's face. She gently cleaned and wiped until he had ceased gasping for breath between sobs. Then she stepped away.

Kara retook her seat and tapped Amberley's knee, "Tell me who Rik is, Francis?"

"I don't know, I really don't know," he pleaded. "I only know his name is Rik. No last name. Derek told me he knew some people that would help him. All I had to do was take him out on my boat. Then he would be gone."

"How?"

"We met another boat. They threw a rope over. Derek took it and jumped in the water. They pulled him across. That's all I know, I swear. I swear."

"Now that's not true Francis. You knew a number to text and how to get a response. Tell me about that."

Amberley remained focussed on her. His eyes were again watery but they weren't darting about. His answers came in rapid, staccato sentences, "Derek gave me it before he left. Told me to memorise it. Told me it was for emergencies. Told me how to use it. I never had to before. But he never told me about no money. Never mentioned an insurance payout. I thought I needed to know about it. That's why I got in touch."

"What's with the Francis 44619 number?"

"Derek told me I needed an identity. He had one too. If I didn't have one, Rik wouldn't pass messages. Wouldn't know who I was."

"And the pin number?"

"Same. He said I needed it so Rik could be sure it was really me. I was to give a wrong one first. That way, I'd know if it was really Rik. Only he would know the right one."

"All seems strange to me Francis," Kara said and hovered her hand across the implements on the table.

"No, no!" he shouted, wiggling within in his restraints and moving the chair from leg to leg. "That's it. That's all I know. That's how it was set up. That's how I had to get messages to him. He said it was all part of the deal for them to get him out."

Jacob stepped forward and put his hands on the man's shoulders to steady the chair and stop it from bouncing. Instead of quieting him, Amberley let out a long wail, "Please, please don't let him hurt me, please."

Kara leant in close, her mouth next to Amberley's ear, "Calm down Francis. He's not going to do anything to you, unless I say so, but you need to calm down and stop squirming."

Amberley again gave a series of protracted nods, but his squirming ceased, the chair steadied and Jacob stepped back. Kara was convinced that she had been told the truth. What she wasn't sure about, was why there would be so contrived a security protocol. She glanced over her shoulder to Tien and raised her eyebrows. Tien spoke from the archway, "What was the name of the other boat?"

Amberley looked across to Tien and Kara caught the strangest of expressions cloud his face. She couldn't quantify or classify it, but it made her feel distinctly uneasy. Then it was gone.

"Answer my friend Francis. What was the name of the other boat?"

"I don't know, I'm sor-"

Kara stood and turning to leave, nodded to Jacob, "Kill him, we're done here."

"No, please, no, God no. Ple-" Amberley's pleading was cut-off as Jacob's hand clamped over his mouth. The muffled screams were frantic and accompanied by a dark stain spreading over the front of Amberley's trousers.

Kara stopped just short of the archway and turned back, "I warned you Francis, lie to me and I have no use for you. You would have spent some time next to the other boat while Derek made his escape. You know the name of it. You tell me and I may let you live," she said and gave a small flick of her head. Jacob released his grasp.

"It wasn't English. Honestly, I couldn't read it, it was foreign. Please, please don't kill me, please. It had an E. It started with an E. Two words, erelike winding. Please, that's the truth."

"Other numbers on the side? A homeport? What type of boat was it?"

"It had a registration mark, VD something. There were numbers, four or five of them. But I don't remember the rest. Please, I don't remember what they were."

"What else?"

"It was a fishing boat, a troller."

"You mean a trawler?" Kara asked.

"No. A troller. It's smaller."

Kara checked over her shoulder and Tien gave a small shrug as she pulled her smartphone out. After a few moments she handed the phone to Kara, who in turn walked back to stand in front of Amberley, careful to avoid the puddle of liquid around the chair. She showed him the image on screen.

"Like this?"

"Yes," he nodded, "like that, only it had a red hull."

Kara sat down again, "Good Francis. Well done. One last question. Answer this and we'll let you go, okay?" she said and waited for the man to look up. She held his stare, "Okay?" she repeated.

He nodded.

"Why did Derek leave?"

"I don't know."

Kara paused. The answer had been given too quickly and delivered with no conviction, but there was a new look to Amberley's face. The timidity and fear was masked by a strange expression. Kara examined the almost instant change that had come over the man. She finally figured that it was defiance. She tried again, "Now that's just not true Francis. Why did Derek leave?"

"I don't know."

Once more the lie was delivered too quickly but his voice was stronger, more assured. Kara wondered what the hell was going on. He should have been getting more compliant, not less. She allowed her hand to rest on the old corkscrew. She nodded up to Jacob, "Hold his eye open."

In a single fluid movement Amberley's head was secured and Jacob forced the man's left eye wide. Kara stood and brought the tip of the rusty metal down.

8

"Now what?" Jacob asked from one of the chairs in Amberley's living room. Kara and Tien shared a threadbare couch that sagged opposite a small fireplace. A forlorn 1970's three-bar electric fire gazed back at them, woefully attempting to heat the room.

"We'll have to go on what we've got," Kara answered.

"Which is not much," Tien said.

"No, but short of tearing his eyes out and cutting his hands off, he's not giving anything else up," Kara said and then paused as she registered that Jacob's complexion was pale. "Are you alright?"

He gave a brief half-smile and nodded, "Yeah, I'm okay. I'm just relieved you didn't actually do anything to him. I'm not sure I could have held him."

"Jesus, Jacob, did you really think-" she stopped herself, aware that she had sounded angry. It wasn't Jacob's fault. Kara hadn't briefed him on how far she would take the questioning and this was the first time he'd been on the inside of any of their jobs. On reflection, his question wasn't out of place. She tempered her tone, "I'm sorry. I should have explained more. Despite what the papers might have you believe, that's not how we're trained to get information as interrogators. The trick is to make it all possible in the subject's mind. They'll imagine much, much more horrendous things than we could actually do. You let them believe what you want them to believe but no, I don't do torture. I was in the same Service as you Jacob, not the Gestapo."

"I'm glad," he said, "And relieved. I mean it, I'm not sure I could have managed that."

"Good," said Tien. "I wouldn't be happy with you if you could."

Kara noticed a distinct brightening of the young man's disposition at the compliment.

"But," Tien continued, "We still have the problem of what now?"

"We need to get Amberley babysat," Kara said. "We can't just leave him here to his own devices, but that shouldn't be too much of a hassle. It might take a while to sort out and that's no bad thing. We'll need some time to get our own logistics in order."

"Do I assume we're off on a trip?" Tien asked.

"Oh I think so. Not sure there are going to be many tulips to tiptoe through in November, but we'll give it a go," Kara looked between Tien and Jacob. "One thing we need to remember though. Francis Amberley is less scared of what we'll do to him if he stays quiet, than what would happen to him if he talks. I don't know why Derek Swift left, but it's one hell of a secret that buys the absolute silence of a timid little man who thought his eyeball was about to be corkscrewed out."

φ

Kara was right about it taking some time to set things up. Her initial phone call was quick, but putting things into place took the rest of the night. As Franklyn called others within the circles he had access to, Kara and Tien went back to their accommodation, saying hello to the indomitable Daphne as they passed back through the bar area.

"Did you find what you were looking for dear?" Daphne asked, her sing-along Suffolk accent returned to the fore.

Kara was aware the old woman had asked in such a way as to maintain discretion in the lightly populated bar.

"Yes thank you Daphne, we did." Kara smiled and winked over at her.

"Shall I send you something to your rooms, or would you like to eat in here?"

"Our rooms would be great. What's on offer?"

"Shepherd's Pie and trimmings, dear. Would have been a lot more, but the night's getting on. Shall I send three?"

"Two's okay, but if you could leave one over for our colleague. He'll be back later."

"I'll plate it up for him. There's a microwave in the small kitchen in between your rooms. I'm sure he'll be able to use that, won't he? A big strong boy like that."

Kara laughed as she neared the door that led out to the converted barn accommodation, "I'm sure he will Daphne, although I doubt he's been called a big strong boy for some time."

"Perhaps not, dear. But he's bigger and stronger than some. I hope he's okay?" the elderly woman called after them.

Kara and Tien were fully aware of the question that had been asked.

"He's fine Daphne. Everyone's fine, thanks," Tien said.

"As long as you're sure dear?"

"As sure as a Hackney girl can be."

Daphne held Tien's gaze for a brief moment before smiling and turning to serve another customer.

φ

It took a couple of hours for Franklyn to come back to them with an agreed plan and quite a few more to get the assets in place. By then Kara, Tien and Jacob had rotated the watch on Amberley a number of times. They could have taken shorter stints, but the look Kara had caught on Amberley's face gave her no inclination to leave Tien alone with the man. She couldn't explain it and hadn't even tried. Her friend would have been furious if she had thought Kara was doubting her ability to keep the man subdued. Nonetheless, Kara hadn't left her on her own. During their non-guarding stints, they verified as much as they could about Dutch trollers.

Now, both women and Jacob were back in the small dining room of the Victorian terrace, with Amberley once more tied to the chair. In the intervening hours they had cleaned up the floor and allowed him to shower, change, eat and drink, all of which he did in a submissive state, offering no resistance. Now the panicked look had returned to his face. He sat with his head down and his eyes locked on Kara. The only noise was the electronic tick of a wall clock in the kitchen.

"You said you were going to let me go?" he said, a pronounced tremor to his voice.

"I lied. Now be quiet," Kara said and checked her watch.

"I suppose you lied about the insurance money too?" he said, pouting.

"Seriously Francis? You have to ask? Of course I lied. Now be quiet or I'll reapply the tape over your mouth and extend it to cover your nose." Kara rechecked her watch. It was one minute past three in the morning. A further minute dragged by. Then another. The door knocker that she had used almost eight hours before, sounded twice. It had been rapped softly yet the noise cannoned off the walls of the small house. Amberley and the chair both jumped a few inches clear of the floor. He let out a small moan of terror.

"We'll be going now Francis. Thank you for your help, or lack of," Kara said.

Amberley's face was still flushed from the shock of the sound of the knocker. He tried to stammer something but stopped when he heard a key turning in the front door.

"It's okay Francis, I put your door key into the lock. Your new guests are just letting themselves in."

Kara, Tien and Jacob walked past him, out the back door and into the small rear garden. As they climbed over the fence and back on to the narrow road, four plainclothes police officers made their way down the narrow hallway and into the dining room. They secured Francis Amberley, led him out of the house and into a waiting, unmarked van. The Woodbridge Police Station had ample facilities to secure a prisoner and was only a mile away, but the van didn't go there. Neither did it go to the Regional Police Headquarters less than half an hour away.

9

Amsterdam, Holland. Thursday, 19th November.

Trains from Schiphol Airport to the Gothic-Renaissance splendour of Amsterdam's 'Centraal' railway station took twenty minutes. Another ten minutes and a taxi, having negotiated the narrow streets, tight turns and unending swell of cyclists, deposited Kara, Tien and Jacob outside a rental apartment next to the Keizersgracht.

Tien gazed up at the buildings lining the banks of the canal, their height dwarfing the British idea of three or four-storey construction. The older townhouses were easily identified by their narrowing roofs and what looked like pulleys and hooks suspended from above the topmost windows. She took in trams, cyclists and cars sharing the same relatively narrow piece of road that was squeezed into a space begrudgingly sacrificed by the gently flowing water. The scent of a roadside flower stall, with hundreds of bouquets and thousands of blooms spilling onto the surrounding pavement, fragranced the street, giving the dulled, late-Autumnal day a fresh, spring-like aroma.

As the taxi departed and Kara made her way to the apartment's door, Jacob asked, "Are you okay Tien?"

She spoke over her shoulder, "Yeah, I'm fine. It's stunning though, isn't it?"

"Haven't you been here before?" he asked, coming to stand beside her.

"No, never. Not sure why not, considering how little time it took to get here," she said checking her watch. It showed 3:00pm. "I mean we only left for Heathrow at ten and we've lost an hour to a time zone change. I could've easily been spending weekends here. Look at it. It's amazing."

Jacob laughed. "You've seen a few streets and a canal. Easily impressed much?"

"Not really. Not usually," she said, turning to him, and aware that she was smiling. "I suppose, it's just that feeling you get sometimes. You know, when you go somewhere and you instantly know it's an amazing place. That it just fits you. Know what I mean?"

Jacob nodded, "I felt that way about Toronto. I went over with the QCS once. Liked it so much I went back on holiday the same summer. Reckon I'll end up there if I can manage it."

"QCS?" Tien asked.

"The Queen's Colour Squadron. We did the ceremonial drill displays for the Air Force?"

"Oh right," she said, "The ones that do it all with no words of command. Very impressive."

Jacob dipped his head in acknowledgment of her compliment, "Thanks. It was fun doing it."

As Tien watched a tram making its near-silent way along the street she said, almost as an afterthought, "I thought you were a proper field gunner."

"We were proper gunners too," Jacob said, too quickly and with a hint of sternness in his voice.

Tien turned back to him and with a warm smile put her hand on his arm, "Oops, my mistake. I didn't mean to offend. So you did that *and* all the normal stuff?"

Jacob reddened under her gaze. "Yeah, we were a field regiment too."

"That's how you ended up in Afghanistan?" Tien asked.

Jacob nodded.

Tien saw the same look in his eyes at the mention of that far-away country that she sometimes saw in her own reflection. She took his hand, "Come on, let's go see where Kara has booked us into. I don't normally let her online with a credit card."

Jacob didn't resist and allowed himself to be led across to the narrow black door that Kara had already knocked on. It opened to reveal a round-faced man, with an even rounder stature. He had the complexion of a shined apple. Sweat was beaded on a forehead barely visible under a riot of dishevelled jet-black hair, and even though his Mexican-styled moustache drooped downwards, Tien desperately wanted to call him Mario. When she realised that he held a large monkey-wrench in his left hand she almost laughed out loud. 'I love this place,' she thought. The man spoke with the peculiar Dutch accent that gave a lisp to his pronunciation of English.

"Good afternoon, you must be the London people, the Wrights, yes?" he asked, wiping his right hand on his jeans and offering it to Kara.

"Yes, good afternoon," she said shaking the chubby hand.

"Please come in. It is so nice of you to be choosing us for your stay in Amsterdam," he said, turning and leading them into a tiny hallway. Jacob remained outside and allowed Tien to step into the tight space.

"I am Bernard, the caretaker."

Tien managed to suppress a sigh. 'You'll always be Mario to me,' she thought.

"I'm just glad we could get it so quickly," Kara said, oblivious to her friend's amusement.

"Oh yes, well it is November so we have vacancies some-times more than in the summer," Bernard said reaching into a small rack of letter pigeonholes and drawing out a set of two keys. He held each up in turn, "This is for the door to the apartment on the third floor and this is for the street door. You are staying three nights, yes?"

"Yes, although we might extend if we need to. Is that

okay?" Kara asked, taking the offered keys.

"Oh yes. It is fine. As long as you are letting me know. We have no booking for another two weeks, so if you want you can stay all that time," he said and then added, "Do you have any questions?"

Kara shook her head, "No Bernard, I think that's it. Thank you."

He raised the wrench slightly, "Well if you will be allowing me, I must continue. I am changing a piece of the heating. So you will be warm in the cold nights. It is nice to meet you. Goodbye." He made for the door at the end of the tiny hall and was almost through it before Tien called out.

"Ma- I mean Bernard, is there Wi-Fi?"

The rosy-cheeked caretaker spun lightly on his feet. Tien almost applauded. "Oh yes. We have the fast Wi-Fi. All the details are in the welcome pack on the table in the apartment." He gave a cheery wave with the wrench and went out through the door.

Kara led them to the stairwell in the corner of the hall.

"Flipping heck," Tien said as she began to climb up, "I'm glad we only have small backpacks. Imagine trying to get suitcases up this." She looked vertically down to where Jacob was following behind and giggled at the sight that greeted her. "You doing okay?"

Jacob, each shoulder brushing the side of the narrow stairwell stopped, not trusting his ability to look upwards whilst finding the next sliver of stair that climbed and twisted at an acute angle. "Yeah, I'm good. Lucky you're not wearing a skirt," he said with a cheeky smile.

"You wish," Tien laughed, and even in the semi-dark of the stairs she saw Jacob go crimson.

Despite them being fit and athletic, they were all out of breath by the time Kara opened the door to the apartment.

"Wow! It's like the Tardis," Tien said as she stepped into an open-plan kitchen and sitting room. Three large windows marked the fact that the apartment held the corner most position of the building. "Those stairs really twist around," she

71

said, moving to look out and reorient herself. The flower stall, the canal and the Hotel Armada on the opposite bank were visible through the kitchen and adjacent sitting room windows. The other sitting room window looked out west along the length of the canal. The sun was already slipping down into a grey, washed out version of a sunset.

Two further stairwells, equally narrow and steep, came off the sitting room. One led back down to half of the building's second floor where the apartment claimed three bedrooms and a bathroom. The other stairs led up to two more bedrooms and a second bathroom. In total the apartment's lease claimed it could accommodate ten, although that supposed a level of intimacy with regard to some of the sleeping arrangements. Modestly, with one of the five bedrooms having three single beds, it could accommodate seven.

Within half an hour Tien had sorted out Wi-Fi access, set up her laptops and was preparing a set of smartphones for use. Seven of them were laid out on the table. One by one she registered the corresponding speed dial numbers into each. Then, using skills acquired while working for a few weeks in the Covent Garden Apple Store, she opened the casing of each phone. A small micro-battery and GPS tracking module, no bigger than her little fingernail, was slipped into a tiny gap under the main CPU. The space looked like it had been left for exactly that purpose, but Tien knew the inventors of the tiny tracker had exploited a quirk of the iPhone's manufacture. It was an ingenious design and one they'd been keen to promote at the device's unveiling a few months before.

The miniaturisation of cameras, microphones and trackers was a boon to Tien's profession, but the explosion of companies, especially within London, offering gadgets like they were some Q-division out of James Bond, made her wince. She wasn't wholly convinced that secret-camera devices, made to look like alarm clocks and pens, weren't being used by seedy, voyeuristic guesthouse owners, or worse. The problem was, that as a registered Private Investigation firm, 'Wright and Tran' were contacted on at least a weekly basis to evaluate what was on offer. Mostly they said no. Politely, but no nonetheless.

The request to see the tracker had come from a new shop called 'Thy Chela' in Knightsbridge. Tien had been intrigued, not least by its name, but by its location. At one hundred yards from Harrods, the new enterprise was likely to be backed by some significant players. Her tech-head also figured that such a device, self-powered and capable of operating even if the main battery was taken from the phone, was worth the trek to the west of the city. When she found out that it could also be monitored through commercial satellite systems, she and Kara had decided to buy a dozen of them. Tien didn't mind spending some of their newly acquired wealth on that type of purchase.

She also hadn't objected too much at spending money on her new lower arm and hand. Prior to the Bebionic model, there was no way she could have manipulated the phones, the screwdriver, the casings and the trackers without a mounting frustration and ultimately having to ask for help. Now, with a simple flick of a sensor within the socket of her arm, she could select the grip she needed, and with a twist, she could move her wrist to any angle. She had become so adept that she could swing her hand against her thigh to quickly switch thumb positions. It was true that Tien had been reticent when she found out the cost, but Kara had insisted that she buy it and it had been worth every penny. Recently some people hadn't realised she had a prosthesis at all. The skin tone match on the 'glove' that covered the futuristic hand was an indistinguishable match for her real skin. Although, one of her young nephews had been disappointed she hadn't kept a more terminator-type look.

Tien had quickly come to love her new arm. Every time she looked at it, every time she used it, she felt the loss of her original limb a little less. She hadn't had to ask for help with any task in months and the value of that happiness and independence was immeasurable. The strength and capability of the prosthesis had even allowed her to get back into attending the gym and she especially loved how she could do push-ups with it.

Flicking her fingers to a tripod-grip, she reassembled the last of the phones, finishing just as Kara and Jacob returned from a quick shopping expedition. While Kara showered, Jacob put the supplies to good use and made tea, toast and scrambled eggs.

As they were finishing their meal, Tien's phone rang. "Hi, yep," she said and rose to look out the kitchen window at two cars pulling into the apartment's designated parking spots. "Black door just behind you," she said and disconnected before looking over to Kara and Jacob. "They're here."

φ

Samantha Davis, known as Sammi, and Charles Randal, known as Chaz, looked like the perfect couple. Sammi stood five foot ten inches, her broad shoulders and slim waist a fitting testament to her love of swimming. Her height, physique, blue eyes and shoulder-length mousey-blonde hair complemented the short, light brown hair and blue eyes of Chaz's six foot, lithe body. Sammi moved with a casual sway and Chaz, two years her senior, moved with what seemed the grace of a dancer, but was actually the result of decades of training in martial arts. The couple's obvious compatibility had been a great cover for their many covert surveillance operations. In reality, their relationship was strictly confined to work. Although once, a long, long time ago, they had tried to sleep together in a drunken haze. That night, a singularly shared secret, never revealed to anyone, had ended with them laughing at each other in their naked awkwardness. They'd resolved then and there to be like brother and sister as opposed to lovers. It was that underpinning stability which allowed them to be so effective.

Kara had first worked with Sammi and Chaz back in 2006, a few months after the tour in Iraq when she had met Tien. Three years later, they had all worked together, along with James 'Dinger' Bell and Aidy 'Taff' Jones, in Afghanistan.

Shortly after that tour, Sammi and the three guys, who were always referred to as Sammi's crew, left the military and joined the world of freelance consultants. As the O'Neill brothers were always Kara and Tien's first choice for security, so Sammi and Chaz were their first call if they needed reliable, specialist intelligence back-up. Taff and Dinger had operated as Sammi's embedded security team, until December 2014 when Taff was killed in a mortar attack in Kabul. Since then, Sammi and her crew had tried to confine themselves to less hazardous locations and take life easier.

"Dinger says hi, but I doubt he'll be joining us," Sammi said, flopping down on the couch next to Chaz and Tien. "It would be a difficult ask to convince his new fiancée that leaving her in Lanzarote while he comes to Amsterdam is a great idea."

"A fiancée? Wow, how much did he have to pay her?" Kara asked from the kitchen.

"I know. The great loutish jock seems to think she's with him for his good looks, personal charm and subtle Gaelic ways," Chaz laughed.

"Aww, don't be mean. Dinger's lovely," Tien said.

"Yeah, but you wouldn't go out with him, would you?" Chaz asked.

"Well, no, but that's 'cos he's Dinger, isn't it?" Tien said, "I mean I wouldn't go out with you either. You're equally weird." She laughed and poked Chaz in the ribs, causing him to recoil in mock pain.

Kara, standing back and observing them, noticed Jacob wasn't joining in. She knew he had only worked with Dinger once before, so probably didn't feel as comfortable slagging off a recent acquaintance. That was quite decent of him, but needless in the present company. "Hey Jacob, what do you reckon?" she called.

"Well, that's hard for me to say. I don't reall-"

Chaz cut him off, "Ah don't be shy. The great lug looks like an albino Viking and talks like a drunken Glaswegian on steroids. Just agree. He's not here anyway."

Jacob shyly glanced towards Tien before saying, "He seemed like a nice guy to me. I mean, he's not my type but I'm sure someone out there likes him."

"Ha, love it," Chaz said. "Yep, he's not my type either. Geez, that poor girl."

"Have you met her?" Kara asked.

"Yes, we have," Sammi answered, with a faked glower at Chaz. "Eloise is lovely. Bright, intelligent and charming. She's a lawyer in Dundee."

"Oh," Tien said. "She's Scottish too?"

"No, she's German, but she's been over here," Sammi paused and corrected herself, "over there I mean, for ages. Beautiful diction."

"Much better than Dinger," Chaz teased again.

"You're not exactly textbook BBC yourself," Tien said, "I mean I'd much rather have Jacob's Essex than your Manc' accent. At least I can understand him. With you, I get about one word in three of that Northern twang," she said laughing and putting her hand out to Jacob's knee.

Kara saw Jacob blush a deep red. She was intrigued by the intensity of the reaction and aware, from a raised eyebrow, that Sammi had seen the same. She thought about teasing Jacob, but something in the back of her mind warned her off. Besides, it was time to move things along. "Right, let's leave Dinger's dalliances in Lanzarote. Toby might be joining us in a day or two, but for now we're just five and looking for a boat that could be in any one of a dozen harbours, if it's still here at all. Once we have a plan then Jacob, Tien and I need some kip. We haven't slept in nearly thirty-six hours."

φ

The two hire cars that Sammi and Chaz had brought from the airport exited the IJTunnel into a wintery sunrise and followed the S116 through Amsterdam Noord. Within ten minutes, the high-rise blocks and closely packed buildings on each side of the road fell away and were replaced by close lines of trees. A few more minutes and the road changed designation to the N247. They were in a heavy, but free-flowing stream of traffic, unlike the nose-to-tail commuter congestion on the other side of the carriageway.

Tien didn't notice the state of the roads. Instead, from the front passenger seat of the second car, she gasped as the trees ended and the road entered into wide-open, flat plains that stretched away to unfeasibly far horizons.

After another twenty minutes, most of which Tien spent as a completely entranced tourist, both cars took the first turn into Volendam. As the road pressed further into the small town the broad horizons began to disappear, crowded out by ever-increasing rows of stereotypical Dutch houses. Tien looked at the distinctly triangular facades and thought they were so much more beautiful than the traditional English terrace houses. Certainly much more attractive than Francis Amberley's had been. She was especially taken by the older buildings and the pronounced steps to their gable ends. She wondered what the proper term was. Pulling out her mobile, she Googled it, only to smile to herself when she discovered that it was simply called a stepped gable.

"What are you smiling at?" Kara said, glancing over from the driver's seat.

"Oh not a lot. Just looking up Dutch architectural terms. As you do," she replied.

"Well, as *you* do," Kara said, her smile broadening. "We good to do this?"

"Yep," Tien said and called the lead car.

Jacob answered, "Hi, what's up?"

"Tell Chaz and Sammi it's the next turn on the right. Follow down there for about two hundred yards and you'll hit the Marina Park. See you later and be careful."

"You too," he said and disconnected the call.

Kara and Tien watched Chaz slow and make the turn. They continued straight past, heading for the historic fishing harbour of the old town. All they had to go on was a potential boat name and the two registration letters, 'VD' which according to the international maritime register led them here. There was no guarantee the boat still sailed from this port, no guarantee that it might not be berthed at some other port and no guarantee they would be able to track its owners even if they did find it, but it was all they had.

No one had responded to Amberley's text message as yet, and as far as they could be sure, no one had tried to contact him by any other means. Tien had put a call-forward on his landline and directed it to her own mobile, so if anyone tried to phone him, she would know. What had slightly disturbed her was that there was no PC in Amberley's house. No iPad or other smart tablets, no alternate mobile or smartphone. The man was as off the grid as she could have imagined. She knew it was possible that he had an email account through his workplace, but he had insisted he didn't and she had been inclined to believe him.

The police that Franklyn had called in had left a babysitter at the old terrace house, in case contact was instigated by a physical visit to Amberley. Again, Kara and Tien couldn't do much if the visitor called for him at work, but they had done as much as they could in the time available.

That left the single lead of the boat's identity. With such scant information, they knew they would have to go and physically look for it. Volendam was the logical place to start. It was certainly a more manageable search task than Amsterdam Harbour proper.

They pulled into a completely empty parking area, end-on to the long rectangle of the old harbour. There was a forest of masts and furled sails in view, but Tien knew the numbers here were less than a tenth of the over four hundred berths that Sammi, Chaz and Jacob were searching in the much more modern marina to the south of the town.

Stepping into the early morning cold, the harbour was almost deserted of people. A couple of schoolbag-laden kids looked like they were trudging through treacle on their slow progress towards school. A single jogger was braving the chilly morning and his accompanying Labrador was the happiest thing in sight. It was certainly having more fun than the young guy fishing off the main quay. He was rugged up in appropriately warm clothing but his face didn't reflect the joy of his chosen hobby. His line stretched out into the harbour and the orange and white dayglow float bobbed on the relative stillness of the water.

The jogger and dog passed behind the fisherman and mounted steps that linked the cobblestoned walkway along the water's edge to another that was fronted by a long row of tourist-orientated business. All, bar one, were shut and boarded. The souvenir shops, gelato cafes, coffee cafes and art galleries gave no sign of having been open since the halcyon days of summer. The alfresco areas were devoid of seats and the only vestige of activity in the whole row came from the Old Holland Hotel. Its broad swathe of full-height glass windows revealed a few guests enjoying breakfast in a warm and comfortable restaurant.

Kara and Tien began to walk along the quayside. It was a good third of a mile long, or as Tien corrected herself, probably half a kilometre. The narrow ends of the harbour were less than a fifth of that. All in all, it would take about ten minutes to walk the full circumference. Or at least to walk out to the gap in the harbour wall that permitted access to the waters of Lake Markermeer. A light breeze was picking up, chilled and constant. Tien pulled her jacket tight and kept her right hand deep in her pocket. As it was, they hadn't gone half the length of the quay before they passed a vintage sailing schooner that had been shielding other boats behind it. Kara pretended to look at the sailboat, but focussed on four fishing boats moored side on to each other. Each hull was painted a different vibrant shade, the furthest from the quay, a bright red.

"They're a lot smaller than I expected," Kara said.

"About right though," Tien replied. "They're definitely trollers. Between forty and fifty feet long. Superstructure set just forward of amidships, trolling beams just aft of that, net bins to the stern, spool gur-" Tien was stopped by the look Kara was giving her, "What's wrong?"

"How do you know this stuff?"

"I Googled it," Tien said and gave her friend a nudge with her elbow. "The specific details are like a signature and these fit precisely. But they don't look rough like the professional fishing ones I researched. They look more kitsch. Sort of touristy. Although they do still have nets on them."

"I thought you said a day or so ago that boats were all wavy navy stuff?" Kara teased.

"Yeah, but that was before I needed to know about it."

"I do adore you," Kara said, before adding, just loud enough for Tien to hear, "Even if you are nutty."

There were no signs of activity on or near the vessels, but each sported 'VD' registration letters and each had a four-digit number. The names, mounted on plinths set above the bridge windows, were quite hard to read on the outermost boats.

Kara looked around casually, her hand up to shield her eyes against the weak sun that was trying to force its way through washed-out clouds. "I guess *'Eerlijke Winden'* is as close to what Amberley said as we're likely to get?" she said, continuing to walk alongside Tien. "What's it mean dear Googler?"

"Hang on." Tien rotated her prosthesis wrist so that she could hold her phone at an easier angle. It didn't take her long to get the answer. "I guess it makes sense, Fair Winds is a fair enough name for a boat."

They reached the end of the main quay and walked along the harbour wall, looking out at the vast expanse of Lake Markemeer. The wind strengthened the further out they ventured. Tien had to raise her voice to be heard, "Are we assuming that's the boat we're looking for?"

Kara nodded.

"Then that was easier than we'd anticipated. Bit of a shame we rented the apartment in Amsterdam."

"Yeah, but we didn't know it was going to be here. It could just as easily have been somewhere else," Kara said, pulling the hood of her jacket up to shield her ears from the biting wind.

"So what now?"

"Rally the troops and go somewhere to get a coffee. I'm freezing. Then we'll try to figure out who owns our fair wind friend there. After that we'll get him to tell us where Swift is, then we'll go find him and be home in time for tea and medals," Kara shouted into what was fast becoming a stiffening gale.

"And you called me nutty," Tien said, hurrying for the shelter of the only open establishment within sight.

ϕ

The waterfront restaurant of the Old Holland Hotel, situated midpoint along the harbour, was welcoming, warm and practically empty. Kara and Tien took two stools at the highly varnished bar-counter and asked the smiling waitress for two coffees. She responded to them in flawless English.

"Puts us to shame, doesn't it?" Tien said as the waitress left.

"How'd you mean?" Kara asked, checking out the rest of the room in the long mirror hanging behind the counter. There was a middle-aged couple at one of the window tables eating breakfast. A suited man, reading a Dutch paper and drinking coffee, sat alone at a table for four in the middle of the room, and the only other customers were a couple of younger men at a corner table. Kara noted they had finished eating and the one with his back to her was on a mobile phone. As she passed her gaze over them the man facing her looked up and made eye-contact via the reflection. She resisted the urge to look away immediately, like a guilty person caught snooping. It was one of the 'giveaway' reflexes that had been trained out of her over the years. Instead, she briefly returned his look and smiled in as friendly a manner as could be managed. She wasn't surprised when he looked away quickly. Like a guilty person caught snooping.

"I mean, no slight intended against her profession, but even a waitress on the early shift in a waterfront hotel can speak at least two languages fluently. Don't imagine her reciprocal in England could do that." Tien said.

"Yeah, although it's probably even more. I reckon she speaks Dutch, German, French and English," Kara said returning her focus to Tien. "We don't do language well in the UK."

"Says the multiple linguist with five or six under her belt. Is it six?" Tien asked, taking her phone out.

"Mmm, eight fluently, or near enough I suppose. Plus English and a tiny, tiny bit of what you taught me in Vietnamese. But not Dutch. Never needed it. Anyway, you're not so bad yourself. You've got three, haven't you?"

"I guess," agreed Tien. "But that's only because Mum insisted we spoke them. She was kind of strict about it."

Kara faced her, "Strict? Your Mum? I can't imagine it."

"Ha," Tien laughed. "All you see is the sweet little lady act she puts on for visitors. Don't let that fool you. She was a right disciplinarian when we were little. We had to speak English when we were outside. She said if Britain was good enough to give us a home then we should be good enough to speak the language in public. At home in the evenings we swapped to French and at weekends we would only speak Vietnamese. Thing is, I never realised other families didn't do that sort of thing until I was in high school and found out that language classes were a choice. I couldn't understand why you needed to learn French at school. I just expected everyone would know it."

It was Kara's turn to laugh, "I never knew that. Seriously, you swapped to French every night?"

"Yeah, regular as clockwork. The six o'clock news would come on and it was bonjour or bust. I don't remember it ever being a problem. We just grew up trilingual. Bit like the Dutch kids, I presume."

The waitress returned to the bar. "Your coffee will be here soon," she said in passing as she went to check on the rest of her customers.

Tien dialled Jacob's phone, told him to call off the search

of the marina and to rendezvous at the hotel. By the time she'd finished the call, a waiter was bringing their coffees.

Kara was mesmerized. The waiter was one of the most handsome men she had ever seen. His skin was a rich dark-oaken colour, his eyes a deep brown and his black hair close-cropped. He stood about six feet, maybe taller. As he approached, balancing the coffees expertly in their saucers, she noticed that his black shoes, black trousers and crisp, white shirt looked like they had come straight from a valeted laundry service. The creases on the sleeves and trousers could have sliced butter and the shoes gleamed with a polish as bright as anything she'd seen in the military. She was reminded of a clothed version of an actor who had been in a series of adverts. "Hey Tien, what was the name of the deodorant the hot black guy advertised, with the horse?"

"What?" Tien asked, looking up from her phone as the waiter arrived.

"Never mind," Kara said, half twisting on her stool to face the man. "Hi, these are ours I assume?"

"Yes miss. I hope you enjoy them. Would you like any-thing else," he said, placing the cups on the counter.

Kara's mind flashed through a range of inappropriate answers. Instead she said, "Well, I was just wondering, sorry, I'm Liz," she said and offered her hand. The man took it in his and held it just a fraction longer than would have been usual. Kara didn't object and held her eye-contact with him for the same fraction over the norm.

He smiled and said softly, "Hi Liz. I'm Henk."

"Are you busy, Henk?" Kara asked and held her hand out in invitation to the empty stool beside her.

Henk gave an overly-emphasised, sweeping look around the restaurant and said, "No Liz. We are not busy. We are redecorating all our bedrooms so we have no staying guests at present. I can be all yours for a few minutes. What can I do for you?" He moved to the stool then paused momentarily and added, looking past Kara to Tien, "And your friend?"

Kara almost laughed out loud and thought, 'Oh, such a

shame and you were doing so well until then.' But she let it slide, "Henk," she said and leaned towards him. He leant in too. "My friend and I are being joined by some other friends soon. We really, really wanted to go out on a fishing trip. The pretty boats out in the harbour, do they hire them or are they all tied up for the winter?"

His expression dropped but, to his credit, Henk managed to hide most of his disappointment at Kara's question. "Oh, I see. Yes they can be taken out. They come with a crew and can be hired, sometimes in the winter. It depends on the weather."

"Oh that's great. Do you arrange it from round here?"

"Yes. There is a small office just along the quay, but it is closed for the winter. We do have some brochures. Wait, wait a second," he said, raising a long, slender finger.

Kara watched him head out the door that led to the main hotel and found herself reflecting that even the man's hands were quite gorgeous. He was back in less than a minute and handed her a glossy tri-fold flyer.

"They have their contact details in there so you and your friends can book." He paused before adding, "Are you staying locally?"

"Sadly, we're in Amsterdam. It's a shame you are not open for business."

"Yes, a real shame," Henk agreed. "We will be again in three weeks. You would have liked it here. Perhaps you stay that long?"

"I'm afraid not. Maybe I shall come back next year? I'd like to spend a few days here. Is it a good hotel?"

ϕ

"Is it a good hotel?" Tien was laughing.

"What? What?" Kara asked, her voice and eyebrows raised in equal measure.

"That was terrible. The poor guy. You had him eating out of your hand right up until Chaz, Sammi and Jacob arrived. He looked crestfallen when he came out to serve us."

"No he didn't. Well, maybe. But then he realised there were only two guys and three girls. I made sure to sit between you and Sammi so he still thinks he's in with a chance."

"And is he?"

"No," Kara said emphatically. Then added, "Well, not until we find out who owns the boat. Maybe we should come back for a holiday after we track down Swift?"

"So you can mix it with a guy half your age?"

"Tien! He's not half my age. He's just a bit younger."

"Oh yeah," Tien teased. "At least a decade." She began to laugh again as their car followed Sammi, Chaz and Jacob's into the IJTunnel and back to the rental apartment.

φ

The phone rang only twice.

"Hi. It's Henk."

"Hello Henk. What can I do for you?"

"He asked me to let him know if anyone unusual was asking about the boats."

"And?"

"Some English were in today."

"Good work Henk. I'll ask Rik to call you."

10

Volendam, Holland. Sunday 22nd November.

Chaz stretched to work the knots out of his shoulders and back. He stood, walked across to the bed and tapped Jacob's foot. The ex-gunner was instantly awake, sitting up and looking around the dulled room.

"Anything?" he asked.

"We have movement on board."

It had been two days since they'd found the boat on the waterfront. The company website had revealed the only office was the one on the quay and, as Henk had indicated, it was shut for the winter. The phone number listed had gone to a message bank that instructed callers to leave a name and number and they would be in touch.

Tien had sent a dummy email from an untraceable account enquiring to hire a boat for a day. As yet there had been no response. Not that any of that was unusual. The website also said that during the winter months it could be a few days before they would respond and that any excursions would be subject to cancellation due to weather.

Meanwhile, Sammi had scouted the streets around the

harbour and found a plethora of holiday-lets but none that were open out of season. She did find one small bed and breakfast that, according to a gaudy neon sign, had vacancies. A quick check on TripAdvisor showed it was clean, neat, reasonably priced and critically, it claimed that its third-storey rooms had harbour views. Chaz had run a number of line-of-sight predictions using available imagery and agreed that it probably had enough of a view to be of use.

He and Jacob booked in with a cover story that they were two friends travelling around Europe who needed some rest and recuperation before setting off once more. The landlady, seemingly thinking they were more than just friends, offered them her last double room instead of a twin. When she confirmed that it had views of the harbour, they decided to play along. Although it was just as well she missed the under-breath, 'Fuck off you twat,' that Jacob had hissed when Chaz had reached out and taken hold of his hand. Sure enough the room did have a view of the red boat's mooring and the two men swapped watch every couple of hours.

On the Saturday, frustrated by the lack of progress, Kara had decided to revisit the waterfront hotel. She reprised her role as Liz and spoke to Henk again but the waiter said he had no other information on how to book the boats. He apologised, flirted a bit more and then asked if she had decided to come back next year. She said she might, before departing with one last lingering gaze.

But now, on Sunday, as the sun struggled to raise itself out of the eastern waters of Lake Markermeer, a man was moving about on the deck of the red-hulled 'Fair Winds'.

"Good morning," Chaz said as Tien answered her phone. "We have movement on-board. One man. No cars in the vicinity so not quite sure how he got here. Assume he was dropped off before sun-up," continued Chaz, not for the first time regretting their inability to get much in the way of surveillance gear across with them on the flight from London.

"No worries. We're on our way," Tien said.

Kara and Sammi, who had been sitting next to her at the rental apartment's breakfast bar were up and moving before she had disconnected the call.

Less than five minutes later they pulled both cars out of the parking bays in front of the apartment and drove to Volendam. Kara trailed Sammi and, given it was the early hour of a Sunday morning, she was surprised at the steady volume of traffic on the opposite carriageway, heading into the city. Even on her side of the road, there were a half dozen cars in her wake. As the only main road between Amsterdam and Volendam she reflected it would have made running a surveillance operation a complete pain. There would have been little chance to turn off or swap trail cars in and out on route. She looked into her rear-view mirror again and, as if to confirm how terrible a surveillance environment it was, the same six cars were there, ever present going to the same place she was.

Twenty minutes later Sammi led them down into the town before turning left to go to the guesthouse, while Kara and Tien continued into the harbour district. Kara checked her mirror. Only two of the half dozen cars were still behind.

The plan was straightforward. Kara and Tien would keep eyes-on the boat until Sammi brought Chaz and Jacob down to the harbour. Both men would make the initial approach. It played into the stereotype that men would book fishing excursions more than women and so would be less suspicious.

Once out fishing the plan was to engage the crew in conversations and try to elicit as much information as possible. It wasn't the best plan, but they had little else.

Kara turned for the harbour. Another sweep of her mirrors revealed there were no more cars following behind. She pulled into the same carpark she had used previously and again theirs was the only vehicle in sight. She supposed it being a Sunday accounted for the lack of schoolchildren, but there were no joggers or quayside fishermen either. The view of the red troller was still shielded by the sailboat so they climbed out of the car.

"Brrr!" Tien called across the roof and pulled her coat tight. "Reckon we can keep an eye on it from the hotel?"

"Suppose so," Kara said. "It'll be better than freezing out in the open."

Kara clicked the remote and the car lights gave a small flash, confirming the doors were locked. As they walked towards the quayside a couple of heads appeared on the deck of one of the recreational boats moored at the near end of the harbour.

"So then, what's one of those called?" Kara said, nodding towards the sleek lines of the vessel.

"I don't know," Tien said. "I only looked up the ones I needed to know about. But at a guess I'd say that's a speedboat-cum-cruiser."

"Very nice too," Kara said as the two heads on the deck developed bodies and moved towards the small gangway and ladder that led to the quay. Both men were wrapped in heavy overcoats and gloves. They didn't look to Kara like they'd been doing much boat work, but as she hadn't much of a clue what that would entail, she didn't worry. The second of the men, much fatter and older than the first, stepped down onto the cobblestoned quay just as Kara drew level. She went to walk around him, just as his younger companion turned to face her. He gave a courteous nod and stepped out of her way. As she passed, he said, "Good morning... Liz."

Kara's brain took a second to process the discrepancy. Then she yelled for Tien to take on the other man as she prepared to take on the one who had greeted her. All she managed to do was step into a full-force punch that hit her in the temple. She was conscious just long enough to see Tien adopt a fighting stance.

11

Tien bent her knees, centred herself and faced the man who had just stepped onto the quay. He was fat, thick-necked, with long strands of grey hair to the sides of an otherwise bald head and was less than three feet from her. She anticipated his right-hand whipping in towards her head and instinctively moved to block it with her left arm. Her speed of reaction was equal to that of years gone by, but the pendulum weight of her prosthesis took her arm higher than desired. The full force punch impacted into the side of her forearm and she felt the light but incredibly strong structure absorb the shock. The man yelped in a voice uncharacteristic of his stature and Tien was aware of the deformity shattering through his hand. She saw at least two of his gloved fingers had broken in the blow. But she was also aware that her lower arm had detached itself.

Her prosthesis wasn't secured with straps or bindings like old fashioned models. Instead, the socket attached to the residuum of her arm, about two inches below the elbow joint, in a precise fit that allowed it to slip on and off like a shoe. It had taken four visits to perfect the fitting and while it was exact and robust, it wasn't designed to withstand a blunt force trauma. Detached and heavy, it was only prevented from falling onto the ground by her jacket's elasticated cuff.

She sensed movement in the periphery of her left eye. Stepping back she saw the second man moving towards her. Tien could see Kara's prone body on the ground behind him. She registered what she was looking at but denied the emotion any space to grow. She refocussed.

This second man, Kara's assailant, was much younger and leaner than his broken-handed colleague. His short hair and goatee beard made his face seem elongated. Tien shifted her gaze up and down the length of his body and ignoring the limp weight in her left sleeve, settled herself again. Both men moved forward slowly, approaching on a split vector that would have presented her real problems if they had been equidistant. But the older of the two was a few steps behind his partner and Tien measured her next move based on that. She was about to launch an attack when she heard the squeal of car tyres entering the carpark behind her.

Rapidly backing up to give herself more room, she glanced over her shoulder, hoping desperately to see Sammi and Chaz and Jacob. But the two men visible behind the windscreen were unknown to her. The car accelerated across the narrow space and as Tien turned back to face her assailants, she knew she was in real trouble. They were still advancing, undeterred by the oncoming car. She realised it wasn't a possible rescue, it was more opponents.

Springing off her heels, she launched forward and sprinted to her left. Avoiding the outstretched arm of the younger man, she positioned herself between Kara's body and what would soon be four attackers. She knew she couldn't reattach her arm as the T-shirt and jumper she was wearing under her jacket would get in the way, so she settled herself again, breathed deeply and forced herself to relax.

The car came to a skidded stop and the two newcomers stepped out. They walked purposefully forward and brushed their colleagues aside. Tien registered the new arrivals were higher in some pecking order than her previous opponents. The man on her left, the passenger from the car, was short, small-framed, with thinning brown hair and large, thick-framed black glasses. He wore Chelsea-boots, jeans and a check-patterned shirt under a half-zipped, expensive looking leather jacket.

The driver, approaching to her right, was the youngest of the four, barely out of his teens. He had dark brown hair and his skin was the colour of milky-coffee. He was substantially taller than six foot, but thin and fragile looking. He wore no jacket, just trainers, jeans and a T-shirt with a faded picture of Einstein on it. Tien decided he was the least of her problems.

She positioned herself to attack the passenger and mentally rehearsed dropping low, taking her weight on her right hand and launching an outside sweep kick. Correctly delivered it would knock him out of the fight. Then she could attack the driver with a series of withering front kicks to what she imagined were spindly legs. The other two would be dealt with after that. Tensing her core muscles, she waited for the passenger to step inside her attack radius. At a distance of four feet, he stopped walking.

Tien watched him reach inside his jacket and withdraw a handgun. Its muzzle swung round to Kara's prone body.

"You will kneel on the ground and put your hands behind you or I will shoot your friend. Then I will shoot you," the passenger said in Dutch-accented English.

Tien made to move between the gun and Kara.

"Fine, I shall shoot you first and then your friend. The order is of no matter. I will not count down or give you another chance. Either kneel, or die."

Tien looked into the man's eyes, boxed within their thick frames… and knelt.

"I have an artificial hand. I can't put my arms behind my back," she said.

The man looked to her limp sleeve and then issued a set of instructions in Dutch. The man with the goatee beard circled around behind Tien, avoiding stepping between her and the handgun. He picked her up in a bear hug and carried her to the car. His broken handed colleague held the rear door open and she was forced down into the footwell of the back seat. A black hood was put over her head and she felt the weight of two men climb into the seat above her. Their feet pressed down harshly on her.

Tien shut her eyes and centred her focus. She heard the click of the car boot opening, felt a weight being placed into it, heard the boot close. She felt the weight of two men climbing into the front of the car, heard all four car doors slamming shut and then felt the car reverse, before it accelerated forward.

There was no conversation in the vehicle and her ear, jammed down on the floor, was engulfed by the roar of the road noise. It reminded her of static hiss, like loud white noise. She shut her eyes and remembered a military training course from long ago.

φ

Kara heard a roar like a rushing tidal wave. The fear of instant death by drowning jerked the sound, from a distant part of her brain, into dead-centre of her consciousness and caused every synaptic nerve to fire for her survival. Her eyes snapped wide open but the blackness was unaltered. Her breath began to catch, her heartbeat raced and her thoughts were swamped in panic. She twisted and squirmed but she was confined in every direction. She tried to raise her head and smashed the side of it into a metal surface. Her breathing speeded up. She was in a box, filling with water. She was going to die. She started to scream but no sound came, her mind yelled to get out, get away. She felt tears in her eyes, her breath coming in rapid but shallow pants, her stomach spiralling in nausea and fear. Then a small voice said, 'Be quiet now Kara and think.'

She knew the voice. It had always been a hidden part of her but had only been revealed by her participation on the worst, yet best, training she had ever undertaken. The voice had been hewn from her, then returned, and finally embedded in her deepest psyche. It was her voice. The real Kara. The only part of her mind that had remained when the rest of her had been broken completely. The core of her, as she was built back up.

It spoke softly, 'Can you breathe?'

Yes.

'Are you hurt?'

Her consciousness detached itself and surged through her body. Her focus settled on her feet. Not hurt, still wearing her boots, not tied but her heels were pressed against a solid surface. She mindfully examined her legs. Not hurt, still clothed in her jeans, not restrained, but cramped. Bent at the knees. She was lying on her right side. The surface under her not quite solid, but not a sponge. A slight spring to it. The whole of it rocking and bouncing. The roar was not water. Kara knew what it was. She recognised it, and her prison, from that same training so many years before.

'Continue your checks please.'

Her arms behind her back, restrained at the wrists by a plastic tie. Her head covered with a dark hood. Her neck tilted at an awkward angle. The top of her head, hard against another restraining surface. Her temple, the target of the punch was pierced by a stabbing, throbbing, aching jumble of pain. But she wasn't dying.

Her core voice asked again, 'So, are you hurt?'

No.

'Where are you?'

I'm in the boot of a small car.

'And?'

And I've realised my situation.

'Good. What now?'

Plan for what could be coming.

'What else do you know?'

He called me Liz.

'And?'

And I'm still alive.

'Good. Let's keep it that way.'

φ

Tien felt the car decelerate and then swing left onto an unsealed road. The wheels bucked and jumped in and out of significant ruts, and bigger potholes jarred the whole chassis. She concentrated and when the car decelerated again she reckoned the rutted road had been no more than a few hundred yards long. She was jostled and rolled under the feet of the men as the car swung around in a half circle before reversing and stopping with a harsh jolt. The engine was switched off and an oppressive silence enveloped her. She heard doors being opened and felt the shift in weight as the two men in the front got out. She heard their feet crunching on a gravel mix. She heard the boot release catch click open. The two men sitting above her got out. She felt hands on her legs and she was pulled backwards. Bracing herself for the drop onto the ground, four hands grabbed her, carried her a short distance and then let her stand on her own.

A foot pressed into the back of her knee. She buckled and sank to soft, damp ground. She wondered if she was in a field. Hands on either side grasped her shoulders and held her upper arms fast. Her head remained hooded and she could hear no noise, no talking.

The muzzle of a pistol was thrust into her left temple. She fought the urge to cry out. Biting down on the inside of her cheek she breathed deeply and tried to calm her thoughts. She heard her mother's voice, 'Don't you dare Tien Margarethe Tran. Don't you dare let these people know you are afraid. You bite down and if this is it, then you will go with the dignity of your forebears.'

Tien realised she was smiling. The thought of her mother scolding her gave her strength. The fear slipped away. She silently recited the Hail Mary and waited for the trigger to be pulled.

φ

Kara lay in the boot of the car, her left leg bent high,

waiting. She heard footsteps on a crushed-gravel surface. She drew a deep breath and tensed. Sensing the change in light as the boot lid was raised, she waited until the flare of light filled her space. Releasing her tensed muscles she exploded her leg out to where she thought her captor would be.

She missed.

Four hands grabbed her and lifted her. She smelled grass and earth, the faintest notes of manure, fertilisers and nearby livestock. A foot kicked her in the back of the knee and she collapsed onto soft, damp ground. Hands grasped her shoulders and held fast. She could hear no talking but as she concentrated she heard a soft rumble. It was another car, coming closer, growing louder. The rutted road made its own cacophony of sound as it attempted to rip the suspension out of the vehicle. Kara stayed kneeling. Listening. She heard the tyres crunch onto crushed gravel as the car came past her, close, then reversed. She heard the engine cut off and one door open and shut. The muzzle of a pistol was thrust into the back of her left ear.

'Breathe.' her inner voice commanded. 'Not one sound out of you. You will not say one word. This is a tactic, but if it isn't then nothing you can say or do will change it. So you will say and do nothing. Are we clear?'

Yes.

'And if it is a tactic, when we get out of this, then we will make this bastard eat his own fucking gun. Agreed?'

Yes.

'We will fuck him and his friends up and make them weep as they beg for a mercy we will not give. Agreed?'

Yes.

She often wondered what it would be like if her inner monologue could become corporeal. She always imagined her inner self to be cleverer and prettier than the woman she provided the commentary for. She could certainly sing better than the voice that came from her mouth.

'Now, think your happy thoughts.'

Kara's mind blanked out the pressure of the muzzle and

conjured visions of the people she most loved. She saw her parents, at the door of their house. Smiling at her as she walked up the path. Her father, arm around the waist of her mum, raising his hand in greeting. His right index finger stained yellow-brown from nicotine. His eyes bright and mischievous, like a five-year old boy, held hostage in a sixty-five year old body. His silver hair still thick and still blessed with the full wave that in summers long ago he had tried to pacify with tubs of Brylcreem, in homage to his Mod idols.

Her mother, elegant in everything she ever wore, dressed in a summery cotton skirt and a brightly coloured top. Her hair, still the vibrant reddish-brown of her youth, albeit now artificially maintained. Her high cheekbones and oval eyes testament to the beautiful girl she had been. The vibrant, youthful hippy-spirit who had fallen for the moped-riding, suited and booted Mod. The only Mod her mum could ever remember seeing out in the wilds of Yeovil in Somerset.

Kara felt the tears welling in her eyes. She switched her thoughts back to the hard muzzle, crushing into the base of her skull. Suppressing the sob that was building and regaining her control, she pictured her brother David with his wife. She saw her nephew and niece smiling up from a Lego-strewn floor. Snatching a breath, her shoulders heaved but she stayed quiet.

The gunman leaned in close and whispered in her ear. Softly, like a lover's murmur, "Not a word. Not one word or you die right now. Nod if you understand."

Kara nodded. It had been a Dutch accent, but different from the man that had greeted her at the harbour. The hands on her shoulders went under her armpits and lifted her back onto her feet. Forcing the images of family out of her mind, she concentrated on building a mental picture of her environment.

She was roughly pushed and guided, her awkward foot-steps tripping on a low step. The light coming through the thick hood changed and she figured she had entered a building. It felt small, constrained, a hallway. She listened and could hear another awkward set of steps being guided behind her. She knew it was Tien, but the muzzle of the gun stayed pressed into her skull and she kept quiet. After a few more steps she was dragged sharp right and into a larger room. There was still no light but she could feel more space. The guiding hands shoved her hard and she sprawled forward, hitting her shin on, and falling over, a low, hard-edged object. She half-twisted on the way down and landed on her back, partially knocking the wind out of herself with a gasp. Her bound hands were trapped between her body and the floor.

She was pulled up and twisted around. Hands delved into her pockets, removing her phone and the small amount of cash she had. She mentally said a thank you for the discipline that stopped her carrying any identification when she was going out on a job. Her jacket was unzipped and pulled down her arms, bunching at her wrists. Then she was pressed back against a wall and forced to sit on the floor. Her feet were brought together and a plastic tie was secured around them. She heard footsteps leave the room and the door shut. She tapped her heels on the bare concrete floor and waited, but there was no reply. Tien had been taken to a different room.

Kara realised that the bunching of her jacket at her wrists made any hope of breaking out from the plastic zip-tie an impossibility. She could also feel that the locking tab of the tie had been placed to the rear of her right hand. She was struck that whoever had placed it on her, knew what they were doing. Well, she reflected, so did she.

Silently and to a long-practised rhythm, she began to count. She knew that each minute estimated would only be out by a second or two at the most. She was her own metronome and while she remained hooded and restrained there was little else to do but count and consider. As the numbers ticked over subconsciously, she put her frontal-lobes to more high-level analysis tasks.

She estimated that if she had been knocked out for perhaps five or ten minutes, then she wasn't more than twenty minutes from the Volendam harbour carpark. They had been waiting for her. They had called her Liz. She had only used that alias with Henk, in the hotel. Had someone overheard their enquiries about boats? She thought back to the two men in the corner of the restaurant on Friday morning. Were they the people who made Swift disappear? Had Amberley's text message put them on alert? Maybe the simple act of asking about the boats tipped them off. How had they known she w-

Kara cut herself off in mid-thought.

She thought about going back to talk to Henk on the Saturday. She had gone alone. It wasn't a set meeting. Just her dropping in casually. She hadn't even known if he would be there. But he had been and she had talked to him. Then she had driven back to the apartment on her own. The road to Amsterdam from Volendam had been as busy as usual.

She realised with sudden clarity that had someone been following her, she would never have picked up on it. She hadn't arranged for Sammi or Tien to operate a trail car coming behind to monitor. She hadn't collated car registration numbers, she hadn't noticed if the same cars had followed her this morning. She had potentially compromised the whole lot of them. They could have been under counter-surveillance for the last day. Or more.

Worse still, Kara, Tien and Sammi had hung around the apartment. They had been easy targets for anyone mounting a surveillance operation. The potential was easy to imagine if Rik, or whoever owned the boat, was already suspicious of out-of-season enquiries coming so soon after an alerting text message from Francis Amberley. This morning would have been a simple trap. Put a decoy on the deck of the Fair Winds and if someone showed up at the harbour, it was too much of a coincidence. She swore to herself.

Her smarter, prettier, internal-self scolded her, 'You stupid bitch, Kara. You've been lazy, distracted and lax. You underestimated the people you were going up against.'

Had she understood how badly she had underestimated, the admonishment would have been a lot more severe.

12

Near Volendam, Holland.

Eighty-six minutes. Her count continuing, her anger festering into a blind desire to get free of her restraints and take it out on her captors.

Kara felt the air pressure of the room change as a door opened to her right. Footsteps, two sets. The plastic tie on her feet was cut. Four hands grabbed her, lifting, dragging and pushing her into the hallway, then right. She was shoved a few feet forward before being thrown left into another expansive room. Once more she stumbled, but this time she was grabbed by a third set of hands. Their owner was smaller. She was twisted around, pushed back against a wall and her feet were resecured with a plastic tie.

"Sit down." A heavy Dutch accent, on a new voice. She figured she had heard three different voices so far. The man who had punched her at the harbour, the gunman from outside and now this *Maitre d'*. Given his approximate size, he wasn't the fat man who had stepped off the boat. In the time she had waited alone she had been struck by the relative professionalism of her captors. They had maintained a fair degree of silence with no excessive talking, no shouting, no hysterics, but she had still heard three of them. She knew there was at least one more and she knew at least one of them was armed.

They had left her alone with no opportunity to talk to Tien. It was a classic interrogation technique that was meant to isolate, subjugate and demoralise. The first time she had been forced to endure it, almost eleven years earlier on the training course where she had discovered her real inner voice, she had indeed felt most of those emotions. Repeated exposure to the techniques lessened their impact. Kara now found that she was examining what was being done to her and rating its effectiveness. She was giving scores out of ten for prisoner handling, maintenance of isolation, clarity of purpose, use of appropriate techniques. Short of them just shooting her, she was beginning to feel a lot more comfortable.

Surprisingly, having thought they were doing well with her isolation, her hood was taken off. She blinked rapidly in the bright light of what was a dimmed room and scanned her environment. Opposite was the door she had come through: standard size, domestic, closed, a young, thin, tall man standing guard in front of it. To his left as Kara looked, a pale green wall was marked by lines of bare plaster that showed where long-gone units had once been affixed. There was a small set of shelves, empty other than a stacked set of towels in blues, mauves and greys and a box that reminded her of an old canteen of cutlery. Next to the shelves was another door, almost diagonally opposite from where Kara was seated. The fat man from the harbour was standing in front of it. The wall to the left hand side of the room had a double-width window. Like the doors, it was domestic in its size and placement. The sun filtered through medium-heavy, unpatterned, grey curtains that didn't quite meet in the middle. Under the window were more bare plaster marks just visible above and to the side of a three-seater couch, its fabric a drab grey. To the left of the couch was a faded half-and-half stable door. The metal bolts and hinges were rusted over and a visible line of dust and grime marked where it met the floor. Kara thought it geographically appropriate that the Americans would have called it a Dutch door. To her immediate left, along the same wall she was propped against, was an old low-level sideboard. Through the gap between the legs of the man who had just removed her hood, she could see more bare plaster marks. The wall to her right was free of furniture but had a mirror, almost identical in size to the window, hung exactly to reflect the light. She looked up to see a lone, unlit, bulb with no shade. She looked down at the floor and her mind jarred. Her eyes widened and for the first time her inner voice sounded less assured.

'Oh what the fuck have we gotten ourselves into here?'

The man who had removed her hood spoke and she recognised him as the *Maitre d'*, "Are you thirsty?"

She kept her eyes cast down and didn't speak, but considered that she had chosen his name well. First he had offered her a seat, now he was offering a drink.

"Are you thirsty?" he repeated, more harshly.

Kara maintained her downward stare and her silence. Out of the corner of her eye she saw his foot moving and was able to tense her muscles to meet the toe of his boot impacting into her thigh. She muffled the desire to scream obscenities at him and instead fell sideways to her right. He bent and dragged her up. Then he reached behind him and retrieved a small plastic water bottle from the sideboard. Twisting the cap off he took a drink and opened his mouth wide to show he had swallowed. He held it carelessly to her lips. She gulped the water, ignoring the excess pouring down her front.

He said something in Dutch before turning away. His two companions laughed and Kara processed the similarities to German. She guessed he had said something like silence wouldn't help her, but she hadn't a clue about the other words laced throughout the sentence. The soreness of her thigh was lost in the frustration she felt at not understanding what he had said. It was relatively unknown for her to be at such a disadvantage. The Maitre d' sat down on the arm of the chair next to her. He wore black Chelsea-boots, jeans, a check-patterned, short-sleeved shirt and large, thick-framed black glasses. Kara guessed he was in his thirties, about five-foot-six, lightly built with thinning dark hair. As she had been trained to do, she automatically personalised her captors. She decided to give him a new name. He would be Buddy.

She eyed the other two men. The one to her far left was the fat man from the harbour. He looked even bigger in girth now his overcoat was gone. He wore deck shoes, beige chinos and a cheesecloth shirt that bulged out trying to cover a substantial gut. He appeared to be in his fifties. Or perhaps he was younger and it was his grey hair, hanging in straggly strands to the sides of a bald dome, that made him look aged. His neck was almost as wide as his head and his forearms ended in rolls of fat at his wrists. Kara noticed he stood with his arms folded awkwardly and had heavy strapping on his right hand. She wondered how he had worn gloves at the harbour. The bulge of his stomach was by far his most prominent feature, so Kara named him Tubbs.

The last man, almost opposite her, seemingly guarding the door through which she had come, was much younger and taller than either of his companions. Kara wondered if he was even out of his teens. He had dark brown hair, skin like milky-coffee and was at least six-foot-four, but thin. Very thin. He was shifting his weight from one foot to the other, unable to remain at peace. He wore trainers, jeans and a T-shirt with a faded picture of Einstein on it. Kara registered it and decided that Albert was a good enough name for now. She realised none of the men had jackets on and that the room was being maintained at a comfortable temperature. She wore a jumper with a T-shirt under it, her jacket still bunched at her wrists, and she was beginning to feel warm despite no visible radiators in the room. Her gaze returned to the floor.

It was covered in old, cracked, dark-brown linoleum. She looked again at the bare plaster lines on the walls and realised she was in what had been a kitchen. All of the fixtures and fittings had been ripped out but it was unmistakable. Her gaze returned to the middle of the floor, where the only discernible anomaly was located. As she half-tilted her head, trying to figure out what she was looking at, there was a knock at the door opposite. Albert jumped a little then stood aside, swinging the door open. Tien was frogmarched in by the man who had punched Kara at the harbour. He was aged somewhere between Albert and Buddy, not as tall as Albert and much leaner than Tubbs. His short hair and goatee beard made his face seem longer than it should be and reminded Kara of Van Gogh. Van would do for his name. He almost carried Tien into the room, before turning her and forcing her to sit against the wall, directly opposite Kara. He removed her hood but kept a hold on her right arm.

The two women made eye-contact and the resolve of both was immediately reinforced, strengthened a hundredfold.

'Well haven't you made a mistake,' Kara thought. She blinked and had the same returned from Tien. Their defence would rely on saying nothing of value to these men. Not one word of truthful information that could reveal anything of use. Not one syllable that would give their identities away. It was all they could do. The force of the women's shared bond, the strength they were enjoying, was practically visible and Kara wondered how the men in the room hadn't realised they had handed the balance of power to their captives. She moved her eyes to the weight hanging in her friend's sleeve and looked again at Tien's face with concern. Tien half closed her eyes and gave a micro movement of her eyebrows. 'No biggie. I'm fine.'

Kara's temper flared and she swore to herself that as soon as she got out of this she would tear these men apart. Clenching her teeth and tensing the muscles in her jaw, she looked around the room, committing the men's faces to memory, but then she refocussed on the middle of the floor. There were four small hollows cut into the linoleum that revealed bare concrete. The indents were spaced in a loose square about three feet apart. In each, offset to the side, was a metal ring half submerged into the concrete. Set in the middle of the square was a narrow-grated drain cover. She was still trying to figure out what it was for when a fifth man walked in.

He wore black shoes, jeans and a red polo shirt. He was trim, Kara estimated just short of six foot, dark hair, neatly cut about a face that was typical of someone who was probably in their mid-forties, except for the dark black of a web-shaped tattoo that covered his throat. Inked exactly on his Adam's apple was the engorged body of a black widow spider.

"Hello, Liz. My name is Rik. I believe we have some mutual acquaintances?"

13

Rik walked through the middle of the room, his hands tucked into his jeans pockets. When he got to the couch he surveyed the space like some old-world monarch before sitting down. Tubbs stood beside him, as if he was Rik's bodyguard. Kara thought, 'My dear, dear Tubbs, you wouldn't last two minutes with some of the people I know who really do that as a job.'

"So Liz," Rik said in his lisp of a Dutch accent, "I want to know who are you and why you want to do the renting of my boat in the cold weather."

Kara looked down at the floor and mumbled, "We're just tourists, honestly, we just wa-" She was cut off by another kick from Buddy.

"Now that's not true Liz," Rik continued. "I want to know where you live in Eng-a-land. I want to know why a friend of mine has not contacted me, as he should have. I would like you to tell me these things."

Kara maintained her downward stare, "I don't understand who yo-" Another kick stopped her again.

Rik leant forward, his elbows on his knees, "Be quiet now

106

Liz. For you see, I was just going to ask you, but then I saw you and your friends in your apartment and I decide it would be more fun to have you visit my house. I want to be polite and have a small... talk? This is not the right word. A small... chit? No matter."

Kara looked up from under her brows and saw Tien had adopted a similar, head-down stare. She thought that these men had no idea who they were dealing with.

"But then I think, the first time my friends in this town see you, you had two men with you. Now these men are not with you. They have gone. So I wondered what they are doing. I wondered if maybe you were watching me. So I set a trap. It seems I am right."

Kara silently swore again for being so sloppy.

"You were caught and I decide to have my friends bring you here. I think we will be able to sort this out with a talk but then I leave you in separate rooms for nearly one hour and a half. One hour and a half and do you know what I find out?"

Kara frowned but this time said nothing. She wasn't sure where Rik was taking the one-sided conversation.

"No? No you do not know and this time you choose not to lie. Yes, that will be it. You choose this time to be quiet and that is the funniest thing. These two women, who I leave alone in big rooms and neither one of them screams or cries or shouts out. Not one word or, how do you say... peep? Not one peep. Like they have been trained not to react. Like they are professionals. Like they are not tourists. Your silence and your discipline show me that you are not usual. Your silence is what has given you away."

Kara couldn't help her eyes half-shutting as she processed Rik's words. She and Tien had stuck to what they knew. They had not veered from how they had been trained. But Rik was right, that wasn't what a normal tourist would have done. She felt sick. Her professionalism had betrayed her. She knew that whatever she and Tien might appear as, normal tourist wasn't it.

Rik continued, "You just sit in the rooms calmly. Then we

bring you in here and you sit calmly. Then we reunite you and you do not call out with joy. You do not call each other's names, you do not make effort to hug, you do not cry with relief. Oh no Liz, tourists you are not. I will tell you what you are. You are professionals. That tells me you know what we do. That tells me you are dangerous to me and my friends."

Kara raised her head and looked across the room. Tien too had lifted her gaze. The two women communicated silently and each knew they had made a mistake. A major mistake.

"So then I think, what type of professionals are these women? But you do not have any identification. Even your phones are blank." Rik stood and reached into his pockets, withdrawing both Tien and Kara's phones. He retook his seat and looked down at the slim black devices. "No names, no, how you say? Contacts? None of these. Just other numbers. This is not usual I think. This is not two tourist women, but also not two police women, I think." He took each phone and flicked them the length of the room. Both smashed against the wall just under the mirror. The cases distorting, bending, the glass screens shattering into a haze of splinters. Despite their training and resolve, Kara and Tien both flinched.

Rik waited for the echo of the impacts to dissipate. "Now you see don't you?" he asked. "Now you see why I think you are unusual. So now you will see that I must find out some things. I must know where Francis Amberley is. He has not sent me another text, like he is meant to after his first."

Kara shut her eyes fully. Nobody had contacted Amberley because Rik and Amberley had a protocol that needed a second text from the originator. Kara felt a tightness in her stomach. Whatever she and Tien had wandered into was a lot more organised than they had thought. She realised her earlier assessment, that the men had no clue who they were dealing with, was truer for her. She had no idea who these guys were.

"I want to know if you are the woman he spoke about. I want to know if you are the one who talks about insurance money. I want to know why you want to hire my boat. Last, I want to know why you are asking about Derek Swift."

Kara went to answer with more of the tourist cover story but stopped. She needed a new tactic and for now she was a blank. She dropped her gaze again and although still furious at herself, she managed to consider that, through his questions, Rik was also giving a lot away. But on balance, the fact none of the men had bothered to cover their faces and the fact he had just mentioned Swift by name, were not encouraging signs.

"So, I shall ask you Liz," he paused and Kara's hair was grabbed by Buddy. Her head was wrenched up to look at Rik. "I want to know, is this your real name? Are you called Liz?"

Kara clenched her teeth against the pain of her hair and through them managed, "My name *is* Liz. Elizabeth, please that's the truth. Please."

Rik held her gaze and then with a dismissive shake of his head said, "Let her go."

Buddy released her and Kara dropped her head back down, but not as fully as before. She kept her eyes on the couch. The room was quiet. Rik laughed, "Even now your training wins out. I ask you a simple question and everyone I know would have said, yes. Or no. But you picked your words so carefully. You think too quickly for your own good. You think you are tough. We shall see soon enough."

Rik gave a small wave of his hand and Tubbs and Albert went out through the door diagonally opposite Kara. They returned a few seconds later, wheeling a wooden framed contraption. It had two end pieces, shaped like upside down Ys, joined in the middle by what looked like the top of a vaulting horse. Its leather surface faded and scratched to a greying brown. Near the base of each leg was a small metal half-ring set into the wood. At the top of each single upright was a strong chain ending in a metal handcuff that rested on the aged leather.

The wooden frame's legs fitted into the floor hollows perfectly. Albert and Tubbs flicked the wheels up and used four metal clips to join the semi-circle of metal in each leg to the semi-circles set into the floor. As they secured the clips the frame took on a rigidity that was testament to precise carpentry skills.

Rik rose from the couch and walked to the box that Kara had thought looked like a canteen of cutlery. He stepped to his right and glanced over his shoulder to check she was watching him. Opening the lid he lifted out a Glock-17 handgun. Buddy stepped across the width of the room and took a second Glock from the box. Both men screwed round-tube suppressors onto the threaded barrels of the pistols. Kara tried to mask her surprise but knew she hadn't come close. She was familiar with both the gun and its silencer. It was military grade and although the attachment awkwardly doubled the overall length of the pistol, its sound suppression capabilities were astonishing. It reduced the normal noisy report of the Glock to little more than the soft metallic clicks of the working parts as they cycled the next round into the chamber.

"Now I see you have the startled look on your face. This is the first I have seen you react," Rik said as he and Buddy cocked the pistols.

Kara thought it was like a stage being set. These men had done this before. Many times. They moved without the need for commands and each was taking up a designated place. Van stood to the right of the strange wooden frame and Rik handed him the loaded pistol he had prepared. Buddy moved back across the room to stand over Kara, his pistol held by his side. Albert returned to stand in front of the door that led to the hallway while Tubbs moved to stand over Tien. Rik moved back into the middle of the room.

"I see your eyes now never leave me. You are like a scared pussy cat," he said. "That is good for I want you to watch. In fact I shall tell you what is going to happen. You will watch everything I do. If you do not keep your eyes open, if you look away, if you look anywhere other than at me, my companion next to you, will shoot you in the foot. After that, if you look away, he will shoot you in the other foot. Then the ankles, then the knees. Then the elbows and the hands. No one will hear for these pistols will be shooting very quiet. Do you understand?"

Kara stared at him. She didn't look away. Her mind was racing and she heard the voice of instructors from the many courses she had been on, telling her not to cooperate, not to acquiesce to any requests. But she held his gaze.

"Still with the no talking. That is fine. Very fine," Rik said and nodded to Tubbs. The fat man reached with his good hand and grabbed Tien's hair, lifting her straight up. Kara watched Tien grit her teeth to prevent crying out. Her right hand reached out behind her, finding the wall and steadying herself as she stood. Tubbs unzipped her jacket and Albert wrenched it off her shoulders. The weight of the prosthesis took him by surprise and he reached into the left sleeve, retrieving the high tech arm. He held it up and whistled in appreciation of the construction.

Kara saw Tien tensing, almost willing the young man to be careful with her arm. But again, no words were spoken. Both women kept silent and watched Albert place the arm delicately on the small shelving unit.

Tubbs reached into the pocket of his Chinos and withdrew a thin black case. The long stiletto blade of the flick knife sprung out and he reached forward grabbing Tien's jumper. In a single swipe upwards the woollen garment was sliced into two halves. Tien tried to recoil away from the blade but Albert stepped up and held her tightly.

"Get the fuck away from her," Kara yelled and the volume of the outburst surprised all the men in the room, except one.

Rik laughed, "Ha! Now we have a reaction. Now we have emotion. How sad it is too late. You *will* tell me everything, but not now. Now you are too late. Now you will watch and after you will tell me. You will tell me all you know just to stop me doing other things. Yes?" He nodded at Tubbs. "Continue."

"Don't you dare fucking touch her you fat bastard. For everything you do to her I'll carve the soul out of you." Kara yelled as Tubbs reached for Tien's T-shirt, reducing it to shreds in a single slash of the knife and leaving only her bra in place.

Rik said something in Dutch. Buddy placed his pistol on

the sideboard behind him and walked forward. He lifted the rag that had been Tien's T-shirt and held it for Tubbs to slice it into a few pieces. Then he walked back across the room. He knelt beside Kara and grabbed her head, forcing a balled piece of fabric into her mouth before securing it with a gag he made from a longer piece of the materiel. Kara resisted as much as her tied hands and feet would allow but Buddy, despite his modest size, was strong. She continued to swear and yell but her voice was suppressed as effectively as the pistols.

"You see, now I do not want to hear you. But you *will* watch," Rik said.

Kara looked to Tien, who responded with a weak smile.

Rik swatted his hand in a gesture to Albert and Tubbs. The fat man reached up and cut the shoulder straps of Tien's bra, then folded the switchblade away against his thigh and returned it to his pocket. He and Albert moved Tien across to the wooden frame and bent her forward over the aged leather. Tubbs kept hold of the residuum of Tien's left arm while Albert secured her right into the handcuff on that side. He hauled on the securing chain and Tien's hand was dragged sideways until tight against the wooden stay. Then he knelt and secured her right leg to the bottom metal clip on that side by a long plastic tie. Reaching over, he tried to take hold of her left foot, but Tien anticipated his movement and kicked backwards. She caught the young man square on the nose. A loud pop, as her heel fractured the cartilage in his nose, was followed by Albert's high-pitched squeal. He toppled over backwards, blood spurting out from between his fingers. Kara felt a surge of victory at her friend's defiance, but it was short-lived. Rik nodded to Van who thrust the muzzle of the suppressed pistol into the nape of Tien's neck, forcing her head down against the leather.

"You do that again and it will be your last act," Rik growled into Tien's ear before looking down at Albert and barking something at him in Dutch. The young man picked himself up and moved to the back of the room, grabbing a few of the last shreds of Tien's T-shirt to hold against his bloodied nose.

Rik bent and removed Tien's left boot before straightening up and leaning into her with his body. He waved Van away and ushered Tubbs back far enough so Kara's view was uninterrupted, then he reached out and unhooked Tien's bra.

Kara's vision was blurred through tears, her screams muffled and choked on the fabric in her mouth. Tien turned her head to the left and looked towards her. The women locked eyes and Kara saw the saddest, most resigned expression on her friend's face. Tien gave the slightest of shakes of her head.

Rik reached around and unfastened Tien's jeans. He pulled them and her underwear down and off her left foot before using another long plastic tie to secure her ankle. Kara saw the plastic cut into her friend's flesh.

When he was sure Tien was completely secured, Rik stepped over to Kara. Grabbing her chin he forced her to look up. "I will so enjoy this little gift you have given me. She looks so young, so pretty and yet she is all woman. A perfect present. You will watch what my friends and I do to her. But I have changed my mind. If you look away I will shoot your friend first." He let her chin go and walked back to the wooden frame. Reaching to his own jeans he unfastened them and positioned the head of his erection against Tien, then looked to the rest of the men in the room.

They began to cheer and bay, save for Albert who stood against the back wall, his left hand to his bleeding nose while he masturbated with his right.

Kara watched Rik begin to press forward. She saw Tien shut her eyes and lower her head, her tears staining the old faded leather to black. As Kara's gagged mouth fell silent, her inner voice broke and wailed for her friend.

The top panel of the half-and-half stable door ruptured inwards as a squat metal milk churn punched through the rotten wood and rusted brackets. The remnants sagged down, tottered on a decaying hinge, then dropped to the floor. Jacob kicked in the lower panel of the door so forcibly that it too separated from its hinge and flew backwards into the room, shattering against the side of the low sideboard, sending long splinters flying past Kara. Buddy, still next to her, jumped at the noise. He began to raise the suppressed pistol towards the onrushing Jacob. Kara fell onto her right shoulder, twisted onto her back, raised her bound feet and delivered a two-footed kick into the back of Buddy's legs. He folded down and forward, the pistol firing as his body spasmed with the impact of his knees hitting the floor. The slightest 'Pfft' sound accompanied the bullet ripping into the linoleum just in front of Jacob's left foot. Buddy adjusted his aim but was woefully slow. Jacob's stocky arms went around the man and pulled him up, turning him to the rest of the room. Kara looked to her right and saw Van, on the far side of Tien, raise his own pistol. Two more 'Pfft' noises sounded and two small whispers of smoke came from the Glock's muzzle. The dull thud of rounds impacting into flesh forced Kara to look back to Jacob, but it was the shocked face of Buddy she saw. The bullets had slammed into the small, bespectacled man that Jacob was now using as a human shield.

Jacob clamped his left forearm across the dead Buddy's throat and held him in place. His right hand grabbed the pistol before it fell and in a smooth movement he levelled the weapon and fired twice. Kara, still on her back, watched two neat holes appear on the lower left cheek of Van, whose raised gun-hand instantly went limp and whose body collapsed straight down.

Jacob let go of Buddy as Tubbs, finally reacting to the intruder in the room, bent for Van's pistol. Jacob fired two rounds into the side of the fat man's grey hair. The bending body continued to topple forward and splayed into the floor like a belly-flopping diver.

Sammi and Chaz came through the wrecked door and Kara registered Sammi's horror at the tableau in front of her. Rik had not moved, he was still positioned behind Tien and his face hadn't yet reacted to the shock he must have been feeling. Tien's eyes had snapped open when the door had been smashed in and now she was screaming for Jacob to stop. Kara heard the shout and saw Jacob drop the pistol before stepping across the room to Rik. Kara tried to mirror Tien's plea but the noise was lost in her gagged mouth. She looked to Sammi and Chaz but they were still in the doorway and not close enough to intervene.

φ

Jacob Anthony Harrop was twenty-six, stood five feet eleven inches and weighed fourteen stone which, according to the BMI scale, meant he was overweight. In fact there was no fat on the stocky ex-gunner. He played rugby and had always liked training in the gym with his older brother, hence he could bench press three hundred pounds easily. His chest was like a barrel, his arms were strong and for a man of his size, he was quick. Yet his natural demeanour was soft and calm, sheltering behind a shy modesty. But since watching the dockside attack on Kara and Tien from his bedroom vantage point, his anger had been gaining momentum.

On first arriving at the isolated farmhouse he had followed Sammi and Chaz's lead. Parking on the main road, they had used the cover of hedgerows to approach the house. Sammi, monitoring the software that was homing in on the beacons fitted to Kara and Tien's phones, reported that the two signals were located close together but that didn't mean Kara and Tien were. Chaz had led Jacob cautiously up to the farm's front aspect, checking the cars, the main door and the windows. They'd made their way around to the back of the house, moving slowly and crouching low to pass under a wide window, the curtain of which wasn't fully closed. Jacob had manoeuvred to get a glimpse into the room beyond and what he had seen impacted him like a physical blow.

A surging rage and intense focus swamped him. Without further recourse to Chaz or Sammi he had grabbed a rusting milk churn that lay on the ground and hurled it at the old half-split door. His actions were automatic and only now, with the fat man slumped like a beached whale, did he turn to the real target of his ire.

He discarded the pistol because it was too impersonal for the fury that was coursing through him. He looked at, but tried not to see, Tien. Beautiful and demure Tien, whom he thought of as a butterfly and whom he couldn't be near without his heart lurching and his pulse quickening. She was his ideal, his personification of perfection. Delicate, smart, strong, stunning. He could see her mouth moving but could hear nothing as his speed of movement, thought and vision sucked the energy from his other senses. His eyes settled on the man now trying to stumble away, trousers caught around his ankles. Jacob focussed on the black widow spider, inked on the man's Adam's apple. In two strides he closed the distance and punched with a straight right. The man tried to raise his hands in defence but the forceful blow tore through his weak palms.

Jacob felt the larynx rupture under his fist. He took one more step and caught the now unconscious man under the arms. Spinning the limp body around so that it faced away from him, he heaved it up, let it go and as the body fell to the floor, he moved his left hand under the chin and his right onto the nape of the neck. His hands acted like the restrictions of a hangman's noose. Jacob put every ounce of his strength into the opposing up and down pressure he exerted and the noise of the vertebrae shattering was audible throughout the room.

ϕ

Kara watched the lifeless form of Rik crumple onto the floor and knew that the one good chance of finding Derek Swift had probably crumpled too. She didn't care. She and her inner voice were cheering for the savagery that Jacob had displayed in protecting Tien. She squirmed to get purchase with her still bound hands and managed to force herself into a sitting position. Jacob was tenderly placing his jacket over Tien's nakedness while Chaz and Sammi were moving into the room. She sensed the slightest of movements to her right

116

before the pistol Jacob had thrown down was pressed hard against her temple. Her body was lifted up with a surprising amount of force and despite trying to resist she only succeeded in having the surreal sight of a smiling picture of Albert Einstein pass by her right eye. The tall thin youngster held her firmly and although she was much shorter than him, he ducked down until his chin was level with her shoulder. Blood from his nose dripped onto her and his now flaccid penis still hung from his open fly. Kara tried to fight him but with both legs and hands bound she had no leverage.

Sammi and Chaz had seen the movement and moved to face the threat but not before Sammi had recovered the pistol that lay to the side of the dead fat man. Kara watched her friend bring the weapon up in a double hand grip.

"Wow there fella," Sammi said. "What are you doing? This is all over. Don't be silly. Just drop the weapon."

The young man's voice was stifled by the damage to his nose. He sounded like he was suffering from a vicious head cold, but he managed to scream, "No. No. You drop your gun. You do it or I kill her. You do it now. I'll kill her, I'll kill her!"

Kara, gagged, bound and with a gun to her head couldn't help but hear the laughter of her internal monologue. Sammi, Chaz, Tien and Kara had all been through the same scenarios in training. She knew what was coming next.

"Just take it easy. Let's all just take it easy. My friend has no intention of putting her gun down mate," Chaz said from beside Sammi.

"I'll kill her. I'll kill her. You put your gun down," Albert yelled again.

"You've seen too many movies, mate," Chaz laughed, holding his palms down and out. "The last thing my mate here," he pointed his thumb at the rock steady Sammi, Albert glanced at the movement, "is gonna do, is put her gun down. That way you'd have a gun and we wouldn't. You'd probably shoot us. You'd definitely win. That's not an outcome I want. So no, we won't be putting our gun down."

"I'll kill her," Albert shouted, the blood flow from his nose increasing with the ferocity of his pronouncements. Kara felt it splashing down on her shoulder but stayed as relaxed as she could. She watched Sammi's eyes.

Sammi blinked slowly and looked, with her eyes only and no movement of her head, almost imperceptivity down to Kara's left. Kara reciprocated the movement. Sammi blinked slowly, a further three times then twitched her mouth, again in a manner that went unnoticed by the increasingly anxious Albert.

Chaz continued, "You see, you won't mate. You won't kill her, 'cos if you do then that's game over. We will definitely kill you. The minute you shoot her your bargaining chip is worthless. It's all over. She dies, then you die in the same instant. Me and my mate here," again he gestured to Sammi with his thumb and again Albert's eyes were drawn to the movement, "we'll be alive and you'll be dead. That's not an outcome you want."

"But she'll be dead," Albert shouted and as if to clear up any confusion as to who he was talking about, tapped the muzzle forcefully against Kara's head.

"Yeah, well that's right. But I won't be," Chaz said, raising his hands to waist height in a half surrender gesture. Again Albert's eyes followed the hand movements. "And to be honest mate, that's all I care about. Me not being dead is a good result. I'll win and you'll lose. But, I do have a good outcome where no one dies." Chaz stopped.

Albert delayed answering for what seemed an age, but was only the time it took Kara to breathe twice, "What outcome?"

"You put your gun on the floor and step away and we'll talk. No one dies. That's a good outcome for all of us, don't you think?" Chaz said. Kara leant the majority of her weight on her left leg.

"No fucking way. No fucking way am I putting my gun down!" The intensity of the young man's reply caused a fresh shower of blood to fall onto Kara's shoulder. She felt the tension surging through him as he pressed into her for cover. "You'll fucking kill me as soon as I do that. You'll kill me or send me to jail and they'll kill me for what we've done. You can go get fucked. I've another outcome. Another way…"

Kara saw Sammi's mouth twitch. She counted one blink. Chaz moved his hands up to a shoulder height surrender gesture, Sammi blinked again.

Albert continued, his voice dulled by his nose yet rising in pitch and intensity, "…I kill you cocksucker. I kill you and then your bitches and then…"

Kara felt the pressure of the muzzle leave her temple. From the periphery of her right eye she saw Albert begin to swing the pistol out in the direction of Sammi and Chaz.

"…when I've killed all of you I'm goin-"

Sammi blinked a third time. Kara twisted her head to the left, driving her chin as far down as possible into the crook of Albert's left arm. A soft 'Pfft' accompanied a 9mm parabellum exiting Sammi's pistol. Even with the reduced muzzle velocity due to the suppressor, the bullet crossed the intervening ten feet and entered Albert's head a mere nine milliseconds later. Given the relative height of her target and the fact the tall young man was crouching down, Sammi had aimed for his top lip. The bullet hit his Philtrum, ripped through the rest of his upper jaw and having shredded through the surrounding muscle mass, obliterated his Medulla Oblongata. The bullet and its resultant expanding gasses caused increasing cavitation, destroying the rest of Albert's brain stem almost instantly. The now misshapen slug, along with an accompanying mass of tissue and bone, blew an exit hole, the size of a small orange, in the back of the youth's skull. Less than two milliseconds after the round hit him and before his frontal lobes or motor-cortex functions could react to pull the trigger of his own pistol, the glutinous mass that had been Albert's brain impacted onto the wall just behind Kara. She straightened and looked down to the corpse at her feet.

14

Kara and Sammi wrapped Tien in their arms and huddled together on the dilapidated farmhouse's stairs. Tien's tears fell onto Kara's shoulder, diluting the red of Albert's blood. Sammi made soft 'shushing' noises while Kara smoothed Tien's straight black hair. There were no words. They simply sat and waited for Tien's tears to cease.

Chaz and Jacob searched the last of the bodies, retrieving a similar set of belongings from it as they had from the previous four. A smartphone, a few euro coins, a wallet holding some euro notes, the normal collection of bank cards, miscellaneous other cards and a driver's licence. All of it was set next to the four other piles atop the sideboard.

"Rik de Vries. Amberley's Rik I presume. Not even using a pseudonym, the arrogant bastard," Chaz said, allowing his fingers to trace over the details on the plastic licence, before reaching for the phone. "It's got a lock screen on it, like all the rest. We'll need software to open them." Jacob nodded his agreement. "Although I'm not sure what good it's going to do us?" Chaz added.

"I'm not sure either. I think we just take it all and clear out as quickly as we can."

"Agreed. But we should probably block that up," Chaz nodded to the gap that Jacob had stormed through only fifteen minutes before.

Jacob pushed the old couch over to the doorway and both men gathered up as much wood from the door as they could find. After a frustrating few minutes of trying to balance the remnants, they achieved a result, of sorts. "Best we can do I guess," Chaz said, looking at the large gaps still visible.

Jacob, his eyebrows raised, pointed to a neatly coiled hose attached to a wall tap that had previously been hidden by the couch, "That's not a good omen."

"Guess this wasn't the first time," Chaz said as he looked at the hose and then back to the drain cover in the middle of the floor. Blood was already finding its own way in small rivulets and branching tributaries, trails of red seeping through the narrow grills.

"A killing room?" Jacob asked.

"Not sure, but probably. Certainly this thing," Chaz hefted a kick at the wooden contraption, "has been well used." He bent and released the metal clasps holding the wood in place.

"What are you planning on doing?"

"I'm going to move it out of the way. Then we can dump the bodies over to one side and use the hose. If nothing else it'll clear the air. All I can smell is blood and cordite."

"It came from in there."

Both men turned at the sound of Kara's voice. She stood between the bodies of Rik and Albert, pointing towards the door in the far corner.

Jacob stepped forward, "Where's Tien?"

Kara put her hand on his arm to stop him, "She's with Sammi. I just came to tell you we're going to head back to the apartment. Tien wants to get out of here and get cleaned up. But we've only got the one car and I need you guys to sanitise this place, that'll take time."

"No problem. Do you," Chaz paused as he manoeuvred the

wooden frame around the body of the fat man, "want me to call you when we're done? Jacob, get the door."

"Guess so," Kara answered. "I'll take the stuff you've found on the bodies and make a start on try-"

"Umm, Kara," Jacob interrupted, his gaze fixed on the room he had just opened the door to. "I think Tien might have to stay. You need to take a look at this."

φ

Tien, her tears dried, prosthesis back in place and wearing Sammi's jumper, sat in front of a desk that took up the whole width of the room. Three pairs of twin-monitor displays were either side of one larger HDTV screen. Under the desk, six tower systems gave away their power-on status by the slight whirring noises from their high-capacity fans. In the rear corner of the room, more fan noises were coming from a glass-fronted equipment rack that hosted six, plain black boxes.

"Kara, this is high-end equipment. It could take me hours to sort out what we're looking at."

"Okay, but it's all we have to go on, so we're going to have to take the time. Sammi, Chaz can you go and recover the car from the Volendam carpark?" Kara received nods of agreement.

"Can you also go past the apartment Sammi? Pick me up some clothes and some soap and shampoo? The shower upstairs here is working and I need..." Tien's voice trailed off.

Sammi placed her hand on Tien's shoulder, "No problems. I'll bring clean towels too. Anything else?"

Tien shook her head.

Kara spoke to Jacob, "We need to put an overwatch in. If we have company turning up I want to know about it before they knock on the door. Until we get both our cars back here we'll have to be prepared to use the ones outside for any quick departures. Can you look after that?"

"Yep. Comms is the only issue. Your phones are bust."

Chaz handed his phone to Kara, "I'll pick up the spare kit

from the apartment, but take this till then."

When they were alone, Kara looked at Tien, "I'm not going to ask stupid questions, like are you alright. I just need to know, can you function?"

Tien eased the swivel chair around and looked up. "You know you asked me that before?"

Kara held her gaze and saw the determination in her friend's stare. She remembered a similar look, years before, when Tien had ignored doctor's orders and come to find Kara. Tubes, trailing from the freshly amputated arm to the portable drip stand, had partially obscured her eyes, but the strength of the woman hadn't been masked. "I know," Kara said. "In the recovery ward of Selly Oak. Do you remember what you answered?"

Tien nodded, "Of course I can function. I'm not going to let them dictate my life."

Kara put her hand on Tien's shoulder, "And this time?"

"Same answer. Funnily enough, same outcome. Those responsible are dead and I'm not. I get to move on."

Kara saw the hesitation in Tien's eyes. "But?"

"But nothing really. I was lucky. Jacob stopped it before it became…" She struggled to find the right words.

Kara waited.

"Before it happened… really. I was lucky."

"But?"

Tien looked away, "I knew Jacob was going to kill him and I knew he was our only chance to find Swift. I knew he wasn't armed. I even yelled at Jacob to stop..." Tien looked back up, "But…"

Kara watched Tien's tears begin to fall again.

"Oh Kara," Tien sobbed and said no more.

Kara knelt and hugged her, "It's okay Tien. It's okay."

After a few minutes, Tien steadied her breathing, sat back and wiped her eyes. "It isn't Kara. It's not okay. It was different when I lost my hand. It was the game. The rules were clear. The enemy died around us and I didn't feel pleased. It was just the job. But this is different. I'm happy he's dead. I shouldn't be happy another human being is dead. That's a most terrible sin. To wish that on him and be happy for it."

Kara felt a rising frustration. She had never been religious. Even when she had been forced to attend some compulsory church service in school or in her early days in the Air Force, she had been a bored spectator. Intrigued more by the architecture of the buildings than the spiritual voodoo the robed-men up front were performing. She had no time for it, or them. Yet she knew Tien's strong moral compass was kept true by her family's faith. Every single Sunday, if Tien was in London, she would attend Mass with her parents and as many of her six siblings as were available. Knowing that still didn't help Kara understand why Tien would feel guilty about Rik. She tried, unsuccessfully, to hide her emotion, "He was about to rape you Tien. Who knows what his friends were going to do. You've every right to be pleased. You ha-"

"No. I don't. It's not right."

Kara stood up, "Maybe not."

"You feel nothing bad about it, do you?" Tien asked, without criticism.

Kara shook her head, "Not a thing. He deserved it."

Tien sniffed and sat straighter in the chair, "Well, I guess I said I can function, so we better get on with it. Eh?" She rotated the chair but Kara put her hand out and swung it back to face her.

"Tien, it's okay to feel the way you feel. It's what makes you, you. Don't envy me my gaping lack of humanity."

The smile returned to Tien's eyes and she put her cheek down onto Kara's hand, "Thanks. Now let's see what these guys are up to." She spun the chair back into place and powered up the television.

The image was of the room next door. Obviously centred on where the wooden frame had been fixed in place, it now showed the drain cover. The legs of Tubbs and Van and the right shoulder of Rik just edged into the frame. The blood, not yet hosed down as Chaz had intended, flowed steadily into the drain.

"Is that a live video feed?" Kara asked.

"Seems that way. I didn't see any cameras mounted in there. It must be small, unobtrusive."

Kara left the computer room and called from next door, "Direct me."

It didn't take many seconds for Tien to have Kara standing in the right position and looking up at the camera.

"It's a pinhole mounted in the old ceiling coving. Weird they would have gone to that amount of trouble," Kara said as she rejoined Tien.

"Not really, when you look here," Tien raised a small remote and flicked the TV image from the room next door to the rooms she and Kara had been separately held in earlier. She flicked again and cycled through the upstairs bathroom, WC and bedrooms. "The whole house is wired up and you'd never know it."

"That doesn't bode well. What the hell have we stumbled into here."

"We'll know soon enough. See that?" Tien stood and took hold of a thin black cable trailing from the rear of the TV. She followed it until it entered the equipment rack in the corner.

"Uh-huh. What's it attached to?"

"A Hard Disc Drive Recorder." Tien followed a thinner cable back from the rack to the first of the computers under the desk. She retook her seat and flicked on the left most pair of monitors. The right screen showed an interface that was a virtual representation of a video-mixer desk. The left screen was a full format video playback display with digital counters running along the base. It showed a duplicate of what was on the bigger television screen.

"Oh dear Lord," Tien said and reached for the appropriate mouse and keyboard.

"What is it?" Kara asked, peering forward to see what Tien had just seen.

"This is professional video editing software. I mean really professional. Top level stuff. I saw the same sort of thing at the

PsyOps School once. They used it to produce cinema quality infomercials."

"And?"

"And it's been on record for the last forty-five minutes." Tien used the mouse and scrolled back across the digital counter at the base of the screen. The image juddered and then a fast rewind of Kara momentarily standing in front of the camera in the adjoining room was followed by a fleeting series of images. Each one displayed for such a small amount of time that Kara's eyes couldn't process what she was looking at, but the overall effect was certain. Tien looked away from the screen but kept the mouse clicked.

"You can stop now," Kara said. The still-image on screen showed Tubbs and Albert wheeling the wooden frame into place. "They meant to record it all."

Tien glanced back at the screen, "Yeah." Her voice was flat, toneless.

"But it recorded us killing them. Is this live streaming?"

Tien was clicking the mouse again and bringing up a series of smaller window displays. "No. Apart from the connection to the recorder, this PC has no other active connections. Not even Wi-Fi. It's air-gapped."

"That's a bit strange in this day and age, surely?" Kara asked.

More windows were opening on screen as Tien said, "We used air-gapped systems in the military Kara. All the time."

"But only for..." Kara stopped as she peered over Tien's shoulder.

Tien made the last window full size and finished Kara's observation, "Only for things that were highly classified. Things we didn't want anyone to have access to. It's the ultimate way to stop anyone hacking into your system. You just stay off the Net."

"What is that?" Kara asked.

"It's an archive store of edited video files."

"But... there..." Kara stammered as her mind processed what she was looking at. "There are hundreds of them."

"Two hundred and nine," Tien said and double clicked on a random file, dating from January 2012.

The screen filled with an image from the room next door. Rik and Buddy were easily recognisable standing behind the wooden frame. They were talking softly, but audibly, in Dutch. Both turned towards what Kara knew was the door that led to the hallway. Rik smiled with his mouth, but his eyes remained narrowed. He extended his right hand in a strange gesture that reminded Kara of an adult reaching out to a-

"Oh fuck no!"

"Two hundred?" Sammi asked.

Kara nodded, "But they're grouped by number sequences. They made a series of videos for each... well... each..." Kara couldn't phrase the right word. She was angry, incensed beyond anything she had ever known, but most of all she was numb. Physically and mentally drained. Her head hurt, a weight in her stomach pulled so intensely that she felt like curling into the foetal position and her eyes were red and puffy.

Tien and she had quickly realised that the videos were grouped by their titles. Some groups had upwards of twenty video files, some just one. Both women knew they had to conduct some rudimentary analysis to determine what it was they had found. Watching only enough to be able to confirm why the videos were grouped, the experience had still been horrendous. They could take no more after opening a file from 2008. Kara had been physically sick in the toilet. Tien had wept and prayed. Then both had sat quietly, tears streaming down their cheeks, holding each other's hand and waiting for the return of Chaz and Sammi.

"Victim?" Chaz offered as a closure to Kara's sentence.

Tien nodded, "Yes. They're grouped by victim. Based on the limited number we viewed, most are girls. But there are some boys. Ages were probably between maybe six or seven up to maybe fourteen or fifteen."

"Oh," Sammi said, dropping her gaze to the floor.

"How many groups of videos in total?" Chaz asked through clenched teeth. Kara could see his jaw was tight, the muscles in his neck tensed and his face flushed.

"Twenty-seven," Tien answered.

"Twenty-seven kids," he said, his voice wavering. "Over how many years?"

"Twelve."

The room was quiet. Kara watched Chaz swallow hard, but that couldn't prevent his tears. The four friends stood and hugged one another. Eventually Sammi straightened up, "We've got to hand this over to the cops. The parents have a right to know what happened. They'll need to come in and dig this whole farm up."

Kara leant against the desk, "We will do, but they won't find anything."

"Oh God, how do you know?" Sammi asked.

"There's a video from 2008. Just one video in its own set and longer than those with multiple files. It showed the whole process. The abduction, they took her from a shopping centre, her time here, we reckon they held her for at least a month and then…" Kara stopped and tried to form words but just shook her head.

"It's okay, you don- " Chaz said.

"Yes we do Chaz," Tien interrupted. "It explains what happened. There's footage of them on the red boat. Rik and the fat man are on camera. That boat is a proper fishing rig. It has an industrial-sized gutting table with knives, bone saws and a chute where offcuts are hosed down before being dumped into the water… There's going to be nothing to find."

"Those poor kids." Chaz's whole body slumped.

Sammi squeezed his shoulder and put her arm around him, "We still have to hand it over to the police," she said.

"And we will," Kara agreed. "But I want to bring down the rest of whatever these bastards are into. I especially want to find Derek Swift. The Dutch Police won't be bothered to go looking for him. The other small matter is, if we hand this all over to the authorities at the minute, we'll be spending a considerable amount of time in a Dutch prison. Despite Rik and the rest of them being paedophiles and killers, extrajudicial executions still aren't authorised. We'll all face murder charges."

"So what's the plan," Chaz asked, his composure partially returning.

"Tien will need time to work through these systems and Jacob will have to stay out on the perimeter. Meanwhile you guys are going to play reservoir dogs."

15

The winter sun had struggled to cling onto the day and by early afternoon the interior of the house was dark. Tien swivelled away from the desk and faced Kara, who sat on a cushion on the floor against the far wall. The room was gloomily lit by the glare from the monitors.

"That's the last one and I think I've finally figured it out. It's sick, but I've got to admit, it's ingenious." Tien said, leaning forward and back to relieve the stiffness that had come from sitting in front of the computers for so long.

"Ingenious? Really? Doesn't sound like I'm going to like this."

"Well, the last system was hooked onto ZeroNet. It used a different chat app from the others but basically, it and the rest of them were the same. All their communications are routed over darknets and they've used five systems, each with a slightly different protocol."

"So this is the darkweb they've hooked into?" Kara asked, not knowing much about the hidden Internet other than it existed.

"Yep. They've used TOR, I2P, FAI, FreeNet and ZeroNet."

Kara held her hand up, "Woah. You know you lost me at the first one. I get they had multiple communication paths but all I need to know is, can we trace who they were talking to? Can we get a lead on Swift?"

"No. That's the ingenious part. Each one of these computers is hooked into a chat room but you can only access it on video. That's what these are for," Tien said, pointing to micro cameras mounted on top of five of the screens. "As best I can establish, they made and edited the videos on the editing PC. Then they uploaded them separately onto file servers buried in the darkweb. That provided the isolation and anonymity."

"So these videos are online? Shared with anyone who knows where to look?"

"Not quite. The added layer of security is opposite to what you'd think."

"How'd you mean?"

"To access the files you need to go through a protocol," Kara frowned. Tien switched tack, "Okay, imagine that the files are in an office, but to get into the office you need to pass through a security check."

"Okay."

"Well, that's what's taken me so long. We'd think these individuals can't afford their names and faces to be known. Every nation on earth would arrest them for what are on these videos. So you'd expect the security procedures to be hi-tech encryption based."

"Yeah. Is that the problem, you can't break it?"

"No. That's just it. There are no encryption methods. Not that I can find and I've looked for," Tien checked her watch, "a good three hours now."

"So the security check is that you can just waltz in?" Kara asked, rubbing her eyes and suddenly feeling very tired.

"No. I think the security check is these cameras. They have to make a video call. The person in this room has to recognise the person on the other end. It's the only explanation that I'm left with and it ties in with the only documentation I can find. Come here and take a look," she said and swivelled back to the monitors. Kara rose and came to look over her shoulder.

"There's a plain text file on each system," Tien said as she opened up a document on screen. "All different content but the same type of information. A list of names and a list of two numbers against each name. See anything familiar?"

Kara leaned in, "They're all first names only and the numbers are i- Oh!" Kara stopped and leaned closer. "The numbers are like the ones Amberley used in his text message. Five figures and then a three figure pin."

"Yep," Tien agreed. "I also think the first two digits of the first number are country codes."

"Like phone codes you mean?"

"Yeah. Amberley and Swift's were both forty-four and I can't find any on here or the other systems that don't start with a number that isn't a country code."

"So that means we can find them?"

"No. Well, probably not. It tells us where they were when they first got given the number. I doubt Swift is still in the UK but he was still referred to by Amberley with a forty-four number."

"Okay, so you have names and numbers. What's that got to do with the videos?" Kara asked, going back to sit on the cushion.

"I think they get identified within the system and then after that it's a human check. Someone in this room has to recognise the person joining the chat room, otherwise they don't get any further. Like I said, it's ingenious. You have a group of people all corrupt, all as guilty as each other, who only allow those they recognise in."

"Like Mutually Assured Destruction?"

"Yeah. It's MAD for sure," Tien agreed, "but more than that. If you do get in and were being coerced by law enforcement, they'd see it in your face. There is nothing better than another human looking at you to figure out if you're distressed."

"So we have a whole ton of paedophiles and perverts congregating in a chat room and no way to get into that chat room to see who is in there, without being a recognised face?"

"Yep and being darkweb means absolute anonymity for the computers they use, so you can't get them that way. You have to be on the inside. The idea that law enforcement could pose as someone and infiltrate the system is unlikely. I can't find proof, because by its design there are no traces, but I would imagine you have to take part in some form of initiation before they'd let you into the inner circle. Apart from no court upholding any case once an illegal act is performed by an undercover officer, I doubt any operative would put themselves through that. So the most you would take down is the single cell you were trying to gain access through."

"But if you did get in, you'd bring down a global network," Kara said, her mind already processing options.

Tien halted her before she had made much headway, "Not really. That's where the separate systems come in. This one," she said pointing to the right most set of monitors, only seems to connect to people with German and Moldovan codes. That one," she indicated the next system over, "connects to the UK, Ireland and strangely enough, Azerbaijan and Cameroon."

"So it's not just MAD they're emulating, but a terrorist cell network?" Kara asked.

Tien nodded. "If you did get into one cell, you'd only be able to remove that particular subset."

"Unless you were in this room," Kara said. "Then you'd bring it all down?"

"You'd bring more down, but I doubt all. This must have been setup like a series of distributed hubs. I'd imagine, no, scrub that, I'm certain that there will be two or three or ten other central hubs like this. It's maximum security with limited risk if compromised."

"Yeah but that's all guesswork, surely?"

"I suppose, but I do know there's even more isolation and compartments. I can't find all the country codes. I mean, I'll have to properly go through them, but it was easy to spot that there are definitely no codes for France or the USA. I doubt very much they are paedophile-free nations and anyway, like I said, I'm certain."

Kara trusted Tien enough to just take her word on it, but she also knew the strength of their working relationship was founded on being able to press each other for justification. She sat up straighter on her cushion, "Why?"

"Because it's what you and I would do if we were setting up a clandestine operation. We'd have the connectivity we needed but the exclusivity and deniability to limit disasters. We'd be doing it because it's how we were trained and it makes the most sense. The people in this network have got self-preservation as a motivator. There isn't really a bigger one."

"Fair enough," Kara conceded. "So how do we break in and find Swift?"

"We don't. The computer nets are isolated and even though there's a bitcoin account, I ca-"

"Sorry Tien. Bitcoin? Isn't that the Internet currency thingy?"

"Yeah. It's an active account."

"Can we get in there?"

"Nope. Bitcoin's probably one of the most secure accounts there is. I haven't got anything anyway near powerful enough to even attempt a hack on it. But the account is active and it must be making a lot of money. Given the list of names and the material they are getting access to, this is a high-end financial operation."

Kara looked around the room, "It always comes down to the money," she sighed. "But this farmhouse is crumbling."

"Yeah, but this isn't anyone's home. It'll just be a random property owned by one of those five next door, or worse, some hidden shell corporation that's untraceable. I'll also bet that all five of them are wealthy. They'll have nice cars and nice houses and nice lives."

Kara shook her head, "And probably nice families and nice wives?"

"Probably."

"I doubt we'll need to research their private lives. Something tells me, like this place, everything will be neatly compartmented. Can you see a way in?" Kara asked.

"Not really. Not at the minute."

Kara pushed herself up and looked around the room. "Well, that's good enough for me. You got what you need to go?"

Tien pulled a thumbnail drive from the last system and walked across to the equipment rack. She pulled the cables from the Hard Disc Drive Recorder and hefted it out. "Do now."

The two left the room, walked through the former kitchen and out the unblocked doorway into the farmyard's rear courtyard and paddocks.

Kara called out quietly in the darkening twilight, "Sammi, Chaz?"

The pair appeared in the doorway of a small concrete blockhouse.

"You all good?"

"Yep," they answered in unison.

"Just need you and Tien to cast your eyes over the scene and see what you think," Chaz said walking towards them with an old can in hand.

The four returned to the house and Sammi turned on the unshaded lightbulb. Kara and Tien took in the staged room for the first time.

Buddy lay where he had fallen, as did Van and Tubbs, but Tubbs had been angled forty-five degrees so that the side of his head, where the bullet holes were, faced side on to where the body of Albert lay. The major difference was with Rik. He had been moved from where he originally died, to lie adjacent to Albert's feet. Given he had no blood dripping from him, his was the cleanest and least forensically difficult move to make. The Glock pistol Albert had held lay between the two, its top slide all the way back, signifying the weapon had been fired until empty.

"Albert fired a full magazine off?" Tien asked.

"Well, Buddy fired a couple first, then Albert fired the

135

rest," Sammi confirmed.

Kara stood where Albert would have and looked across the room, "Where?"

Chaz walked across and pointed out the bullet holes in the walls and in the couch that had been returned to its original position.

When Kara was satisfied that the spread of bullets was feasible, she asked, "Residue?"

Sammi indicated Albert, "He's covered in it. It was a bit difficult, but Chaz held him and I managed to get his right hand to grip the pistol. Not only that but Rik will have quite a lot on him as he was lying underneath when we did it."

"Van and Buddy had already fired and Tubbs, just like the original never got a chance to," Chaz added.

"You know the gunshot residue won't be traceable afterwards," Sammi said.

"Yeah, but it makes a complete job, just in case," Kara said as she had one final look around the room. "So Tien, talk me through it."

"As long as we pile the wood from the door in the right semblance of order, then the ash pattern will look plausible. With what will be left, I could make the scenario of a fight between three versus two. One of the three gets their neck broken, others fire wildly all over the place. Our only issue will be the accurate headshots in the middle of spurious aiming but the investigators will see what they think they see."

"So final thoughts?" Kara asked. "Do we do this or make them completely disappear? Sammi?"

"I liked the idea of taking them down to the harbour, nicking their boat and sinking it in the middle of the North Sea, but it's way too complex and will end up with someone asking awkward questions."

Kara looked to Chaz.

"I agree with Sammi. The boat idea seemed plausible at first, but we'd risk being seen getting them on board and we'd need to delay until we could get people we trust over here to crew it. That's way too many risks."

Kara surveyed the room again. "Tien?"

"We can't just take them out and bury them in a paddock," Tien said. "The ground disturbance will be too noticeable and then we're left with the same problem. If the police think someone else was involved they have to come looking. If we make it reasonable enough that nobody else was here, then they won't waste the effort. Added to that, if we go ahead it solves the problem of our DNA being all over this house."

"Okay then," Kara said, happy that her team were decided. "Final questions then. Are we completely sanitised and how do we initiate the fire?"

Sammi answered, "Yep, Jacob and Chaz have covered all the tracks in and out that got us here and we have a route planned back down to where the cars are. We'll be spotless." She pointed across to the small set of shelves. The stacked set of towels and the box that had contained the guns was still there but next to the towels was an old fashioned, double-glass-bowled oil lamp.

"Nice," Kara said. "Where did you find that?"

"Out in one of the stable blocks. The burner and wick housing was rusted to hell and back but we got it working well enough."

Chaz held up the small can he carried and shook it, "Only problem was kerosene but we finally found some in a small storage shed."

"How are you going to light it? None of us smoke any-more." Kara asked.

"No, but the fat man did. He had this in his pocket," Chaz said, holding out a cheap plastic lighter.

"Oh, that's a point. Have we put back all their belong-ings?"

"Yep, all good," Sammi said. "We've cloned their phones with the software Tien gave us, so we can take a look at it all later and we've photographed everything else."

Kara took one last look around, "Okay then, let's get it done."

Kara, Tien and Sammi made their way to the doorway and

arranged the fragments of the shattered door on the ground. As the last piece was placed in like a crazy jigsaw, Tien straightened up, "You know a really close examination will reveal it was off its hinges before the fire, but I doubt they'll look that close."

Kara stepped into the open doorway, "I hope not. Right Chaz, you're on."

Chaz filled up the lower bowl of the lamp with the clear liquid, replaced the burner, extended the wick and tried to ignite it with the lighter. The first two attempts failed to catch. He picked up the can again and drizzled some of the fuel directly onto the old cotton wick. The threadbare, dry material soaked it up. He flicked the lighter again and this time the wick flared. When he was sure it was fully caught, he reached over and slipped the lighter back into Tubbs's trouser pocket. Then he replaced the delicate glass chimney carefully onto the lamp and moved the whole assembly on to the shelves, between the towels and the box that had housed the pistols. He walked to the door, handed the kerosene can to Sammi, switched the room light off and went back to the shelves. Giving the unit a sharp nudge with his hip he jumped back. The pistol box shifted sideways, a couple of the towels dislodged and fell to the floor and the lamp wobbled, made a click-clacking sound against the wooden shelf and then settled back into place.

Kara heard Chaz swear under his breath.

He moved back and gave the unit a harder nudge. This time the lamp wobbled, teetered and just when it looked like it would regain its equilibrium, it finally toppled. Chaz had made it to the doorway by the time the lamp plunged to the floor. The lower bowl shattered and liquid cascaded over the towels and the linoleum. There was a momentary pause before a small but satisfying 'whump' accompanied a small but spectacular yellow fireball that mushroomed up. The peeling ceiling paint blistered and caught almost immediately. On the ground, the towels were well alight and fingers of fire spread across the old linoleum.

The four friends stood in the doorway and watched as the fire took hold. When the turn-up bottom of Tubbs's beige chinos were burning, Kara, Sammi and Chaz made to turn away. Tien stayed still.

Kara put her arm around Tien's shoulders. "C'mon Tien, let's go."

"Not yet. Wait."

Kara looked back to what Tien was watching. A small rivulet of fire was snaking across the room, reaching out for Rik. The smoky yellow flame began to lick at the sleeve of the red polo shirt. As the flame strengthened and the material succumbed, Tien finally turned away.

"Having seen what he did to those kids Kara, I've got no more qualms about feeling happy he's dead."

16

Central London. Monday, 23rd November.

Franklyn walked into the meeting space with two minutes to spare. His shoes tapped a formal rhythm as he walked across the white Portland stone floor, patterned with hundreds of Welsh slate inlays. The deep black oak of the church pews, pillars, wood panelling and altar that filled the bottom half of the space, stood in stark contrast to the glistening white of the vaulted ceiling adorned with ornate gold work. The whole interior was bathed in the early afternoon sun that flooded through clear, Reamy antique glass high windows. He slid into the third pew from the rear.

"Good afternoon. Let us pray?"

She turned towards him and gave a half-smile.

Franklyn looked startled, "Good grief Kara, I hesitate to say this, but are you alright? You look shattered."

"Yeah, I'm fine. Just tired. We've had a rough few days and I haven't caught up on my sleep."

It was strictly true but the reason she hadn't been able to sleep was kept to herself. After leaving the farmhouse, the team had stayed in the Amsterdam apartment overnight.

They'd sat up late watching the local Dutch news but there had been no mention of the fire. There was still no mention by the time they had left for the early morning flight back to London, their presence lost in the mix of hundreds of others making the early morning hop.

But the late night news and early start were not to blame for Kara's tiredness. There had been the opportunity to get at least a few hours of sleep during the night, but each time she had closed her eyes, the faces of the children from the videos swam in front of her. At about two in the morning, she had heard someone moving about in the apartment's kitchen. Rising quietly so as not to wake any of the others, she made her way down to find Tien, sitting at the kitchen bench, tissues in hand, sobbing. They made cups of tea, talked for the next couple of hours, and both felt better for it. They also knew there would be similar nights coming up if they were to get through the damage the videos had done to them.

Eventually, their conversation had turned to Derek Swift. Tien, as was her want, opened a laptop and was distractedly going through the call logs of the cloned phones they had taken from the men at the farm. She wasn't surprised to find that Rik's phone was as sanitised as Francis Amberley's had been. No recent calls, no recent messages, but when Tien applied her recovery software to it she scored a lot more history than she had back in Woodbridge; almost a year's worth. The rest of the hours before they left for the airport had been spent examining one deleted message exchange in particular. Once back in their Camden office they had initiated a meeting with Franklyn. The date meant the location would be St Clement Danes, a 17th Century church designed by Wren, which dominated a small island of calm in the middle of the bustling Strand and Aldwych at the heart of London. Kara thought the contemplative setting, with its overtones of forgiveness and redemption, was most fitting for what she was going to ask for.

Franklyn was still looking at her. Kara knew the bags

under her eyes and the pale complexion would not be painting her in a favourable light. She gave another weak smile.

"Well if you're sure," he said. "Shall I assume your request for a meeting means that you have news of Swift?"

"Yes, but not the whole story yet. We do know that he didn't die at sea by drowning. He was transferred from Francis Amberley's boat to another vessel and made it to Amsterdam."

"I knew it. I knew it, that son of a bitch," Franklyn said it quietly, in keeping with the surroundings, but Kara could see his fists clenching.

"Now, now Franklyn," she teased in an affected accent, "Even I don't swear in church, tisk, tisk."

He laughed, "I apologise. That's good work Kara and so quickly done. I knew there was something not right with it all."

Kara took a deep breath, "Seriously, you have no idea how not right it is. For now, though, I need you to take something from me and do something for me?"

"Okay," he said without hesitation.

Kara reached under the pew and took out the Hard Disc Drive Recorder that Tien had removed from the equipment rack of the farmhouse. The box, fifteen inches wide by ten deep and two in height, was surprisingly light given its 1Tb recording capacity. "This needs to go to someone on the right side of the line," Kara said referring to the fact Franklyn's organisation had contacts inside established law enforcement.

"May I ask what's in it?"

"On it," she corrected him gently. "It's a digital video recorder and it has movies containing child pornography on it. The imagery is vile, Franklyn. Totally vile and sickening. The movies show a total of twenty-seven separate child victims and I'm guessing they'll all be listed as missing in police databases, somewhere." Kara stopped as she watched the colour drain from the old man. It was her turn to ask him if he was alright.

He nodded slowly and raised his hand to his mouth. "I'm sorry. I wasn't quite expecting it to be that bad. Sorry, go on."

"It's our assumption that all of them have been killed and their bodies disposed of in a manner as to make them unrecoverable."

"My good God. Are you sure?"

Kara set the recorder down on her knees, "We're fairly certain because there's one particular file on this that gives the method they used. But the parents could still have some closure if the police can track the victims' families down."

"Okay," Franklyn said, "Will you be able to come and talk to them. The police I mean?"

"No."

He turned to face her directly. His complexion was returning to more normal shades as he half-cocked his head in query.

"The recorder is from an isolated farmhouse in Holland. Near Volendam. There was a fire. The Dutch Police will probably have found five bodies by now and I guess it will make the news soon, if not already," she said glancing at her watch and registering that it was just coming up to two in London, three in Holland.

"Do I assume the men didn't die of smoke inhalation?"

"Not quite. The identification of the bodies will take some time as the police will only have recourse to matching dental records, but I can assist them with that. I can give them full IDs and I can provide a full operating model for what and how the men did what they did."

Franklyn pursed his lips, processing what he had heard. "First things, Kara. Are all of your team okay?"

"Yes... Well, physically. Mentally it might take us a while to work through it, but we'll cope."

The old man reached out and placed his hand on her forearm, "If you need to talk to people we have some contacts. Discreet, trustworthy."

"Thanks, but you know what it's like. We'll try our own ways first. Whining and wine always had the edge on trick cyclists."

The old man tried to muster a smile but it faltered. "Secondly then. Was Swift one of the five that died?"

143

Kara shook her head, "No. He's long gone and that's what we're hoping to find out about, but we need the Dutch Police to do us a favour. If it hasn't hit the news yet, I want them to suppress any mention of the bodies."

"How long for?" Franklyn asked and Kara was struck that he hadn't pondered the difficulty of getting a request like that fulfilled. He had just accepted it could be done and moved on to specifics. She wondered again just how powerful his organisation was. Whatever the answer, she knew that she and Tien were but minor parts in it. She also considered that he hadn't questioned her with regard to how she had found the farmhouse or why she and her team had killed the men. He had just accepted it as an obvious necessity. She felt the strange frisson of excitement and anticipation, knowing that she was going to be given the means to get an operation into motion and no one would interfere with her team's planning. It was a weird sense of freedom that she knew would allow her to rush into danger.

"I'm not too sure. At least a week, maybe two. In return they get all the evidence on that drive, a full set of IDs and all the credit for taking down a truly terrible group of people."

"Is there any chance you can be linked to the deaths?"

"No, we're clean. The fire would have removed any of our traces. The weapons were owned by the men and it was staged to look semi-convincingly like an in-group fight."

"This," Franklyn said, patting the recorder box, "being handed over and the offer of help for a maintenance of silence will destroy all of that illusion. Is that what you want?"

Kara handed the box over to him. "We need the silence to give us a chance of infiltration. That will give us a chance to perhaps track down Swift. The shattering of the illusion is no big deal, but I'd prefer the police still didn't know who we were. What I'm really asking for is to be absolved in absentia and that they don't look too hard for us. I don't fancy my team spending years in prison for what was effectively disposing of five pieces of human excrement."

"Quite," he agreed. "I'll make sure it's handed over in a

way that will ensure anonymity. I'll also make sure the request is processed quickly. Now, is there anything else you need?"

"No. That's it really. We'll be a bit tight for personnel, as some of my guys are unavailable, but we should be fine. We just need to set the wheels in motion once we receive confirmation the police will play along."

"I'll call you as soon as I know. Umm," Franklyn paused, "I have some security chaps, young keen types, working with me. I could lend a couple to you if you are in need."

Kara worked hard not to laugh out loud at Tien's voice sounding in her ear with an assessment of the skills of Franklyn's security detail. Instead she managed to say, "No, that's kind, but we'll be fine. Thanks Franklyn. I'll wait to hear from you. Good luck."

φ

Kara was more than a little impressed at not just the obvious reach of Franklyn, but his efficiency, when the call came in at only 21:20. She hung up and looked around her office, "We're on."

Tien walked over and picked up the cloned phone that was for all intents and purposes Rik's original. She typed a message in French and hovered her thumb over the send button, "We all agreed?"

Jacob, Toby, freed from his child-minding duties, Chaz and Sammi gave her a mix of hopeful grins and thumbs-up.

"Jacob, you sure?" Kara asked.

"Yes. Positive." There was no missing the conviction in his tone.

Tien pressed send.

17

Camden. Tuesday, 24th November.

Sammi had slept in Tien's spare room, Chaz in Kara's and Toby had gone home for the night. Jacob had insisted on sleeping on Tien's couch so he could be nearby if needed. Sammi had said it wasn't necessary but Tien had said she liked the idea.

Now they were all gathered together again in Kara's office. Takeaway cups of coffee, wrappers from McMuffins and hot pancake plastic trays were balanced precariously in the small wastepaper bin, like some fast food house of cards.

The Harrop brothers were both reading sports pages they had separated from a tabloid, Chaz was looking at his Facebook, while Tien painted Sammi's finger nails.

"It's a shame I never get a chance to do fancy designs anymore," Tien said.

Sammi held her left hand out and admired the work, "Plain is fine. I still forget how good you are at this."

"Wasted youth in this very room," Tien laughed.

"Really?" Sammi asked, looking around at the office with its functional working desk that Kara sat behind, the small coffee table and three occasional chairs off to one side and the open door off to the other side that led to a kitchen area. "You learnt to paint nails with Kara?" The surprise in her voice made Kara look up from the Kindle she'd been reading.

"Oi, I have my nails done, thank you."

"Yeah, course you do. You're the epitome of the girly-girl aren't you?" Chaz chimed in without looking up.

Kara raised a middle finger to his bowed head.

"No, not with Kara," Tien laughed. This was my Mum and Dad's original nail salon business when they first came to London. When we got older, my sisters and I worked in here after school. Then my oldest sister and her husband took the business on when Mum and Dad retired."

"But not here?" Sammi asked as she placed her right hand in Tien's prosthetic palm.

"Oh no, they had seven other shops by then and this place was in need of a bit of tender loving care."

"And they thought Kara was the woman for that?" Chaz piped in again, still without raising his head.

Kara raised her finger again.

"No. It stayed empty for a while and then when I got out of the Army, Mum offered to have the top floors converted into an apartment for me and asked if Kara would be interested in leasing the office space."

"All like it was meant to be," Kara said and looked across at the other two women. "I can onl-"

She was interrupted by the chirped tone of an incoming message on the cloned phone. The echoing ping caught everyone off guard and they all held position like someone had shouted freeze.

Chaz slowly raised his head, "Well, what's it say?"

Kara checked her watch. It was precisely twelve hours since Tien had sent the opening message to a conversation they hoped would determine their next moves in finding Derek Swift. Now the response was in.

It was a gamble and they knew it, but it was based on the recovered messages from Rik's phone. Most of them had been written in Dutch, taken Tien some time to process through Google Translate, and turned out to be superfluous. But one exchange, dating from the day before Swift had vanished, had piqued Tien's interest. Not least because it, and the responses received to it, were all in French. The initial message from Rik had simply asked for 'The extraction of a package' and had been sent to a French mobile number. The resulting conversation, while not mentioning a person or a specific destination, was obviously the setup for getting someone out of Europe. That, combined with the date of the messages, was enough for them to postulate they might have stumbled into something significant. It was worth the gamble.

Kara reached for the phone and opened the text, "It says, 'Where to'." The relief that the response to their text was the same as that to Rik's original, was reflected in the various shouts of 'Yes' that went around the room. Jacob and Toby high-fived each other.

"Okay Tien," Kara called, "You're up."

Tien took the offered phone and, referring to the transcript of the original messages, began to type in French.

Don't care, but like last
time, outside of UK Extradition

There was a short delay before the reply popped up.

When?

Within 24 Hours

This time the reply took longer to come through.

This is all same as last time?
I'd like a security check.

Tien looked up, "Well that's not in the script. What's that mean?"

"We know that their security is good. Unorthodox, but good. Maybe because everything is the same they're concerned the mobile has been compromised," Sammi offered.

"Probably," Kara agreed. "Whatever it is we need to respond sharpish. If we get it wrong then we get it wrong, but we have to try. Just send 'Okay'."

Tien typed *d'accord* and sent it.

The five of them had migrated to a tight semi-circle behind Tien, peering over her shoulder, watching the phone. Kara was willing a reply to appear.

"If they ask for a face time call we're stuffed," Toby said.

"Yeah, but I really don't think they will," Tien said looking up at him. "I think the reason the Dutch operation only deals with certain countries is because it acts like another sort of air gap. They don't have any French contacts in their chat rooms, so I don't reckon the Dutch and French sides know what one another look like, and there were no deleted face time calls on the original phone."

Kara thought Toby's idea was a distinct possibility but she also knew she had no control over what would be asked. That meant she didn't have to worry about it. She'd always run her operations by controlling what she could and reacting to what she couldn't. 'Until a couple of days ago,' she thought. The dull ache in her stomach returned and she bit down on the tip of her tongue as she reconsidered how her laxness and laziness had almost cost them everything. She began to replay her second visit to the waterfront hotel, her conversation with Henk and all the security holes she had created in not controlling that operation. She felt a rising wave of guilt and disappointment within herself. The ping of the phone rescued her.

```
Previous Package
Provide Pin.
```

"That's clever," Tien said. "That assumes we not only know who the previous person was, but that we have access to the chat room lists. There was no pin disclosed on the original text messages, so you'd only know it if you knew who it was."

"What pin?" Chaz asked.

"I'll explain later," Tien said.

"How would they expect Rik to know it?" Kara asked.

"Because whoever the previous package was would have been a member of the Dutch chat rooms. The French would know that Rik would have access to it," Tien said as her thumb pressed down on the send button.

> I need to get that from my
> system. One moment.

"Are we sticking with the big assumption that Swift was the last person," Sammi said.

"I don't see we have an option. Anyway, if he wasn't then we don't really want to be following this trail anyway," Chaz countered.

"You're both right," Kara said, before turning back to Tien. "Do we *have* Swift's pin number?"

"Yeah. He was still on the access list I showed you. The one with the names and numbers, remember?"

"But they were only first names. There must be more than one Derek?"

"Of course there is, but we have Amberley's text that told us Swift's id number. It's all good Kara. I have it, I just need to get the text file from my thumb drive."

Not for the first, or the thousandth time, Kara was so grateful that she had Tien as a partner. She was about to smile and thank her when a physically painful stab of remorse tore through her. She saw the image of the wooden frame and the tear-stained leather. The intensity of the emotion caught her breath and stifled the 'Thanks' in her throat. All she could do was pat Tien on the shoulder.

Tien read the number '175' off her PC screen then picked up the phone. She typed it in and was about to press send but stopped.

"What's wrong," Sammi asked.

"Just a hunch," Tien said, deleting what she had typed and entering a new number.

> 826

> Not quite.

```
Excellent.
But security tight after
Recent terrorist attacks
Controls back in force on all borders
Complicates journey in and out
Price will be more
```

"What shall I say?" Tien asked, looking around to Kara.

Kara pushed her guilt back down and refocussed on the phone. "Ask them how much in total, I guess."

Tien sent the message and then gave a small whistle before holding the phone up for them to see.

```
90,000 euro
```

"Seems it's not cheap to get trash out of the country," Chaz said. "Now what?"

"We wait a couple of minutes. If we are Rik we'd have to talk to the, umm, runaway, client or whatever they'd call him. They'd have to make the decision," Kara said, looking at Tien and knowing from the frown and the twist to her lips, that there was a problem. "What's up?"

"If they ask us to transfer money we're busted. They'll use that bitcoin account I found and I've no way of getting into it."

"Well, like we said at the start of this, we go as far as we can."

The phone beeped again.

```
?
```

Kara nodded and Tien responded.

```
                                              Agreed
Do you need more time?
```

Tien shrugged and again looked up to Kara, "For what?"

"Don't know. Difficult to have half a conversation with no idea about what we're getting into. Suppose you'll just have to ask them."

```
                                            For what?
To get the cash together
Package must have it
```

```
on arrival or no go
```

Tien smiled, "That's handy."

```
                                    No, we are good
Restaurant de George
Rue Damrémont, Montmarte
rendez-vous 21h00 tonight
```

"Paris anyone?" Chaz asked.

"That's different from the original message," Tien said. "We might not be handled by the same people."

"That's a chance we'll have to take. Send what Rik sent the last time," Kara said.

```
                              Agreed - Safe travels
```

Kara stepped in front of her team. "We have less than twelve hours. We'll need to take kit, so Toby and Jacob, I want you driving the van. The rest of us will go in by plane and train," she paused while she considered the logistics of what they would need. "We'll hire cars and bikes when we get there but Jacob, you're going to have to see them so you recognise them as ours. We'll also need to get the euros and hand them off to you. It means meeting up, but I'm not sure where yet. Toby, keep your phone on and I'll send the location later. Once done, Jacob, we'll get you into the outer suburbs and from there you'll make your own way in, completely independently. I don't want the remotest chance of anyone seeing you in our company. The rest of us will figure out our surveillance options and be in place before you arrive. Questions?"

They shook their heads.

"Right then, let's get busy."

Their reaction was immediate and sent a different emotion through her. She was going to be responsible for them and the operation and this time she would not screw up.

18

18th Arrondissement. Paris. Tuesday, 24th November.

Chaz imagined that the awning of the establishment wouldn't have looked as inviting if it had said *'George's little restaurant welcomes you'*.

"Amazing isn't it," he said quietly, but knew that his voice would be perfectly audible over the radio net, "how *Le petit restaurant de George vous accueille*, sounds so much more romantic. Honestly, I reckon the French could make the idea of dropping nuclear weapons on beautiful Polynesian islands seem like a good idea."

"Very droll Chaz. How's it looking?"

"Same as half an hour ago, Tien. No noticeable counter-surveillance assets, no noticeable problems. But then again, we know what that means."

"Yeah. Maybe they're as good as us."

"Mmm…," Chaz let the rest of his sentence go unfinished. He knew he had dropped the ball in Holland. He knew that he had been too relaxed, thinking that they were up against amateurs. His attitude had meant that Jacob had relaxed too. But, it was all Chaz's fault. He was meant to be the senior operator out of the two. He was meant to have led Jacob and kept them both switched on. Instead they'd nearly lost Tien and Kara. As it was, what Tien had had to endure was down to him. He wanted revenge on anyone and everyone involved with the organisation that Rik and the others had been part of.

As if reading his hesitancy from the other end of the street, Tien said, "It's okay Chaz. We won't underestimate them again. If we all just do our jobs we'll be fine. We need to remember, we're good at this stuff."

"Does anything ever get you down girl?"

"Sitting in the back of a van in a Parisian street with the smell of cafes and restaurants wafting all around while I get to eat cashew nuts and drink water. That's getting up there on my list."

"Try being the homeless bum sleeping in a doorway."

"Yeah, fair enough. You win that one."

"Don't I get to enter?" Sammi said, joining the conversation from the other end of the street.

"Oh please," Chaz responded, "you're in a four-series beamer. What's the hardest thing you have to contend with?"

"I accidently switched the heated front seats on. It got quite warm for a while."

Tien's laughter made the other two smile. Sammi felt a small lightening of the guilt she felt from the Dutch operation. She knew that Tien had had a truly lucky escape from a terrible experience and she was sure that she would bounce back, but she was still relieved to hear unhindered laughter from her friend. She was about to give Chaz a bit more stick when Jacob, his shoulders hunched, head down and hands in his jacket pockets, walked past her car, heading directly for the restaurant opposite Chaz. "He's inbound," Sammi said.

Chaz didn't move, he didn't look round, he just held his place and waited for Jacob to appear in his field of vision. Less than a minute later he saw Jacob cross the road in front of him and go into the restaurant. "He's in Kara." There was a single click in acknowledgment.

φ

154

Jacob allowed himself to loiter in the doorway of the small restaurant, unzipping his heavy leather jacket while his eyes adjusted to the low light of the interior. The Parisian streets he had walked through for the past half an hour had been cold, but brightly lit. He checked his watch. It was ten minutes to nine but they'd decided a bit of slack in his timekeeping would add to the overall effect. He looked about, remembering the lessons Chaz had taught him back in London.

"You ever see David Attenborough and the gorillas?" Chaz had asked.

"Yes," Jacob said, wondering how this was relevant.

"You walk and stand like an Alpha-Male, Jacob. You need to be a broken man-on-the-run. I can't change your height or your build, but just like Attenborough did, you need to become subservient. Lower your head, hunch your shoulders, stoop and walk less confidently. You need to shuffle, be non-threatening. Speak quietly, avoid eye contact, but not furtively, more like you're afraid."

Jacob had felt like he was in an acting class rather than a quick introduction to fieldwork and said the same to Chaz.

"Yeah. You're right, but your stage debut is going to be up close and personal with your audience, and there's no second chances."

Jacob dropped his shoulders and stooped his head, then made his way to the restaurant's counter. The room paid heed to the description on the awning. It was certainly little, but it used its space to maximum effect. The raised counter at the far end was dressed in dark oak and hosted a number of what Jacob guessed were 'specials of the evening' boards. More boards, with elaborately chalked pictures of grapes and flagons surrounding crammed wine lists, were mounted on the low walls. Below these were benches that provided one half of the seating to the three tables that lined each side wall. On the room side of each table were two tall dining chairs. In the middle of the room, four round tables with six chairs at each completed the dining area. Interspersed throughout, tied to the backs of chairs, table legs and wall-mounted light holders were bunches of herbs and small sheafs of wheat and corn. On top of the already small counter were wicker baskets overflowing with vegetables and peppers. Behind the counter, filling the rear wall of the room in width and from just above counter height to ceiling, were shelves teeming with bottles, only a small number of which Jacob recognised. He thought that if he ever wanted to open a French-themed restaurant anywhere on the planet, then this place would be a great model. It reminded him of a pub he'd gone to in Dublin. It had looked like all the themed, plastic-Irish-pubs he'd ever been in, but it was the real thing.

There were only four other people in the place. Two couples, one elderly sitting at a table to the left and one young, sitting to the right. Jacob reached the counter just as a thick-set man, dressed casually in an open-necked, short-sleeved shirt, came out from a door set into a niche to the side of the bar. Jacob reckoned he was in his fifties, his hair was clipped to at least a Grade-3 cut, he was about Jacob's height and both his broad forearms sported faded tattoos.

"*Bonsoir, que voudriez-vous?*"

Jacob gave him a nervous smile, looked around self-consciously, leant forward and said quietly, "I'm sorry. I don't speak French. I was wonder-"

"Did you have an appointment time," the man interrupted in flawless English.

"Umm, eh, yes. Nine. I was to be here at nine."

"You are early." The man turned, retrieving a glass and a bottle of red wine. He poured a generous amount and offered it to Jacob. Jacob shook his head to decline. The man stared at him and held the glass out. Jacob still didn't reach for it. The man looked discreetly towards the other diners, then back to the glass then pointedly at Jacob. Jacob nodded as if he had finally realised why he should take the glass. He reached out and with a distinct tremor in his hand, raised it to his lips.

The barman poured himself a glass, took a small sip then said, "Who arranged for you to come see me?"

"Eh," Jacob hesitated, looking around the room again.

The man behind the counter reached out and touched him on the arm, forcing Jacob to look back to him.

"Who told you to come here?"

"Eh," Jacob lowered his head, leaned into the bar once more and whispered, "Rik. Rik told me to come here."

The man let go of his arm. "And what did he tell you to tell me?"

Jacob's first thought was, 'Oh fuck, that's screwed it'. He had no communication system on him as they had decided it was far too risky. A physical search or a quick counter-bug scan would have revealed even the most discreet system and they couldn't risk that. He was truly on his own with regard to the content of the conversation. He improvised with the continuation of the nervous and self-conscious fugitive. "I, uh, I don't remember. I'm sorry, I'm uh… not too sure what…"

"His name. Rik told you his family name. You say, eh, surname in English. Rik told you it. What is it?"

Jacob was about to continue the stammering obfuscation but stopped as he remembered the moment in the farmhouse, just before they'd discovered the computer room. He saw in his mind Chaz running his fingers over a license lying on top of the sideboard. Jacob reached for the red wine and took a long, slow sip. He concentrated on the memory.

"I need a name from you," the barman said, moving his own glass to one side and folding his arms. He suddenly looked like a doorman that would provide security to the roughest of bars. Jacob slowly set his glass back down and willed the man to try and start something. He would so gladly rip him and the restaurant apart, but he also knew that wasn't what he was here for.

"De Vries. His name is Rik de Vries."

The big barman relaxed and unfolded his arms. "Good. Have you eaten?"

The question surprised Jacob, but he decided to tell the

truth, "Umm, no."

"Fine. Do you eat meat?"

Jacob nodded.

"I will get you some food. Go and sit in the corner table."

"Thanks," Jacob said and offered his hand, "I'm-"

The barman held his own hand up, index finger raised, and shook his head, "No. No. I don't want to, or need to, know your name. I don't wish to know where you come from either. You will be Pierre from Paris for tonight. You will eat and drink here and stay tonight and tomorrow. Then you will go. In the time you are here I wish to know as little about you as possible. Now go sit."

Before Jacob turned away and the barman went into the kitchen, the young couple approached the bar. She was attractive, in her mid to late twenties and was saying something in German to her partner who looked like he could have been a poster boy for a different time and place. He was tall, athletically built, had short blond hair, blue eyes and generally light colouring. The woman swapped to French and, as Jacob took his seat, he watched the blond man hand over a bunch of euros which she used to pay the bill. Amidst a chorus of *Merci* and *Au Revoir* the barman returned to the kitchen and the couple turned to go. Jacob barely noticed the subtle movement as the man passed his hand under the lip of the counter top. He looked down at a menu as the young couple left the restaurant.

φ

"Kara?"

"Go ahead."

"Dinger and Eloise are clear," Chaz said from his increasingly cold and uncomfortable doorway.

"Okay. You all heard the copy from inside. He's going to be there for a day. We need to find somewhere to stay."

"Chaz raised himself on one elbow and peered down the street. "Kara?"

"Yes Chaz?"

"I'm looking directly at a Holiday Inn. It's less than fifty yards away."

Kara, from the confines of the observation position she and Toby had established to monitor the rear of the restaurant, said only, "Tien?"

"On it. Give me half an hour."

19

Jacob had finished his meal and been taken to a well-furnished bedroom in a spacious apartment on the fourth floor above the restaurant. The room, and the adjoining bathroom, had windows, but they were covered by internal shutters secured by padlocks. Having been told to wait until the restaurant shut, he took his leather jacket off and lay down on the bed. At midnight there was a knock at the door. The barman and a smaller man, who carried a black brief case and wore round, thin-frame glasses that perched halfway down his nose, came in without waiting for an answer. Jacob sat up and swung his legs onto the floor.

"I need you to stand up and undress," the barman said.

"What?" Jacob asked, much too aggressively for his cover story. He relaxed his stance as best he could.

"I need to search you. Before we give you the details of what will happen and what you must do. Empty your pockets and undress."

"Oh. I see," Jacob meekly nodded and did as he was asked. He concentrated on the discussions he, Kara, Tien, Sammi and Chaz had had when they were trying to figure out what the mindsets of these men would be like. They had no inclination to understand, or try to analyse what drove them to do the things they did, but they were interested in how they would react if they were forced to run. The best that they could come up with was that they were used to being incredibly careful. Hiding what they did from their families, their friends, society and the police was second nature to them. That meant security precautions and anything deemed a necessary measure wouldn't be objected to. Searches, scans and intrusive questions would all be understood as serving the purpose of trying to protect them and the wider network they were part of. It was decided that the reaction should be one of meek compliance with all requests. That and the fact Jacob wouldn't carry any covert surveillance or communication equipment would hopefully allow a chance to establish some trust. One-way trust, Jacob reminded himself as he stripped off the last of his clothes.

The search was quick and efficient. As an experienced personnel-searcher himself, although never having conducted one with a naked prisoner, Jacob was aware that the barman had been trained by someone at some time. He first searched Jacob's jacket, removing four envelopes from the inside pockets. Each contained forty-five €500 notes and the barman took the money out, counted it, held up sixteen of the notes to show the small man, and laid them on top of the bedside cabinet. He returned the rest of the money to the envelopes and put them on the bed. Next he examined the remainder of Jacob's possessions that totalled an empty wallet, save for a few hundred euros, a watch, a black plastic comb, one cotton handkerchief and finally, a money belt that Jacob had worn under his shirt. In it were another four separate bundles of notes that looked to total a substantial amount, but the barman didn't count it. He merely laid the money on the bed and turned the belt inside out, running his fingers over each seam and join.

Moving onto the rest of Jacob's clothes he rolled the fabric of each garment, checking for any hidden wires or transmission devices and was as thorough in his examination of Jacob's shoes. He was equally efficient and completely unabashed when he donned latex gloves and conducted a full body cavity search, beginning with Jacob's mouth, before moving on to his nose, ears, armpits, navel and finally asking him to bend over. Jacob said nothing and complied with all instructions.

"You can get dressed again," the barman said, removing the gloves and rolling them into a ball. He walked to the bathroom and dumped them into a small bin. Returning, he asked, "You have no telephone?"

Jacob felt his pulse quicken. Chaz had suggested that if he was a man on the run, he'd have been advised to ditch anything that could trace him. But they had no real idea if that was what would be expected. He tried to answer as calmly as he could. "I was told not to carry anything that could identify me."

"Yes, I know that," the barman answered. "I'm not stupid. I was making sure *you* have not been. You are sure you have not bought a replacement so you can phone home and put us all in jeopardy?"

"No. Of course not." Jacob allowed a trace of annoyance into his voice. "Rik made me leave it and all my bankcards and other papers."

The barman stared hard at him, then relaxed. "Good. Tomorrow, you can sleep as long as you like, but you will have to go out for breakfast because the restaurant is not open in the mornings. I do not care if you take all day to look about Paris, but you have to be back here by five at the latest. You will meet some others who will take you the next part of the way. Do you have any questions for me?"

"No," Jacob said, "Just thank you."

"Don't thank me. You have paid Rik and now you have paid me." He picked up the sixteen notes he had laid aside, and tucked them into his shirt pocket. "This is just a job." He gave a shrug that Jacob thought was like the restaurant downstairs; so stereotypically French as to be almost comedic. "One last thing," the barman continued, "before you go out tomorrow, you must come and knock on the door of Apartment Two, downstairs. You must let me know when you are leaving so that I am aware. Yes?"

"Yes," Jacob said.

The barman gave a curt nod of his head and left the room.

The small man placed the briefcase on the bed, flicked the catches and removed a compact digital camera. "Now lad, sit yourself down over there, with your back to the wall," he said in a broad Yorkshire accent that landed on Jacob's ears like a punch. He stared at him and the man gestured to a chair next to the window. "No need to look so surprised, we're not all bloody French, but don't be asking questions. Just get yourself over there, sit down and stare straight ahead. No smiling, just a neutral expression please, there's a good lad."

Jacob finished dressing and did as he was asked but as the small man went to take the photo, Jacob turned his head and shied away. "Hang on, hang on. What's this all for?"

The small man lowered the camera and sighed. "Look, you can recognise my accent and I can recognise yours. I don't need details, but you've fled England and come to us via Rik. That means he got you out by sea and across to Holland. That's how he operates. We all know that lad. You didn't need a passport because he picked you up, and landed you, in his own boat far away from prying eyes. You still didn't need a passport when he got you into France. Normally it's because of our bloody idiotic European brethren and the stupid Schengen Agreement, but now, after these here recent terrorist attacks, I imagine he'll have used some pretty unconventional methods to get you in to the city." He paused and Jacob nodded his agreement.

"The thing is, we need to get you out of France now and it's all a bit screwed up at the minute."

Jacob gave him his best confused frown.

The small man stifled another sigh. "Look, what's your first name?"

"Umm, I thought you didn't need to know it?"

"No, our thug of a Frenchy barman who thinks he's running the *'ello 'ello Café*, doesn't need to know it, because he's the first and most inconsequential step on the Path. But I'm going to need it. I have to get you a passport and other travel documents and we want you to answer promptly when someone calls your name. We'll invent surnames but your first name stays the same. Understand?"

Jacob nodded slowly.

"Well?"

"Oh, yeah, Jacob. It's Jacob."

"Great. Well, Jacob, if you'd decided to do a runner a couple of weeks ago, then we'd have taken you on a small round trip through some pretty European states. It was easy. There were no border controls and the more countries we moved through, the more complicated it got for any police that might have been trying to follow you. Finally, when we were happy any police were long lost and when we had produced a good passport, we'd have spirited you away to where no one is going to find you. But, this damn state of emergency has complicated things. Big time."

"So what's going to happen to me?" Jacob asked, trying desperately to control his temper and make his voice sound pathetic. He realised this man wasn't concerned with, or sympathetic to, the deaths of so many people in the recent terrorist attacks that had left Paris reeling. It was just an inconvenience to him.

"Oh don't worry lad. We'll still get you out. You're one of us and we look after our own," he said with an air of pride and joviality.

Jacob's control slipped and a furious rage surged through him. This piece of crap was happy to belong to a bunch of paedophiles and rapists, like it was some elite club. He was basking in their ability to protect each other. Knowing his flush of anger would be visible, Jacob half turned in the seat and put his head in his hands. He concentrated on lowering his voice and again speaking in a semi-whine, "But you're saying it's all going to be more difficult. I might get caught?"

"No. No. Nothing like that. It just means we have to be

more direct. Less time to do what we'd normally do and bloody typical of foreigners, that means it gets more expensive. Happen you have to pay more for express service."

"I don't understand," Jacob said, feeling the redness leave his face. He turned back to the smaller man, reverting to his bewildered on-the-run persona again. "I just need to get away. I need to go somewhere they can't find me. It wasn't my fault. She was meant t-"

It was the small man's turn to hold his hand up and indicate Jacob should say no more. "Shush now Jacob. I don't need to know what happened. It's safer I don't. But, yes, we'll get you far, far away."

Jacob looked crestfallen, "I'm going to be so alone. What will I do?"

The small man sighed again. "Here, don't be silly. We wouldn't let that happen. If we did that you'd be wandering around like a lost soul. People would notice. Police would notice. So stop worrying. We're sending you somewhere that's outside the extradition treaties with good old Blighty, but everyone speaks English and there are lots of western faces. Relax."

Jacob knew he had to balance his bewildered act with the need to get information, but without raising the small man's suspicions. He wished he could cry on demand; the tears would have been a good convincer. Instead he just focussed on keeping his voice like a whine.

"But I'll still be alone. I won't know what to d-"

"Here now, stop it, I said," the small man interrupted him. There was a frustration and an edge of sternness to his voice, "I told you, we wouldn't do that. You'll be met at the airport by another British guy who lives out there now. He's a Londoner, but I suppose we can't hold that against him. This isn't the first time we've done this. He meets all the new arrivals and makes sure they get settled in. You'll stay with him for a few months until you're comfortable. Nice secure house that you'll be safe in. Happen that's why they call it a safe house," he said and gave a grin. "He'll help you arrange bank accounts and find a place to stay eventually. So stop it. No more feeling sorry for yourself."

Jacob made a show of wiping his eyes, though there were no tears. He sniffed and with a slightly less whining pitch said, "Oh. I didn't realise. That's really good of you."

The small man laughed with an unusually deep baritone sound that didn't fit his body size at all. "Not me Jacob. Not me at all." He raised a finger and waggled it strangely in the direction of the roof.

"Upstairs?" Jacob asked, properly confused.

The man gave another deep laugh. "No. Not upstairs. The higher-ups. The men who first established the Flight Path. That's who to thank."

"Oh, of course," Jacob said.

"Aw dear, you're such an open book," the small man said and Jacob stiffened, wondering where this was going. "You've no idea what I'm talking about, have you?"

Jacob shook his head.

"The Flight Path. It's what you're a part of now. It was first setup in the Seventies. Like the underground railway during the war when the resistance used to smuggle all those allied pilots out of occupied France. We're just the same, only better, because we have way more police chasing us than they ever did." He gave another incongruous laugh.

It was all Jacob could do not to reach out and snap the small man's neck. The previous surge of anger was nothing compared to what he felt now. How anyone could compare the heroics of the Dutch, Belgian and French resistance to a bunch of criminal scum that helped other scum escape justice was beyond him. He bit his lip and clenched his fists, fighting to calm himself. The small man didn't miss the physical reactions, but totally misinterpreted them.

"Now, now, there's no need to feel embarrassed. The whole point of us, is that no one knows about us. There are rumours sometimes in the chat rooms, but mostly we go under the radar. On a couple of occasions, when we were helping celebrities get away, they almost revealed the extent of it, but

166

we managed to cover it back up." He stepped forward and patted Jacob on the shoulder, "Now come on. I need to get some photos taken so we can get you nice new passports and identities."

Jacob swallowed hard and struggled to suppress his intense anger. He swallowed again and concentrated on making his voice sound sad and broken, "Yeah, but I'm not being sent home like those pilots were. I can't ever go home, can I?"

"No. No you probably can't. Like I said, I don't know what you did and I don't want to know. But, if you've had to pay to get to a country with no extradition, then no lad, you won't be going home." The small man gave Jacob another friendly pat on the shoulder. Jacob imagined standing up and putting his fist through the bespectacled face. Instead he breathed deeply and brought his temper back under control. He straightened in the chair and looked towards the camera, "Okay then. Let's do it."

The small man took a series of photos, checking the digital display after each one.

"How come so many photos?" Jacob asked.

"Just me being overly pedantic with the composition. It's the OCD coming out in me," he grinned. "One would do, even for the four passports."

"Four?"

"Oh yes. You'll have one for the first flight. Then someone will meet you when you get off it and look after you until the next one. They'll give you your ticket and a second passport. Same for the next one. Given what I said about this damn state of emergency, it's the best we can do to confuse your trail."

"What's the fourth one for?"

The small man was looking down at the camera display, raising his glasses from his nose and concentrating on the images, "Oh that's for your new identity when you get to where you're going."

Jacob decided now was the right time to push things, "And where will that be?"

The small man straightened up and looked back at Jacob,

"You'll find out when you get your final ticket. You understand, it's just safer that way."

"Oh. Of course, sorry."

"Nope. No need to apologise, it's fine. Perfectly natural to be curious. Right. They're okay, I can use them. Very photogenic."

Jacob gave him a pathetic smile.

"That's better, chin up." He moved across to the bed and began to pack the camera away in the briefcase. When finished he lifted the envelopes with the money in them. "Now, a few things you need to do tomorrow. Okay?"

Jacob tried to convey a sense of attentiveness and a keenness to please.

"Travelling light is great but people with absolutely no luggage get noticed. I need you to buy a small suitcase and a carryon back pack. Outfit yourself for what you would expect to take on holiday to somewhere warm. Make sure you don't pack anything that's going to cause any problems. Just normal holiday clothes, shorts, tops, underwear, sandals, toiletries. That sort of thing, but get one light jumper and a light jacket. Especially for the flights. For your carryon think about what will make you fit in and not raise any suspicions. Maybe some sweets or a pack of cards, a book, or some of those puzzle magazines. There's places round here will sell them in English. It just needs to look normal. Only nothing that's electronic. We don't want something, no matter how remote, that might be traceable. I know you wouldn't, but on a stopover, you might be tempted to check Facebook, or look at emails or something that would give you away. Okay? So no electronics. Very important. For security. It's just saf-"

"Safer that way," Jacob finished for him.

"Yes. Exactly. Got it?"

"Yes," Jacob said.

"Well then. Keep your chin up. Good luck Jacob."

The small man started to leave but turned back, "Oh, almost forgot. What year were you born?"

"Umm, sorry?"

"The year of your birth, what is it?"

"Nineteen eighty-nine. Why?"

"It's for the passports, that's all. Now I don't want to know the day or month but I do need to know if it was in July?"

"No."

"Great. Right. Get some rest. Big few days ahead."

When the small man had left, Jacob went back to lying on the bed. He shut his eyes but couldn't sleep.

His anger at both the man's pride in helping people escape and the resistance remark was bleeding off, but his underlying anger, present since he had looked through the farmhouse window, hadn't so much dissipated as refined itself into a purpose and been channelled for effect. Purposeful anger gave him a focus but wasn't the reason for his restlessness. It was the gnawing guilt that weighed heavy in his chest and was much more difficult to ease. It caused his thoughts to replay the events of the past few days. He saw so clearly the mistakes he'd made by allowing Tien and Kara to approach the waterfront alone. He should have been aware of the risks and he knew it was because of his oversight he'd almost lost Tien. Almost lost both of them.

His failure rankled so deeply within him because that was his job; now and before in the military. He was a Force Protection specialist. His whole reason for being anywhere was to protect the main assets of an operation and he'd always done it. From Basra to the Battle of Bastion, when he had fought alongside his older brother, that had been his mission. The Bastion raid had caused its own guilt and regret, but it hadn't been as personal as this. Tien was his main concern. She was what had to be protected at all costs and he'd let her down. And Kara, he reminded himself.

That's why, when they had discovered there was a chance to infiltrate the network, to perhaps discover how Swift had disappeared, maybe even find him, he had instantly volunteered to take on the role of the scared fugitive. He saw it as an opportunity to make it up to her; them. Even when Sammi & Chaz both suggested that Chaz should do it because of his experience and capabilities, Jacob had held firm. They all knew Chaz was superior to all of them when it came to skills in unarmed combat. The guy was a force of nature at fighting and given that the mission would be solo, with no communications and no chance to call for help, it had almost swayed the argument in Chaz's favour.

But it had eventually come down to Kara and Tien. They'd both agreed that Jacob, being from Essex and knowing Swift from television, might have the advantage over Chaz if he ever found himself close enough to the target. Kara told him later, in private, that Tien really appreciated him volunteering. A calming sense of contentment washed over him as he remembered the conversation.

"Dark hearts," he said softly and concentrated on slowing his breathing and quietening his thoughts.

"Dark hearts," he repeated, closed his eyes and eventually drifted off to sleep.

φ

It was Paris on a cold, overcast November night so Tien had no difficulty securing three rooms. Dinger and Eloise had accommodation already and it was important that they stayed separate from the rest. Sammi, Tien and Kara checked-in together and while the receptionist completed the paperwork the three women laughed and talked about their day. By the time they were being handed the room cards, the receptionist, had she been interested, would have known that the three English couples had had a change of heart and instead of rushing back to catch the London train, had decided to stay in Paris for another night. The husbands would be along later, they'd just gone to extend the rental on the minibus they'd hired for the day. Once upstairs they quickly met in Kara's room and were joined by Dinger via phone.

"Any difficulties getting the bug back out?" Kara asked Dinger.

"Nope," he said. "It went under the counter when we

ordered and came off when we paid the bill. Easy as."

"And Eloise, she was okay with all this?" Sammi asked.

"Happy? No," Dinger said and waited until he heard at least one concerned 'Oh' in response. "She was delighted. Thrilled in fact. When I explained what you wanted us to do she was completely up for it. Thought it was 'incredibly exciting', and the fact she got to come to Paris was a bonus. Lanzarote's lovely, but I think booking for three weeks was a mistake, so yeah, cutting early was good. To be fair, I'm not sure she's in the right job. She took to tonight really well."

"I just thought, with you and her speaking German, it gave us good cover and a chance to have some on-site presence when Jacob made the first contact," Kara said. "Just in case."

"And it worked. She was cool. Given she's never met Jacob also helped. She didn't react at all to him when he came in, just stayed completely relaxed. Like I said, maybe the law isn't her calling," Dinger laughed, more than a little proud of his fiancée's performance in the restaurant.

"Yeah, but a lawyer's going to be good for you to have Dinger," Sammi said. "You never know when you're going to need bailing out."

"Yeah, fair enough," Dinger laughed in agreement.

"Right, what next?" Kara asked, bringing them back on topic.

"Well, Eloise heads home tomorrow morning and then I can be wherever you need me to be," Dinger said.

"Afraid not on this one Dinger," Kara said. "We're going to assume these guys are top-notch on their counter-surveillance. When I say good, I mean equal to us. That's why I wanted you in there tonight as a couple, but given you've been visible to them, then that's the last you can play close-quarter-reconnaissance on this. It'll also be better if you travel to the airport and depart together. That's what they would expect to see and we're going to assume they'll have put assets on you. It's what we would do if an unknown couple turned up at a site we had set for a high-value meet."

"Yep, understood. No problem," Dinger said and Kara

again thanked her good fortune at being able to work with the best professionals she knew. There was no dissent or ego getting in the way of the job.

"What we would like you to do is head to the Camden office and be our coordination if we need it?" Tien asked.

"Too easy. How do I get in?"

"I'll text you my brother's number. He has spare keys," Kara said.

"You mean David? The cop?"

"Yeah," Kara hesitated, "Is that a problem?"

"Nah," Dinger laughed. "Just thought the last time the cops came to your office they didn't need spare keys, did they?"

"Funny bugger aren't you?" Kara said. "Just you be careful going in. That paint job in the foyer was expensive," she added with a chuckle, thinking about the new doorframes, doors and paint that the Cambridgeshire Constabulary had had to foot the bill for after a raid in July.

"Okay, no worries. Do you need me anymore then?"

"Nope. Thanks again and thank Eloise," Kara said.

"No problem. I'll talk to you when I'm in Camden. Bye." The call cut-off. Sammi, Tien and Kara gathered round the room's coffee table and studied a map of Paris for the next hour.

φ

At two in the morning, Kara went on a one kilometre walk to end up less than fifty metres from her hotel. She entered a darkened alley that, halfway along, was lined with a deep hedgerow. Penetrating through it, she crossed a clearing of grass to a pitch black tree line that separated two blocks of buildings, the western most of which housed the restaurant Jacob had entered five hours before. She knelt on the ground and waited until she attuned to her immediate surroundings. Taking a set of binocular night sights from her small hip pouch, she turned the black to a deep green haze. Despite the clarity of vision they provided, the tree line still revealed nothing of note.

"Toby," she whispered into the night.

Her voice-activated mic transmitted and less than ten steps from where she knelt, a hand appeared from the darkness.

"Here Kara."

"Jesus, that's impressive camouflage," she said.

"You know how it is. Once a sniper..." Toby said as he manoeuvred out from his observation post.

"Anything?" she asked as she moved to take his place.

"Nope. Chaz reports all quiet too. If nothing bad has happened then he's still in there."

Kara could hear the slightest of tonal changes in Toby's voice as he spoke about his younger brother's safety.

"It's okay Toby. He can look after himself and we'll be in there in minutes if anything looks wrong. Now, go get something to eat and drink. Room 428," she said and handed over the hotel room card.

"Thanks. Have we figured out what we'll do at dawn?"

Kara knew the tree line afforded a great observation post during the night, but in the daylight the trees in the small inter-building park were much too thin to provide any cover.

"Yep, all sorted. Even if they come out the rear door they only have two streets that they can exit onto. We have plans in place. Talk to Tien back at the hotel. Dawn's at eight so I'll withdraw from here by seven and catch up with you then."

"Chaz'll be knackered by then," Toby said, stifling a yawn of his own.

"Yeah, but he'll cope. It's not like we can change homeless bums in the middle of the night. He's in his doorway and he's happy."

Chaz, forty metres on the opposite side of the trees, in a direct line through the building and across the road, turned over under his cardboard blanket, feigning restless sleep. "Happy is one word for it, I suppose."

Tien, back in the hotel and listening in to all the communications through a base station that also amplified the signals to prevent interference from the tightly packed Parisian buildings, said, "Come on back Toby. I have hot chocolate and marshmallows waiting for you."

"You're a cruel woman," Kara said, settling down to watch the back of the restaurant as Toby disappeared into the night.

20

Wednesday 25th November.

The door to Apartment Two was opened by the barman.
"You are going out now?"
Jacob nodded.
"Back by five. No later. Better if you can stay out most of the day. Keep a low profile. Don't draw attention to yourself and don't act suspiciously. Whoever you are running from does not know you are here. You can relax. Yes?"

"Yes."

"Go down the stairs and through the hallway. It will bring you out to the rear of the restaurant. When you come back, come in that way. There is a bell. Yes?"

"Yes."

The barman shut the door and Jacob turned for the stairs. Once outside he walked back around the building to the street in front of the restaurant. The sun had only been up for half an hour and the damp of the night still clung to a morning that was overcast, grey and cold. He swept his gaze up and down like he was completely unaware of his surroundings. In reality he had committed most of the 18th Arrondissement, and the neighbouring 9th, 10th and 17th to memory while travelling across in the van from London. That van, a non-descript white transit, had been parked in a town an hour's distance from Paris and swapped for an equally non-descript hire van that boasted French plates and right-hand drive configuration. Without dwelling on them, Jacob's sweep of the street registered at least four similar vans parked within one-hundred metres of where he stood. Given the strange and extremely close nature of Parisian parking, he couldn't see any of the registration plates, but he was fairly sure one of them would be theirs. Likewise, although he couldn't see the other car and motorbikes that Kara and the rest of the team had hired, he knew they'd be close by.

He also noted that the homeless man who had been sleeping in the doorway opposite the restaurant had moved on, or been moved on, as daylight had dawned. He turned left towards the centre of the city. The nearest Métro station was about a kilometre away, but he wanted to stay above ground and on foot for longer than that. He figured his appearance on the street would have surprised Tien and Kara but they would be mobilising to follow him and he had to give them a chance to make contact.

It took him seven minutes of browsing store fronts and walking casually, yet not too slowly, to reach the end of Rue Damrémont. Doglegging right he joined Rue Caulaincourt and walked along the narrow footpath of a wrought iron bridge. He paused to look down through the high-sided blue metal lattice that was a favourite canvas for the local graffiti artists. From studying the maps of the area he knew what to expect, but was still surprised at the view in reality. Broad tree-lined avenues ran between clumps of majestic tombs and grand mausoleums. The great and the good of 19th Century Montmartre had been buried in a secluded town of the dead, then forced to endure the domination of a strange metal viaduct that town planners of later years thought a necessary improvement for progress.

He lingered for an amount of time that he thought balanced the curiosity natural for a first time visitor against his need to allow Tien and Kara a chance to catch up. After a few minutes he set off south again.

A short distance later he came to a confusing intersection of eight different streets centred on a small, paved island that was a parking space for mopeds and bicycles. The brown-coloured tourist signposts showed the Moulin Rouge was to his left along the wide Boulevard de Clichy. Sure enough, the red tip of a windmill sail was visible, peeking out from behind the dozen or so buildings between him and it.

He turned around slowly, as if realising for the first time that the building dominating the corner of the intersection was a café serving breakfast. The long stretch of pavement wrapping around the semi-circular frontage would no doubt have catered to a large number of tables and chairs during the Parisian spring or summer, but in the drabness of a winter's morning it was empty. The lack of alfresco tables afforded an unbroken view into the windows of the café. He could see a number of empty tables inside and the reflection of the busy street scene behind him. As he walked into the Café de Luna he had the first confirmation that being sent out to do shopping wasn't all the small man wanted from today.

φ

Sammi had been startled when Jacob came out of the restaurant. She was in the rear of the white van parked down a small alley that ran at an obtuse angle to the main Rue Damrémont. As Kara, Tien and she had worked out the previous night, owing to the bizarre layout of the streets in this area of Paris, the alley afforded a view of the restaurant's entrance and oversight of the two streets that were the only access to the rear of the property. Its only disadvantage had been that it was packed with cars. That meant they weren't going to be able to get a parking spot until some of the residents left for work. At six-thirty that morning, Chaz, his cardboard decidedly wet and his back cramped, reported one early riser had just driven out of the alley and there was a gap if they moved quickly. Sammi had left the hotel, recovered the van from where they had originally parked it, raced around three city blocks and managed to squeeze it in. That allowed Chaz and Kara to pull out of their respective posts and make their way, circuitously, to the Holiday Inn. Chaz especially had to take the long way round to allow him time to transform from a homeless tramp into someone that could be seen walking through a hotel foyer.

The plan was to rotate the watch duties throughout the day and wait until Jacob eventually left the restaurant. What they hadn't expected was for him to walk out on his own at eight-thirty in the morning.

"Tien, you there?" Sammi called into her mic.

"It's Toby. Tien's gone for some kip, go ahead."

"Get everyone up. Right now. Jacob's out and on foot. He's walking south on Rue Damrémont."

"Oh fuck. It's going to be a chunk of time before we're fit to follow."

"I know, but get the- Whoa!" Sammi stopped abruptly and reached for the digital SLR camera that was next to her in the van. She manoeuvred the 800mm telephoto lens up to the glass.

"Sammi?"

"Hang on Toby, I mean, don't hang on. Make the phone calls. Get them up and moving but…"

"Sammi?"

"Wait a minute. Make the calls, but give me a minute."

"Okay," Toby said, crossing to the other side of his hotel room and shaking Chaz awake at the same time as ringing Kara's room. Tien's was next. By the time he hung up and returned to the radio, Chaz was already half dressed and heading to the bathroom to soak his head in water.

"Sammi, they're all moving. What's up?"

"Tell them to standby, I'm going to come back to the hotel. Jacob is out on foot but he has company. A lot of company."

φ

Sammi took five minutes to walk around to the rear of the hotel, passing between blocks of buildings whose triangular fronts looked like majestic battleships, intricately carved from the cream-grey Paris stone, and sailing headlong into narrow streets that threatened to confine them. She thought the wrought iron balconies, perched under tall windows, transformed the early rising Parisian coffee drinkers who stepped onto them into living figureheads.

As she came up a final, twisting side alley she checked to her right. The much wider and straighter Rue Damrémont allowed her a great sightline and confirmed what she thought. When she got to Kara's room the rest of the team were already there.

"What's the story?" Kara asked.

"Jacob left on foot and about a minute after he walked away three guys came out of the restaurant. A fourth came out from the apartment block opposite and crossed the street to join them. I got good shots of all of them," she said handing the camera's small Secure Digital High Capacity memory card over to Tien, who slipped it into a PC and opened up the images.

Four men, aged in their late twenties to early thirties were pictured in exquisite detail. A couple of group shots were followed by four individual head shots. "Sorry two of them are only profiles, but they wouldn't turn around." Sammi said. "Anyway, these two got into that Citroën," she said pointing to the photos on the screen, "and the other two set off after Jacob."

"That's a surveillance team, no doubt," Chaz said.

"Yep. The two in the car will leapfrog forward and pick Jacob up at the next intersection," Kara agreed. "Right, how long's it been?"

Sammi checked her watch, "Eleven minutes. Given Jacob was dawdling and to draw things out he'll look in every window and at every interesting thing he can find, then we should be good."

Kara turned to Chaz, "You gave him the crash course.

Does he know what to do?"

"Yep. He'll loiter, always stick to the main routes and if he hits a T-junction he'll alternate left and right."

"Okay. We'll leave the car and the van where they are and use the bikes. Toby with me, Chaz with Sammi. Tien you're on comms until we get a fix on him."

"We'll have to swap to open phone lines Kara. The radios won't have the range in the urban area and we can't take the amplifier mobile if the van's staying put. They're all good to go," Tien said, pointing to the line of smartphones on the desk.

"Okay, then once we find him, I might get you to come in ahead of us. Anything else?" Kara asked.

Tien clicked a couple of buttons on the PC, opened a message program and clicked again. All the mobiles pinged at the same time. "I've just uploaded the photos of the men and the car to all the phones," she said.

"Good. Anything else?" Kara asked again and this time received shakes of the head in response. "Right, let's do this and don't forget, we make sure we're spotless. We stay in the background and if we need to engage with him, it's a one-off occurrence. No repeat opportunities. We do not get seen."

The four moved to the door, grabbing the motorcycle over leathers and helmets that had come with the bikes they'd hired.

φ

Jacob pulled the warm croissant apart and took a bite. Raising the cup of coffee to his lips he peered over the rim and was satisfied he had made the correct assessment. Standing on the bridge over the cemetery he had counted fourteen people pass by. The foot traffic hadn't been considerable and he'd put it down to the fact it was almost nine in the morning and most people would already have been in, or well on their way to, work. He certainly hadn't remembered all fourteen faces but their body shapes and clothes were much easier to log. When he had turned to continue his walk all bar two, a young mother and her child of about five, were well in front of him. By the time he reached the complicated interchange all fourteen should have been long gone. Yet when he had turned to enter the Café de Luna and saw the street scene reflected in the windows, two of the men that had passed him were still in view. One sheltered behind a strange piece of street art that was a red and green rectangular box with a large silver apple on top of it. The other was sitting at a table behind the glass front of the Palace Café directly across the road. It was perfectly reasonable for both men to be where they were, but as Jacob had his back towards them he thought they had made eye contact with one another. It was a fleeting moment, reflected in a window at distance so he hadn't been sure, but it was worthy of further study.

Now, as he peered over his coffee cup he saw the man behind the silver apple reach up to his ear. Jacob recognised the movement. He'd done it himself when the small earpiece of a radio system either unseated itself or was suffering from poor reception. It was an instinctive reaction and one of the clearest giveaways for covert operators. When he had completed a close-protection team training course after leaving the military, the instructors had slapped the back of the students' hands with hazel rods every time they touched their ears. It was a crude, aggressive and effective correction device. The two men he was watching obviously hadn't taken that course. Final confirmation for Jacob was when the men once more made definite eye contact with each other from across the street.

He considered that despite the surveillance tail being badly executed, it placed him in an awkward position. His bewildered, poor-man-on-the-run persona wouldn't notice it, bad or not. That meant he had to continue as normal. It also meant he couldn't use active methods to shake it off. That wouldn't be in character and what's more, would raise the suspicions of the small man and any others in the Flight Path. Lastly, and much more worryingly for him, it meant that Tien and the rest couldn't attempt to make contact with him. He was sure that they'd notice the tail too. It would be impossible for them to miss it, but it did mean he wouldn't be able to tell them what he had learnt about the journey he was going to embark on. He attracted the waiter's attention and ordered more coffee as he tried to think of a way to solve that particular puzzle. Out of the window to his right he saw a black and silver BMW motorbike glide to a stop at the pedestrian crossing, less than ten yards from where he sat. The rider and pillion passenger were both clad in black over leathers and black full face helmets. Their single distinguishing mark was the name of the helmet manufacture, 'Yohe' outlined in white and only visible because the visors of both helmets were fully down.

Jacob raised his hand to his mouth and coughed a couple of times, then patted himself on the chest twice with a closed fist, like he had just choked on his croissant. Reaching to take another sip of coffee, he saw the pillion passenger move their left hand from the waist of the rider to their own left thigh. Four fingers were extended. It was a fleeting movement and they gripped the rider again as the bike pulled away, turning left, towards the Moulin Rouge. He didn't follow its path and merely continued to hold his gaze towards the crossing point. From the corner of his right eye he could see a stand of postcards that also supported a tight stack of tourist prints, trying to look like Lautrec originals, but that were no doubt mass-produced in China. The shop that owned the stand had various signs above and to the sides of its doors, including the prolific 'Tabac' that in Paris seemed completely undeterred by the rest of Europe's crackdown on smokers. Jacob twisted around in his seat to look more closely at one of the signs.

He stood and walked over to the waiter who was watching a repeat of a football game on a screen set high up in the corner of the room. After explaining he would be back momentarily, Jacob left the café and walked across the street. He saw, in the reflection of a passing car, the man behind the silver apple make to follow him then stop as he realised where Jacob was going.

Inside the small newsagent and tobacconist's Jacob selected 'The Times' from the stand of English newspapers that he had seen advertised. He bought it, a pen and pencil set and 'The Bumper Book of Puzzles' also in English, then returned to the café. Retaking his seat and moving his freshly arrived coffee to one side, he opened the paper at the crossword puzzle and sucked the end of his pen in quiet contemplation.

An hour later, with another croissant and yet another coffee under his belt, he paid the bill, received his change and made to leave. The waiter called him back and pointed to the table. Jacob, with an overly expressive gesture of thanks went back and picked up the paper and his puzzle book. Exiting the café he turned left, walked across to the wide, tree-lined median of the Boulevard de Clichy and made his way towards the Blanche Métro station. Walking within ten metres of the silver apple he stifled a laugh at the way the man manoeuvred to keep the statue between them.

Jacob sauntered, allowing his tailing pair to sort themselves out. He noticed a strange and eclectic mix of adult shops off to the right side of the wide street, balanced by a procession of bars and clubs to the left. He thought it odd that there were four Irish bars within touching distance of each other. He wondered if they were the stereotypical plastic-Irish versions of that old pub in Dublin.

A few minutes later he stopped and looked up at the famous red windmill. Having never been in this part of Paris before, he was genuinely surprised that the whole building wasn't bigger. The entrance foyer to the right was just the width of a normal townhouse, although the row of gilt-handled entrance doors to the left gave some clue that the home of the can-can was bigger inside than out. He decided that a closer look was warranted, not least because those gilt-handled doors were also full-height black glass that made perfect mirrors. As he pretended to gaze up at the billboard advertisement, with its real Lautrec inspired drawings, he saw a matt black Z800e Kawasaki motorbike turn up the next street to the right. In the reflection of the door furthest to his left, he saw the original silver apple man cross to a grey Citroën that had pulled up on the far side of the boulevard. As he got into the front of the car, a new man got out of the rear. Jacob committed his shape, size and clothes to memory, then turned and continued on his way.

Just across from the Moulin Rouge, set in an island in the middle of the boulevard, an ornate metal sign with the word '*Métropolitain*' artistically depicted on it, arched over a flight of steps that disappeared below ground. There was a steady stream of people going down and a small knot of newly ascended people loitering at the top, getting their bearings. Jacob navigated his way around most, but stepped back to allow an elderly woman, and a much younger Asian woman, to gain the steps first.

When he descended he found himself in a circular ticket hall, similar to a London Tube station but different enough to be confusing. He didn't have to fake an unfamiliarity with the Métro system. In the few times he'd been in Paris before, he'd never used it. Attempting to comprehend the ticket machines set into the white brick walls, he struggled to find a language button that would transform the instructions to English. Eventually he gave up and took his place in the queue for the ticket booth behind the Asian woman he had allowed to go down the steps before him. As he stood behind her he placed his puzzle book and the copy of 'The Times' under his left arm. He patted the paper as if to ensure its safekeeping.

When the woman reached the ticket window, Jacob listened with pleasure to her melodically beautiful French. Peering over her shoulder he watched her place a €20 note on one side of a circular plate. The formidable looking lady behind the partition rotated the plate, took the note and in its place put a stack of white tickets. The plate spun again and the tickets were presented, ready to be taken. As the woman moved away from the window, one of the tickets fluttered down to the ground. Jacob nearly stooped to help her, but she had already knelt to the side and retrieved it, so he straightened back up. Stepping forward he bent his head so that his mouth was in front of the serrated plastic insert of the speech grill. The already stern looking ticket-lady adopted an even more severe countenance.

"Hi, can you help me please? I'd like to get to the Champs Élysées."

Even Jacob knew that his pronunciation had managed to butcher the words. To his ears it had sounded more like *'Sean's duh lease ee'* and to the ticket-lady it obviously sounded like someone was attacking the heart of the Republic. She glared at him and Jacob got the distinct impression that had the plastic grill not been in place she may have reached through and punched him. As it was she just glared at him before saying something in French with the delivery of a barking dog.

Jacob tried again, "I'm sorry, but I don't speak French. Can you tell me how much it is and how I get there?"

The ticket-lady heaved her shoulders and gave an audible sigh before saying in heavily accented English, "One euro eighty. Get off at Champs Élysées Clemenceau. There is a map on the wall."

Jacob felt annoyed, but he remembered the barman's advice on keeping a low profile. He put a €5 note on the turntable and in return received a single cardboard ticket, his change and another glare from the charming ticket-lady.

"Mercy buckets," he muttered. 'The French Tourist board called, they said you've missed your calling,' he thought, but didn't say as he walked over to the Métro map. A few minutes of looking at the coloured, numbered lines identified the station and how to reach it with only one change of train. He slowly traced the route with his finger, then retraced it to make sure. Finally he headed for the westbound Line-2.

The wide, double-sided space was much brighter than its London counterparts. There were also opposing direction trains running side-by-side, an interesting twist on what Jacob was used to. The eastbound train was just pulling away as he stepped onto the westbound platform. He looked about him, once more the interested tourist. Various international advertisements, similar in style to those on the London Tube decorated the walls, but beneath them, at irregular intervals, little outcrops of strangely shaped orange seats sprouted in groups of five. None of the relatively few passengers who stood waiting for the arrival of the next train used the seats. Jacob elected to stand as well. The information board suspended from the ceiling said the next train was due in three minutes. He clamped the puzzle book upright between his feet and unfurled his copy of 'The Times'. On the third turn of a page he glimpsed the man who had replaced silver apple standing at the far end of the platform. The diner from the Palace Café was further along. Jacob thought these guys were amateurish, then stopped himself mid-thought. 'That type of thinking is what caused the problems in Amsterdam. You switch on to these people or it all goes wrong again,' he told himself. However, he did admit that they could have learned a few things from the masterful way Tien had managed to establish where he was going next.

φ

Tien had picked up her dropped ticket, heard Jacob ask for his destination and then had descended down to the eastbound Line-2. She needed to get distance between herself, him and his followers and would take no further part in the surveillance, but it had been nice to see he was doing okay.

The train she took had barely picked up speed before it decelerated less than a minute later. When the doors opened she got off, climbed the exit steps from Pigalle station and found herself only a few hundred metres east of her original starting point on the Boulevard de Clichy. She reached for her phone and dialled Kara, Sammi, Chaz and Toby. As each answered she pressed 'add call' and once all four were on the line, pressed 'merge calls'. They were back to having linked communications.

"He's heading to Champs Élysées Clemenceau," she said, her pronunciation flawless and the memory of Jacob murdering the language made her smile.

"Great. Thanks for doing that," Kara said. "Just saves one of us having to ditch the bike gear yet."

"No problem."

"How'd it go?"

"Good. He saw me from the other side of the road and made it look smooth. I'm impressed, considering he's not really trained in any of this. Although his French needs a bit of work. I think the Académie Française would be mortified had they heard him. He has two tails in company."

"Yeah we saw them going down the steps. One popped back up and then the Citroën left, so at least we know where they're all destined for. He'll arrive before us, but so far he's been sensible. I was pleased he realised he was being followed before we even got to him. His wave-off when he first saw us outside the café was neatly managed."

"Yeah, he's doing well," Tien said, before adding, "Oh, one thing. He has a copy of 'The Times' with him."

"Mmm, bit weird," Toby said in reply. "It's not the usual thing my brother would be reading. What's with that?"

"Not sure, but he indicated it's important. You'll have to setup a drop for him."

"Okay," Kara said. "I'll work on it."

"Right, well I'm off back to the hotel, I'll see you all back there. Keep the line open."

"Will do," Kara said.

As Tien walked away, the to and fro chatter of Chaz, Sammi, Kara and Toby allowed her to mentally track the progress of both bikes into the city centre.

21

Jacob exited the Métro and turned the collar of his leather jacket up to fend off the drizzling rain and cold wind. He stopped at the top of the steps, disorientated by his immediate surroundings. The imposing statue of General de Gaulle was to his right, the larger-than-life bronze looking as if it was about to step from its plinth and continue striding down to the Place de la Concorde. A pedestrian crossing, seemingly in the perfect place to assist the General should he need it, was to the quarter-right, but directly in front of Jacob, where he had expected to see the broad avenue of the Champs Élysées, was a wall of white wood. It took him a few moments to realise he was looking at the rear of a long row of small cabins with gently pitching roofs.

He walked to the crossing and looked to the other side of the road. A similar line of wooden cabins stretched up and down the pavement. Despite the drizzle Jacob couldn't help but smile. A huge Christmas market had been erected along both sides of the road. Each cabin and stall had lights that weren't doing themselves justice in the greyness of the day. Jacob didn't doubt they would look spectacular at night. In the distance, on the other side of the road, he could make out the brightly painted, big-top-like roof of an old-fashioned carousel. The smell of freshly baked donuts, the sharper tang of roasting chestnuts and the heavy aroma of Glühwein defied the drizzle and filled his nostrils. He breathed in deeply.

Jacob was a sucker for Christmas. He knew it was because Toby, being the elder brother by seven years, had done such a good job of not spoiling it for him. All the Christmases he could remember as a small child, his big brother had been there, helping him leave out carrots for reindeers and milk and mince pies for Santa. Toby had never once tried to ruin the magic of it, even when he was in his early teens and probably had better things to do. Jacob's love for the season had been ingrained and Toby had played his part to perfection. A role he was getting to reprise with gusto now he was the father to a boy and two girls. Jacob, as the doting uncle, was always allowed to join in the fun and it all served to reinforce his love of the season. He was slightly startled to realise Christmas was only a month to the day away and knew he would struggle not to buy all manner of gifts in his walk through the fair. He decided that when the operation was over he was going to come straight back to Paris. As he set off towards the distant Arc de Triomphe he imagined, perhaps, maybe, the possibility of asking Tien if she'd like to come back with him.

The cabins ended when he reached the intersection of Franklin D. Roosevelt Avenue. He also realised that the Métro station of the same name, and another he could see further ahead, were much closer to the main shopping area of the Champs Élysées. The charming ticket-lady had probably sent him to Clemenceau in the hope he would have a longer walk in the cold. As it was, Jacob considered that by showing him the Christmas Market, she had done him a favour.

He used the next pedestrian crossing to negotiate the ten lanes of traffic and walked until he came to the first chain store that he recognised. A quick ten minutes in 'Gap' and he had his first purchase. Or the first five, as he liked the style of T-shirt he found and bought one in each available colour. Taking a roundabout route through the shop he caught the man from the Citroën paying close attention to a rail of winter jackets. Jacob blithely ignored him and went to the counter.

Back out on the street, he checked his watch and saw it was just after eleven. He walked past the Disney Store, struggling to resist the temptation of the window display with effort, crossed over the Rue du Colisée and entered the next café he came to. Ordering more coffee and managing to point at a ham and cheese sandwich, he settled down at a corner table by the window and resumed his pondering of 'The Times' crossword. From the corner of his eye he saw two of his watchers move into oversight positions on the street outside. Another man, different to those he had seen before, but definitely part of the surveillance team, and so had to be the fourth follower Kara had indicated was out there, entered the café and sat at a table in the corner.

A half hour later and following a trip to the café's toilet, Jacob resumed his meanderings, criss-crossing the ten lanes of traffic and pottering in and around various shops. The tails stayed constant, less than invisible but achieving their main goal which he was sure was to monitor his every move. Even after his quick nature break at the café, the new man, whom he had uninventively named 'Four' had gone into the facilities, no doubt to check Jacob hadn't scrawled a message on the walls. The Flight Path organisation might well have been efficient at getting people out of countries, but it seemed they didn't instinctively trust their cargo.

After another two hours, he had only added a pair of sandals and some swimming shorts to his haul of T-shirts. He was slowly realising a Parisian winter was not the best season to shop for warm-climate holiday clothes. He was also becoming anxious that unlike his obvious tails, he had only seen Kara and Toby when they'd pulled up on their bike next to the café and only glimpsed Sammi and Chaz on their bike turning up the street next to the Moulin Rouge. Time was running out and he needed to get a message to them.

By now he was two thirds of the way towards the Arc de

Triomphe and was considering doubling back to one of the larger malls just off the avenue. He paused on the side of the kerb and waited for the Parisian version of a bin-lorry to trundle past. Once it was clear, he found himself staring directly at a Marks and Spencer storefront. Heading into it, arm in arm, with not a trace of motorcycle apparel anywhere, were Sammi and Chaz.

Jacob entered the store and went upstairs to the menswear section. Approaching the counter, he spoke to the attractive sales assistant who, according to the two badges she wore, was called Marielle and spoke English. He told her what he needed and she responded in beautifully accented tones, happily taking his previous shopping bags for safe keeping and pointing him towards the rear of the shop for the more summery items still on display. With just his much folded copy of the newspaper in his jacket pocket, Jacob set about fulfilling his shopping needs. He visited the fitting rooms a few times and when happy with an article, took it back to Marielle who placed it on a small, but growing pile. After less than an hour he had everything he needed including a couple of pairs of lightweight trousers, a few light shirts, one pair of beige cargo shorts, a full set of toiletries, a small suitcase and a backpack.

Looking about the racks for any final purchases, he noticed that 'Four' was positioned perfectly to cover the floor space and had a direct line of sight to the fitting rooms. He was quite impressed with this guy. He hadn't even noticed him in the shop until then. About to return to the sales counter, Jacob was relieved to see Sammi and Chaz rising up on the escalator from the ground floor. Sammi, laden with Marks and Spencer shopping bags, was hanging on to Chaz's arm like a grateful recipient of gifts.

"Oh honey," she said in a remarkable rendition of a New York accent, pitched just too loud for conservative European tastes, "you are simply the best. The best."

Chaz patted her arm and smiled.

Breaking from his grasp and pawing a rack of expensive looking knitwear, she added, "But seriously hon, we need to get you one of these here sweaters. Look, at that, would you believe it? It's made from a goat. Oh! This would look soooo good on you. Your cheek bones will just explode."

Chaz responded with a non-committal grunt.

"You have just got to go and try that on. I absolutely insist."

Chaz made a show of looking at his watch.

"Oh honey, don't give me that old, 'we don't have time'. Go and try it on. You'll look drop-dead gorgeous."

Chaz dithered next to the knitwear.

Jacob strolled over to the sales counter and saw that Marielle had a fixed expression on her face. He rolled his eyes, then glanced sideways at Sammi. Marielle broke into a grin and shied away, so as not to be seen by her new customers.

"Marielle," he said leaning on the counter, "you've been great. I'm nearly finished, just one last thing. Do you think I could try on another pair of shorts?"

"Why certainly. Which do you wish for?"

"They were down on the end, quite bright."

"But yes, a good choice," she lied smoothly, for Jacob knew they were anything but. He imagined that particular pair were still on the rack in mid-winter for a reason. He surmised they'd still be there next mid-winter too.

Marielle handed him a single article token for the fitting room and Jacob set off, picking up the fluorescent pink cargo shorts on his way past.

A few minutes later he came back out, hung the offending items back on the rack and returned to the counter.

"No, Monsieur?" Marielle asked.

"No, Marielle. Sadly too small for me," he said patting his tummy.

She giggled as she prepared his bill.

Once out on the street, with all his purchases packed into the suit case and backpack, Jacob walked to the George V Métro station, only a couple of hundred metres away. Prior to descending back underground he decided to stop into a final café and treat himself to some decadent looking pastries. Once more he took a seat next to the window.

He retrieved his copy of 'The Times' from his pocket, turned to the back pages and read the sports news. When he had finished his coffee and a second chocolate eclair, he paid his bill and walked straight to one of the numerous waste bins affixed to the pavement of the Champs Élysées. Jacob understood why modern cities had replaced ornate bins with clear plastic bags attached to simple metal hoops. The obvious advantage for security over style made sense. In this case, it was exactly what he needed. Even better he thought, as his act of dropping his copy of 'The Times' into it was done in clear view of Citroën man, watching from an adjacent bench.

Jacob looked up in the direction of the Arc de Triomphe, shielding his eyes from the drizzle that was beginning to grow heavier. He looked from the arch to the entrance of the Métro. To anyone watching him, it looked like he was contemplating more sightseeing against the potential of not getting any wetter. In the end, the tourist lost out and he walked to the station entrance. As he was about to descend the steps he turned a full circle to look one last time at the broad majesty of the Champs Élysées.

φ

Chaz and Sammi continued their amble around the menswear department and both watched the fourth member of the French surveillance team go into the fitting room area after Jacob had left. He didn't even bother to take a garment in with him as an attempt to cover his real intentions.

Before he had reappeared Sammi had already opened the side pocket of the pink shorts and removed a single page of 'The Times'. She folded it and put it in her bag. Then she and Chaz went to the counter and spoke to Marielle about the benefits of a plain cream Cashmere sweater. By the time they had finished, the French man had departed.

"Kara, we've got it," Chaz said as he and Sammi exited the store and made their way back to the underground carpark in the Rue de Berri.

"What is it?" Kara said from her vantage point in the motorcycle parking bay on the corner of Rue Quentin-Bauchart.

"Appears our Jacob has being doing the Times Crossword. What's more he seems to have completed it, but it reads like gibberish and I haven't got a clue what it says."

"Okay, get back to the hotel. Jacob's just gone into the Métro but gave the signal that he was heading back to his start location. His little band of followers have gone with him but I don't think we need to expose ourselves. We'll pick him up back in Montmartre. Sammi, you get back to the van and set up a watch on the restaurant again. The rest of us will try and figure out the crossword puzzle."

"You mean we're going to give it straight to Tien," Sammi said as she was getting back into her leathers.

"Yeah, that's what I meant," Kara said.

22

18th Arrondissement, Paris.

The crossword page was on the bed of Kara's room and at an arbitrary first glance looked like a properly completed puzzle. A closer examination revealed it was filled in with a random collection of letters that didn't seem to make a single legible word in any of the available spaces.

"Tien?" Kara said.

Tien lifted the page and went across to the small writing desk set to the side of the room. Taking the hotel's thin notepad, she copied down all the letters from the crossword. The rest of the team were quiet as she bracketed the page with her elbows and leant her head in her hands. After a few minutes she began writing again, then paused, her pencil hovering. Another five minutes ticked by before she smiled, looked around at Toby and said, "I see what he's done. Your brother's quite clever, isn't he?"

"Yeah, for an ex-gunner," he laughed.

"Well, ex-gunner or not, he's been commendably logical," she said, flipping another notepad page and writing more words. After a few more minutes she stopped and her look of concentration was replaced with one of concern, "Oh no way is that happening."

"What is it?" Kara asked, "Have you deciphered it?"

"Yes, but I don't like his message." She held up the note-pad and pointed to the first block, "These are the across words if you follow the clue spaces."

mtiinodn   ewrasr
ymwahteerseadfe
tsteosneic   guhr
eexetfr   leimgeh
sotcmao   tnitohn
nios   winoenvmea
roopcmeoendiitn
dkehse   tairntas

She pointed to the next block, "And these are the down words."

meyette, imw, nvhpotttmd, dcehn
wleo, ardruyglokm, rieurrh, eraitlst
tixftuodoge, hirienpdar, rionieed, ssnrrod, ncatnrs, oseea, ycrs,
idt

"Yep, still makes no sense," Kara said.

"I thought maybe it was a replacement cypher but which-ever way you read it there are just too many double letter combinations to be sensible. So, then I just wrote all of the letters in sequence, line by line, and got this."

mtiinodnewrasremvcelriymwahteerseadfeephaoru
tsteosneicguhrtitthyreexetfrleimgehftisrlsotcmaotnitohn
sudnekcnioswinoenvmeardyesptroopcmeoendiitnogrdeadr
dkehsetairntas

Kara peered at the letters, "Mmm, if we were in parlia-ment, I'd be saying that I refer you to my previous answer."

"Well, if you ignore the word and line breaks and run

everything together in a continuous loop, then extract every second letter, you get this," Tien said and flipped to the next page.

MtIiNoDnEwRaSrEmVcElRiYmWaHtEeRsEa
DfEePhAoRuTsTeOsNeIcGuHrTi
TtHyReExEtFrLeImGeHfTiSr
LsOtCmAoTnItOhNs
UdNeKcNiOsWiNo
EnVmEaRdYeSpTrOoPc
MeOeNdIiTnOgRdEaDr
DkEhSeTaIrNtAs

minders everywhere depart tonight three flights
location unknown every stop monitored destination
warm climate safe house security extreme first months
decision made proceeding dark hearts

"There's no way we let him leave to go somewhere we have no idea about, without any communications and with no way to back him up," Tien said.

Kara was surprised by Tien's tone. The calm and relaxed manner that normally ruled her every word and action seemed strained. "Okay," she said, somewhat hesitantly. "Chaz what do you think?"

Chaz sat down on the bed and looked up at Kara, "It's a high risk proposition. If they're going to fly him here, there and everywhere, then we'll have no idea where he ends up. We can't hope to just follow him to the airport and buy a ticket for the flight he checks-in for. It's unlikely to work and we'd be relying on luck to get close enough. We could easily lose him at the first hurdle. Then add another two flights and he could be in deepest Mongolia. We won't know and like Tien says, he won't have comms. If things go bad he'll be completely alone."

"Granted," Kara agreed. "But he must have a concept of how he's going to get in touch with us. He wouldn't just launch into the unknown, not from what I've seen today. He was switched on and a good, smart operator. I th-"

"That's as maybe," Tien interrupted. "But what we're contemplating is on a different level. He knew we were nearby today. This is different. He'll be completely on his own,"

Kara wasn't too sure how to respond. She was aware that Tien was still holding the pencil, but in a clenched fist. As Kara considered how to continue, Tien did it for her.

"Sammi, what are your thoughts?" she said towards the radio mic.

"I'll be honest, if it was one of us, or the O'Neill brothers making the call, I wouldn't question it. But you all know we haven't had the depth of experience with Jacob, or you Toby. No offence, but is he up to it?"

Sammi's question caused Kara, Chaz and Tien to turn towards Toby who sat in a chair next to the bed. He looked relaxed. "I'm naturally biased," he said, "but yes, he's capable. What you saw today is my brother doing what he does best. Adapting, learning on the job, becoming capable in techniques he's only just been shown. I know we haven't done much in-depth stuff with you guys previously, and it's good that you're looking out for him, but the conversation's wasted."

"Why's that?" Tien said before anyone else could respond.

"He wrote dark hearts, didn't he?"

"Yes," Tien confirmed, looking back at the notepad.

"Then it's a done deal. He's going to do it and us wondering if we think it's a good idea doesn't matter."

Tien glanced at Kara but she just shrugged back at her, "I don't understand. Isn't he just meaning the men he's with are bad men, with dark hearts?" Tien asked.

Toby shook his head, "Nope. Dark hearts means something specific to Jacob."

"What?" Tien said, her obvious frustration more than apparent in her tone.

"There's a bit of a story to it."

"Probably best we hear it," Kara said.

Toby sat forward, "You've all done basic training in the military and you all know how seemingly pointless it is. But then, when you graduate and look back, you see the reason for the running and marching and cleaning. Especially the cleaning. What seems completely useless for military training is actually all about team work, attention to detail and building moral character."

"Yeah, but how is this relevant?" Tien said, not attempting to mask her growing agitation.

Unseen by her, Chaz and Kara swapped a look.

"Well, after basic I got sent to RAF Honington for the Trainee Gunner's course. Chaz, Sammi and Kara know about it Tien, but the closest I can put it for someone who was army, like you; well, the TG has a reputation. Not as bad as P-company, but it's still known for being a hard course. Physical, tough."

"Where's this going Toby?" Tien interrupted.

"Tien," Kara said.

"Yes."

Kara walked over and knelt beside Tien's chair. She reached out and took the pencil from her friend's still clenched fist, "Let Toby finish his story, eh?"

Tien looked down and blushed. "Oh. Yes. Sorry. Sorry Toby."

"No problem," he said, before continuing, "Anyway, as well as the physical stuff we did all the normal crap, including a bull-night every week. You know, cleaning everything and getting ready for an inspection the next morning."

They all nodded, Tien included.

"The block I was in had white tiles in its ablution areas. They had to be spotless, but in the middle of a set of six washbasins, one tile had a series of dark smudges in the shape of three small hearts. They were rough, raised up on the surface and felt like tar or rubber had been melted onto the tile. The guy who was on that section of the block got torn a new arsehole on the first inspection. We all had to do extra physical training that day and the next. All the blame was put on to him and everyone was left in no doubt that if he fucked up again there'd be hell to pay the next week." Toby paused and smiled around at them. Kara was pleased to see Tien reciprocate his expression as they all recalled similar experiences.

"Needless to say, on the next bull-night we all pitched in to try to get those damn marks off the tile. We failed and we went for more long runs. It went on like that for the first six weeks. Every week, another inspection, every week, more long runs. I think we must have used every chemical under the sun, but all to no avail. Then, we moved accommodation blocks and the dark smudges were a distant memory."

"I want to know who comes up with shit like that. There must be a secret school where military instructors lie around thinking up things to clean," Chaz said.

Tien leaned forward as if she was going to interrupt, but Kara put her hand on her knee and she relaxed back into the chair. "Go on Toby," Kara said.

"Jacob joined up a good while after me, but the training was much the same. He phoned one night, early on in his course, and somewhere in the midst of the call he asked if I had any good tips for getting dirt off a tile. I asked him why and he told me about the dark smudges. Obviously I remembered them, laughed a lot and told him my story. He said exactly the same was happening to his course. Then I told him what the instructors had told us at the end of our Passing Out Parade. Back when the block was being built a box of tiles had turned up with a design flaw in them. Just one box, but every tile had three little heart shaped smudges that looked like a stain. Some bastard thought it'd be a great idea to put one in each ablution area in the new recruit's block. The rest as they say was history."

Kara, Chaz and even Sammi on the other end of the radio laughed along with Toby. Tien merely said, "So?"

This time Kara watched Toby look at Tien. She wondered if he'd seen the obvious.

"So, I told Jacob and said that he and his mates could save a lot of time by not trying to get the marks out. He'd be a hero. There was a long pause on the line and then my kid brother, who had just turned eighteen said, 'Nah. I don't think I will.' I asked him why not and he said that those dark hearts were making a loose bunch of kids into a team. He knew, even then, at that age, that it was way more than cleaning. He ended the call by saying, 'Those tiles will help us help each other, even when things seem bleak.' I was pretty proud of him that night. Still am."

Kara looked to Tien. She had bowed her head and was smiling.

"Good on him," Chaz said.

"Yeah, it was good," Toby agreed. "But the reason he still uses the phrase with me is because of what he did next." Toby's face had broken into a grin.

Tien looked up and tilted her head just enough to prompt Toby to continue.

"On the morning of the last inspection of his Phase One training, their CO walked into the ablutions with the Sergeant in tow, ready to deliver the reaming that was to be expected, but the tile was a glistening, unblemished white. There were a lot of double takes and stuttered umms and aahs, but they couldn't say anything. Jacob and his mates had chiselled out the flawed tile and replaced it."

Chaz gave a cheer, "Ha, brilliant, I love it."

"I went to his Passing Out Parade and at the end of it, when the students were all together for their final photograph with the instructors, and all the friends and families were looking on, Jacob presented his CO with a small parcel. He said it was the flawed tile and it needed to go back on the wall to help the next guys coming through. Then he said, what he and his mates had done on the final inspection was proof that however difficult a task, however bleak the prospect of success, hard work, a dose of ingenuity and a good team would always prevail over dark hearts. It became his personal motto when things got tough. 'Dark hearts' for Jacob means he won't give up. Ever."

The room was quiet for a few moments. Kara looked sideways to Tien and saw the sadness in her eyes.

Sammi, at the far end of the street and not witness to the room said, "Well, if that's what he thinks then I don't see we can do anything but back his decision."

"Agreed," said Chaz.

"Agreed," Kara said. "Tien?"

Tien just nodded and got up. "I'll be back in a minute." She lifted the smartcard to her hotel room and left.

When the door shut, Toby asked, "Is Tien okay?"

"Yep," Kara answered. "She's fine. I just think, ah, never mind. Yeah she's good. Right," Kara said, rising from her kneeling position, "If we're going to support this mad dash into the unknown, what do we need to do?"

The next fifteen minutes passed with the four of them throwing ideas around with regards to how they could best help Jacob, when he finally figured out a way to let them know where he had ended up.

As they were agreeing on a course of action, there was a knock at the door. Chaz answered it and let Tien in. She had a single sheet of paper in her hand.

"Ah, Tien, good timing," Kara said. "We reckon Chaz is right. The chances of getting on the same flight as Jacob is unlikely, so we're going to trail him to the airport and try, but if that doesn't work out we'll head back to London. Wait until he contacts us, then go straight to Heathrow and take the first available flight to wherever he is. What do you think?"

"Shit no!"

Kara saw Chaz's head whip round so fast she thought it might detach. She heard Sammi let out a small gasp, audible enough to be picked up by her voice-activated mic. Even Toby, who hadn't worked with Tien for as long as the others, looked surprised. 'You should be' Kara thought. 'I've worked with this girl for almost a decade, she lost her hand in a firefight that she pulled me out of and I've never once heard her swear. Shit is huge'. What she managed to say was, "Oh, okay. Umm, what do you suggest?"

"If we do what you said it could be hours, maybe even a day or more before we get a plane to the right part of the world. He'll have disappeared again. We need to be in a position to track him when he gets off at his final stop. I think we use some of that precious money we have and charter this." Tien handed the piece of paper to Kara.

"Wow, nice. Umm, yeah, okay by me. How much?"

"To have it on standby for five days and for it to go anywhere on the planet and back again, that much," she pointed to the six figures scribbled at the foot of the page.

"Oh. Okay. Is that in pounds?"

"Yes, is that a problem? It's not like we can't aff-"

Kara held her hands up and Tien stopped. "I'm not arguing Tien. I think it's a great idea. Have you already booked it?"

"No," she said and looked shocked at Kara's assumption. "We need to agree on it."

Kara stepped forward and gave Tien a tight hug. She gently whispered, so the men didn't hear, "Of course I agree. It doesn't matter how much it costs. We'll be there for him."

Tien squeezed her back, "Thanks."

Sammi's disembodied voice asked, "Umm, someone want to tell me what's going on?"

Kara let Tien go and referred to the sheet of paper in her hand, "We're going to stay in Paris Sammi, and hire a corporate jet. It means we can leave at short notice and get to wherever we need to quickly. I think it's a great idea and by the look of what Tien's just handed me, it's going to be way nicer than commercial cattle-class and definitely better than the back of a C-130."

"Good. Glad to hear it. Always thought I should join the jet set. So what else do we need to do?"

Kara sat down at the desk and picked up the notepad Tien had written on. "He doesn't know the final location but he does say it's going to be a warm climate. I've looked at the countries that don't have an extradition treaty with the UK. Apart from Belarus and a few others, the majority fit that criteria. They range from desert to jungle so we'll need some different gear. If we're going to stay in Paris I'll get Dinger to bring what's useful from Camden and he can go shopping for the rest."

"So he's coming back on the op?" Sammi asked.

"No reason why not. We'll relocate nearer to," Kara paused and looked again at the details of the aircraft charter, "Le Bourget airfield. That's where the charter company operates from. We won't be exposed to the same people from then on so it'll be okay."

"Are we going to need weapons?" Chaz asked.

"I hope not, 'cos even in a private jet, I don't think they're going to allow us to bring them," Toby said.

Kara thought Chaz had made an interesting point. She was about to ask Tien her thoughts when Sammi came on the air again.

"We might have to answer that later. Black Peugeot, three male occupants, just pulled-up, rear entrance to restaurant. Two passengers have gone inside. The driver hasn't moved and the engine is running. Wait."

Kara reached for a small backpack.

23

Jacob had rung the bell to the rear entrance of the restaurant on his return and been greeted by the small man.

"Ah Mr London. Welcome back."

Jacob frowned in a way that the small man found amusing.

He gave his deep, discordant laugh, "That's you Jacob. You're Mr London. Follow me." He led Jacob back up to the fourth floor apartment.

Once inside, the small man took Jacob's case and backpack. "You don't mind if I take a look at what you bought?" he asked, handing over a beige envelope.

"No, not at all," Jacob said, opening the envelope and finding a New Zealand passport, a collection of bank cards, a UK driving license, a Nectar card and a small photograph of a beautiful looking Asian woman. His heart lurched. He knew instantly it wasn't Tien, but the woman's complexion, the shape of her mouth and the long, straight dark hair were so similar as to be disconcerting. He held the photo and felt his heart beginning to race. Thoughts jammed in to his head, 'Had they seen her at the Métro station? Was his cover blown? Was

205

she alright? Had they gotten to her?' As this last one occurred to him he felt nauseous.

"Oh, I see you've found her," the small man said.

"Uh, what?" Jacob asked, completely numb with the thought she was in harm's way again.

"The photo. Beautiful isn't she?"

"What the fuck's this all about?" Jacob was no longer the confused fugitive. His anger was clear and he realised the look on his face alone had startled the small man.

"Hey, hey, calm down. It's all okay Jacob. It's just a photo. It's like the cards and the driving license. It all adds texture to your wallet. To you. You know?"

"No, I don't know," Jacob said, still angry.

The small man sat down on the edge of the bed, "When you go through security at airports, you need to appear like the average man. Like your luggage. You need luggage to look normal. You need things in your wallet to look normal. The photo's just an addition. She's meant to be a girlfriend. We've given her a name and an identity. Even an address. She's the reason you're travelling to your first stop. You need to fill in arrival documentation and it asks for things like where are you staying and why you are there. Do you see?"

Jacob nodded, trying to rein his emotions in, "Sorry. It's just… well, it's…" he paused and tried to think of a reason he would have become so angry. He fell back on something Chaz had said about mixing lies with lots of truth. "I'm sorry, she just looks like someone. Someone you shouldn't know about. You said last night you didn't want to know about why I was running."

"Oh! Oh hell! I'm sorry Jacob. It wasn't meant to give you a shock. I didn't, I mean, I don't know. She's just a random photo we took from a catalogue. I had no idea."

"No, you couldn't have known. I'm sorry. Really, I am. I'm sorry for reacting the way I did," Jacob sat down on the chair next to the window and looked at the photo again.

"Are you going to be okay with it?" the small man asked. "It's just I don't have any other photos with me that we could use."

Jacob decided to try to be as appalling sick as the men he was dealing with, "No. I'll be fine. I mean, this one is a good bit older in all honesty." He ended with a laugh that the small man joined in with.

"Oh, that's very good. I like it Jacob. Well done."

Jacob thought he would enjoy seeing this bespectacled, little bastard swinging at the end of a rope. He used the thought to maintain his smile.

Crisis over, the small man went back to looking in the suitcase. Jacob noticed that he was taking each item out, removing the price tags and other labels that identified it as 'just bought'. He then folded the clothing and packed it neatly back in the case. Except for one set of underwear, socks, a T-shirt, the light jumper and the light jacket. These he set carefully to one side of the bed. Jacob turned his attention back to the envelope.

He emptied its contents out and picked up the passport. Turning to the back, he found a picture of himself with the name of Jacob London, born in Auckland on the Fourth of July, 1989. The cards showed the same name and the driving license had the addition of a home address in Grays, Essex, England. All the items bore the same signature.

"This is all nice gear you bought," the small man said, zipping up the suitcase and the backpack. "You did well lad. It looks exactly like what it should."

"Thanks. It wasn't a bad day. Nice to not have to be looking over my shoulder to see if the cops were there," Jacob said before holding up the passport. "So, I'm a New Zealander from Essex?"

"That's right. You lived in England for a few years. Hence your accent."

"And the signature?"

"You'll have to practise but I wouldn't get too stressed. Even those people who try to compare a signature haven't got a clue. If it's close enough, then it's close enough."

"What does Jacob London do for a living?" Jacob asked.

"Whatever you do. No point making up stuff we don't need to."

"And this address in Essex, it's real?"

"Well Maple Road exists, but there's no actual number sixty-nine. If you Google it though, it'll show up. It'll even put a flag on the map. That's just a quirk of the system."

"And I was born on the Fourth of July. Really?"

The small man smiled. "It's easy to remember. Like the number sixty-nine. We just need it to be enough to get you through a few simple questions if you get asked them."

"That's why you wanted to know if I'd been born in July?"

"Yes. It would be a coincidence but a complication we could do without. Dates of birth and real names are the keys to most police databases worldwide. If we avoid showing up on them, then we have the advantage."

"And these?" Jacob held up two debit cards, two credit cards and the Nectar card.

"They're purely for appearances. People carry cards and a wallet without a collection of bank cards and other cards looks strange. You've got enough to look right, but sadly there's no money and no points on them."

Jacob took out his wallet and slipped all the cards, the license and the photo of the woman inside. "You're right. This feels a lot more like my wallet did before I had to ditch everything."

"You see," the small man said, cheered by the recognition finally being shown for his work. "This is what we do Jacob and we're good at it. Everything will be fine." He checked his watch, "Now, you have just enough time to get a shower and change clothes. Wear the shoes and jeans you have on but put this lot on," he said pointing to the clothes he had laid out on the bed, Just leave what you take off and we'll get rid of it."

Jacob looked at his leather jacket, draped over the back of the chair, "I need to leave my jacket?"

"Yes, especially the jacket. It makes you look like you. Anyway, where you're going you're not going to need it." The small man grinned at Jacob's look of disappointment. "It's okay Jacob, there will be compensations. I promise. Especially if you…" he trailed off.

"If what?"

"Well… I shouldn't say, but that photo in the wallet?"

Jacob nodded slowly.

"Let's just say if you like that look, you'll be pleasantly surprised. Now go! Get ready!"

Before Jacob could ask anymore the small man left the room.

φ

Showered and changed he was putting his shoes on when there was a knock at the bedroom door. Again, without waiting, the small man came in. Behind him were two other men. One was in his early twenties, average height, average build, his long brown hair secured in a ponytail, he wore black boots, black jeans and a heavy black duffle coat. His only distinguishing feature was a set of three silver loop earrings through his right eyebrow. The other man, older, was Jacob's height and heavily built. Sturdy was the word Jacob thought of. His hair was similar in length to the barman's. In fact, as Jacob looked more closely at him, he decided there was a definite family resemblance. He wore brown boots, blue jeans, and no coat, just a heavy dark brown jumper, the sleeves of which were pushed up. Unlike his potential brother he had no tattoos, faded or otherwise, but he did wear a small gold hoop earring in his left ear.

The two new arrivals flanked the small man. "This is Jean-Paul," he said, indicating the younger of the two, "and this is Thierry." As if on cue Thierry folded his arms and gave what he must have thought was his best, most intimidating stare. Jacob saw he wore two gold rings on his right hand; a medium sized square cut, black onyx set in gold on his ring finger and the other, also gold, also square but larger and with a diamond solitaire set centrally, on his index finger.

Jacob gave a weak wave to the men.

"You're leaving now," the small man continued. "There's a car outside. When you get to the airport Thierry will accompany you. You'll travel together. When you get to the next place, Thierry will hand you over to the next courier team."

Jacob struggled to keep his alarm and frustration hidden. His plan for communicating back to Tien and Kara was dependent on not having a minder in the air. He had to try to dissuade the small man. "Oh really, that's so much trouble to go to. Surely that's not necessary. I can co-"

"Now, now Jacob. You have paid and this is what we do. Besides, it's safer this way."

Jacob wondered how much more a real fugitive would protest. He decided to switch tack, "It's just, almost like, you don't trust me."

"I trust you Jacob. But those…" He pointed up with his finger as he had done the night before.

Jacob filled in, "The higher-ups?"

"Exactly, the higher-ups. They don't trust anyone. Nothing personal. Just safer."

Jacob knew it was a lost cause. He managed a shrug, "I see. Well, I suppose it makes sense. Thank you, it's kind of you Thierry."

Thierry moved his head the tiniest fraction which Jacob figured was his way of saying, 'Don't mention it'.

The small man reached forward and shook Jacob's hand, "Great, well, here, Jean-Paul, take Jacob's bags and let's get going."

φ

"We're rolling. Black Peugeot, I'm on point, north on Rue Damremont," Sammi called as she scrambled into the driver's seat and pulled the van out into the traffic flow.

"They're on it Sammi," Tien called as the others made for the vehicles. "Swapping to telephones, and I'll coordinate them into the chase. How is it out there?"

"Sun's dipping rapidly which is good, Should be dark before much longer. What I need are eyes on me to clear my back."

"They'll be minutes out Sammi, hang tight."

As it was, it took six minutes for Chaz, on the Z800e Kawasaki, to weave his way through heavy traffic and pick up Sammi, less than three kilometres from the restaurant. A series of turns, combined with narrow streets and rush hour congestion had slowed the progress of both her and the Peugeot. Toby, on the other bike, arrived a few seconds later. With the sky blackening and the Peugeot slowing to turn off the Boulevards des Maréchaux,

Sammi pulled out of the pursuit. "He's on the on-ramp of the highway, Tien. Looks like he's going to Charles de Gaulle Airport. Chaz and Toby, I'm gone, all yours."

Tien routed Kara, in the BMW Four-series, to the Place Auguste Baron. She paced her driving by Chaz's non-stop commentary on the road signs and distance markers he was passing and intercepted the pursuit seamlessly twelve kilometres later. "Chaz, how's it looking?"

The Bluetooth mic and earpiece, Jerry-rigged to fit inside the bike helmet, worked well enough but the roar of the powerful Kawasaki engine meant Chaz had to shout his answer, "Good Kara. He's clear. He has no other cars providing cover. They're running solo."

"Okay, I'll take it from here. I'd say it's almost certain he's going to Charles de Gaulle, so you and Toby get ready."

"Roger that," Chaz yelled and first he, closely followed by Toby, powered past her.

Kara was left to maintain the pursuit alone. It called for considerable effort and concentration as twilight had given way to darkness and all three lanes of the motorway, although congested, were fairly free-flowing. She had to balance the need to identify and keep in contact with the target, against the risk of getting too close.

After a further five kilometres, the Peugeot made the turn for the airport and although the traffic was still significant, it had thinned considerably. Kara allowed some more distance and a few more cars to get between her and Jacob.

"Chaz, Toby, we've just pulled off to the airport. According to my satnav, I've still got seven clicks to run before I get there. Have just passed a large sign for the Hyatt Regency. Where are you?"

Chaz's voice was clearer and the background noise much less, "Just keep coming, we're in the Total service station, about two minutes ahead."

The traffic was slowing and bunching and the two minutes took nearer four, but as she passed the service station she saw Chaz's Kawasaki, with Toby riding pillion, come up the on-ramp and join the main road.

"Kara, we're two cars behind you," Toby called.

"Roger that, seen."

The road followed a long right-hand turn and then straightened out, becoming much more brightly lit. Kara allowed another few cars to get between her and the Peugeot. The bike also slowed considerably and fell back. Multiple off-ramps, on-ramps and side lanes of traffic appeared and disappeared and Kara, with one eye on her dashboard satnav display, wondered how anyone had ever managed to build such a complex series of roads and interchanges. Her leftmost lane gently peeled away and the now narrowed carriageway, down to just two lanes, went under a series of bridges. Kara remembered a photograph she had once seen of aircraft taxying across bridges with cars passing underneath. She wondered if it had been here. She got her answer when the distinctive nose of a 747 peeked into view above her. Markings to her immediate left indicated a widening of the road into three lanes again.

"Decision time coming up," she said as they passed under a sign that pointed Terminal One and Three traffic to the left and Terminal Two to the right. The Peugeot held its position in what was now the middle lane. Kara slowed more to give herself the most room and the least need for a violent manoeuvre whatever way the Peugeot went, but there was no need. As the newly appeared left hand lane veered away to the other terminals, the middle and right lanes turned in a wide sweep towards Terminal 2 and the Peugeot went with them. The road ducked under another taxiway bridge with multiple concrete supports, testament to a lot of built-in redundancy, or the overly cautious mind of an overly paranoid engineer.

A sweeping left hand turn brought her up onto an elevated section of road. It gave the most incredible views of even more complex road interchanges, backed by an ocean of concrete, lit by hundreds of gantry lights. Aircraft stretched as far as she could see, taxiing, or parked nose-on to gates. The Peugeot moved into the left lane and Kara followed suit.

She passed terminal buildings to the right and left before following the Peugeot past an unusual, wedge-shaped hotel, lit up like a cruise liner set in the middle of the carriageways. Distracted by its strangeness, she almost missed the Peugeot moving across to the exit lane for Terminal 2E's drop-off point.

"Chaz, Toby, you ready?"

"Yep, we have you."

The Peugeot slowed and went through one of three automatic security gates to the set-down area. Kara still had five cars between her and the target, so by the time she got through, three men had already stepped out of the Peugeot and were standing at its open boot. Pulling in five bays back from them, Kara watched Jacob lift out a suitcase and swing a backpack onto his shoulder. The older of the other two men did likewise.

She switched off the BMW, stepped out and went to the rear of the car. Opening the boot she lifted out her own small backpack and waited, watching Jacob up ahead. Before he and his new companions had made the entrance to the terminal she heard the bike pull up behind her. She handed the car keys to Toby and set off to follow Jacob.

The first thing she noticed once inside the building was the number of heavily armed security personnel visible in every direction. There was a majority of blue-clad police, but here and there were small patrols of camouflage-wearing army personnel. She recognised the red berets of the 11th Parachute Brigade and considered that the French were certainly making a robust response to the terrible attacks that had occurred.

As one of the patrols passed by she saw Jacob, flanked by the other men, move towards the check-in area for Air France. She followed along, casual, yet direct, mirroring the demeanour of almost every other traveller in the terminal, barring those few who rushed about, evidently late. The majority of people were all walking in the same direction, but occasionally she had to sidestep those who elected to go against the consensus, or those who determined it was a good idea to stop right in the middle of the thoroughfare and check their luggage for something or other.

Ahead she saw a long row of check-in desks, perhaps forty or more, each with a high-mounted display screen, a single seat and a small gap where luggage would be placed for weighing and tagging. Kara could see most of the desks were not staffed, the seats empty, the screens either blank or displaying a static Air France logo. Only half a dozen or so desks at the far end were open and she reckoned it would be easy to identify Jacob's flight from where he queued up. If she followed that with a quick trip to the Air France ticket sales counter, she might just be in luck.

Her luck took an immediate blow when Jacob, halfway to the desks, had his elbow tugged by the man to his right and was steered towards an angled row of baggage drop-off counters. Kara looked at their suitcases and could see white labels with barcodes printed on them hanging from the handles. She took out her phone, the line still live, "Tien. Look up Air France check-in procedures. Find out if you can home print your boarding pass and baggage tags."

"On it."

Kara angled her path to swing outwards and approach Jacob from his rear-left quarter. As he was carrying his suitcase in his left hand, she figured, if it was a baggage label, then that would give her the best chance to see it up close.

"Kara, yes. You can print it all out and check-in online.

Why, what's going on?"

"I think they've done all of that. Have you got a picture of one?"

"Yes, I'm looking at it now."

"Is the three-letter airport code printed on it?"

"Yes, but small. Really small. It's set to the top of a big barcode."

"Great, I'll just have to get closer."

"Be careful."

"Always."

Kara kept the phone up to her ear, helping to mask her face and was within ten strides of the three men when the one to Jacob's right again tugged his arm and turned them both to the first bag-drop point. At the same time the man to Jacob's left, the younger of the two men, wearing a duffle coat and with his hair tied back in a ponytail, turned around and stopped in the perfect position to act as a block and prevent anyone getting close.

Kara adjusted her feet and barely managed to avoid bumping into him. She felt like a stone that had been skipped off a pond.

Stopping a short distance further along she spoke into the phone and meandered about, appearing lost in conversation. She saw Jacob place his bag on the conveyor. He tapped the touch screen panel set to the side of the bag-drop point, but Kara couldn't see it from where she stood and the ponytail block would have prevented her from seeing it even if she had been on the correct side. The bag lurched as the conveyor sped it away and then the older man followed the same procedure.

All three set off again and Kara tailed them at a distance. Entering back into the central space of the terminal, Ponytail walked to the exit, while Jacob and what she now understood to be his travelling companion, made for the central concourse and joined the queue under the sign for 'Immigration et sécurité'.

She had no options left and she couldn't risk joining the queue without a boarding pass of some sort. Not given the heightened alert levels. She considered lining up just to be close to him, maybe starting a conversation, casually asking where he was going, leaving before the first check, but again, in a heightened state of security that would draw attention and spoil Jacob's good work to date. In the end she stopped walking and looked up at the huge departures board. At least twenty Air France flights were leaving over the coming three hours. She looked back and saw Jacob reaching inside his jacket pocket. The act of withdrawing a passport made him twist slightly. As he looked up their eyes met, fleetingly, but Kara hoped it had been long enough. She willed him to realise, they'd be there for him as soon as they could.

24

Charles de Gaulle Airport, Paris.

He was comforted by the fact she'd been there, but knew she probably hadn't discovered his destination. He felt Thierry nudging him, "Here. You will need this," he said, passing Jacob a boarding pass.

Jacob knew from the luggage tags that his bags were en route to Singapore on an Air France flight, but at least this confirmed he was going too. "Twenty-L? Is this business class?" He asked.

Thierry didn't respond.

"Where are you sitting?"

Again he got no response and decided to give up trying to establish some rapport with the surly Frenchman. Instead he focussed on being as natural and relaxed as he could for the moment he would hand over a completely fake passport in the middle of a declared state-of-emergency, when border controls in France were as tight as anytime in recent memory.

A yellow line marked where each passenger had to stand until called forward. Jacob looked ahead but tried not to stare. He swept his gaze over the four immigration officials behind their glass partitions. He thought it unusual. He couldn't remember passport desks in the UK having glass, but he couldn't be sure as most recently he'd used the E-Passport gates. Then he realised that most times he had been abroad in the past few years, he had travelled courtesy of military transports. He hoped that seat Twenty-L would be an improvement on them.

The green light on the counter to his far left blinked. He took a breath and walked over. The official's position was raised so that the already tall and lithe black man loomed large over Jacob's head. With his best smile, Jacob slid his passport and boarding card through the small gap at the bottom of the glass. The check was swift, the passport was scanned, the photo was held up to compare and without a word of acknowledgement, a question or a smile of recognition, the documents were handed back to him and he was waved through.

The security checks, metal detectors and X-ray stations, although slow, and with a cordon supplied by French paratroopers, were equally uneventful.

Thierry was waiting for him on the other side. Jacob hoped that the ninety minutes they had before boarding might give him a chance to get a message out to Tien and Kara, but Thierry once more gripped his elbow and led him off. This time to the Air France Business Lounge. Thierry, it turned out, could speak more than monosyllables, and he did so to the Air France representative on the front desk. They were ushered into an extremely plush area and one that afforded Jacob's minder the best prospect of monitoring his every move. This was no sprawling departure gate concourse with cafes and fast food outlets surrounded by duty free and gift shops. This was a controlled, quiet, refined space with limited numbers and a small, albeit not cramped, footprint.

"You have before been in place like this?" Thierry asked in passable English, while directing him to sit down at a table.

Jacob shook his head. "No. Never." It was the truth. He reckoned the departure lounge at RAF Brize Norton, although definitely an exclusive lounge, didn't quite come up to the same standards.

"You drink and eat?"

"Sorry?" Jacob asked.

"You drink and eat. You want to?"

"Umm, yeah. I could eat something."

Thierry waved a hand in the direction of a long counter running almost the length of the room. "It is all, umm, how you say? Eh, *gratuit*, free. You go, help yourself. But, do not get drunk."

Jacob began to stand, but Thierry's hand gripped his arm, "Also, do not leave where I can see. And do not go near them," he said pointing to a long row of computer terminals, half of which were in use.

"Why would I go near them?" Jacob asked, trying to sound offended.

"I am sure you do not, but I just tell you. That is all."

"What if I need to go to the toilet?"

"You come tell me. Like in school, with the teacher. Yes?"

"Right. Okay, got it."

Jacob grazed up and down the length of the buffet table and the open bar, taking his cues from the other diners. He knew he was on a potentially dangerous mission, he knew it was likely he would mix with more people that would sicken him, but just here and now, he was impressed with his surroundings. He liked the exclusivity of it. He liked the ability to have free wine and spirits, served by smart waiters and waitresses. He could see why those with power and money found it intoxicating, but as he looked around him, at the slightly bored looking customers with their matter-of-fact'ness expressions, he also realised how quickly anyone could become inured to anything. He had a tiny inkling as to why, once used to their surroundings, they would continue to push for more. Quickly becoming dissatisfied by this lounge and jealous of First Class exclusivity. The vaguest thought teased him. He wondered if it was the same for those men in Amsterdam. Did their need for new experiences, evermore reckless pleasures, mean they constantly had to push and stretch the boundaries of what they were prepared to do? Until they stepped over the line. The line that, once crossed, surrendered their right to be called men.

φ

The ninety minutes passed quickly and when their flight was called Thierry led them to the departure gate and stepped back to allow Jacob to go first. Handing his boarding pass over, he was directed by the ever-smiling flight attendant to the far aisle of the aircraft. With a quick glance into the luxury of First Class, he turned right and made his way through Business Class before entering a separate section of seats. Not quite as luxurious as the business ones, but certainly more upmarket than normal economy class. He looked up at the seat numbers on the bulkhead and was surprised to find himself staring at Twenty-L. It was the window side of a pair of what looked more like upright shells than seats. Thierry nudged him to move in from the aisle and then sat down next to him.

As the rest of the passengers embarked, Jacob took the time to examine his surroundings. The little area was a midway point between business and economy. He took out his boarding pass stub and for the first time noticed the words *Premium Voyageur.* 'Premium economy?' he thought. Turning around like he was examining the seat he was in, and stretching up to turn the airflow on, he noticed the discreet cabin had tied back curtains that he guessed would be drawn as soon as the flight departed. It had its own toilets and only twenty-two seats in total. He figured only First Class would have been smaller. It was like the business lounge they had been in. Comfortable, plush and giving Thierry the most control of his charge. Jacob would have no excuse to wander thirty or forty rows to get to a toilet when there was one in reaching distance. He sighed inwardly and knew that if this continued for the rest of the flights, he was never going to get a message out.

φ

The Air France flight left the ground twenty minutes after its scheduled departure time of seven-forty at night. It touched down in Singapore a little early, some twelve hours and twenty minutes later, but at a local time of three-twenty in the afternoon of the following day.

The only conversation Jacob and Thierry had throughout the flight was in regard to the disembarkation cards handed to them by the cabin staff. Jacob was told that he was visiting Shu Ying Tan, his girlfriend of one year. She lived at 22 Lor Batawi, Hougang, Singapore and he would be staying with her for two weeks. Shu Ying was a twenty-six year old school teacher he had met when she had been on a six-month exchange program in his home town of Grays, Essex. This was his first time visiting her, or Singapore. Jacob filled in the disembarkation card with the corresponding details.

Once happy he had memorised the backstory sufficiently, Thierry ignored him and began to watch a movie. Jacob did likewise and patiently waited for Thierry to go to the toilet. He thought that would provide his best chance to slip a message to one of the flight attendants. It would be a long shot but worth trying. They might just pass it on for him on landing.

But when Thierry finally stood and ambled up to the toilet, Jacob was immediately aware that he would have no such opportunity. The big Frenchman had timed his absence right to the start of the first in-flight food service.

The flight attendants were all busy, their attention focussed on the quick and efficient delivery of food to the masses. When Jacob ducked his head through the curtains to look down the aisles of Economy, he saw multiple trolleys blocking any hope of making it to the rear galley, where there might have been some spare staff. He turned back and sat down. His last hope was to pass it to the Premium Economy flight attendant who was making her way slowly down the aisle towards him, but by the time she arrived, Thierry was back. Jacob's only consolation was being served the best airline food he had ever tasted.

After the meal he was sure Thierry wasn't likely to doze off, so he decided to take the chance to rest. Reclining the shell-like seat he managed to grab about five hours' worth of fitful sleep. The rest of the long flight he watched more movies and listened to music. As they landed, Thierry leaned over to him, "You stay with me all the way through. We go through immigration together, get our bags together, we go through customs together. I will take you out to meet the people who will look after you tonight."

"Tonight? Am I not just flying straight on?"

"No. You have to leave the airport, then come back later. You use a different passport. It's safe-"

"Yeah, I get it. Safer that way," Jacob said.

Waiting for the aircraft doors to finally open seemed to take longer than the passage through the vast arrivals terminal of Changi Airport. Jacob knew the reason for the swift and simplified path he followed was because the Frenchman had no need to refer to signs or directions. He wondered just how many people this man had escorted on the Flight Path. Relieved of the responsibility of navigating, Jacob noticed the numerous Christmas decorations on display. They surprised him as he hadn't expected massive trees and frosted, crystal reindeers pulling wooden sledges inside an Asian airport. As he took in the stars and holly wreaths, huge baubles and garlands, he admitted to himself that he had no idea if Singapore was Islamic, Buddhist or whatever. He figured that by the decorations on show, there must have been some Christians. Or maybe just some commercialism.

At the top of an escalator, Thierry stopped and pointed down to the ground floor. A series of eleven lanes, marked out by standard security barriers, but with tinsel twisted around them, led up to eleven passport control desks. Numbers ten and eleven were marked for aircrew and diplomats only.

"We go into lane four. Both of us. You behind me. Clear?"

"Yes. Clear." Jacob stopped, then thought he had nothing to lose, "Umm, why exactly?"

"Because she has some of your money," Thierry said and

tilted his head in the direction of the female immigration officer sitting behind desk four.

"But I thought the passport was good enough."

"It is, but we like to have, eh," he struggled to find the right word.

"A guarantee?" Jacob offered.

"Yes, *une garantie*. That is it. Come along."

25

Changi Airport, Singapore. Thursday 26th November.

Passport control, baggage reclaim and customs were uneventful and Jacob followed Thierry out to the waiting faces of a large crowd standing along the edge of a wide walkway. Jacob had always considered the passage through waiting crowds at an airport arrivals a strange experience. Even when he knew there was no one waiting for him he couldn't help but look at the faces and read the printed names on cards. Just in case. This time, although he knew someone was waiting, he still had no reason to scan the faces or read the cards. He wouldn't recognise anyone. So he didn't try. Instead he watched Thierry and saw him give a subtle nod to a pair of smartly dressed, middle-aged, Asian men near the end of the greeting line. Both men walked towards the exit door at the furthest corner of the terminal building. Jacob followed them, and Thierry, outside.

The wall of heat and humidity hit him like a physical blow. There was a smell that he couldn't identify. It reminded him of smoke. He could taste it, like a bitter-sweet heaviness in the air. By the time he walked the modest distance to the short-term parking and the silver Nissan Teana the two Asian men were standing beside, he was drenched in sweat. He remembered the heat of Kandahar and Basra, but it had never felt this oppressive. A weight of hot dampness was pressing down on him. He looked across at Thierry, who had removed his heavy sweater on the plane. He may well have escorted many others on this journey, but the Frenchman's face was beaded with perspiration and dark stains were already showing under his arms.

The man on the driver's side, dressed in a business suit that Jacob thought would have melted him to a puddle had he been wearing it, leant in and released the boot catch.

"Put your bags in there Jacob, then get in the back please," he said in an accent that surprised Jacob as much as the man's ability to wear a shirt, tie and jacket in this climate. There was no trace of Chinese, or other stereotypical Asian pronunciation. The man spoke like he had been born and raised in Surrey, or Hampshire.

The other man, on the passenger side of the car, who also wore a suit but with no tie, held the rear door open for him. Jacob did as he was asked. Outside, he could hear the driver speaking to Thierry in French. He twisted around and saw Thierry hand over a single piece of paper. There were a few more words in French then Thierry walked over to a taxi rank on the other side of the road. Jacob guessed that his part in this was over.

The driver got in and turned to face him. "Good afternoon Jacob. My name is Gerard and this," he held his hand towards the passenger who was just taking his own seat, "is Lim. You will be staying with us for a short time. Then I shall accompany you on your next flight."

"When will that be?"

"Tomorrow morning, very early. We shall be back at the airport by ten tonight."

"Can I ask where we'll be going?"

Gerard just smiled, "All in good time. What I would like you to do now is two things. In the door compartment next to you is a black hood. Do you see it?"

Jacob held the heavy cotton material up.

"Good. Now I'd like you to lie down on the back seat and slip that hood over your head, if you would be so kind."

Jacob considered it the most polite and potentially most threatening thing ever said to him. He stared back at Gerard, who must have easily read the astonishment on his face.

"I assure you, my dear chap, you are in no danger. We are simply the latest steps on the Flight Path. It is a necessity that we keep things as isolated as possible. There are only a few links, like our French friend there," he gestured in the direction of the taxi rank, "who know people at either end of a step. Even then it is limited. I do not know his name, he does not know mine. But, the men who pass from one end of the Path to the other, men like you, get to see all of us. We need to have safeguards if we can. One such safeguard is that you do not know where you will be staying for the next few hours. It is safer for everyone. Do you understand?"

"Right, of course. That's a good idea. Much safer."

"Good. I am glad you agree. Hood on then, and lie down please. I shall turn the air conditioning up to full so you will be more comfortable."

Reaching up to slip the material over his head, Jacob managed to get a quick glimpse of his wristwatch. It was 16:10. The car pulled away, but never having been to Singapore, he had no concept of a mental map to refer to. The little he knew of the place was the circumstances of its surrender in the Second World War, the fact it once had an RAF base and that there was a bar called Raffles; somewhere.

He decided to start a count of lefts and rights, but other than the initial right turn out of the carpark and another long sweeping right-hander that felt like an on-ramp to a major highway, the rest of the journey, for a long time, was without any noticeable deviations. Eventually, the car decelerated and stopped. He heard the tell-tale ticking of an indicator and the noise of other cars around him. 'Traffic lights' he thought and then the car moved off again, turned right, drove a short distance, turned right again, stayed straight for another few minutes, and went up a considerable incline. As it levelled out, it took a pair of left turns in quick succession then slowed and stopped, before reversing back and left. He felt the bump of the wheels as the car mounted a low kerb, heard the handbrake being applied, the engine switched off and sensed Gerard and Lim step out of the car. The rear door was opened and a hand was placed on his arm.

"Now, Jacob, please keep your hood on, but sit up and shuffle this way," Gerard said and helped him out. He was guided forward, told to step up and guided forward again. He immediately felt the coolness of air-conditioning. He heard a door close behind him and the hood was removed.

Blinking rapidly, he ran his hands through his hair. His wristwatch told him it was twenty-seven minutes since he had put the hood on. He considered the information he had gained about the journey was likely worthless.

As his eyes adjusted he could see he was standing in a small open plan living area with two steps leading up to a kitchen on his left, a dining table with six chairs to his front and a lounge area with a red leather sofa and matching armchairs, two steps down to his right. A coffee table was in front of the sofa and triangularly offset was a low television unit on top of which was a flat-screen TV that Jacob thought was twice as big as the room needed. Other than it, an electric kettle on the kitchen bench, and a white fridge jammed into the corner next to the sink, he noted a lack of any other appliances, pictures or ornaments. The three windows, one for each section of the space, looked out onto what he assumed was a high-walled courtyard. He could hear nothing of interest and neither could he smell the tang he had at the airport. He felt a waft of cool air pass across his head and looking up, saw two air-conditioning vents in the ceiling.

Lim and Gerard, both standing behind him swapped a few sentences in what sounded like Chinese. He turned to see Lim carrying the suitcase and backpack up a flight of stairs that rose from the right hand side of a small hallway.

"Come, Jacob," Gerard said with a sweep of his hands

towards the stairs, "I will show you your room. I am sure you are tired and would like to have a shower, then some rest perhaps?"

Jacob was suddenly aware of how tired he was. He hadn't had a proper night's sleep since before Amsterdam and a flight to the other side of the world hadn't helped. He nodded and followed behind Lim.

The room he was shown into had a double bed, a single bedside cabinet with a lamp and, like downstairs, no ornaments nor pictures. It did have a window that was shuttered on the inside and secured with a padlock in the same manner as the room in Paris had been.

"The bathroom is shared, I am afraid, but please, feel free to use it first. Lim and I shall prepare some food. Do you care for pizza?"

Again Jacob's surprise must have been evident in his expression. Gerard gave a discreet, polite laugh, "You thought maybe I would offer you some noodles, or rice, or fish head curry?"

"I... well, I..."

"Come, come now Jacob. I am not offended, but I find that our western guests need carbohydrates and familiarity after they have endured the rigours of a long-haul flight. We have Dominos, just like in the UK, so what would you like, Hawaiian, chicken, peperoni?"

"Umm, peperoni would be great," Jacob said, still struggling with the weirdly amusing prospect of being in a tropical Asian paradise and getting a fast-food pizza delivered like he would in Essex.

"And to drink?"

"A Sprite?"

"Very good. I will make the arrangements. Now, before we eat you must shower, change and relax. Get out of those heavy jeans and put on something cooler, but first, I need you to give me your wallet and passport, if you would be so kind."

Jacob didn't hesitate. He reached both over and Gerard put the passport and the contents of the wallet, except for the picture of the woman, into his own jacket pocket. From the drawer of the bedside cabinet he took an envelope and handed it and the wallet to Jacob. "This is your new identity. There are also some Singaporean dollars. Just enough to look like you have been here for a while. Lastly, the backstory that you will need to know. I'd like you to read it and be familiar with it please. Now wash, change and rest. I will call you once we are ready to eat." Gerard turned and ushered Lim out of the room.

Jacob opened the envelope to find a similar collection of items to the ones he had been handed in Paris, but with enough differences to lose Jacob London for ever and introduce Jacob Poole.

His passport was Canadian. His driving license, still from the UK, but the address had shifted to Clacton-on-Sea and Maple Road had morphed into Maple Close. His date of birth was the same, but now he had a Boots Advantage Card, an Air Canada loyalty card called 'Aeroplan', one credit card and three other bank cards. The last item was a single sheet of paper that transformed Shu Ying Tan, his girlfriend of one year, into Audrey Huang, his fiancée of two years. She was English and he had met her when she worked in London for the Hong Kong and Shanghai Bank. Now, she was temporarily working in Hong Kong and he had come out to visit her in a block of apartments on Tai Man Street in somewhere called the Chai Wan district. Jacob had less clue about Hong Kong than he had about Singapore, but at least he knew where he was going next. Not that the information was of any use to him. He had resigned himself to the fact that he might well be screwed. Even if he could find a way to get a message back home once he found out his final destination, the chances of Tien and Kara being able to get there before he did were next to none.

Filling his wallet with the new cards and putting his passport away, he listened at the door to make sure both Gerard and Lim were downstairs. Recovering his washbag from his suitcase he quietly eased the bedroom door open and stepped cautiously into the landing. Any thought that the other rooms might have held secrets was dispelled immediately.

There were two other bedrooms in the house and a bathroom with a toilet. All their doors were wide open. The other bedrooms were furnished and shuttered like his. The bathroom, stocked with fresh towels, shower gels, soaps and a new pack of disposable razors, also boasted a shuttered window. 'Nothing to search if there's nothing to hide,' he thought, shutting the bathroom door and starting the shower.

φ

The Nissan pulled back out of the driveway and Jacob, once more hooded in the back seat, was happy in his own abilities as he managed to reverse plot the turns they had taken earlier in the day. As the car came down a sweeping left-hander, that he presumed would lead them off the major highway and back to the airport, Gerard told him he could sit up and remove the hood.

He checked his watch. Twenty two minutes this time. He figured the traffic, at what was now approaching ten at night, was less congested. In the almost six hours since he had left the airport, he had showered, changed, eaten pizza, fallen asleep for a couple of hours, then showered again. In all that time Lim had said nothing directly to him and only a few sentences in Chinese to Gerard. Conversely, Gerard had been the politest host he could have wished for. He struggled to remind himself that this man was in every way as culpable as Rik, or the small man or Thierry. He and, the mostly silent, Lim, were paid to smuggle evil men out to a freedom they didn't deserve. Yet the middle-aged man in the tailored suit, with the accent of an Eton school boy and the manners to match, neatly presented with trimmed black hair, conservatively cut, cleanly shaven and with no jewellery, could have passed for... Jacob wondered at just what Gerard could have passed for. He physically shuddered as clarity dawned on him. This man could have passed for almost anything. He was the trusted neighbour, friend, teacher, role-model that you wanted your children to be like. He was the man you'd let look after your kids when you were late home from work. Jacob understood that of all the men he had met so far, Gerard could well have been the most dangerous, because of his normality. He was shaken out of the darkening thoughts by the sudden realisation Gerard had been talking to him.

"I'm sorry, Gerard, what did you say?"

"I said, we will be checking in using the self-service kiosks. I have all the paper work. You just need to stay with me. We will drop off the bags and proceed to passport control. No need to worry, it will all go smoothly. Follow me throughout if you would be so kind, Jacob."

φ

Gerard led them through the terminal as Lim, with not even a word of farewell to Gerard, drove off. Jacob knew this flight was likely to follow the example of the last when he was handed a boarding pass showing seat '17A Business'. His only real surprise was at departure passport control. There were fewer lanes in comparison with the arrival area, but as Gerard lined up, Jacob was intrigued to see the same female immigration officer up ahead. He leant forward and asked quietly, "How can she be on here?"

"These passport officials work a twelve-hour day. She works half on arrivals and half on departures. We choose these flights for a reason my dear chap," Gerard explained.

"But how can you be sure she'll be working?"

"We have a few, shall I say, spare pieces on the board of play?"

"So she knows me and what I look like?" Jacob asked, putting what he hoped was a sufficient amount of alarm into his voice.

"Gosh no," Gerard said quietly over his shoulder. Even after six hours, Jacob was still bemused at the Englishness of the man's speech. "Our dear lady knows what our French friend looks like and what I look like. She knows whomsoever comes after us will be someone for her to pay less attention to.

Simple really."

"Do you have the same in place at all the airports?"

"Where we can. Sometimes the logistics makes it impossible. But we try our best," Gerard said and Jacob noticed the same pride in the operation that the small man in Paris had shown.

Once through all the preliminaries, Gerard led them to the Cathay Pacific Skyview Lounge. After checking in with reception, he ushered Jacob through an open plan arrangement of chairs, tables and self-service counters, past a table with six unattended PCs, the screen savers of which said, in English, 'Free Internet for your Use', and upstairs to an even smaller lounge. Once more, Jacob knew the exclusivity came with increased security.

"Please sit, my dear Jacob. Relax. Help yourself to food and drink. Although please remember what I daresay our French friend will have impressed upon you; do not get drunk and do not go where I cannot see."

Jacob sagged into a half-circle tub-chair opposite Gerard and sighed.

"What is the matter?" Gerard asked.

"All through this it seems I'm not trusted. From when I first started on the Flight Path, I've been watched and monitored. I feel like a prisoner yet I'm paying good money. It just saddens me."

"True, very true," Gerard agreed, nodding slowly. "But of course Jacob, there is a chance that you are not who you say you are. There is a chance you might be police or some other form of agent." He held his hand up to stop Jacob's attempt at protesting. "I know. I know. It is most unlikely and given our security we have never had one successful breach. Not in all our years, but we have had attempts. These measures we use, protected us then and protect us now. We'll only relax when you get to the end of the Path and…" he trailed off.

"And what?" Jacob asked.

Gerard leant forward, "And you prove you are one of us."

"Can you explain further?"

"When you get to wherever you are going, the men who are there will manage your life into your new identity. They will help and assist you. At some point they will be able to tell if you are who you say you are. That's all, really," Gerard said and gave a wry smile.

Jacob was aware that, for the first time since he had met Gerard, the man was being coy with his answers. He tried to get him to clarify, but Gerard said only, "All in good time Jacob. All in good time. But, rest assured, once that is done you will be given complete autonomy. Until then, we must watch over you closely. It is the Flight Path way. We are cautious. You have lived with this caution all your life, so you must see the sense in it, no matter how frustrating. Does that explain why we do what we do?"

Jacob said nothing for a long time. He thought about Gerard's last sentence. Nothing would make him comprehend what or why these men did what they did. It sickened him to think how any adult could betray the trust of an innocent. Images of last Christmas, spent in the company of his brother and sister-in-law, his two nieces and his nephew flooded his mind. He saw the two older kids with their beaming faces, reflecting their happiness and their excitement. He heard their squeals of laughter as they put up their stockings and then their soft breathing as they slept peacefully, waiting for Santa and the surprise of the morning. He saw the tiny bundle that had been his youngest niece, oblivious to the season and totally dependent on the adults around her to provide protection. He knew he had to follow this Path to its end, but he also knew that being in the company of these animals was wearing him down.

"Jacob, do you understand?"

"Yes. Of course. I see. I'm sorry to have asked."

"Oh no, my dear chap. It's alright. Perfectly fine. Now why don't I go and get us both a nice cup of tea?"

Jacob managed to nod. As Gerard stood, he found his voice, "Gerard, you said wherever I am going. Do you not know?"

"Oh no. Absolutely not. For all I know, you could end up in Timbuktu and I would have no clue."

φ

They departed ninety minutes late, at ten to three in the morning. Jacob guessed Gerard would be as watchful and controlling as Thierry had been, so he tried to sleep for a part of the almost four hour flight, but the sharp ache he felt when he considered the normality of Gerard and others like him, kept him wide awake.

Forced into a holding pattern they finally touched down at 06:50, but at least there was no time zone change. Jacob followed Gerard once more, but other than noting Flight Path had at least one Hong Kong immigration official on their books, evidenced by the scant examination he gave the forged Canadian passport, Jacob wandered through the arrival's process in a semi-daze. He knew it was a combination of tiredness and the fear he felt at the casual way Gerard, so refined and respectful, could probably walk into any child's life and destroy it. The same man would then offer friends a cup of tea, like it was the most natural thing in the world.

He shook his head in an attempt to clear the fog and watched large glass doors slide apart to reveal a broad concourse thronged with meeters and greeters, welcoming relatives and business associates. A young girl, of no more than six, broke free of what Jacob presumed was her mother's hand and ran to hug, what Jacob also presumed, was her father. The man swept her up and twirled her around in a moment that made Jacob's heart lighten.

"Jacob," Gerard called.

He looked away from the family, "Yes?"

"This way," Gerard said and began to follow a much younger man, dressed in black trousers, a white shirt and black tie.

They followed him through a series of moving walkways and tunnels before entering an immense space of shops,

234

cinemas and food courts. Lavish Christmas decorations, even bigger and more prevalent than the Singaporean ones, gave Jacob more pause for thought on the universal nature of the festival. He was so distracted by the displays that he was halfway through the complex's upper level before he realised it was almost empty. Other than the staff in the retail outlets, he could see only a handful of other people. He remembered the noise inside a Heathrow terminal and compared it to the relative silence here. A silence that was broken only by piped music, currently playing '*Rockin' around the Christmas Tree with Mel and Kim*'. The Christmas song stopped him. He looked up at the phenomenally complex ceiling architecture, adorned with golden chandeliers and brightly illuminated stars. Looking down, through the glass-sided walkway, he could see the ground floor stretching away in wide concourses, vast and mostly empty. The building, that could have comfortably accommodated thousands of travellers, seemed to be hosting less than a hundred.

He felt a hand on his arm, "Come along Jacob, Keep up. We have a change of plan," Gerard said, moving off again.

On the far side of the building they took an escalator down to ground level and out into a huge carpark. The humidity again made Jacob feel like he was walking through a fine mist, but he was relieved that the temperature of a Hong Kong morning was at least ten degrees cooler than a Singaporean night had been. He was also relieved not to have jeans on anymore. Cooler or not, he was still drenched in sweat by the time the three of them had traversed rows of cars to finally stop next to a white Toyota Camry.

The younger man and Gerard talked rapidly in Chinese while Jacob stood apart, put his case on the ground and looked up to the peaks of high mountains off to his left. He knew, from the small map display that he had studied on the in-seat entertainment, that he was looking south-east to Lantau Island. He had been surprised, and disappointed, to find out from the travel guide that played in the plane during their time circling around in the holding pattern, that Hong Kong Airport could be an hour's drive away, depending on traffic, from the main Hong Kong harbour and skyline that he had seen on television. Although he did think it probably didn't matter as another hooded journey through unknown streets was hardly going to give him an opportunity to sightsee. As he looked at the mountains, Gerard came over to him.

"It appears that we have a small problem."

"Which is?"

"Your escort for the next leg of your journey has been, umm, delayed."

"Umm delayed? I don't like the umm, if I'm honest."

"Yes, rather. It turns out she has-"

"She!"

"Yes, a woman. We do have women who share... Well, let's not talk about that here. She has been delayed because the documents she was collecting were not ready. This has been a lot more of a rush than normal. Because of the events in Paris."

"Yes, I was told that things are different,"

"Quite. Well, she is waiting for them to be finished. The thing is, by the time you drive into Hong Kong, to where you were meant to be meeting her and then back out here, it all gets tight for time. So, I am afraid you will have to wait here."

"Here, as in the airport?" Jacob asked.

"Here as in the car. I do apologise Jacob, but it is the same as we spoke of before. Security and confidence."

Jacob knew not to object again, "That's fine Gerard. All is fine. But..."

"Yes?"

"What happens if she doesn't show up?"

"Oh she will. She may have to change some travel plans, but she will show up."

"Fair enough."

"Then, if that is settled, this is where I shall bid you fare-well. I doubt our paths will ever cross again, but if they do, I shall certainly enjoy your company," Gerard said and held his hand out.

Jacob automatically reached out. He felt the clamminess

and willed himself not to break the man's fingers. Instead he mustered a smile and said, "Thank you for getting me this far. I do hope we meet again." The last half of his sentence, truly meant.

Gerard walked off, back in the direction of the terminal building and Jacob looked to the young man who stood next to the car. "Can we get in?"

The doors unlocked at the press of a key fob and Jacob put his bags in the back before getting into the passenger seat. The young man got into the driver's side and turned the ignition on, not to start the engine, but to allow a gentle breeze of air conditioning to flow through the car.

"Okay, what's your name?" Jacob asked.

"We no speak now," the man said in heavily accented English.

"At all?"

The man shook his head. Jacob turned and stared out the window to the far off peaks.

φ

At 09:20, a black Audi A5 came roaring up the line of cars one over from the Camry. The noise of its engine woke the dozing Jacob and he sat up straighter in his seat. The Audi braked to a halt and a woman, western looking, medium height, slim, with a blonde bob-haircut and wearing low heels, silver-grey slacks and a fitted green blouse, stepped from the passenger's side of the car. She moved with a sense of urgency, recovered a single suitcase from the boot, then leant back into the passenger footwell and brought out a leather handbag, slinging the strap over her shoulder. She slammed the car door shut and the Audi pulled away, rapidly.

The silent young man stepped out of the car and walked over to the woman. He spoke a few words before walking a short distance away and lighting up a cigarette.

She in turn hustled over to the Camry, threw her case in the back and got in the driver's seat. Jacob estimated she was about thirty, she wore make-up but not overly applied and, had he met her in a bar, he'd have considered her pretty. Not plain, not stunningly attractive, just pretty. He knew she reeked of Poison.

26

Hong Kong International Airport. Friday 27th November.

Jacob was by no means an expert on perfumes but he knew this one. His first girlfriend, back when he was growing up in Chelmsford, had thought it was the height of luxury. On every birthday, Christmas or Valentine's Day during the two years they had dated, she had wanted Poison. He remembered saving up the money he got from his after-school job in Waitrose, and buying her the heart-shaped bottle with the fancy crystal top. He could still see the deep green shade of the box, but most of all he had never forgotten the potency of the heavy scent. It was Poison, at the age of sixteen, he'd breathed in so deeply while losing his virginity and it was Poison, at the age of seventeen, he'd breathed in when he caught her shagging Mickey Ronaldstone in the back of the Odeon Cinema. He couldn't watch *Pirates of the Caribbean* or smell Poison without being reminded of those days. He was whisked back from his memories of Tanya Brown by the slap of an envelope against his chest.

"Jacob, I'm Kelsey. Take this and give me your wallet. Put your passport in there," she said, pointing to the car's glove box.

He couldn't quite place her accent. It was a mismatch of English, maybe American, or even Australian. He put the envelope between his legs and did as he was asked. He saw that she took everything from his wallet, including the photo of the Asian woman, then without warning, leant across him and put all the items on top of the passport in the glove box. Shutting it and pushing herself back up by placing her hand on his thigh, she said, "You're a hell of an improvement on the usual. Such a shame I'm probably twenty years too old for your liking. We could have made the most of our time together."

His emotions, stretched from the last few days, didn't have the capacity to muster a response. He just stared back at her blankly and wondered how his world view of decency could have been turned inside-out and upside-down so drastically in such a short time.

Kelsey just gave a weak, 'ha-ha' that carried no real emotional content. Her eyes, a pale, washed out blue, didn't carry any hint of amusement. "Don't worry handsome, I'm not judging. Hell, I'm a ways partial to the young 'uns myself. It's just that most of the men I escort on the Flight Path are old, fat, bald, or rancid. Some of them, all four at once with bad teeth as a bonus. You look like a God compared to them. So chin up. Don't be so scared."

Jacob still couldn't think of an adequate response. Instead he opened the envelope she had given him. Inside was a South African passport in the name of Jacob York, who apparently had been born in South Africa, with no other details given. Behind the passport was a small wad of Hong Kong dollars, some US dollars, three credit cards, an RAC membership card and a card for an online betting firm. There was another UK driving license with yet another different address, Maple Avenue in Heybridge, Essex. He held it up and looked at it. He knew Heybridge, he had friends there. He'd cycled to and from the village when he'd been in his teens, before Tanya had come along with her Poison and distracted him.

"Do you actually speak?" Kelsey asked.

He looked away from the license, "Yeah. Just been a long few days. I'm a bit tired. Sorry. I'm Jacob," he put the license down on his lap.

"Yep, I know that my big friend. Apology accepted. I'm sorry too, 'cos I got held up with some complications in Shenzhen and now we need to get a skedaddle on. So, listen quick and get your head in the game. You are Jacob York, from Johannesburg but have been living in the UK for years. You flew into Hong Kong, with British Airways yesterday and stayed on a one night stopover at the Marriot Hotel," she twisted around in her seat and pointed out the rear window, "It's that building there. Okay?"

"Yeah okay," Jacob said, hunkering down to see the hotel on the far side of the airport's inner ring road.

"Now you're off to Bali for a three-week holiday. You'll be staying in the Hard Rock Hotel in a town called Kuta. Got it?"

"And am I?"

"Are you what?"

"Staying in the Hard Rock Hotel?"

She frowned, "No. Of course not. You'll be in a safe house somewhere on the island. Handsome you may be, but smarts ain't all there now, are they?"

Jacob ignored the insult, "So I'm travelling alone, no fake girlfriend photo or travelling companion?"

"Nope. Single guy going on a bit of an Asian adventure. You'd be amazed how many do it. But, when you say no travelling companion, I'll be shot-gunning you on the journey. You play nicely, handsome, with the same rules as you should be used to by now, and we'll get on fine. Don't leave my sight, don't do anything strange or unusual, clear?"

"Clear," Jacob said.

"Good, now repeat back who you are, what you've been up to and where you're going."

Jacob did so and other than stumbling over the name of the town that the Hard Rock Hotel was in, he got through it to Kelsey's satisfaction.

"Okay, I'm going to get our young chauffeur there," she pointed out the window at the young man who was still smoking, "to drive us to the departure entrance. I didn't get a chance to check us in online so we have to do it the old fashioned way and we need to get a shake on. Any questions?"

"Only what I know I'm not meant to ask, but where are you from originally?"

"Why do you wanna know?"

"No reason, other than your accent is sor- "

Kelsey laughed and this time her eyes properly reflected the emotion, "Oh my accent is peculiar as hell. It's a mismatch of everywhere. I was born and raised in Texas until I was fifteen, but since I escaped from the hellhole that was home, I've lived in a lot of different places. More than I can recall and some that I don't want to. Anything else you'd like to know?"

"No. I'm good."

"Great. Got to admit, I'm not. I've been on the go since four in the AM and I haven't stopped." She stepped out and shouted to the young man in Chinese. He dropped his cigarette on the ground and returned to the car. Kelsey got in the back, moving their bags and as soon as the driver was in she said, "Let's go. I really need to pee."

φ

The car dropped them off outside the entrance for departures and pulled away. Jacob thought, given Kelsey's remark about needing to go to the toilet, she would avail of the first opportunity, but she didn't. On reflection, he figured she would never have left him unescorted in the vast terminal building. Instead, she led him through the check-in procedures for Hong Kong Airlines and all the immigration and security procedures that he was becoming so used to.

Finally he followed her into the Hong Kong Airways VIP Lounge. It was plush and exclusive, just like the other two he had been in and he realised his thoughts on entering the French lounge had been correct. It was incredibly easy to become used to the level of service on offer. Each of the women behind the reception desk smiled, gave small bows of their heads and generally welcomed him like he was their long-lost and dearest relation. The waiters and waitresses couldn't do enough, the food looked superb and the wine list extensive. It slightly saddened him to realise that, in only his third visit to a lounge like this, he was used to it all and bored by most of it.

Kelsey made her way to a row of two-seater tables next to the windows. The panoramic view of the aircraft apron perked him up. He'd always loved planes and the sight of at least five different airliners manoeuvring and taxiing towards the main runway, at the threshold of which was a Korean Air 747 just about to start its take-off run, had him enthralled. So much so that he wasn't looking where he was going and bumped into the rear of a seat occupied by a middle-aged woman.

With her book in one hand, she had just lifted her glass of wine with the other. The jolt to the chair forced a mini-tidal wave to slop up the sides of the glass. The shallow rim couldn't contain it and a large 'sploosh' hit the table to her front. Jacob apologised immediately and beckoned to one of the waitresses to come over. The lady was busy balancing her book while lifting her phone that was still plugged into a USB power slot. She managed to rescue it from the advancing liquid. Once the efficient waitress had soaked up the wine with a pile of napkins, the lady looked round to Jacob. He apologised again and her stern expression, relaxed.

"Oh, don't mention it, free top up service even at this time of the morning, ain't it," she said, in as Essex an accent as Jacob had, while giving a wink to the young waitress who dutifully went off to fetch a bottle of white wine. "No bones busted. Jus' don't fall on me 'cos then there would be an' I'd need a crane to lift you off," she laughed and continued, "Where you from then?"

Jacob was aware Kelsey had sat down at a table further along, but was watching him closely. He stuck with his cover story.

"Heybridge."

"Oh! Don't think I've 'eard of that. Where's it at then?"

"Small village near Chelmsford. What about you?" he asked, knowing that he could always explain to Kelsey that he had to be polite.

"Oh I'm from up Saffron Walden way, luv. Small world init?" she laughed and reached out for her freshly refilled glass, giving him a small toast with it. "You off home then?"

"No, I'm going to Bali on holiday," he said.

"Very nice. Well, enjoy yourselves," she said, looking over and toasting Kelsey, before returning to her book.

Jacob sat down and Kelsey leaned in, "Smoothly done. You handled that well."

"Thanks. But," he looked over his shoulder at the woman before turning back around and leaning nearer to Kelsey, "you don't think she's police or anything, do you?"

Kelsey shook her head. "God no. There's no way you've been followed or tagged. We'd not have gotten this far if you had been. Anyway, you bumped into her. Remember?"

"Yeah, right. Of course," he said, happy that he had managed to stay in character.

"Are you hungry," Kelsey asked.

"A bit."

"Well, go and get whatever you want, then come back here, but make it quick."

Once more he did as bid. As soon as he returned Kelsey said, "Normally, I get myself all squared-away and sorted out before I get to the airport, but this morning was a complete cock-up, so I'm busting and I can't hold it anymore. So you just sit yourself down there and enjoy your food, I'm off for a pee." She stood and walked towards the rear wall of the lounge, where a dark-purple door had the international symbol for a female toilet etched into it in gold.

Jacob looked around at the small row of 'Free Internet' iMacs he had passed as he came into the lounge, but all four were in use. The business centre, overflowing with PCs and which he'd also seen upon entering the lounge, was down at the far end and he'd never make it there and back. He figured Kelsey had chosen well when it came to where to sit and when to leave for the toilet. Frustrated, but resigned, he turned back to his plate of food just as the Essex woman passed him by.

"It's all this free wine luv, goes right through ya. Here, would you be a dear and just keep an eye on me stuff, so no one nicks it?" she asked.

He looked round and saw a small carryon case next to her table.

"Of course," he called after her as she walked to the end of the room and went through the dark-purple door.

He got up and walked back to her table.

"Yes," he said under his breath when he saw her phone still plugged into the charging port. He looked around but no one in the lounge was paying him any attention. He grabbed up the phone and held his breath while he pushed the home button. The lock screen came up and he swept it sideways, hoping that his new friend from 'up Saffron Walden way' had no clue about telephone security and hadn't locked her phone with a passcode. A home screen teeming with icons appeared. He looked up to the far wall. Another woman was going into the toilets.

The message icon was along the bottom of the phone's home screen. He opened it and began a new message, remembering that he needed to add the country code for the UK. As he typed the thought dawned on him that he knew practically no one's mobile number anymore. When he had been younger he had known lists of numbers, but he'd forgotten most of them because his phone remembered them for him. Nowadays he only knew two numbers by rote, his own, and his brother's.

The door at the end of the lounge opened and his heart pounded as he looked up. A small Chinese woman appeared and turned towards the lounge's exit. He checked the message and the number.

"For fuck's sake," he said quietly when he realised he'd added the country code but forgotten to delete the leading zero from the phone number. He tapped to edit it, but deleted the whole number.

"Fuck it."

The dark-purple door opened again and once more his heart surged. A mother and baby came out and turned towards the lounge's main seating area.

He looked back down, slowed his actions and took a breath. He retyped the UK country code and added Toby's number, properly, without the leading zero. He reread the text and pressed send.

The little green line showing the progress of the 'send operation' crawled from one side of the screen to the other. "C'mon, c'mon."

Finally it hovered millimetres from the end, teasingly, with the tiniest gap of white between it and completion.

"Come on," he said, more loudly. At his prompt, the line leapt across the gap and completed its journey. There was a confirmatory tone, which sounded like a sigh.

"You're not wrong," Jacob said. He returned to the main message screen, swiped left on the message he had just sent and deleted it. Then he pressed the home button and then the on-off button briefly to send the screen back to darkness. He set the phone back on the table and returned to his seat. He was raising a glass of wine to his lips when Kelsey stepped back through the dark-purple door.

27

Le Bourget Airfield, Paris. Friday 27th November.

Toby was asleep when the ping sounded on his phone. He reached for the dim light being given off by the new message notification. The clock on the screen showed 03:23 Central European Time. He read the first line of the message, threw aside the blanket that had been over him and sat up. "Guys!"

In the dim light he saw four blanketed shapes on the other couches around the room, doing much as he had. The door to the small lounge opened and the lights were flicked on. Kara stood in the doorway.

"We've got him," Toby said holding up his phone.

"What's it say?" Tien asked, wiping sleep from her eyes.

"Safe house is Bali. Dpt HKG 1225 ETA DPS 1735L"

"Bali. Fucking hell, how far away is Bali from here?" Kara asked, walking into the middle of the private passenger lounge. The room and the adjacent dining area, with its own 24-hour catering facility, were complimentary with the hire of the charter jet. Since their arrival on Wednesday night, they had turned the place into a mini operations room. Four laptops and two printers were on tables next to a wall that had a large map of the world stuck up on it.

"Where exactly is Bali," Sammi asked, rubbing her hands through her hair and yawning.

There was quiet. Kara looked to each in turn. "Seriously, we have lifetimes of operational experience and none of us know where Bali is?" she asked.

"I know it's a tropical paradise thingy Roberts made a movie about, but we've never fought a war there, so nope, I've no idea," Dinger said.

"It's somewhere in Indonesia," Tien said, pushing her blanket aside and moving towards the computers. "One of my Mum's friends went there for a wedding anniversary. That's all I know." She sat at a laptop and brought up a map. All of them looked from the screen to the large map on the wall.

Kara picked up a small red sticker and placed it on the tiny island, the shape of which reminded her of a greyhound in full flight. It nestled in the middle of a curving line of other islands. "Guess this is the famed Indonesian Archipelago," she said and without any more prompting, Chaz and Sammi sat at two of the laptops, Tien walked to the other side of the room with a phone in her hand, Dinger hustled through to the canteen and Toby went out to a large storage hangar.

"HKG is Hong Kong and DPS is Denpasar," Sammi called out as she typed into open search boxes. "Time difference is plus seven from us in Paris, so it's currently 10:26 with him. Given the times he's told us, he's on a Hong Kong Air flight scheduled to leave at 12:25 and arrive into Bali, also seven hours ahead of us, at 17:35. Basically seven hours from now, give or take."

Kara moved behind Chaz and watched him open a Google map and scroll out. Right hand clicking on Le Bourget Airfield he selected 'measure distance' then zoomed in and clicked on the airport in Bali. The number that came up was 7699.

"That's in miles, Kara, so," he paused and opened a new search window to do the conversion, "6690 nautical miles."

He and Sammi looked up at her.

"We're not even close, are we?" she asked.

Tien, her call finished, joined them, "Not even remotely," she said. "The charter crew are up and on it. They'll have the necessary flight plan approved in an hour, just like they promised us, but the pilot gave me a choice. The jet can either go at maximum speed but then we'll need to refuel, or it can go for maximum cruise range and we get there in a single hop, but at a slower speed. Bizarrely, going slower, gets us there quicker because we miss out the fuel stop, but it's only half an hour's worth of difference."

"Do they have any alternatives?" Kara asked.

"No. I picked out the Gulfstream G650 because it was their fastest and longest range jet. Whatever way we try it we get to Bali between twelve and thirteen hours from now. If we get wheels-up in an hour, depending on wind conditions we'll be on the ground at about 23:00 Bali-time tonight. Jacob will have disappeared Kara. We'll not be there for him."

"How big is the place?" Kara asked. "It looks small."

Chaz turned back to the keyboard, "Population four odd million. Land size is…," he scribbled down some numbers on a pad next to the laptop, then brought up a list of English counties on Wikipedia, "…between the size of Devon and Somerset."

"We've lost him," Tien said and put the phone down on the table. She walked away and sat down on one of the couches. Sammi and Chaz went across to her.

Kara could hear them talking but she was staring at the large map on the wall. She was vaguely aware of Dinger calling that the chef had breakfast on the go and of Toby saying that he had all their kit ready for loading on the aircraft. She felt Sammi's hand on her arm.

"We're still going, aren't we?"

"Yes, of course. It doesn't matter how long it takes, we'll go out there and find him."

"Good. Come and get something to eat."

"Yeah, I'll be there in a minute. You guys go ahead."

Kara continued to stare at the map and then sat down at one of the PCs. She opened a search engine and after a few minutes she reached for her mobile phone.

The number took an age to connect, but, eventually, she heard it ringing.

"Hello?"

"Hi, Dan?"

"Kara?"

"Yep, it's me. How's things?"

"Umm, good… Kara, you do know wh-"

"Yeah, I know exactly where I'm ringing."

"This is going to cost you a fortune."

"Not important. Tell me, how was the wedding?"

"Eh, great. Yeah fantastic."

"Did Aisling look the part?"

"Yeah, she was beautiful. It was a great day, thanks for asking. But Kara, there's no way you're calling me all the way over here to talk about my big sister's wedding. What's going on?"

"I'm just wondering, where you are at the minute?"

"Right now, I'm sitting on a grass mound, in a place called Kings Park, looking out over a magnificent view of Perth and waiting for my brother to come back with a couple of coffees. Why?"

"What are you and Eugene up to for the next few days?"

"Bit of brotherly bonding. We're thinking of hiring a four-wheel drive and going native in the Australian Bush. We've still got two weeks out here and now the wedding's done and dusted we thought we'd try and see some stuff."

"Do you fancy seeing Bali?"

"When?"

"Your flight leaves in just under three hours."

28

Ngurah Rai International Airport, Bali. Friday 27th November.

Dan and Eugene O'Neill had been adopted from Nigeria by an Irish couple living in Mill Hill, London. The effect of the disconnect between their names and their appearance was evident on the faces of everyone they met and had been a source of amusement for them throughout their lives. It was also the reason they had learned to box at an early age. Their dad had told them that if they were going to get into fights because of their skin colour or their adopted heritage, then the least they could do was to win, and win quickly. The brothers had taken to the task with relish.

Eugene, the youngest but biggest of the two, won the Under-16 British schoolboys heavyweight title and Dan, the English ABA Middleweight Championship. Surprisingly, they gave up their promising amateur careers, as first Eugene, quickly followed by Dan, joined the British Parachute Regiment.

Nine years later, with a wealth of operational experience behind them, they left and established a private security firm. Kara, who had served with Eugene in Basra at the same time as she had met Tien, used them as her first choice for security back-up. It was through Dan that Jacob and Toby Harrop had been introduced to 'Wright & Tran Investigations'.

The flight from Perth touched down into Ngurah Rai International Airport, just outside Kuta, Bali, slightly ahead of schedule. As the aircraft gates stretched out in a single line for half a kilometre on either side of a newly extended terminal building, it took the brothers a brisk five minute walk just to reach passport control. There, the queue for the four desks that had immigration officials in attendance was a bizarre zig-zag that funnelled all arriving passengers into a single stream. The resultant line, herded into the middle of a huge arrivals hall, stretched back at least one hundred metres.

"This is the single worst use of space I think I've ever seen," Dan said and checked his watch. "How does that happen? We landed five minutes early and we've spent fifteen minutes just getting this far."

"Landing doesn't mean arrived," Eugene said, looking down at his iPad.

"Thanks, that's helpful. Where is he?"

Eugene looked up from the flight tracker app that showed a small, red, aircraft-shaped icon representing Jacob's flight. It was following an almost straight line from north to south on the screen and had already cleared the southern tip of Borneo. "He's still in the air, still set for a scheduled arrival of 17:35. Assuming worst case and his aircraft taxis straight to a gate that is closer than ours was and they open the doors as soon as possible, then I reckon he'll be standing where we are now in forty minutes."

"That doesn't give us a lot of time to hook up transport options."

"Seriously, I think transport's going to be the least of it." Eugene looked about the massive hall that formed only a tiny corner of the terminal complex. He and Dan had spent the three and a half hour flight studying every file that Tien had managed to email through before she and the rest of the team had boarded their own jet and left from Paris.

"Given the size of this place and where the hire cars are, I reckon it's a miracle if we get to follow him. We've got to assume he's being met and they'll have a car waiting nearby. If they're smart it would be right outside in the pick-up area and that will knacker us. I'd have said a cab would have been the best option, but from the Trip Advisor file Tien sent through, you have to go to a counter and get a ticket, then you wait for the driver to bring the cab round. Or, you go with one of the guys that hang about outside and walk with them to a parking area. Neither one lends itself to jumping in and yelling, 'follow that car' does it?"

"I guess not. But we're it matey boy. We have no fall back and if we lose him, he's in the wind."

"Shame we didn't have more time, or the chance to get any clever kit from Tien."

The line to the passport desks shuffled forward a few steps. Dan turned around and watched the latest gaggle of passengers join the queue. He stepped to the side of his brother and saw that the line now zigzagged at least another fifty metres back. Some people, a mother with a couple of small children, an older couple and a group of four young guys, had decided to drop out. They were sitting on the floor, to the side of the hall, obviously deciding to rest and wait for the queue to die down.

The line moved forward again.

"How many desks are open now?" Dan asked.

Eugene, at six foot three, peered over the crowd and said, "Five, out of a possible ten. Seems they think this is only half busy."

"How many people between them and us?"

"About… sixty."

If it takes three minutes per check that's about half an hour before we get through. He'll be landed by then."

"Yeah, but then he has to do all this too. He's still half an hour behind us."

"Unless all the desks open and things speed up a bit."

"Always the optimist Daniel," Eugene said.

"I'm not the one saying we've no chance of getting a car

in time."

"True."

The line moved forward again.

Dan pondered their circumstances. Eugene went back to looking at his iPad. The little red icon was moving closer.

φ

Twenty minutes later Dan and Eugene were within touching distance of the front of the queue.

"Hey?" Dan asked quietly.

"What?" Eugene answered, his head down, looking again at the red icon, now almost on top of the airport.

"Do you have your phone on you?"

"Yeah, of course."

"Is it linked to your iPad?"

"How'd you mean?"

"Do you have 'find-my-phone' activated?"

"Yeah, of cours-" Eugene stopped and looked up. "Oh, that's clever. Do you think it's possible?"

"I do, maybe. Depends. Kara said he'd have minders in tow, but it might be possible. Jacob's sharp on the uptake and a drop is easier than a pick."

"Puts him at risk."

"Losing him puts him at more."

"True," Eugene said and took another two steps forward.

"It means one of us has to drop out of this line and go all the way to the back," Dan said.

Eugene looked over the crowd to the end of a line that had increased, not decreased, in length. "Paper, rock, scissors?"

"Nah. It's okay bro. I'll do it. I'm less conspicuous. See if you can get some wheels sorted, but I'll Facebook message you when we're almost out. Here, give me that." Dan held his hand out and took the iPad.

In turn, Eugene took his iPhone out and disabled a few settings. After less than a minute, he handed it to Dan and took his iPad back, "That should be safe enough. Good luck."

Dan pocketed the phone and, apologising to those in his way, made it to the belted-barrier. Ducking under, he crossed the hall and sat down on the floor, his back against the wall. He positioned himself not quite next to, but near enough to give a false impression of association with, a group of ten teenagers and what he assumed were their three teachers. He looked at the group without staring and wondered if the adults were, in fact, teachers, or maybe scout leaders, or youth coordinators. He couldn't be sure, but all the kids had similar tops on. Not an actual uniform, but the same colour and general appearance. He saw they all wore pin-sticks with 'WYIFC 15' on them. He had no clue what it meant, but as he looked across to the slowly moving queue he noticed distinct groups of young people with adult supervisors. Their happiness and enthusiasm for whatever it was they were attending was infectious and he couldn't help but smile along with their smiles and laughter. Looking closer he identified at least twelve separate groups, some with more adults than others, but all with ten young people. They were a broad range of ethnicities. He picked out African, Asian, Indian sub-continent and Latino groups. There was a group that he guessed were from the Middle East or perhaps North Africa, the girls in it wearing a range of dress, from simple veils to full burqas, and a few groups of mixed ethnicity, that Dan thought might have been European or North American.

Looking to his right he saw another group of teens embedded in the middle of the latest flock of passengers streaming into the hall. This new contingent were easy to identify and also gave the answer to what was going on. A young man Dan guessed was about fifteen, tall, broad, with a shock of red hair above golden tanned skin, had a green flag draped over his shoulders. He turned to talk to his fellow travellers and the flag revealed a cartoon kangaroo with a speech bubble coming from its mouth that said 'G'day from Australia'. The roo held a gold balloon on which was written 'World Youth Interfaith Convention 2015'.

Dan stood and walked further along, keeping in rough line

with the end of the queue. Off to his left he saw a number of immigration officials come out from a side door. They walked with no haste but after a few minutes they had opened the remainder of the passport desks. He also caught a glimpse of Eugene's back as he exited to the next hall.

A few minutes later, he received a Facebook message notification on his own phone. 'Baggage reclaim smoother than passport control. All bags, including carryon have to go through a security scan. But not people. Plan still good to go. Queues not too bad. Bottle neck is passports.'

Five minutes passed before another message arrived. 'Am through. Massive crowds of people waiting out here. Seems a youth church thing going on. Marginal chance of keeping tabs on Jacob before he leaves building let alone in a car. Lot of armed police and army in attendance. Maybe aftermath of Paris, maybe protecting church crowd.'

Dan sent back, 'Okay. Get the paperwork done on a hire car, then wait.'

The passport line was moving a lot more swiftly now and a number of people who had been sitting to the sides of the hall began to re-join it. Dan watched the first group of WYIFC15 teenagers he had been sitting near make their way across. To his right, the latest group of passengers appeared at the broad entrance to the arrivals hall. Third into sight was Jacob Harrop.

Dan swung his small carryon case over his shoulder and in a couple of strides fell in at the back of the WYIFC group. He cast a casual glance to his right and saw the recognition in Jacob's eyes.

Jacob didn't alter his gait, but he raised both hands and gripped the shoulder straps of his backpack. His put his left index finger flat against the left strap and at the same time pointed with his right index finger at the blonde woman who was walking just ahead of him. The actions were swift and to anyone other than Dan, would have looked like he was simply adjusting the lie of the straps on his shoulders.

Dan raised his right hand to his face and quickly wiped his mouth from left to right.

Jacob glanced down at the ground and back up. The movement, once more looking like nothing in particular, provided confirmation that although Jacob knew of no other minders in his vicinity, there might be undisclosed, silent assets tracking him.

Dan paused, swung his case down and knelt as if checking an external compartment. The ten teenagers and their adult chaperones were at the side of the queue and beginning to filter into the zigzag. The newly arrived passengers slowed to allow them in. Dan, still checking his case, waited.

The flustered looking Asian business man, who had been the first through from Jacob's aircraft, stepped closer and as soon as the last of the youth group straightened out into the queue, he tagged onto the end. Dan stood up and slung his bag back over his shoulder.

The blonde woman covered the last few steps and joined the line. Dan stepped forward and allowed Jacob to pass him, before he swung into the queue ahead of a young couple.

The line was twisting forward steadily now. At the fourth turn, Jacob leant forward and said something quietly to the blonde woman. So quietly that Dan, only three steps back from him, didn't hear it. She shook her head in response. Jacob moved his hand behind his leg and gave Dan a quick hand signal to wait.

After ten more minutes the line zigged into the last leg before the passport desks. Dan saw what he hadn't noticed the last time he had gotten this far. The person at the head of the queue stood behind a yellow line. When a desk became free, the incumbent immigration official would signal for them to step forward. It meant a few seconds delay until either the person saw the gesture, or the person behind them in the queue drew their attention to it and pointed them on their way. Dan couldn't understand why they wouldn't just have separate lanes going to each desk, but was grateful they didn't.

The flustered business man, who seemed even more flustered now than he had on arrival, gained the yellow line. He scanned his head back and forth like a Wimbledon spectator, and when a hand went up he was away like a greyhound out of the traps. The blonde stepped forward. Jacob held his place, as did Dan.

The seconds stretched into minutes. Dan shuffled a step forward. A hand went up on the far right. The blonde saw it and walked towards it. Jacob stepped up to the line. Dan stepped closer and using Eugene's iPhone simulated making a call. It allowed him to talk quietly without drawing attention.

"Jacob, when the next official signals, stand still. Don't move until I point out the open desk. I'm going to plant a phone in your left trouser pocket. Keep it turned on. All tones and vibrations are off, lock code's disabled. We'll use it to track you but don't put it in your bag before you leave the airport. Security scans for luggage up ahead but not the person."

More seconds stretched by. Dan saw the blonde was paying attention to the immigration official.

"My number is first in the list of favourites if you need the cavalry. Only issue might be battery life but we should be okay for a good few hours. We're the advance guard, Kara and the rest are on their way too."

The immigration official two desks to Jacob's right raised his hand. Jacob stood still. Dan stepped forward almost bumping into him. He tapped Jacob on the right shoulder and pointed to the waving official. At the same time he slipped the iPhone into Jacob's left trouser pocket. As he withdrew his hand he delved into his own left hand pocket and grabbed his own phone.

Jacob did a double-take, saw the raised hand of the official and said, "Oh thanks."

When he walked away Dan was standing, phone to his ear, looking to anyone, other than a very close observer, like he was continuing the same call he had been on.

He 'hung-up' as the official on the far left of the line waved him over.

29

Bali.

Kelsey was waiting for Jacob at the entrance to the baggage reclaim hall. The delay at passport control meant both their bags had been lifted off the carousel and set in the middle of a jumble of others. Jacob clambered his way through and retrieved them, before walking across to another line of security stations. He dumped them and his backpack on the conveyor and waited as they trundled their way through the X-ray machine without incident.

"Why do they scan the bags on the way out of the airport?" He asked.

"Not sure, drugs maybe. They don't like them much here," Kelsey answered, scooping her handbag and suitcase up.

"Why not search the person as well?"

"No idea handsome, but not my concern. Come on," she said and set off down another long corridor. At the end it turned a sharp right and opened into a wide concourse that in turn led through to a thronged hall packed with hundreds of people, police, army and media crews. An impressively tall, gaudily painted statue of a fearsome half-man, half-dragon creature with huge eyes and larger fangs, held aloft a banner welcoming the delegates to the Youth Interfaith Convention.

"Surely is different to how the Baptists would welcome you in Texas," Kelsey said over her shoulder as they made their way towards the end of the area that divided the waiting crowds from the arriving passengers. "Although the number of police and army probably make the gun count about comparable," she said, slowing up and drawing him to one side. "It's going to be crazy busy out here, but you stick with me and don't go getting lost. We need to get to the front of the airport, there'll be a car waiting. Okay?"

"Okay," Jacob said.

He followed her through the press of people who semi-blocked the thoroughfare, before they emerged into the afternoon heat and humidity of Bali. Jacob was grateful for only wearing cotton trousers and a light T-shirt, but was still drenched in sweat after a few steps. He wanted to reach for the handkerchief in his pocket but he knew it was the only thing hiding the outline of the phone. He wiped his brow with his hand.

Kelsey glanced over at him, "What's the matter white boy, you no lik-ee the heat-ee?" she said and laughed.

"I don't mind heat, but this is like a sauna."

"Yeah, well, you'll be getting used to it, I have no doubt. Now come on, hurry it up. We're late as it is and the people you're meeting are particular about their time."

After a few more steps he realised the walkway they were traversing had the flow of direction for pedestrians marked out in coloured butterflies. It was subtle, but somehow calming. He thought Heathrow could have benefitted from a similar idea. What was less calming was that every two steps a blue-shirted man would ask him if he wanted 'Taxee? You need taxee?' Within twenty steps he had stopped answering politely and merely raised his hand and shook his head before they had asked the question.

The further he followed the butterflies, the thinner the crowd got until there was just a handful of people, including some of the 'Taxee' drivers, heading to a parking area on the opposite side of a single-lane road. Down on the left, in a small layby, was a black Mazda people carrier. A man about Jacob's age, slightly taller, though not as stockily built, stood at the side door of the vehicle. He wore sandals, blue shorts and a white T-shirt. His head was bald and he held his arms down in front of his body, his hands gripped together at groin height. Both arms showed tattoos that Jacob thought looked like the crude prison attempts he'd seen in TV movies. As the man turned to slide the side door open, two professional tattoos, one of a harp and the other a pair of crossed rifles, showed on his calves.

Kelsey stopped before crossing the road and Jacob almost walked into her.

"This is as far as me and you go handsome."

"What do you mean?" He asked.

She tilted her head towards the Mazda. "That's your ride. I don't need to see who else is in it. I've done my bit. You take good care of yourself now. Ya hear?"

"Umm, yeah. I mean, thanks."

She flicked a casual salute at the bald man, who returned the gesture, then she walked off towards a sign pointing to departures. Jacob walked towards the car.

By the time he reached it the bald man had gone around the front of the vehicle and climbed into the driver's seat. Jacob looked inside the rear passenger compartment. On the right of the vehicle, taking up two of the plush leather seats with his immense bulk was a man that Jacob thought must have been at least thirty stone in weight. He was reminded of the fat man in Amsterdam, but this guy was almost twice the size, and older, maybe sixty or more.

He wore a huge black, short-sleeve shirt, black shorts and sandals. His legs were massive mounds of flesh, and deep blue thrombotic veins laced towards knees, that were almost lost within rolls of fat. Flabby hands dangled from arms that looked fit to burst and a long, chunky gold bracelet, hung from the left wrist. A huge neck that reminded Jacob of Jabba the Hutt transitioned, with seemingly no distinction, into a double chin and a relatively small head, with grey hair shaved almost as short as the bald-headed driver. The man's nose was bulbous and threaded with red veins, his cheeks hung in jowls like an old basset hound and his eyes were underslung with bags of grey. The smell coming from the car, and from the man himself, was a strange mix of body odour and a strong, almost overpowering, smell of peppermint.

"Well, don't jus' fuckin' stand there mate. Get the fuck in. Fuckin' 'eats killin' me," the man said in harsh Cockney.

"Right, sorry," Jacob mumbled, about to step up into the cabin.

"Put your fuckin' bags in the back before you go fuckin' climbin' in and makin' me 'ave to move. Fuckin' 'ell."

"Right, sorry," Jacob repeated, stepping down and going to the rear of the vehicle. He opened the back door and hefted his luggage into the gap behind the last row of seats. Out of sight of both the fat man and the driver, he took the phone from his trouser pocket and slipped it into the side pouch of the backpack, making sure the zip was secured.

"Well c'mon, I 'aven't got all fuckin' day."

Jacob slammed the door, went back round to the side and climbed in. He'd just managed to close the sliding door and sit on one of the single seats to the left of the cabin, when the vehicle pulled away from the kerb.

"Welcome to fuckin' Bali, Jakey boy. I'm Tommo. You ever been 'ere before?"

"Umm, no, never."

"Well you're gonna luv it mate. How was the trip?"

"Yeah, not too-"

"I don' really give a shit Jakey. Jus' bein' sociable. All I wanna know; you on the run for killin', fuckin', or both?"

Jacob said nothing and looked down at his hands.

"Oi!"

Jacob looked up.

"That one wasn't fuckin' rhetorical. So?"

"Both," Jacob said through gritted teeth.

"Good, glad to fuckin' 'ear it. Right, well you're 'ome

now, so sit yerself back and relax." He took out a small tin of mints from his shirt pocket, flipped the hinged lid and emptied some into his mouth. "Fancy some?" He asked while crunching noisily.

"Umm, no, thanks."

Tommo dragged his bulk forward and raised his right buttock. He reached into the pocket of his shorts and took out a pack of cigarettes and a brass Zippo lighter.

"Do ya smoke Jakey?"

"No. Gave up."

"Ah well, you might refhink that out 'ere. Cheap as fuckin' chips mate. An' you can smoke anywhere you fuckin' like."

Tommo took a cigarette out of the pack, flicked the lighter, inhaled deeply and blew the smoke out. The enclosed cabin filled with the smell. Jacob thought it strange how much he disliked the smell of cigarettes now, considering he'd been a dedicated smoker since his days with 'Poisoned' Tanya right up until his early twenties.

"Yeah, maybe," he said without conviction.

"Relax Jakey boy. Don't be so fuckin' tight. We're on our way to a nice pad that you get to live in for free for a good few months. I'll look out for ya until we get you set up. No bovver. Even got a fuckin' pool. You ever had anyfink like that where you're from? Eh?"

"No, definitely not."

"Nah, wouldn't 'ave 'fhought so. Not an Essex boy like you. It is Essex, ain't it?"

Jacob nodded.

A set of exit barriers slowed their progress until the driver leaned out and handed some coins to an attendant. The red and white pole went up and the car turned onto the main road. Jacob looked through the windscreen and was shocked at the congestion. There were literally hundreds of motorbikes, or more correctly, mopeds and scooters. The majority of them with just a rider, but some were managing to support a couple of adults and a couple of kids, all balanced precariously on one small seat. The surprise on Jacob's face made Tommo laugh and cough at the same time.

"Yes mate. 'Elf an' safety not made it this far yet. Wait till you see your first mad bastard wif' a chicken coop on the back of his bike. Mind you, they're all fuckin' mad, the little brown bastards."

Jacob knew he had to stay in character, but he wondered just how long he could put up with Tommo before the desire to kill him overcame his need to play along. He nodded and forced himself to laugh.

"You don't talk much, do ya?"

"Sorry, I'm just knackered. It's been a long few days."

"Yeah, s'pose," Tommo said, flicking his ash straight onto the floor.

The car weaved its way through a crush of traffic, accompanied by high-pitched horn beeps, swerving scooters and other cars that somehow didn't touch despite edging through gaps that looked impossibly small. Jacob was equally appalled and impressed. No one seemed to be dying, nor were there hundreds of car wrecks pulled over to the side of the road, but he was sure it must happen. It couldn't not.

The sun was getting low in the sky and he reckoned twilight's diminishing visibility wouldn't improve the situation. He checked his watch and saw it was almost six-thirty. It had taken nearly an hour to get out of the airport and the truth of what he had said about being tired was becoming apparent. He also felt calmed and relaxed, more so than he had at any stage since leaving Paris. The surprise of seeing Dan O'Neill in the airport had been accompanied with a sense of wellbeing. It came from knowing the two men he trusted the most after his own brother, were somewhere in the vicinity.

"Tommo?"

"Fuck! It speaks. Yes mate, what can I do for ya?"

"How far have we got to go?"

"About an hour once we get clear of the worst of this fuckin' traffic. Why's that?"

"Just thinking I might shut my eyes. Is that okay?"

"Fuck yes mate. Nuffink you're gonna see anyway."

Jacob looked out the window again and watched the twilight fade rapidly to dark.

φ

Eugene was at the wheel of a light-golden Toyota Kijang, that wouldn't have been his first choice of rental, but as it turned out, had been his only option. The Toyota could at least seat six adults comfortably, whereas the only other car offered by the rental desk had been a bright pink Suzuki Splash that would have struggled accommodating Eugene on his own.

Dan, the iPad on his lap, tried his best not to look at the myriad of scooters and motorbikes that drifted in and out of the car's headlights. It was like driving in the middle of a swarm of fireflies and had not become much better even after leaving the centre of Kuta, heading north out of town.

"How many a year do you reckon get killed on the roads here?" Eugene said, breaking sharply to avoid a man on a tiny scooter that had two side panniers draped over the rear wheel, under what appeared to be a small oven for roasting nuts. It even had its own neon sign.

"God alone knows. You need to take the right hand turn off this next roundabout."

Eugene started laughing as he slowed at a set of traffic lights. "Yeah, good map reading bro. I think this is your roundabout."

Dan looked up to see a split, offset junction with five lanes converging. "Umm, I guess that one," he said pointing to the road on the far right. "I can't see any sign posts so we just keep going where this thing points us and hope he doesn't drive for the next twelve hours."

"How far ahead is he?"

"It's daft, but only about twenty clicks considering he must have left the airport half an hour before we got moving."

"No real surprise, when you consider the state of the traffic," Eugene said, moving off on the green light, then leaning on the horn to stop the oncoming cars, which, oblivious to the red light on their side, had continued forward just as he was about to swing right.

Dan looked up to see two cars and four motorbikes flow around them as they made the turn, like water would flow around a boulder in a stream. "Fuck's sake. This is fun."

Eugene didn't answer, his concentration fully on the road.

Another kilometre further and a badly moulded and dilapidated whitewashed wall showed up in their headlights and in the overspill from a small tower perched on the wall's corner. About fifty metres further along was a bigger, centrally mounted circular construction, also with light spilling from it. The outline of a man was visible in its small windows. The wall, only about two metres tall, was heightened by sharp metal stakes lined with razor mesh and topped off with tight rolls of barbed wire.

"What's that?" Eugene asked.

"Just checking," Dan said, swapping the display to a satellite-map hybrid. "It doesn't say. Just a big square of mixed buildings and a couple of tennis courts according to the image I'm looking at. It does have a double perimeter wall though."

"Maybe it's army?" Eugene speculated.

"They're not that interested in spick and span then. That wall's a disgrace," Dan said, looking over his shoulder as the strange facility passed by. "Turn left at the next junction."

φ

"Oi, sleepin' fuckin' beauty. Wake up and get yer arse in gear," Tommo shouted.

Jacob was instantly awake. He looked over to the big man who was shuffling himself to the edge of the seats he filled.

"Open the door and grab yer bags then. We're 'ome 'oney," Tommo said and laughed.

Jacob slid the door open and stepped out from the cool, air conditioned car into the heat of a Bali night. Storm clouds, threatening in their size, were clearly visible scudding across a virtually full moon, the light from which cast everything into sharp relief. Cicadas chirped incessantly and the bright lights illuminating the driveway he stood on were swarmed with insects of all shapes and sizes.

To his front were another two Mazda people carriers, parked to the side of a set of long, shallow steps. These led up to the entrance portico of a beautiful, golden-lit villa. Caught in the intermittent glare of the moon, Jacob could see the single storey building appeared to have a small 'hat' structure set atop the main, thatched, roof. Silver-grey silhouettes of tall palm trees surrounded the villa on three sides and beyond these he could sense, rather than see clearly, more buildings. Their dark shapes huddled amidst more trees and looked as if they were trying to hide from the moonlight.

He heard the springs of the car sag and then recover as Tommo extracted himself.

Jacob turned and opened the rear door, retrieving his bags. He hoped the battery on the phone was still working and he willed his luck to hold. The last thing he needed was someone deciding to search him, or his kit, like they had in Paris.

"Where you got to ya little fucker?" Tommo called.

"Here," Jacob said shutting the rear door and stepping back around the car.

Tommo was just an inch or two shorter than him, but about half the width of the people carrier. He threw a vast arm around Jacob's shoulders. The effect of the body odour, the peppermint, a breath of stale tobacco and the dampness of the man's armpit on Jacob's shoulder were almost enough to make Jacob shrug him off, but he doubted he would have been able to. The weight felt immense.

"C'mon. I'll show you to your new 'ome," Tommo said, swinging his legs up the shallow steps and dragging Jacob along with him.

The bald driver unlocked a solid double front door and stood aside.

"Oh, yeah." Tommo stopped and let go of Jacob. "This 'ere is Mutt. He's part of the security. There's two more jus' like 'im. They're called Bonce and Nasti. All 'free of 'em are

Paddies like, but not bad lads for a bunch of thieving Irish," Tommo laughed and ran his hand over Mutt's head. "Only kiddin' me old mucker."

Mutt gave the big man a genuinely warm smile.

"Anyway," Tommo continued, "you'll need to talk to 'em if you wanna go outside."

"How'd you mean?" Jacob asked, following Tommo into a wide, short hallway. His body temperature instantly dropped as he felt the air conditioning wash over him. The hallway walls were painted a cool cream colour and the floor was Italian white marble. Looking up, Jacob saw exposed beam work and a woven effect of what he assumed was the underside of the thatched roof.

"Well, me old son, you're on probation of a sorts. You got the cash to get you on the Flight Paf', but to be 'onest Jakey, I wouldn't trust you as far as I could 'fhrow you at the minute. I mean you could be fuckin' anybody, couldn't you?"

Jacob said nothing as he turned right and entered a subtly lit, large lounge room that he supposed took up nearly the whole length of the villa. The marble floor that flowed in from the hallway offset perfectly the comfortable furnishings that included three twin-seater futons, a good sized dining table with eight chairs around it and an elaborate sideboard that hosted a number of bottles of spirits, various decanters and two in-cabinet fridges for beer and wine. The whole lounge and dining space was immaculately finished with hanging art works, occasional art sculptures on small plinths and an appropriately sized television mounted on the far wall. Jacob took the details in peripherally, for his attention was captured by the two large windows and expansive glass doors, looking out to manicured lawns. Spots of light came from stone holders, shaped to look like miniature temples. Beyond the lawns a sapphire blue pool glistened and shimmered in the beams of underwater lights along its edge. Surrounding the pool in an arc were three villas like the one he stood in, but marginally smaller. These were the buildings he had sensed were in the shadows of the palm trees.

"Did you 'ear wot I said son?" Tommo asked as he puffed and struggled to sit down on one of the futons, which, even as a two-seater, barely managed to fit his bulk.

Jacob pulled his gaze from the gardens. "Yeah, I know. Ge-," He stopped himself. "One of the people on the Path, told me how it was."

"An' wot you 'fink of it?"

"I think it's a good thing. Makes perfect sense. You never know what the police are going to try and pull, so I've no problems with it."

"Good. Good lad. Well said. Anyways, you shouldn't 'ave long to be nurse-maid'ed by Mutt and 'is mates. Jus' don't go pissing 'em off. They're not what you'd call civilised." Tommo let out another laugh, then raised his hip and let out a long fart. While still up on one buttock he took out his cigarettes and lighter again. "You might wanna fuck off to yer room before I light up 'ere. That ripper could blow the 'ouse up." Tommo started laughing and coughing again as he waved him away.

Jacob couldn't imagine a more obnoxious clash than the slob that was Tommo, sitting in this beautifully cultured villa with its wondrous gardens and pool. He forced a laugh and turned to find Mutt standing by the door. Without a word, the security man walked into the hallway, turned right and made his way through to the rear entrance. He stopped and unlocked the door, allowed Jacob to step out, then relocked it.

"Are all the doors locked all the time?" Jacob asked.

Mutt spoke the first words Jacob had heard since meeting him at the airport, "Yes. You heard what Tommo said. While you're on probation, this place is locked down."

Mutt's soft Southern Irish lilt, caused Jacob to reflect on how many nationalities were involved in this network. It sickened and saddened him that humanity could have sunk so low, with the failings so widespread.

The entrance to the next villa along was not quite as elaborate as Tommo's but it wasn't shabby by any means. Mutt unlocked, then relocked the door before stepping ahead of

Jacob. He walked through the opening to the right. "Lounge, almost the same as next door. Smaller dining table, not as much nice art. No booze. You can ask me to get you some," Mutt said like a bored tour guide.

Walking to the far side of the room, he approached what Jacob at first thought was a gloss-white recessed panel in the wall. Mutt flipped a cover to access the handle of what could now be seen was a cleverly concealed sliding door. He eased it backwards to reveal a kitchen. Jacob ducked his head into a medium-sized space which looked to be equipped with the basics, but high-end basics. A stainless steel double fridge with built in water and ice dispenser, a dishwasher, four-slice toaster, matching kettle and a block of dimple-handled, single mould, chef's knives he recognised as being of top-quality Japanese design.

Mutt pushed the sliding door shut and led Jacob back into the hallway. Three doors faced the lounge entrance. Opening each in turn from left to right, Mutt said, "Bedroom with its own bog and shower, main bathroom with another bog and finally, another bedroom. Any questions?"

Jacob looked back into the lounge and through to the pool.

"Am I allowed to go for a swim?"

"Yeah, during the day when me or Bonce or Nasti are with you. Or anytime if Tommo and the others are around."

"The others? Are the rest of the villas occupied?"

Mutt turned away, "Nah. No one but you and Tommo here now. But when they have their parties, then most of them get full. Anything else?"

"Where do I eat?"

"There's snacks in the kitchen, but there's breakfast, lunch and dinner provided by the staff Tommo has come in."

"How do I get over there?"

"Easy, you just ask me, I'll be in here," Mutt said pointing to the bedroom on the right. "Well, me or one of the others. We get to babysit you until Tommo says you're good."

Jacob nodded, "Right. I see."

"Anything else?"

"No, I think that's it for now."

"Right, well dinner's at eight," Mutt checked his watch, "That's eighteen minutes, and you're invited."

Jacob felt awkward, given who these men were, but he figured he better check, "Is there a dress code?"

Mutt gave a wry smile and pointed down to his T-shirt, shorts and sandals, "Yeah, this is considered formal."

"Fair enough. I might just go and grab a shower."

"Okay, but don't be late. Tommo doesn't like his meals delayed."

Jacob took himself and his bags into the main bedroom. He wandered around the room like he was admiring the fixtures, but despite his best efforts, he couldn't be totally sure there were no surveillance cameras. He decided to leave the phone where it was. Better that than give himself away. He lifted his washbag from his case and went for a shower.

30

Eugene dropped down a gear and pulled in just past a bend in the road. Killing the engine but leaving the parking lights on, he joined Dan on the other side of the road. The moonlight, battling the increasing storm clouds, still managed to turn the world pewter.

"We're not particularly equipped to go dancing into danger," Eugene said, moving cautiously. The single-width road was lined with a strange mix of grass, trees, dense bush, the occasional shack with corrugated shutters and directly opposite where Dan and Eugene stood, a beautifully ornate medium height wall, in a much sounder state than the dilapidated white one they'd passed. The wall had an intricately carved archway that allowed them to see through to an inner courtyard, gardens and a central building only just visible as the clouds won temporary ascendency against the moon.

"What do you reckon?" Eugene asked.

"Temple maybe. Some of the background Tien sent through had pictures of places like that. Anyway, not going to be an issue, we're up here," Dan said and pointed away from the temple, to a dark laneway at their backs.

The narrow road, hemmed in at first by the walls of some adjoining buildings, then by thick clumps of trees and denser bush, was humped in the middle with indented tracks running either side. Its surface was crushed gravel and a thin ditch, filled with rubbish, ran along the right-hand side.

Eugene led off. The lane ran straight for two hundred metres then turned in a relatively sharp left-hand bend.

"Here," Dan said, pointing across the road to the apex of the curve.

Eugene looked to where his brother was indicating. Apart from having to negotiate the rubbish filled ditch, the lane was now exclusively lined with thick-set trees and low bushes.

"How far on the other side?"

"About thirty metres, maybe forty. Then you're through to tended lawns and a swimming pool. But that's all based on the Google imagery and it could well be out of date. According to it, there's four houses clustered around the pool. The bigger one has the driveway going up to it."

"How far down the lane till you get to it?" Eugene asked.

"As far again as we've just walked. It bends out and around before coming back in on itself."

"Do you want to try pushing through these trees and see what we can see?"

Dan considered it then shook his head, "No. We've no idea how thick this gets and we could end up creating more noise than a rampaging bull. We also have no real idea what's on the other side. The phone location shows him roughly in that group of houses. Actually it shows him in the middle of the swimming pool, but I guess it's not that accurate."

"Okay, so now what?"

Dan checked his watch, "It's almost nine, Kara and the rest of them are due to arrive in a couple of hours. I reckon we go and book a hotel somewhere close to here and wait for their call."

φ

His dinner plate was taken away by one of the two elderly Balinese ladies who worked as Tommo's cooks and maids.

"Thank you," Jacob said.

"Welcome," the lady said in a sing-song lilt. "I go now Mr Tommo. Wayan will draw your bath and tidy up."

Before she had made it back into the kitchen, similar to the one in Jacob's villa but much larger, Tommo said, "I told you mate, you don' need to keep 'fanking 'em. They get well paid to be 'ere. I'm far too generous, if I'm 'onest. Probably fuckin' up their whole economy by paying what I do, but it's all cash, so no tax to worry about. Know wot I mean?"

Jacob fought the desire to tell Tommo to go fuck himself and managed to give a light laugh, "Very good Tommo, nice one."

The big man reached forward for his cigarettes and lit his third since he'd been at the table. A ring of carelessly flicked ash surrounded a metal ashtray to his right.

"You sure you don't want one Jakey?"

"Nah I'm good. Maybe see how I feel after being here a while."

"Good lad, that's what I like to 'ere." Tommo pushed back his chair and looked about the lounge. "So, do ya like me gaff then?"

"I do mate, love it. Must cost a fortune."

"Nah. cheap-as mate. Well, cheap-as if you know the right people and can slip a few quid their way when you need somefink sorted. Get me drift?"

"Yeah, but still, must have cost. Can I ask you?" Jacob stopped.

Tommo, cigarette halfway to his mouth, frowned, "Ask me wot?"

"How'd you get your money? How'd you manage to get set up here?"

"Aww that? Fuck yes mate, I've no secrets. Well, that's not true now, is it?" he laughed loudly and ended it in a fit of coughing. Jacob waited.

Tommo sniffed and rubbed his arm across his nose. "Nah,

it's okay, I'll tell ya. I 'ad to get out of England back in the nineties. Very dodgy goin' ons so there was and a whole lot of us nearly got snaffled up by the old bill. Flying Squad an' all sorts came in on it. Like a fuckin' episode of the Sweeny," Tommo stopped talking and studied Jacob. "You're too young to 'ave watched the Sweeny, ain't you son?"

Jacob nodded, "Yeah, but my old man told me about it," he said.

Tommo laughed again, "Ha, very good. You're all right boy. I 'fink me an' you'll get on like a fuckin' 'ouse on fire... Anyways, the old bill did a roundup and I got out to Spain. But I 'ad names and numbers of a good few people and they was all getting a bit squeaky bum time. There weren't no Internet nor nuffink back in 'em days, so they was keen to see me get rid of all their details. Said they could get me out and far away if I'd clean 'ouse for 'em. Lose all their information." Tommo took a long drag on the cigarette and blew the smoke up towards the ceiling. Jacob's gaze followed its rise and saw the woven ceiling just at that spot was stained a dark yellow.

"So I says," Tommo continued, "yeah 'course I will and they puts me in touch with this old geezer in Paris. Long story short turns out he, Serge was his name, fuckin' dead now like, but back then, turns out he was in charge of this 'fhing called Flight Paf'. Not only in charge, but Serge was the fuckin' founder of Flight Paf' weren't he. Said he'd set it up back in the seventies to 'elp some of his mates fuck off after a couple of girls died. Wasn't like it is now. Back then there was all border patrols and Iron Curtains and the Ruskies gonna nuke everybody. Moving people out of Western Europe was very dodgy. Expensive too. So the Flight Paf' was like for all the snobs and toffs who could afford it. No way could I get on it normally, but 'em same type of fuckin' toffs back in London, wanted me to do 'em a favour, so they paid. See?"

"Right," Jacob said, not sure Tommo had managed to answer his original question. He was going to push it, but Tommo stared talking again.

"So I'm there and old Serge says to me that he needs

someone at the Asian end of 'fhings. Says he 'ad a fella running it out 'ere but he went and died on 'im. Says he wanted someone wif' a bit of street smarts but all the people who used the Flight Paf' weren't the right sort." Tommo took another drag on the cigarette.

"But you were?" Jacob said, as upbeat as he could.

"Yes mate. See, I'd been banged up for bein' a bit naughty wif' me fists. I know, I know, you're 'fhinking, that fat bastard, really? But see I was a bouncer down in the East End. Fuckin' very tasty I was. Mutt and his boys are good, but I'd 'ave skinned them in my day. Fast I was. Still am under all this," he said and clapped himself on his chest, sending ash flying from the end of the cigarette.

"Anyways, Serge says I'd be set up in a villa. Lump sum cash to get started and I'd be paid for every person comin' 'fru on the Paf'. Seemed okay to me. I mean, wot the fuck's not to like eh?"

"Fuck yeah. Sounds sweet," Jacob managed to sound envious.

"So, that was me, I was in. But, before I even got a chance to say yes, he says that I'd also 'ave all the girls I can 'andle. Free perk. He had lots of contacts up north and over east. Said when they got girls, I'd get sent some. Fuckin' sweet, like you said. I was in. Been twenty-two years now. Still fuckin' sweet. Got a bit fatter though. All this good livin' I'm doin." He took a last pull on the cigarette and crushed it out in the ashtray.

"Wow! That's fuckin' awesome Tommo. You lucked in there didn't you?" Jacob enthused and then added, "I don't get it though. You mean they get girls from up north of England and ship them out here?"

Tommo looked perplexed. "Nah, ya daft bastard. Up north of 'ere. On the island. Over east too. Real fuckin' remote areas. Couple of head-honchos in some of the villages set up a steady supply. They takes the little fuckers from the families when they get ripe, if you know wot I mean. Still going now all these years later, passed down from father to son like a weird brown mafia. Mind you, no fuckin' wonder it's still goin' 'cos they use real extreme methods to keep the rest of their people schtum. Makes the Krays look like fuckin' pussies."

"That's some life you fell into, ain't it?" Jacob said, feeling sick at the sound of it.

"It is and now you're out 'ere too you'll get to reap some of the rewards me old son."

"But I'm not sure how all of it's going to work. I mean, I don't have unlimited cash."

"Don't you worry about that Jakey. We 'ave a whole circle of us out 'ere. We all 'elps and we all contributes. We 'ave some lucrative little sidelines. I mean, you don't 'ave to go and work a nine to five nor nuffink. You look like a big boy that can 'andle yourself. We 'ave need of that. Sometimes, some of our little dalliances gets out to the public. Police and judges sometimes can't be bought off, so we need to remind anyone that might be 'fhinking of telling tales, that talking can be bad for their 'earts. And their fuckin' 'eads." Tommo leant his bulk on the table and pushed himself up. "But no bovver Jakey. You'll get to meet all the lads soon enough. But for now, I'm goin' to go and have me a baff. Always 'ave one, every night. Add peppermint oils to the water. Lovely. Ever tried that son?"

Jacob stood and shook his head.

"Nah, ya see, more stuff you'll 'ave to try out 'ere. Okay then, fuck off and I'll see ya tomorra'. MUTT."

Mutt appeared in the entrance to the hallway.

"Take our boy back to his room."

With the lights off, Jacob folded the duvet back and raised the side of the mattress. The bedframe consisted of a series of bowed slats, tensioned by virtue of being held in slots at the sides and in a central stave that ran the length of the frame. He lifted the mattress onto his shoulder. The iPhone fitted on the central stave and couldn't fall through the tightly packed slats. He checked the battery and saw it still had 46% showing. Then he gently lowered the mattress back down and got into bed. He tried to close his eyes but the thoughts of the last few days were spinning in his head. He knew that using the phone would decrease its life but he decided it was more important to get the things he'd seen and heard recorded.

Slipping back out of bed he recovered the phone, opened up the notes app and began to type. It was almost two in the morning by the time he'd finished. Detailed descriptions of all the people he had met, the route from Singapore airport to Gerard's safe house and every detail he had learnt about the operation of the Flight Path. Lastly he added everything Tommo had revealed tonight.

He replaced the phone and lay down. The full implications of what Tommo had said about the remote villages and how they supplied children into a network of vice, played over and over in his mind. He saw his nephew and nieces, happy in their safe and protected childhood. Unless they ever came into contact with men like Tommo, or Gerard or women like Kelsey. For the first time in as long as he could remember, he cried himself to sleep.

31

Saturday 28th November.

Kara and Tien were in the back of a second Toyota Kijang. This one, black and newer than Dan and Eugene's, was parked behind the brothers' light-golden model. Both cars were two kilometres from the laneway that led down to where the 'find-my-phone' app said Eugene's iPhone was located. Sammi was in the passenger seat and Chaz was behind the wheel. Dinger and Toby were in with the O'Neills.

Tien tested the comms and boosted the amplifier nestled on the third row of seats behind her, "All callsigns, I have it as 03:40"

A series of clicks acknowledged her.

The Gulfstream had touched down at 23:05, slightly later than estimated due to strong headwinds, but the team had arrived completely refreshed. During the flight, the on-board attendants had laid their seats down into fully horizontal beds, dimmed the cabin and nurtured them like they were children in a nursery. After a solid eight hours, they'd been wakened, fed, and allowed to indulge themselves with the in-flight entertainment systems. Sammi had summed up the whole experience most simply by saying it had ruined normal air travel for her, forever.

They'd phoned Dan and Eugene on landing, rendezvoused with them at the hotel Dan had booked them into and spent the last few hours getting ready for what was coming. Toby had inconspicuously distributed the necessary equipment between the two cars so that when they had walked out of the hotel lobby they looked like eight friends, dressed for a night out in the clubs of Kuta.

Now, dressed head to toe in black, equipped with night vision goggles and radio mics, they all climbed out of the cars and made their way silently along the edge of the road. A sky filled with heavily laden storm clouds had effectively switched off the earlier brightness of the moon and although those same clouds also threatened a massive downpour, they had, as yet, held off.

When Chaz reached the point that Dan and Eugene had stopped at previously, he led the team through the first line of tightly packed bushes and trees. Much more detailed and up-to-date imagery, downloaded by Tien in the hotel room, had shown that what, on the older Google maps, had looked like twenty metres deep, almost impenetrable semi-jungle was in fact a narrow line of vegetation. On the other side it opened into lightly covered scrub. It also revealed that Dan and Eugene would have walked into a series of flooded Paddy fields had they gone in a straight line. Chaz, the imagery committed to memory, and his night vision goggles painting the landscape green, moved silently across the open terrain. He scouted around the Paddy fields and manoeuvred around a series of low walls, remnants of some long ago dwelling.

He stopped and crouched when he came to the next out-crop of dense vegetation. The other seven spread out in a line to his left.

"All set?" he asked.

Kara, from her position on the end of the line, made her way up to Chaz, patting each person on the shoulder and getting a thumbs-up in return.

Crouching next to him she said, "Okay. Let's get this done."

All eight rose together and went through the tree line. The tightly packed leaves and close-knitted branches were a slight cause for concern noise-wise, but there was nothing to be done for it. Breaking through they crouched again and took in the view ahead. Perfectly manicured gardens, dotted with strange little temples that, from the imagery, Chaz and Sammi had assessed were likely to be light fixtures, now lay in complete darkness. As did a large, mostly rectangular, pool. The four surrounding villas also showed no lights. It was as they had expected it would be at this time of the morning.

Kara clicked her mic and all eight set off again. She and Eugene skirted the side of the pool and approached the rear door of the second villa. Chaz and Toby moved to the one on her left, the biggest of the four. Sammi, with Dinger, approached the one on Kara's right and Tien, accompanied by Toby moved to the villa farthest to the right.

Kara tried the door handle and as she had mostly expected, found it locked. She bent and removed a set of skeleton keys from her pocket and laid out the black felt roll on her thigh. Selecting a small angular pick with a series of notched bumps, she pushed her goggles to the top of her head. The new binocular-goggles were a huge improvement on the old monocular ones she and Tien had mostly used in the past, but for close work they still made depth perception hard and hindered her judgement as to how close the pick was to the lock. The pitch blackness she now had to deal with wasn't as much of a concern. Kara knew that picking locks was mostly done by feel and instinct. She also knew that frustration at not getting it first time was not a help. She breathed out and started again. After another minute she heard the satisfactory soft click as the tumblers aligned.

Eugene followed her into a cool, marble-floored hallway and they both stood still. They remained like that for a good three minutes. Not to adjust their sight, as the building's interior was as pitch black as outside, but to grow accustomed to the sounds and the feel of the house. Kara, her goggles back in place, sensed the place was occupied. She didn't know by how many or by who, but she knew there was at least one person somewhere in the darkness.

She moved down the hallway, slowly sweeping her vision left and right. Directly ahead of her was the main, front door. To her right she passed a closed door, then one that was ajar. Looking in she saw a bathroom. Further along from it was another closed door. Opposite the bathroom was an open entrance to a lounge room. She looked in and confirmed the spacious room was empty. With hand signals she told Eugene she was going to check the closed door to her left first, then the one to her right. Fully aware that these were likely to be occupied bedrooms, she moved excruciatingly slowly.

The handle was a lever action and she took half a minute to depress it fully. Another half a minute went by before she put any pressure on the door in an attempt to move it inwards. It took a further three minutes for her to ease it open sufficiently to look inside. She withdrew her head back out of the room and clicked her radio three times. She didn't expect, nor did she need, any confirmatory clicks. Eugene, less than two feet from her, but who had also heard the clicks in his earpiece turned and took up a blocking position between her and the closed door further down the corridor.

Kara moved into the bedroom and as slowly as she had opened it, she eased the door closed. She walked silently across the tiled floor and moved into position to do the most dangerous part of her night so far. Bending low, she reached her hand out, tentatively, knowing that her depth perception was likely to be off and therefore she could well miss her target. A final steadying breath and she plunged her hand down onto Jacob's mouth. She did miss and hit the bottom of his nose before flopping her palm over his lips.

Leaning in close and pressing down as much as she could to stop him reacting and rearing up, she whispered in a voice so quiet it didn't activate her mic system, "Jacob, It's Kara. Be quiet. Tap my hand when you're ready."

Kara was impressed when the tap came almost instantly. It wasn't a usual thing to be assaulted in your bed at night and most people she'd done this to had struggled and fought for at least a few seconds. It was rare for someone's brain to process the facts so quickly, while in that strange state between asleep and awake.

She took her hand away and when Jacob had pushed himself up in the bed, she leant in sideways to have her mouth as close to his ear as possible, without hitting him in the head with her goggles.

"You doing okay?" She asked.

"Just about. We need to take these people down," he whispered into her ear.

"Is Derek Swift here?"

"No. Just me and the boss man of the Balinese end of the operation. A Brit called Tommo. Huge guy, must be at least thirty stone. Plus three security. Only met one so far, but meant to be three on site."

"Well, get up and get ready, we're extracting you now."

"No Kara. No way. They'll go to ground if I disappear."

"But Swift's not here so what's the point in dragging it out?"

"Tommo says I'll get to meet the rest of what he called 'the lads' soon enough. If Swift is in Bali then he's bound to be invited."

"And if he's not?"

"Then we still get to sweep up a whole host of bastards."

"So what's your plan?"

"I don't have one. I wasn't expecting you to drop in on me."

Kara, her cheek next to his, felt him grin.

"But I might have an idea, now you're here. It's going to be tough. They have judges and lawyers sewn up and when they don't do that, they have intimidation. I'm not sure, but there's a chance none of them would go down for what they've been doing. But we've got to try."

"So what's the idea?" Kara asked.

"I wrote down, on Eugene's phone, what I know so far. If you take it and talk to the authorities, then it might be enough for them to act on. I'll stay here so they won't be suspicious. I assume you'll put an overwatch on me?"

"Of course."

"Then when the rest turn up, whether Swift is with them or not, I'll signal you and you can have the cops come charging in."

"You're sure?" Kara asked.

"Absolutely. Now take the phone."

He slipped out of bed and raised the mattress. Kara retrieved the phone then waited until he'd climbed back into bed. She leant in close again, "You be careful Jacob. Tien will be upset if you're not."

"Tell her I'm doing fine, will you?"

"Course I will." She went to get up, but stopped. "Jacob?"

"Yeah?"

"Is this a case of dark hearts?"

"Toby told you about them then?"

"Yeah. So is it?"

"Never more so."

She made her way to the door and just as slowly as she had eased into the room, she eased back out into the hallway. Eugene was standing in exactly the position she had left him. Kara wasn't surprised. Dan and Eugene were the most disciplined security team she had ever known, but her admiration and respect for the Harrop brothers was growing daily.

By the time she and Eugene had made their way back to the edge of the lawns and the thick undergrowth of the tree line the rest were already there.

"Where's Jacob? You signalled you'd found him, where is he?" Tien asked.

"We did, but he's not coming out. He wants us to try something but now's not the time or place to discuss it. We need to get the fuck out of here and let Chaz and Sammi find us decent surveillance positions before dawn. Then we'll figure out a shift system."

No one, not even Tien, who Kara knew would be tearing herself apart at leaving him on his own, put up an objection. They all accepted that the decision had been made and it was time to sort out how to manage it, not moan about it.

φ

By ten in the morning, Dan and Eugene had been in their covert hide for four hours. Chaz and Sammi had used the available imagery to pick a position which was a compromise between the need for complete invisibility and the need to be close enough to provide security to Jacob. The result was situated within a dense stretch of what could have passed for a piece of rainforest someone had forgotten to chop down. It gave clear sightlines across a thirty metre gap to the swimming pool and three of the four villa's lounges and was approached from the rear by crossing a section of dense scrub that itself was accessed from a small roadway that ran up the side of a deep ravine. Toby was in one of the Toyotas parked two hundred metres back along that road.

Dinger was in a similar, if much smaller covert hide position, on the other side of the complex. He was only ten metres from the top of the driveway and the entrance to the biggest of the four villas.

By half past ten, Sammi, Chaz, Tien and Kara, back at the hotel, had taken a break from discussing Jacob's notes and what could be done with them. They weren't the least bit hopeful there was enough to secure a conviction.

Tien put the in-room kettle on and began to make cups of tea.

Chaz opened up his laptop intending to search for the exact meaning of 'circumstantial'.

"What's that?" Sammi asked, looking at the image on his screen.

"It's just the local prison," he said going to shut the window down.

285

"Oh let's have a look," Sammi said, sliding onto the seat next to him and almost pushing him off.

"Geez Sammi, you're so delicate," he said and got an elbow in the side for his trouble.

"Why are you looking at this anyway?" She asked.

"Dan and Eugene asked me to. They'd driven past a place last night, didn't know what it was so Dan had tried to figure it out from his iPad Google map, but with no success."

Sammi chuckled.

"Yeah I know," Chaz said, "how could you not know it's a prison."

Kara wandered over, intrigued by his last comment. "I don't get what you mean."

"Well of course you do not, my little non-imagery, dark-side intelligence sad-ling. You are not gifted in the mysterious ways of enlightenment."

Kara raised her middle finger, "Don't start your normal bullshit about how imagery analysts are the Jedi mind warriors of the Intel world. I'm not in the mood. Just tell me what you meant about the prison, Obi One Ball" she said, giving Sammi a wink.

Chaz pouted, then said, "Fair enough. You see this whole area on the screen? It has a double wall running around it. Clear area between the walls. A guard tower at every corner and in the mid-section of each outer wall, except the wall that sits to the north. That one faces a car parking area and the main road. It has a larger, probable administration reception centre sitting amidst it. There's only one entrance into the whole place. Inside the walls there's a distinct divide. The place is split into two. That makes it likely to be a joint male and female facility, or a semi-secure and real bad-ass prisoner split. The low-level accommodation blocks surround a central compound, probably accessible to all, with a couple of areas for fitness and recreation including a tennis court and a prominent Mosque, perfectly aligned to Mecca. Aside from the Mosque, which would be a church or a synagogue depending on what country you're in, to anyone trained in imagery the rest of this place shouts prison like, oh I don't know what like… Sammi?"

"Like a bear coming out of the woods with an Andrex puppy under its arm," she said.

Kara laughed and took the cup of tea that Tien handed to her. "Thanks, Tien. Anyway, I missed the beginning of this conversation, why are you looking at a prison?"

"Because Dan didn't know what it was. They'd driven past it last night. He said it had tall railings on top of the outer wall, razor mesh and barbed wire but that the outer wall was minging. All peeling paint and mouldy. He thought it might have been an army camp but for that."

"So what is it? I assume you've run a check." Kara asked.

"Course I have. Oh thanks," Chaz said taking the offered tea. "It's Kerobokan Prison, described by some as a hellhole and by others as a cesspit. There's not much in the way of good PR for the place. It's where the Bali bombers went and a whole bunch of hi-profile Aussies."

"Do you remember Schapelle Corby?" Tien asked.

Kara thought for a moment, "The surf board full of drugs?"

"Yeah. She went there. It's not a fun place."

"It's where that British woman is too," Sammi added. "You know the one that's been sentenced to death for drug smuggling. Made the news a couple of years ago because she was expected to get a term sentence but got death by firing squad instead."

Chaz shrugged, "The court said she had taken the piss out of their anti-drug stance."

"I doubt they said that Chaz," Tien said, handing Sammi her tea.

"Yeah, they may have worded it a bit more upmarket, but that's what they meant."

"So what you're saying is that if you get done with drugs over here you either do hard time, or you get killed?" Kara asked the three of them.

"Basically, yep and sometimes you do the hard time and

287

then get killed," Chaz said. Sammi and Tien nodded.

"And yet we have a bunch of the worst scum on the planet, with a full rundown of their activities and how they spirit people away from justice, but not one shred of real evidence so they'll likely walk scot-free?"

"Yeah," Chaz said, a lot more downbeat.

The four of them drank their tea and Chaz started the search that he had intended before the conversation had turned to the prison.

Tien stood and walked to the far side of the room. She looked out the hotel window to the gently shimmering water of the Indian Ocean. "Kara?"

"Yeah?"

"Do you reckon the police in Britain have got any spare drugs?"

32

Victoria Oxford was still serving in the British military but had left her Royal Navy beginnings far in the past. As Kara and Tien's boss on the deployment to Basra, and later in subsequent operations, she was trusted by Kara above everyone else, bar Tien. The only issue was that being still active, getting in touch could be problematic. So it was that four hours went past between Kara ringing an emergency contact number and her own mobile beginning to vibrate on the table.

The incoming call merely said 'Overseas'.

"Hello?"

"You rang my dear?"

"I did. Can we talk?"

"Do you mean can we talk securely?"

"Yes."

"No," Victoria said. "If you need to do that we shall have to be cleverer. Have you got Internet access?"

"Yes."

"I'll text you a link. Ciao."

The line went dead. Kara waited and a few minutes later a

text arrived.

Tien copied the web address and posted it into a browser. A secure padlock appeared on the screen and under it a terminal server interface with two boxes asking for username and password.

Another text arrived on Kara's phone giving not a username and password but two questions.

"She wants the first name of the Police liaison officer we worked with in Northern Ireland," Kara said.

Tien typed in Demi.

"And the name of the puppy we sponsored in 2009 down in Hereford."

Tien typed in Rasputin and pressed enter.

The screen blanked, then refreshed. A sharp feedback tone with treble echo sounded in the speaker before Victoria's voice came through clearly.

"Hi, can you hear me?"

"Oh, wasn't expecting that. I need to activate the laptop's built-in mic," Tien said, clicking on a settings screen and rapidly accessing menus. Kara waited patiently.

Victoria repeated herself twice more before Tien said, "Yeah, sorry, didn't know we were doing comms. Can you hear us?"

"Loud and clear Tien. So, Kara my dear, you rang?"

"Yeah. You back in London?"

"No. Actually I'm in the same place I was when last we spoke. Well, not true. I'm a little further into no-man's-land but near enough."

"Ah, that's a shame."

"Why, what do you need?"

"Access to a diplomatic pouch."

"Where's it going to?"

"Bali."

"Indonesia?"

"Yeah, but I've checked, we have a consulate here in a place called Denpasar," Kara said.

"I might be able to help you out. I'm not in London but I

can probably call a few chaps and arrange it from here if we're quick. I have to head out in a few hours. Do I want to ask what we're transporting?"

"Not really," Kara said.

"Okay. I'll text you 'go' or 'no-go' in an hour or so. If it is a go then get whatever it is to Box. Ask for Jamie Birch. Got it?"

"Yeah. That's great, thanks."

"Don't mention it. Only issue will be if Jamie's not around. No one else I trust to do it. Right, got to dash. Love to all."

"Bye," both Tien and Kara said to the laptop screen before Victoria disconnected.

φ

Franklyn answered his phone on the fifth ring.

"Yes, who is it?" he asked, the sleep still evident in his voice.

"Me. I need you to call a number but not from your normal phone please."

His voice was instantly alert, "Certainly. Send it through."

Kara disconnected and texted the number of an unregistered Indonesian mobile she had bought from a 7-11 across the road from the hotel. It rang a few minutes later.

"Good morning. I'm sorry to have woken you at this early hour," she said, knowing it had just gone 04:00 in the UK. She put the phone on speaker mode.

"That is alright. I assume it is urgent. What do you need?"

"I want the official side of your contacts to misappropriate some evidence."

"Go on."

"I need a quantity of drugs. The harder the better."

Franklyn didn't even pause, "Okay, how much of it?"

Kara looked over to Tien, Sammi and Chaz. They looked as surprised as she felt at the way the man had just accepted this strangest of requests.

"One or two kilos would be good. Ten would be better but that might be noticed if it walked out the door."

"Where do you need it to be?"

Kara told him the details that Victoria had confirmed by her 'Go' text message, sent through minutes earlier.

"Fine. Leave it with me. I cannot see it presenting too much of a problem. Do you need confirmation?"

"No. The courier will provide that for us. Keep things simple."

"Well, I could think of simpler things than what you are suggesting, but yes I concur," he said and chuckled.

"My, aren't you in a good mood at such an early hour?"

"I am. Surprisingly. Is there anything else?"

"Yes. Tien will send you a link to a file soon. It contains notes on everything we've found out to date. You may want to pass it through to the appropriate people."

"I shall look forward to reading it. Any word as yet on Swift?"

"None, but if we're likely to find him, then we're currently in the right place."

"I do not doubt it. Anything else?"

"Not for now."

"Excellent. Stay safe."

"You too,"

The call disconnected.

"We need to hire another car," Sammi said.

φ

Chaz took over from Toby, who in turn took over from Dinger, while Dan and Eugene were replaced by Tien and Sammi. The kit that Dinger had picked up in London and brought to Paris was now proving invaluable. The jungle pattern combat clothing allowed them to blend in with their surroundings, the long range surveillance glasses meant they had an up-close view of everything going on in the majority of the villa complex and the soft-skinned water bladders they wore on their backs, kept them hydrated in an afternoon sun that was pumping oppressive heat into the day. Soft shimmers of localised mirages rose in the air, but they didn't prevent a clear view of Jacob, swimming in the pool.

Sammi whispered, "Oh my, he is a well-built boy, isn't he?" She looked sideways to Tien and could see a flush of colour rising in her face.

"Sammi!" Tien said in a forced whisper.

"Ah admit it. You like him."

There was quiet for some time before Tien turned her head slowly, "Yes I do. I can't explain it, but I was horrified at first by what he did in Amsterdam. Then, I, well… I suppose I realised that for such a sweet, shy guy, he must have cared for me to have gotten so mad."

"Cared for you?" Sammi said with a gentle play to her voice. "The guy is besotted with you. Can't you see that?"

"No. Well, I mean… I know he… aww stop it Sammi."

"No Tien, I'm not teasing you. He seriously is. It was written all over his face when I first got to Amsterdam."

"Really?"

"Yes, really. Anyway, he's a nice guy. Good for you."

"Well it's not like we've gone out or anything. We just talked, that's all."

"I wouldn't have thought anything different of you Tien," Sammi said.

"Aww, now you are teasing."

"Maybe I a- Oh for fuck's sake!"

"Sammi!" Tien said, surprised at the sudden, although still quiet, expletive.

"Well… that's just not funny, is it?" Sammi said and pointed with a slow nod of her head, to her own left hand.

The women, lying side by side on their stomachs in the hide, had both of their arms out in front of them. It allowed use of the long-range binoculars while ensuring they stayed as flat as possible. The key to successful and therefore unnoticed observation, was minimal movement. Certainly no fast movements. Everything needed to be done with a calmness that allowed the surrounding environment to envelope the observers. That way, those being observed would be completely unaware. It called for a lot of self-discipline.

Tien looked to where Sammi was indicating. A fat, almost thumb-width-fat, black millipede was crawling across the back of Sammi's hand. Its front legs were rippling over her thumb nail and the last of its back legs hadn't even reached her little finger.

"Oh!" Tien said. "Mmm, I can see what you meant now. No, not all that funny. But quite a size, isn't it?"

"Yeah and it tickles, but I don't think I'll laugh."

The women watched the insect traverse over the peaks of Sammi's knuckles before it bumped its back legs on to the ground. It hunted around with a head section that possessed impressively large pincers and then headed for her right wrist. Sammi raised her hand slowly to allow the wanderer to pass underneath. After a few minutes it left their little clearing and disappeared into the undergrowth.

"See, that's why I should have filled up my water bladder with vodka. How come we're doing this and Kara's swanning around in the city?"

"We're just lucky, I guess," Tien said and returned to watching the villa complex. And Jacob.

φ

"I'm just lucky, I guess," Noel Stewart said.

"I agree. Surely it's not a bad posting though, is it? Beats some other places you could be in," Tien said, sitting next to the British consular official on the grass in front of the Bajra Sandhi Monument in Denpasar.

"Oh yeah. Although, I have done my time in some right holes. So yeah, it's nice to do it easy'ish."

"Speaking of easy, how easy is what I want?" Kara asked.

"Very. The pouch comes in direct to Jakarta on a British Airways flight. Then it and whatever the Jakarta Embassy need to send me gets put on a Foreign Office charter and flown here.

Picked up by our in-house security and ferried directly to my office. Full diplomatic status throughout."

"Timings?"

"Flight leaves Heathrow at midday every day. With the stop in Jakarta and the transfer to the charter, it arrives about seventeen hours later. So, normally around 13:00 local."

"Great."

"Except, as soon as I hand it to you, whatever it is, and no, I don't need or want to know, but as soon as I hand it over, you lose the diplomatic protection of the pouch. If what you have is illegal, then you're on your own."

"Yep. Understood." She began to push herself up from the grass. "Eh, Noel?"

"Yes," he said and gave her a quizzical look, squinting up at her and shielding his eyes from the sun.

"If you drove it to a spot on the island and I took it from you there, that would limit the time it was outside diplomatic protection, wouldn't it?"

"Yes Kara. It would... Is that what you're asking me to do?"

"Yeah. What'd ya reckon?"

"Shall I assume this is going to benefit Her Majesty's Government?"

"It certainly won't damage it and I think she'd be pleased at the outcome."

Noel stood up, "Fine. Tell me where and when."

33

Monday 30th November.

The rest of the weekend had been spent rotating shifts in and out of the two hides. The off-shift team changed back into normal holiday attire on their way to the hotel, showered, ate, slept and then rotated back out, once more changing from holiday-makers to covert observers in the back of the Toyotas.

During their time in the rear hide, they'd seen Jacob do a lot of swimming in the pool, saw the huge man called Tommo occasionally stand at the side of the pool and watched three guys, who they presumed were the security Jacob had told Kara about, reclining on the loungers near the pool. The front hide saw no one come or go apart from two older Balinese women who seemed to do all the cooking and cleaning. The team designated them as Nigella and Delia.

On the Saturday night, Jacob and Tommo had eaten dinner together from 20:00 to 21:00. The lights of the lounge were bright enough, and not interrupted by curtains, giving a clear view of the scene. The same ritual played out on Sunday.

Kara had met Noel Stewart on the ravine road on Sunday afternoon and taken delivery of three kilos of cocaine. It had been divided, carefully, back at the hotel, into four large, treble wrapped freezer bags, secured with heavy duty tape. Now, on Monday night, those bags resided within a single backpack that lay between Dan and Eugene in the rear hide.

Kara was stepping out of her hotel shower when her phone rang. She quickly wrapped herself in a towel and hurried into the bedroom, grabbing the phone up from the side table.

"Yep?"

"Kara you need to get over here. I think we've got something happening," Dan said, his voice soft and unhurried.

"Go ahead."

"Jacob and Tommo had their meal as usual but instead of getting up from the table like Saturday and Sunday, they've stayed sitting. Now Toby's just called in that a car's arrived on the driveway. Two men, white, middle-aged getting out and going up, wait."

Kara could hear Eugene whispering to his brother, "Okay Kara, these two have joined Tommo and Jacob in the lounge room. Tommo made a big fuss of them. Handshakes all round. I think this is the get together happening, wait."

This time Kara heard nothing while she waited.

"That was Toby again, we have another car turning up. Another white male. Nigella and Delia have already left so this isn't a late night supper with friends."

"No worries, we'll be there in twenty. Call Chaz in from the ravine road car and send him to join Toby at the front. The rest of us will come and join you."

She hung up and speed dialled Tien. "How long before you're good to move?"

"Five minutes?"

"Great, ring Sammi and let her know we're moving now. We'll meet in the lobby and go as soon as we're all there. I'll ring Dinger." She hung up.

Six and a half minutes later the four of them climbed into the black Toyota.

φ

Kara crawled into the small hide next to Dan, while Tien, Sammi and Dinger crouched just behind, in the cover of the trees.

"What's happening?"

Dan passed her a set of binoculars and whispered, "We've had another guest turn up. You might want to take a look."

In the large lounge room Tommo's great bulk sat at the head of the dining room table, his back to Kara. To his left, three men drinking beers. All were white, all were in their forties or fifties. Two of them were dark haired, one grey. To Tommo's right was Jacob. He also had a beer. Next to him was the last man present. Kara moved the binoculars a fraction and stared into the face of Derek Swift.

"Oh you son of a bitch!" She said.

"Yeah, thought you'd like to see it before I called you on the radio. We all set?"

"Hope so. We'll just watch and wait, get the lay of what's occurring and look to make a mov-"

She was cut off by the radio earpiece making a small 'Tic'. Chaz's voice came through to them all.

"We have a small panel van coming up the driveway. Two male occupants in the front. Look like they're Balinese."

No one spoke, waiting patiently for Chaz to continue when he had more to report. The Cicadas played a constant theme in the background, before even they were drowned out by a long, low roll of thunder that lasted for a good fifteen seconds. Kara gazed up but the sky was cloudless. The full moon bright and unimpaired.

"Kara, we have a problem," Chaz said. At the same time they all heard Toby, alongside Chaz, say "No fucking way."

"Explain," Kara said.

Chaz sounded rattled, "Confirmed, two Balinese men, but they've just opened the rear door of the van and made six kids step out. They're all little girls Kara. Not one of them more than ten, can't be. They're tiny. They're taking them inside. Kara, we can't ha-"

"Quiet Chaz," she said, slewing the binoculars over to look at the entrance to the lounge. Sure enough six little girls were being shepherded into the room. Tommo was getting up from the table. He pointed and gesticulated to the futons and the Balinese men made the girls sit down. Then the big man waved Jacob and the rest of his guests forward. They all rose and stood in a line. Kara saw Jacob take a single pace backwards. Tommo, still animated, moved over and pulled Jacob forward to stand in front of the rest. Kara could see him waving his hand at the girls and turning back to Jacob.

"Oh my fucking God," Kara said as the truth of what she was looking at hit home. "They're making him pick which girl he wants. This is how they prove he's one of them."

She watched Jacob take a pace forward, then slowly turn round to face the other men.

The time for whispering was over. Dan and Eugene who lay beside her and were seeing what she was seeing were already moving by the time she yelled, "Plan's changed. We need to get in there right now. Storm the fucking place, GO, GO, GO."

As she rose to her feet, Jacob's fist connected solidly with the face of Derek Swift. The lounge room erupted.

ϕ

Being only ten metres from it, Chaz and Toby hit the front door of the villa ahead of everyone else. It hadn't been locked since the children had been taken inside and was still ajar. Toby slammed it back with his shoulder and sent it rocketing into the cream coloured wall. Chaz bypassed him and, bathed in the golden lights of the hallway, saw one of Tommo's security men, the bald one with the prison tattoos, only five paces ahead of him.

The man turned quickly, shouted something Chaz didn't catch and began to raise his hands. Chaz's speed closed the distance in a second. He hit him with straight fingers to the throat, crushing the man's windpipe and causing the tattooed arms to flail and claw, leaving the body undefended. Chaz kicked him in the groin, physically lifting him off the ground with the force. As the man began to collapse, Chaz spun to the right, grabbed, twisted and thrust the man's head down towards the knee he was ramming up to meet it. Somewhere in the back of his mind, honed and trained by decades of practise, Chaz knew he had never delivered three strikes with more fury. He also knew it was a corpse he was letting go of.

He gained the open entrance to the lounge and saw three little girls cowering and screaming on one of the futons. Another hid behind it, a fifth was standing frozen in the corner. The unconscious body of Derek Swift lay to the side. Tommo was standing halfway between the dining table and Jacob, who was on the ground, curled as tightly as possible, hands protecting his head, with a frenzy of kicks being aimed at him by the other three men.

Chaz was wearing a pair of high-leg combat boots, the soles of which squeaked against the marble floor. He planted his right food hard, used the forward momentum of his onrushing frame and spun just past one hundred and eighty degrees. The squeal of the rubber on the marble was the only warning the nearest man to him had, before Chaz's left heel impacted into his right eye socket.

The man cannoned backwards, knocked two of the dining chairs aside, fell and bounced his shoulder off the table. That caused his body to pivot and he face-planted into the white Italian marble. It discoloured with a vibrant splash of red.

The other two men who had been kicking Jacob stopped.

Jacob, realising help was on hand, rolled towards the futons and regained his feet. His head was a mass of pain with the blow that Tommo, of all people, had landed on him. It was true. Big Tommo must have been fast in his day. Jacob saw Toby coming through the entrance to the lounge, then saw him turn and go back out. He looked to Chaz and what he saw made him take half a step backwards. Chaz's pupils were fully dilated, his face was serene, not twisted or angry looking, yet in his expression, there was a menace that was unquantifiable. Jacob saw in his periphery the two Balinese men, who to this point had not moved, begin to run. He saw one of the men who had been kicking him, run. He saw the last, the grey-haired guy, start to back away, but Chaz was almost on him. Jacob moved to shield the little girls from what was about to happen, but the action of him turning towards them broke their spell. They shrieked even more. Then ran.

Chaz was aware of the man furthest from him bolting for the door. He saw the two Balinese men also run, but mostly he heard the cries of children and watched the last of the men who had been assaulting Jacob, trying to back away towards the large windows. In the ten steps it took to reach him, Chaz played through his options. In the end he kept it simple. He dropped his hands to his sides. The man, who Chaz noticed had a full head of wavy grey hair, came at him with a swinging right. Chaz moved left, parrying the oncoming fist by applying a light touch with his left hand to the back of the man's right elbow. At the same time he placed his right hand on the inside of the man's right wrist. With both hands now on opposite sides of the man's arm, he applied a full force snap and simultaneously dislocated the man's shoulder while breaking the elbow joint. Maintaining his grip on the arm, Chaz stepped forward and pivoted. The man's own momentum caused him to turn a full half-somersault, ripping the last of the shoulder joint and surrounding tissue into a useless pulp. He landed on his backside, sitting up and facing away from Chaz who, by a final twist to the wrist, broke it as well. Letting go of the irreparably damaged limb, Chaz smashed his left elbow back into the grey haired man's face and watched with satisfaction as the unconscious body fell straight back on to the floor. Its short journey ended in a crack of head on marble. Chaz felt his senses relax. He was aware of higher-pitched screaming coming from the kids and looked back to where Jacob was standing. He called on the radio, "Tien, Sammi, Kara, the kids are terrified of any man. You're going to have to find them and calm them down."

Kara heard the call in her ear but was trying hard not to get her face smashed in. She and Dan had got to the back door of the villa first, only to find it locked. Eugene arrived at full tilt and the door didn't so much open as disintegrate. Dan followed his brother up the hallway to the lounge. Sounds of a fight were also coming from the first bedroom on the right. She saw Dan begin to enter the bedroom but further ahead the two Balinese men ran out of the lounge and turned towards the front door, closely followed by one of Tommo's guests.

Dan shouted, "Eugene, with me," and the two O'Neill brothers set off in pursuit.

Kara reached the bedroom door and saw Toby grappling with one of Tommo's security men. She knew, from Jacob's notes and observations over the last few days, that there were three of them. She even knew, again from Jacob's notes, what their names were, but she didn't know which was which. Other than Mutt. Jacob had described the bald, tattooed Irishman to a tee. Looking up the hallway she could see him lying unconscious on the floor. About to move in and help Toby, she looked again. Mutt's eyes, open and unseeing stared back at her. She thought, 'Oh, you met angry Chaz, didn't you?' at the same time she heard feet behind her. Expecting to see Tien, Sammi and Dinger, she glanced over her shoulder in time to see the third security guy launching himself at her. This one was thin, wiry, about the same height as she was and currently only wearing a pair of shorts, a pair of trainers and a pair of knuckledusters, one on each fist. The first skull crunching punch was already halfway to her. She dropped into a crouch, threw her right hand out for support and as she heard Chaz calling on the radio about the kids, flung her left leg forward. Her boot connected just below the oncoming man's right knee. The effect wasn't as she'd hoped. He'd anticipated and pulled his leg back. She knew he'd have a bruise but that wasn't much compensation. He gave a small hop and transferred his weight onto his right leg. Kara knew he was about to aim a kick at her head while she was still crouching. She waited until he had committed to the action, than she fell flat, rolled three-quarters to her right, under the oncoming foot, and delivered a powerful sidekick into the man's groin. He collapsed onto his knees in front of her. Pushing backwards she started to stand when Tien, Sammi and Dinger came through the remnants of the rear door. Tien strode down the hallway and as she got to the unsuspecting man, put both her hands on the left side of his head and slammed it, and him, into the wall. He slumped unconscious in front of Kara. Tien walked past. Sammi followed.

Kara saw Dinger move into the first bedroom on the right. The noise of the fighting stopped soon after. Dinger walked back into the hallway and moved to the front door.

Kara called, "Report."

"Lounge room. Clear. Three down. No kids," Chaz said.

There was a pause, as they waited for a response from the next in their reporting sequence.

Kara retransmitted, "Dan, report."

Still no response.

"Eugene?"

No response.

Kara pointed to Dinger and then the open front door. He began to move into the darkness, but stopped at the sound of Dan's voice, "Sorry Kara, we were being a bit quiet so we could catch the second of the Bali guys. He was hiding under a car. Anyway, we have him now." As he finished speaking, Kara saw Dinger step back and let Eugene pass. He was carrying one Balinese man under each arm. Each time they wriggled he squeezed them in a way that reminded Kara of someone playing bagpipes. Dan strode in behind his brother. He carried the unconscious form of one of the guests over his shoulder.

"Sammi?" Kara called.

"Tien and I are in the master bedroom. We have five of the girls here. They're terrified Kara."

"Okay, Sammi, you stay there. The rest of us, meet in the

lounge.

Jacob was sitting on the edge of a futon, bleeding heavily from his nose and ear. Chaz stood next to him holding tissues in place.

Kara surveyed the unconscious bodies on the ground. Derek Swift had sustained at least a broken nose and cheek. She couldn't see what mess his teeth were in and she didn't care. Anyway, in comparison to the havoc Chaz had unleashed on the other two, Swift had gotten off easy.

"You okay Chaz?" she asked.

"Never better."

Toby and Dinger dragged the two unconscious security men into the lounge. The body of Mutt stayed in the hallway.

"We're missing a kid and we haven't got much time. Dan, go back to the hide, get the drugs and bring them back here. As soon as we find the kid we'll take all the girls away, put the drugs in each villa, call the cops and withdraw out the back as they're coming in the front. All good?"

They all nodded except Jacob. He sluggishly raised his head and looked around, "Kara?"

She knew exactly what she'd missed just as he said it.

"Where the fuck's Tommo?"

34

The glass doors leading to the lawn were wide open. The little temple lights gave enough illumination to show Tommo wasn't anywhere in sight.

Kara's frustration threatened to swamp her thoughts, but she consciously forced her mind to quieten. She looked at Jacob, his ear and nose still bleeding and his face beginning to swell.

"Tien, stay with Jacob, patch him up as best you can. Sammi, can you still hear me?"

Sammi's voice was clear in her earpiece, "Yep, go ahead."

"You stay with the rest of the girls. Eugene, secure those two" she said pointing at the Balinese men he still held under each arm, "then join Chaz and search next door. Toby, go with Dinger and take the third villa. Dan, you and me will take the grounds and the last building. We're looking for a thirty stone man and a scared little girl and I have to hope they're not together. We have no time for niceties, if the doors are locked, smash them in."

Tien took the small first aid kit she carried on her belt and began to dress Jacob's ear.

"You okay here?" Eugene asked when he'd finished binding the hands and feet of the Balinese men with cable ties.

Tien nodded and Eugene left at a run to join Chaz.

As she wiped more blood from Jacob's cheek, Tien looked at the still unconscious Derek Swift, on the floor to her front.

Jacob followed her gaze. "I know why he faked his suicide," Jacob said.

"Really?" Tien asked, looking at Jacob with concern.

"When he came in tonight I told him I recognised him off the telly. He liked that. I played to it, telling him that everyone back home thought he was dead. How it had made all the papers in Suffolk and Essex. Made it sound like he was bigger than he was."

"Let me guess, he loved it?"

"Oh yeah. So I said, how come he'd pretended to die. The room went quiet and Swift looked to Tommo."

"What for?"

"Permission to tell me I guess. That was the first inkling I had something was wrong."

"How'd you mean?" Tien asked,

"Well, Tommo said, yeah, you can tell him. He's gonna be proving he's one of us soon anyway and if he doesn't, well then it definitely won't matter."

Tien finished securing the dressing to the side of Jacob's head, then reached out and took his hand.

"I know what he meant now, but at the time the others laughed and I joined in. I had no clue what was going to happen. Swift said-" Jacob's voice caught. He swallowed hard and took a deep breath. Tien could see a glassiness in his eyes. She squeezed his hand and waited. After another deep breath Jacob tried again.

"Swift said he'd abducted a girl in Ipswich. A schoolgirl, thirteen years old. He'd killed her after a couple of days. That's what he said. After a couple of days. Didn't even give her a name. He said it like he was telling an old fishing story and the rest of the men round the table just smiled and nodded and laughed. Then he said he'd dumped her body where he thought it'd never be found, but it was. He spent a few hours trying to figure out if he'd made any mistakes but he couldn't be sure. The bastard said, you all kn-" again Jacob stopped and checked his emotions. Tien waited.

"He said, you all know what it's like. Trying to remember if yo…" Jacob's voice wavered and he closed his eyes. Tien leant her head on his upper arm. He breathed deeply and coughed.

After a minute, he started again, "It doesn't matter what he said. You don't need to hear it Tien, but it was disgusting. When they'd all stopped laughing, he said, he couldn't be sure the police wouldn't trace her back to him. He was only fifty-fifty if he'd get away with it, so he'd decided to run."

Jacob leant his head down gently on top of Tien's. "I asked him if the papers were right, had he taken all the charity money. He said, yeah, but it was alright, it wasn't like they needed it. They were all going to die anyway."

Tien straightened up, "He said what?"

"He said the kids didn't need it, they were all going to die anyway. That was it for me. I'd had enough. I was about to stand up and signal for Toby or Dan or whoever was outside watching to crash the place, but that was when they brought the little girls in. Tommo dragged me forward and said that as the guest I had to choose first and they'd all watch. Then they'd welcome me to their club. It was their way of testing what he called, graduates of the Flight Path. I decided that for what he'd said, even if I only got one good punch in, it was going to be aimed at taking Swift's head off his shoulders."

She reached up and gently kissed his cheek, "I'm very proud of everything you've done Jacob. Are you sure you're okay?"

"Yeah I'm fine, but thanks for asking."

"Your head still sore?"

"Yeah, but it's stopped pounding. Anyway, we can get me checked out before we go home if you want."

"I'd like that, yes." She tilted her head and smiled at him, holding his gaze. She felt the intensity of her heart as it pounded and the lightness of her stomach as it flipped cartwheels. She broke into a wide smile and leant her hand against his cheek. He lowered his head towards her and she waited for him to graze his lips against hers but instead he pulled back.

"Sorry," he said, holding his hand up to his nose, which had decided to start bleeding again.

Tien giggled and raised a new dressing to his nostrils, "Gosh, is that what's always going to happen?"

"I hope not."

She kept her hand in place and tilted his head down. As she waited for the bleeding to stop she leant her head to touch his. They stayed like that for a little while, even after the blood had stopped and she had removed the dressing.

She stood up and looked about. "Is there no bin?"

"Probably in the kitchen," he said.

"There's a kitchen?"

He pointed over to the recessed gloss-white panel on the far wall. She began to move across the room.

Jacob looked casually to where she was. His eyes were blurry. He blinked and looked again. This time he focussed and recognised the hidden sliding door. A massive dump of adrenaline cleared the fog from his mind and accelerated his body up from the futon. He jumped to his feet, ignoring the renewed pounding in his head and the fresh flow of blood from his nose.

"Tien, stop! No one's checked the kitchen," He hurdled over the prone form of Derek Swift.

Tien's hand was almost touching the surface of the gloss panel, feeling for the catch that she knew had to be there, but she paused at his shout.

Jacob was three steps behind her. She had taken a pace backwards, glancing over her shoulder with a look of concern on her face. The door began to slide open from the other side. Tien turned back around. Jacob smelt the unmistakeable aroma of peppermint.

"Tien!" he called as the door opened. The massive bulk of Tommo was revealed in the darkness of the kitchen.

Jacob leapt forwards and shoved Tien sideways with his shoulder. She careered into the wall as Tommo, his left hand wrapped around the mouth of a terrified little girl, loomed out of the doorway. Jacob felt a blow against his chest but his fury at all that had gone on in the past week, topped with what had just so nearly happened to Tien, brought his own right fist through in the most powerful punch he'd ever thrown.

It hit Tommo centrally on the face, smashing the big man's nose and most of his teeth. He staggered backwards, then fell, his head striking the kitchen bench on the way down. The whole villa shuddered under the impact of his bulk. The little girl, thrown to one side, picked herself up, screamed and ran. Tien, recovering her own feet, went after her and scooped her up in the hallway. Jacob felt a pain where Tommo had hit him.

He looked down and saw the dimpled-handle of a Japanese carving knife sticking out of his chest. His shirt, bought in Marks and Spencer on the Champs Élysées, what seemed like an age ago, was turning red.

He leant his back against the wall. Glancing right he saw Tommo's chest rising and falling, each expelled breath raising a crimson and white cloud of blood and tooth fragments. Glancing left he saw Tien, in the entrance to the hallway, her back to him, cradling and soothing the little girl. He sank slowly to the floor.

"Tien?"

φ

Franklyn stood by the mantelpiece, staring at the deep red of the dying fire and considering whether he should add more logs, or let it go out. The lights of the Christmas Tree illuminated the room in a way he found most pleasing. Shadows and highlights danced around in gentle ripples, reflecting off the crystal decanter and glass that sat within reach of his favoured leather, wingback armchair. It all reminded him of some Dickensian illustration. He considered which character he might be. As a younger man, he would have aspired to the fully realised ideals of the grown Pip, or the gentle good natured being that was Joe Gargery, but he wondered now, if he wasn't Fagin. The ultimate puppet master of younger, more able hands. He glanced at the clock and turned the radio's volume up.

"This is the BBC news at ten o'clock. Five British and two Irish men have been arrested on the holiday island of Bali, in Indonesia, on a series of alleged drug and child abuse related offences. Those detained include former East Anglian radio and television host, Derek Swift, who was previously believed to have committed suicide earlier this year. The arrests were carried out by a specialist unit of the Indonesian Police, following a tip-off that the men had allegedly abducted six under-aged girls and were holding them in a luxury villa complex."

"The subsequent raid, which apprehended a total of nine men, including two Balinese locals, also resulted in the death of Dermot Moylin, a native of County Kerry, Ireland, who allegedly opened fire on the police when they attempted to enter one of the villas. Further searches of the complex allegedly uncovered three kilograms of cocaine with a street value of between one hundred and fifty and two hundred thousand pounds."

"The Indonesian Minister for Law and Human Rights hailed the success of the operation as further proof of their serious, robust and never-ending efforts to crack down on child-sex offenders. He said it was due entirely to the professional actions of the police that all the children had been rescued unharmed."

"He went on to say that, given the concurrent seizure of a major quantity of drugs, the Government would be seeking the Death Penalty for all those arrested. The men, expected to go to trial in six to nine months, have been remanded to the notorious Kerobokan Prison. The British and Irish Foreign Secretaries are expected to issue a joint appeal for sentencing

clemency for their citizens."

"In an unrelated event, the British Consulate in Bali confirmed a decorated hero of the Iraq and Afghanistan conflicts, has been killed in an accident while scuba diving just south of the island."

"Jacob Harrop, twenty-six from Chelmsford in Essex, a former Corporal in the Royal Air Force Regiment, was fatally injured by a malfunctioning spear gun, being carried as a precaution in the event of shark attacks. Mr Harrop was awarded the Conspicuous Gallantry Cross, second only to the Victoria Cross, for his actions in defending Bastion Air Base during a Taliban raid in September 2012. Mr Harrop's brother, who was also on the dive at the time of the incident and was himself a former member of the RAF Regiment, said, 'The loss of Jacob is a tragedy, but we will remember him for the kind, loving and courageous man he was.' The body is due to be repatriated back to the UK within the next week and the Chief of the Air Staff has confirmed that as an RAF recipient of the Conspicuous Gallantry Cross, Corporal Harrop will be buried with full military honours."

"In European news, Dutch police have now confirmed the identity of all five men who died in a house fire outside Amst-"

Franklyn turned the set off and reached for his glass of single malt. He raised it to the dying embers.

THE END

Acknowledgements

Once more I am indebted to a host of individuals who have generously given of their time, expertise and good humoured tolerance. Without them the story you are about to read would be a weaker version of itself.

To my fantastic editing 'team' of Angeline, Helen, Lauren and Sara. Thank you for taking the time out of your incredibly busy schedules to help me. Any remaining mistakes in here, are mine alone.

To Sara again, and Kirrilee, my *accomplices* in crime and to Kirrilee's anonymous neighbour. Thanks for your continuing advice and guidance on police procedures and mortuary forensics, it is invaluable.

To Chris and Amy, thanks for keeping me straight on Int Corp training and deployment guidelines.

To Steve Harland and all at Ottobock® Australia, Tomie Pfeiffer at Orthopaedic Appliances Pty Ltd and especially to Nicky Ashwell, the first recipient of a Bebionic hand. The information you provided was superb and more importantly, your enthusiasm for the field of prosthetics is inspiring.

To all the readers, family, friends and Facebook followers who loved the first Wright & Tran and in doing so encouraged me to write the next, thank you, I am humbled. Thanks also to Dotty McLeod, Siobhan McGarry, Meghan Woods and Debbie Davies for the fantastic media coverage they have afforded me.

Finally, as ever, to Jacki. Thanks honey, for everything. None of this gets done without you. Also, congratulations on all you've achieved this past year. You make me very proud.

About the Author

Ian was born in Northern Ireland in 1966. At eighteen he joined the Royal Air Force; originally training as an aircraft technician he was later commissioned as an Intelligence Officer. Throughout his Service he had the pleasure of working alongside some "right eejits" whom he still feels lucky to call friends. On leaving the Service he relocated to Western Australia and is now surrounded by a resident mob of Kangaroos who bounce past his house each day. They remind him of his previous colleagues.

His first novel **A Time To Every Purpose**, an alternative history with a religious twist, was published independently in 2014 and gained positive critical acclaim.

He is currently working on the next in the Wright & Tran Series of detective novels.

Enjoyed the Book?
Leave a review

Follow Ian at:

Web: www.ianandrewauthor.com

Blog: www.viewsfromtheridge.com

Twitter: @ianandrewauthor

Facebook: facebook.com/viewsfromtheridge

Email: ian@viewsfromtheridge.com

Fall Guys
The Third Wright & Tran Novel

Kara Wright and Tien Tran, combat veterans of an elite intelligence unit, now make their living as Private Investigators. Often working the mundane, just occasionally they get to use all their former training.

"We want to know why the Brits
are selling weapons to ISIS"

When a break-in threatens Britain's National Security, Franklyn calls on Wright & Tran but Kara will have to take this case on her own. Tien wants nothing to do with the world of Private Investigations and less to do with the world of Franklyn. Kara goes solo, but finding who is responsible for the break-in is the easy part. Finding who the real criminals are is much, much harder.

Isolated in a world of half-truths and lies, international arms deals and power politics, she is quick to discover that she's been working for the wrong side. What she didn't figure on was that making amends will place her, and those she loves, in the sights of those who have everything to lose.

Face Value
The First Wright & Tran Novel

When siblings Zoe and Michael Sterling insist that their middle-aged parents have gone missing, Kara and Tien are at first sceptical and then quickly intrigued; the father, ex-intelligence analyst Chris Sterling, appears to be involved with an enigmatic Russian thug.

Using less than orthodox methods and the services of ex-colleagues with highly specialised talents, Wright & Tran take on the case. But the truth they uncover is far from simple and will shake Zoe and Michael as much as it will challenge Tien and anger Kara. Anger she can ill afford for she is being hunted by others for the killing of a street predator who chose the wrong prey.

The only constant in this darkening world is that nothing and no one can be taken at face value.

"Ian Andrew is an author who can be relied upon to deliver a good – no, much more than that – a great read. Face Value, once again proves Andrew to be a versatile and gifted writer who delivers books that hold readers from beginning to end."
Elaine Fry, The West Australian

A Time To Every Purpose

What if Jesus hadn't been crucified?

For two thousand years humanity has been enveloped in Nirvana. But in the early decades of the 20th Century, natural disasters, famine, disease and economic collapse bring catastrophe and a fledgling Nazi Party sweeps to power. Now, almost a century later, their brutal persecution of millions is a never-ending holocaust.

Yet a few heroes remain.

Leigh Wilson, the preeminent scientist of her generation, has kept a secret all her life. But plunged into the aftermath of the cold-blooded murder of a Nazi official, she is forced to make a choice. Will she destroy what she loves to save what she can only imagine?

A Time to Every Purpose is a thrilling mix of science and action, good versus evil, and the eternal question all humans face: Is this my time to act?

"A Time To Every Purpose by Ian Andrew deals with huge concepts, looking at the broad sweep of history... a well-executed alternate history novel with some great action scenes."
John Wyatt, News UK

The Little Book of Silly Rhymes & Odd Verses

An illustrated collection of humorous, daft, sometimes sad and occasionally thought provoking verses from the pen of Ian Andrew. Illustrations by Alison Mutton.

Lightning Source UK Ltd.
Milton Keynes UK
UKOW01f0857020317
295709UK00002B/13/P

9 780992 464172